I would like to thank my sister, Deena, for her help in editing this book.

mwstevenson2023@gmail.com

"Do You See What I See"?   © 2018 / 2022

This unique story will appeal to teenagers, everyone that was ever a teenager, U.F.O. buffs and fans of the 1970's era. The story's central date coincides with the actual historic date that President Nixon was in Moscow, one day ahead of a scheduled conference with Premier Brezhnev. Nixon met with Brezhnev in the Kremlin's equivalent of the Oval Office. No one knows what was actually discussed and no other American president has ever been invited to the executive Russian office.

May 1972, two teenage boys John and Mark decide to hitchhike west. Ninety-eight other American teenagers are also compelled to travel to the center of the country – fifty boys and fifty girls; a similar occurrence is happening in Russia.

President Nixon and Premier Brezhnev have been visited by the "Others", aliens that will not tolerate many more nuclear explosions, for testing or otherwise. The world leaders have one week to comply with the Others demands, or a plague will descend and kill every human on Earth, it's said to have been done before. The Others demands are threefold – to reduce nuclear arsenals and testing, to deliver 100 young adults from the U.S.A. and Russia, and for both countries to cooperate with one another. The task is dubbed Project Noah's Ark.

General Brandon is chosen by Nixon to head the American side, Brandon will be forced to trust his instincts and his personal assistant, Captain Duffy, to make difficult decisions. Colonel Nikolai will lead the Russian operation. Nikolai is not at all pleased with the mission and is convinced that the Americans are running an elaborate ploy to weaken Russia; he will not allow it.

Curtis Knapp is the Assistant Director of the Department of Defense, and he has never been able to escape his suicidal thoughts. After being briefed on the matter, Curtis is struck with a compelling idea for a perfect suicide. He can check out and take every other asshole on Earth with him. All he has to do is, make sure the operation does not go smoothly.

Ivan and Victor are the Russian spies assigned to General Brandon's team; they are recalled by Colonel Nikolai and forced to defect. Colonel Nikolai and Curtis Knapp are not the only complications to Project Noah's Ark.

For John and Mark, strange and dark feelings begin to develop while they are on a bridge – outside Omaha, Nebraska. After a few wild rides, the boys are left stranded on a deserted swamp road; then, suddenly, the road is no longer deserted. They are surrounded by police, subjected to testing, and are integrated. Eventually, John and Mark are released and ominously told to "walk that way".

The boys do as they are told and walk directly into Betty and Sandy – two teenage girls who are running away from men who want to enslave them. The four teens quickly become two couples, with a shared goal – to get "there", wherever "there" is. The two couples are drawn to a railroad yard, then to a caboose where they meet four more teenage travelers, Walt, Louise, Brownie, and Christine.

Like a commandment from God, ordinary people have vivid dreams, compelling them to help and protect the teenagers. Railroad men transport and shelter the teens on cabooses, church ladies make sure they are clothed, clean and fed. And then, in the dead of night, it happens.

One hundred young adults are indeed abducted and returned by the "Others" with the signing of the S.A.L.T treaty. Plans to sabotage the mission are foiled.

President Nixon personally thanks all of the teenagers and swears them to secrecy by recruiting them into the Department of Defense. He tells them, "Fifty years, that is the contract with the Others. You will be mentored and groomed to be in positions of power and influence, to negotiate the next fifty-year lease on the planet, in the year 2022.

One

The 1968 Plymouth Roadrunner is the hottest car of the day. That is our next ride. The four women in the car are older than us, of course and beautiful. I am pretty sure they are hot women, as they paw at me even more aggressively than the black guys in the ride before. I hear the big-block engine kick down with that unmistakable sound and feel of power. As the engine winds up the girls are becoming more excited, they are having a blast. The brunette driver is expertly weaving the car in and out of traffic. She takes the downtown ramp and turns left, too fast and against the red light. The engine kicks down; again, I can feel the power and speed of the car. She doesn't let up on the gas. She maneuvers through traffic and intersections; it doesn't matter if the lights are green or red.

I'm not sure if the car is wanted, or if it is the driving that attracts the entire city police force. The driver and girls are immensely enjoying toying with the police, ripping back and forth through the city. The brunette loses them because she knows every street and ally in the city of Omaha, Nebraska. She also knows the surrounding countryside as we are about to find out.

The view changes from city to suburban, to rural; next, it is becoming desolate. We are now in the middle of nowhere and going fast, over 100 most of the time and probably now. I won't know until much later why she slams on the brakes, but that is what she does. The car slips sideways and starts to spin like a toy top. I am being crushed by the three other bodies in the back seat, but somehow the car is staying on the road. The Roadrunner stalls and stops sideways.

A cloud of dust and smoke overtakes the car; it looks like fog but makes me choke. I am snapped back to reality by the brunette driver. She gets out of the car, bends over and splays her hands on the hood. After a moment she says in a loud, monotone voice, "Take their shoes, we are to leave them here. They are to come of their own free will."

The pretty red-headed girl on my left looks at me and smiles; then her face twitches up, making her not beautiful anymore. She reaches down and removes my sneakers, I don't resist. The bucket seat flips forward and the blonde girl from the front takes my hand and pulls me out. I can't believe it; she is stronger than me, by far. She is holding me strong and firm and at arm's length. She is intensely looking into my eyes. I can't help thinking that she is gorgeous, model-like; they all could be Playboy centerfolds.

The car is rocking. It's John, he doesn't want to give up his shoes, and he is resisting – bad idea; the other girls have pulled him out of the car and they are beating the hell out of him.

The brunette is trying to start the car. The engine is turning over slowly. It doesn't want to start; it's hot, probably flooded and close to being overheated. The big-block catches and stumbles, then roars to life. I can't help but plead, "My sneakers! Please! My shoes!"

The gorgeous brunette driver revs the engine and dumps the clutch, burning rubber and fishtailing the car back straight; it is going, going – something flies out the window, I can't see what it is. Was it my sneakers? God, I hope so. I hear the big four-barrel kick in, and the car is gone.

"John! Where are you!?" It's quiet – no noise; it's a far cry from the noise and chaos of the past half hour. I notice that it is not quiet at all. The frogs and crickets are making their swamp noises, and I hear John moaning on the other side of the road. It sounds like he is in the ditch, or maybe the swamp. "John!" I cross the road still calling his name and see him climbing up the bank. He is dazed and confused. I help pull him up. "You, ok?"

"I think so," he says, "Shit! My shoes! They must be in that car. What just happened? I thought they were going to kill us." "Yeah," I say, "Or do something worse."   John asks, "What could be worse than getting killed?" "I don't know," I answer, "But I think those girls were possessed, or high, or something." John says, "They couldn't have been too high, or that brunette could never have driven that well. Where are we?"

"Hell, I don't know," I practically scream. "I'm freezing and I don't have any shoes!" I'm getting upset as my adrenaline is starting to wear off. John says, "Don't feel like the Lone Ranger, that blonde hit me in the head with something hard. Man, my head hurts; I think she knocked me out. And, the bitch has my sneakers."

"What the fuck are we going to do?" We both say, at exactly the same time.

It's cold; not the New York freezing-winter kind of cold, but the Midwestern early-spring kind of cold; and, standing there with no shoes is making it feel even colder. "Let's do something, even if it's wrong; it can't be any more fucked-up than what we just went through. Can It?" I don't even know where that came from, I just said it. "Can you walk John?" "Yeah, I think so, give me a minute."

I walk a few feet in each direction up and down the road, there is nothing to see. I point and say, "Well, we know that we came from this way; so, this direction should get us back toward town. I'm going up the road to look for my sneakers. I hope my redhead girl took mercy and threw my sneakers out. Come on."

John says, "But, I don't have any shoes!" That makes me mad, "Shoes? Neither do I! Get up and come on!" I help John up and we start to walk in the direction the car was last traveling. We're not walking fast; in fact, we are walking very gingerly in our stocking feet. The road isn't all gravel, but it sure has plenty of small stones that hurt with every step. Plus, my socks are getting wet. We are getting close to where my sneakers might be. Damn, I wish I had more light.

John is still bitching about his shoes. I feel like punching him, but I tell him to check his side of the road really good. His blonde girl may have thrown his sneakers out the window. John won't stop freaking out about his shoes. I tell him, "Damn-it, we are lucky to be alive! And, I don't have any shoes either."

I think, no I know, we are getting on each other's nerves. Did I say it was dark? Well, it is. My eyes are adjusting somewhat, but not well enough to find my shoes or I should say my sneakers.

I'm scared of snakes. Don't see any, but I know there are plenty of them in this swamp. Shit, I have to go in there and kick around with bare feet if there is any hope of finding my kicks. Don't want to; damn sure don't want to go down there. Think... Ok, I'll mark this spot with a pile of rocks then I'll check up and down the road some more.

John is starting to break down. He is panicking about being abandoned in the middle of nowhere. He might be crying, I can't tell, and he sure doesn't want me to see. I wonder why I am holding up better than John. He is supposed to be the tough one. I take a little bit of charge and tell John to stay here and calm down; I am going to walk a little further and see what I can find.

Did I say it was quiet before? Well, I guess it was, comparatively. But now, noise is coming from every direction, and it's almost deafening. How to hell can they be so loud? There are swamp noises from frogs, bullfrogs, and crickets, along with the hooting of owls; and, I swear, I hear coyotes, wolves, or whatever howling in the distance. There is something else too. What is it? I don't think it should be this loud. All of these bugs, frogs, and animals seem to be upset, urgently calling out at their maximum decibel level.

I leave John and walk on tender feet up the road in the same direction the Roadrunner was last traveling. I walk about a half a step at a time, straining my eyes, and hoping to see what I am looking for. After about 50 feet, I see a wide spot in the road. Is it a parking area in the middle of nowhere? I walk around it. I am confused but of course, that's nothing new. And I hear another noise on top of all the others. It is water; running water, it has to be a stream or a river.

Oh, now I get it. My father used to take me fishing in rural New York and there were parking pull-offs for fishermen. Ok, that's what it must be. As I circle around the area and get back to the road, I find a sneaker in the roadside ditch. That's good. I wipe the stones off my right foot and put the one sneaker on. Now, I am hopeful now of finding both.

With a big stick and a funny hop, I investigate down into the ditch; I'm still scared of putting my barefoot down there. Luckily, I am quickly rewarded with my other sneaker. I climb the bank and put it on. Man, it sure is nice to have something on my feet again.

I can see a little better now, must be getting used to the darkness, but I can't see John. I holler for him, "Hey John!" He calls back to me, "Mark I can't find my shoes!" There is a note of panic in his voice. Is he losing it? Maybe he is. "Work your way back to the rock pile. I'm coming and I'll help you look," I call back to him.

I walk slowly down the other side of the road. So much better with shoes on! With my stick I poke around in the grass as I make my way all the way back to the rock pile, nothing. I find John sitting next to the rock pile; his hands are covering his face and he is definitely crying. He is way past caring if I see, or not. "We'll find your shoes John." I say, trying to console him.

We are novice cigarette smokers and, since John has a half a pack of crumpled Marlboros, it seems like a great time to have a cigarette; so, we do.

I calm down John and myself too by just being still for a few minutes. I say to John, "Remember that creepy feeling we had when we were on the bridge?" John says, "Yeah like we were being watched?" I say, "I still have that feeling and, something else. Something feels really strange. Shit, something is really strange." In a shaky voice John says, "Yeah, I'm hip to that. I sure feel it too."

"I can't find my shoes! How far can I walk with no shoes? My feet are already bleeding!" I can understand, because 30 minutes ago I felt the same way. "Ok," I say, thinking out loud. "You're going to have to put my sneakers on and go down into the ditch. Look good, and work your way up to the parking area that I told you about." "I'm not going down there!" John shouted.

Again, he is making me mad. "Damn it! Don't be such a baby! You want your shoes, go find them! I'm not doing it for you!" I take off my sneakers and hand them over. John whined, "They don't fit! They are too small!" "Goddamn-it John, just put the sneakers on the best you can and get down there!" "There are snakes down there!" John protested. "Yeah, I know. Take my stick; I'll check down the road and back again but, you're going to have to go down there and beat the bushes." John agrees, but mostly because he has no choice.

I slowly make my way back to where the Plymouth dumped us out; I am trying to find his shoes. I check and double-check the area where we landed, nothing. I search both sides of the road all the way back to the parking area with no luck. I find John sitting down crying again. "What the hell. You have to keep looking; this is where I found my shoes. What are you doing? Giving up?"

"That crazy bitch didn't give a shit about me or my shoes!" "Ok," I say, "So what's your idea?" John says "The next car that comes by, I'm going to stop them and make them give me a ride out of this place!" "Oh, great idea," I say, "We haven't seen a car come down this road since we've been here! You don't want to look anymore, give me my back my sneakers!" "No! Fuck you; I'm keeping them."

Naturally, that pisses me off, mad enough to make a preacher cuss as my father would say. I'm about to make a dive for him and I'm regretting giving him that stick when we see headlights on the road. True to his word, John stands in the middle of the road in the classic big X position. His legs and hands spread wide and his palms are flat out. He is damn-sure telling this car to stop. It does. It's the police.

Lights flash on. Every light on the cop car comes on, flashing blue lights, high beams and spotlight. Everything comes on except the siren but, he makes up for that by using his bullhorn.

"You boys, move to the center of the parking area and put your hands up!"

Two

We do as we are told. Why the center of the parking area?

The cop circles the cruiser around the lot, then angles the car toward us and turns off the strobes. Over the bullhorn, real loud - the officer says, "Stand where you are and don't make a move!"

I shield my eyes from the painful light and think about moving away from the glare.

"I SAID DON'T MOVE!"

Ok, got it.

We stand there not long, it seems like less than a minute and then we see more cars coming up the road from both directions, lots of them, two, four, six, eight, ten? Maybe more than that, they are moving fast. As they enter the parking lot, I can make out that they are cop cars, hard to see because of my sensitive eyes and the glare - but they don't all look the same.

Some are black and white some just black, white or brown. I can see that some have the badge of authority on the doors and some are big and boxy. And more of them, how many now? I can't tell, but lots. Holy shit where are they all coming from? How did they get here so fast? What did we do?

As they race in, they kick up dirt and dust. All come to a stop - just about door handle to door handle, in a complete circle around us - like an old fashion wagon train circle. I can see now why he wants us in the center of the lot.

Did I say the lights were blinding before? No, I only thought they were. Now they are. Every one of these countless cars have their high beams on us, and their spotlights too. They all stay in their cars and I don't see any of them, for a while anyway, but they make use of their bullhorns. Questions are asked loudly by the faceless men, one after the other, fast and confusing and from every direction.

We are split up. My interrogation starts.

"What's your name?"

"Who were those girls?"

"How do you know them?"

"What did they tell you?"

"What do you know about it?"

"You boys raped those girls - didn't you?"

"Admit it; you little punks are going to prison!"

"They told you a secret - didn't they?"

"What did they tell you?"

I am told to go to the driver's side of the black boxy suburban thing, up close to the front bumper. I can't see my interrogator as the vehicle's spotlights are shining in my face.

A nicer voice, from a different car says "Son, lay your hands flat on the hood and look down - close your eyes if you have to." I do and it's funny, it still seems bright. Of course, I can't see John, he's somewhere else in the circle. I can hear similar questions being shouted at him. I haven't answered or said anything yet; to this point everything said is rapid-fire, with no time between questions to even answer. Hard Ass continues with the questions.

"Again, what's your name?" "Kevin Olish," I said. I lied.

"How old are you?" "16." I lied.

"Do you have any I.D.?" "I lost my wallet in the swamp." I lied.

Why is he still using the bullhorn?

Even though I can't see him, I know that he is only six feet away, standing just inside the driver's door.

"What other countries have you been to?"

"None."

"Are you sick?"

"No."

"Have you ever been sick?"

"Well, yeah, sometimes."

"What did you see?"

"You mean the car, the girls?"

"Damn it, boy! I know that you are lying to me! Everything you say is a lie! Do you know what we do to lying little punks like you?"

"I have heard enough," the nicer voice says. "Proceed."

The Hard ass (cop?) comes to the front of the vehicle and says "Don't dare to look at me you little punk. You do and I'll make you sorry; I'd like it too, you little punk!"

"Enough I said!" The nicer voice is a little bit sharper now. "Proceed!"

I'm still looking down at the hood of the car, but I open my eyes - just a crack. I see Hard Ass put a black bag on the hood. It looks like a gym bag to me. He unzips it and takes something out.

"Goddamn it! I told you not to look!"

How did he know?

Hard Ass roughly grabs my hair and yanks my head back. Snip; I know that sound. He's cutting my hair. Why? Just one snip, that's it – no, it's not. He takes out a small pair of locking pliers and locks them on some hairs close to the scalp and pulls out more than a few strands of my hair by the roots. He yanks my head back a little bit more and whispers in my ear - so the others won't hear. "There is nothing I'd like more than to have you to myself for 48 hours, I'll show you pain that you never knew existed. You fuck with me now or fuck with me ever, I'll find you and give you what you deserve. Understand punk? Just nod." I give a little nod with some help of his hand pulling at my hair.

"Don't move." I hear him rustling in the bag. I hear cha-chink – cha-chink it sounds like a stapler. I'm being a good boy, being quiet and still, eyes shut tight as I can. My eyes are shut so tight I feel wrinkles in my cheeks, even though I'm only fifteen. He takes my glasses off. Boy, I'm lucky to still have them I think, not for the first time.

Hard Ass slides something over my head, it feels like a big rubber band on the back of my head and something heavy snaps over my eyes. He says "Open your eyes real wide, like you are trying to see something off in the distance." I do. I don't see anything, black as black can be.

Flash!

An unbelievable bright light, it hurts my eyes all the way to the back of my brain. I think of a civil defense film I'd seen in school, that's what it looks like. It looks like a nuclear explosion, right in my eyes. I think he blinded me and I'm freaking out, I held it together up until now - but that puts me over the edge.

I turn and bolt as fast as only an athlete or an adolescent can. Why wasn't Bad Ass expecting that? Oh - he did expect it, he just wanted a reason to tackle me and slap my face, really hard. I know at this point he wants to punch me – a lot, maybe beat me to death - but his boss is watching.

"Victor! Goddamn it contain yourself! We have to stay on track!" Boss Man is starting to lose his cool, maybe he's having a bad day at work. "You know the ends justify the means! Now get back and finish the job or I'll send you back where you came from and get another!"

That's the second time this guy has saved me from this lunatic.

Before Victor gets his knee out of my chest, he has to give one more, not so gentle nudge to my solar plexus. My vision is clearing, thank God, but I can't catch a breath. Man, this guy is mean, and I'm starting to be able to make him out. I'm nearsighted and thankfully, not blind so I see him. That is not supposed to happen. Victor sees me looking at him. He grabs me up like a rag doll and throws me on the hood of the car.

It's too late; I have a picture of him burned into my mind - black hair turning grey at the sides, big head, flat nose, and square chin. He looks Russian; the scar on his face is the most unforgettable part. A pink scar line goes from his forehead, down his nose to his chin. It's not a large scar, just a pink pencil line, except where it goes through the center of his lips. The lips took most of the damage, from whatever happened to him, as they are not lined up evenly, side to side. I won't forget that face or see it again, for a while.

The boss is taking over, he is making sure I don't see his face and I don't care. I'm just glad that he is being nice to me. The other guy reminded me of a Nazi or a prison guard like I had seen in old movies. "Get the other kit" he orders.

I say to him "We are not arrested, are we?"

"No, no, everything is ok, we're just about done and you both can go afterward."

The angle of the light changes and it's not quite in my eyes anymore.

"What did we do wrong?" I ask?

"Nothing, just be quiet and let me finish. Everything is ok; no one is going to hurt you."

A different man brings the "Kit" and sits it on the hood. It's like a small suitcase; he opens it and turns on some switches. Red, yellow, and green lights are blinking and then they burn steady. I see him take out a plastic face-mask like the one grandpa had in the hospital. He hands it to Boss Man. The boss says, "All I need is for you to give me three deep breaths - in and out, through the mask - ok? It's no big deal, promise."

It doesn't sound so bad, and what choice do I have anyway? I do it. In-out, in-out, in and out. Done.

"That wasn't so bad, was it?"

"No," I say. I can't see his assistant's face, but I can see his profile clean cut, nice suite and muscular build. He looks like an army guy.

Boss Man says, "The other analyzer."

Suit Guy pulls a square notebook thing from his case and lays it on the hood.

"Put your hand on it" the boss says. He assures me again that it won't hurt.

Of course, I do. It makes a whirring sound and a light moves slowly back and forth– twice. He says "Not so bad, right? Now the other hand please." The same thing, the light moves slowly back and forth twice, it doesn't hurt.

"Ok," he says to himself and holds his hand out for the next instrument.

point he wants to punch me – a lot, maybe beat me to death - but his boss is watching.

"Victor! Goddamn it contain yourself! We have to stay on track!" Boss Man is starting to lose his cool, maybe he's having a bad day at work. "You know the ends justify the means! Now get back and finish the job or I'll send you back where you came from and get another!"

That's the second time this guy has saved me from this lunatic.

Before Victor gets his knee out of my chest, he has to give one more, not so gentle nudge to my solar plexus. My vision is clearing, thank God, but I can't catch a breath. Man, this guy is mean, and I'm starting to be able to make him out. I'm nearsighted and thankfully, not blind so I see him. That is not supposed to happen. Victor sees me looking at him. He grabs me up like a rag doll and throws me on the hood of the car.

It's too late; I have a picture of him burned into my mind - black hair turning grey at the sides, big head, flat nose, and square chin. He looks Russian; the scar on his face is the most unforgettable part. A pink scar line goes from his forehead, down his nose to his chin. It's not a large scar, just a pink pencil line, except where it goes through the center of his lips. The lips took most of the damage, from whatever happened to him, as they are not lined up evenly, side to side. I won't forget that face or see it again, for a while.

The boss is taking over, he is making sure I don't see his face and I don't care. I'm just glad that he is being nice to me. The other guy reminded me of a Nazi or a prison guard like I had seen in old movies. "Get the other kit" he orders.

I say to him "We are not arrested, are we?"

"No, no, everything is ok, we're just about done and you both can go afterward."

The angle of the light changes and it's not quite in my eyes anymore.

"What did we do wrong?" I ask?

"Nothing, just be quiet and let me finish. Everything is ok; no one is going to hurt you."

A different man brings the "Kit" and sits it on the hood. It's like a small suitcase; he opens it and turns on some switches. Red, yellow, and green lights are blinking and then they burn steady. I see him take out a plastic face-mask like the one grandpa had in the hospital. He hands it to Boss Man. The boss says, "All I need is for you to give me three deep breaths - in and out, through the mask - ok? It's no big deal, promise."

It doesn't sound so bad, and what choice do I have anyway? I do it. In-out, in-out, in and out. Done.

"That wasn't so bad, was it?"

"No," I say. I can't see his assistant's face, but I can see his profile clean cut, nice suite and muscular build. He looks like an army guy.

Boss Man says, "The other analyzer."

Suit Guy pulls a square notebook thing from his case and lays it on the hood.

"Put your hand on it" the boss says. He assures me again that it won't hurt.

Of course, I do. It makes a whirring sound and a light moves slowly back and forth– twice. He says "Not so bad, right? Now the other hand please." The same thing, the light moves slowly back and forth twice, it doesn't hurt.

"Ok," he says to himself and holds his hand out for the next instrument.

The assistant hands him something. He says "I need you to tilt your head back, and open your mouth - wide. Don't bite me, and don't look at me." He doesn't say it mean, like the other guy Victor would. But the way he says it and the authority he emits leaves me with no doubt that it is in my best interest to obey.

"I'm just going to clean your teeth a little bit" he says. That reminds me I haven't brushed my teeth for days; I am embarrassed, but I do as I am told. I feel something like cotton being rubbed hard over my teeth, but mostly my gums, it didn't last long only about ten seconds. "Good" he says, then hands Suit Guy what looks like cotton on a stick.

"Only more thing," Boss Man says as he is already reaching for the next instrument. Suit Guy
hands him something I can't see. "Give me your hand please," he says in his nicest voice.

Now I can see what he is doing, he is letting me watch. He puts two Popsicle sticks on my middle finger, top and bottom and wraps them tight with some kind of tape. There is a wire coming out the bottom and leading back to the machine. Suit Guy is studying the suitcase, or I should say what's inside of it. After a short, while he says, "Good. Ok, ready."

The nicer guy takes my finger into the cup of his hand and squeezes, just a little. Suit Guy says, "Now!" And my finger is squeezed - hard – Something pokes, jabs or cuts that finger and it hurts. "OW"! I say, and try to turn and run, as I did before. But this guy is ready for it, and holds me fast and firm. Damn that hurt and these guys are strong! I'm starting to freak out again; this is all too much for me - for anyone!

The still nameless boss puts on his soothing voice again and says "It's ok, it's ok, that's it we're done." In a different voice he says, "Analyze! Go or no go?"

Suit Guy says nothing for what seems like a long time, and then he says "It's a Go!"

The Boss Man says to check with the blue team. I hear muffled voices in the car and a few seconds later a man calls out "Blue team is a Go!"

I know now that if it had been a no-go, both John and I would have been killed deader than dead, on the spot. We would have been nothing more than two more runaway kids that are never seen or heard from again.

"Wrap it up!" Boss Man says. He is giving rapid-fire orders as he walks away, I can hear some of them... double check, analyzes, notify, --- something com. Confirm position, get a fix on - - -?

I reach for my glasses and put them on, nobody stops me. I wonder where that crazy bastard is. Maybe he was ordered away. I hope so. The circle of cars is breaking up and leaving. Some are turning left and some are turning right down the swamp road. I move to the side out of the bright lights in front of me. Nobody stops me. Should I run? I'm thinking about it. Where is John? Is he all right? I think so; whatever this is we are in it together. More cars are leaving, there are only three or four, maybe five left.

I can hear snippets of the nice guy's voice coming from across the parking lot. Yes, sir. It's underway sir. He is standing outside a black car talking into a microphone. Yes sir, 03:00 sir. I can't see his face but I can see flashes glinting off his chest. Are those medals? And a bright gold color decorating his uniform, is it a uniform? Yes, I'm sure it is. There are gold strips running all the way down his legs, there are more strips on his shoulders and in squiggly lines across his hat. I've seen enough movies to think, this guy looks like a general, and he acts like one too.

My arm is twisted behind my back in the classic - move and I'll break your arm hold. "Hey punk, I haven't forgotten about you."

Shit, I know who this is; it's the accented voice, Bad Ass.

"Move!" He forces me around to the back side of the big suburban and to my surprise, he doesn't break my arm. "Sit down and stay there. I'm watching you boy." He talks funny; he's not from anywhere I've ever been or like anyone I have ever met, so far.

I hear footsteps crunching on the gravel, coming my way. A cop, a no doubt about it cop, then another one. Big badges, big guns and big guys, they stand there looking at me for a minute then, without a word, turn around and leave. That was weird, but what hasn't been tonight? More footsteps in the gravel, two more cops. One has on a blue uniform and the other has a brown uniform. They have John in the middle, and wow, he is a mess. Do I look that bad? His long hair is dirty and there is a large chunk missing from the left side. I don't think even my lunatic interrogator took that much off me, but then again, I don't have as much hair. Or could his interrogator be even meaner than mine? Na, couldn't be. Damn, he is filthy dirty from head to toe and speaking of toes, the son of a bitch still has my sneakers on! I'm glad to see him, but I'm mad as holy hell about the sneakers and about him being such a baby in the swamp.

I look in his eyes and I see redness; he has been crying. And what else, fear? I think to myself I'm hip to that and what else? Oh, the little fucker is glad to see me. He is really not so little, but I have been thinking of him that way lately. Can't he talk? Can I talk? One of his escort cops tells him to sit down. The cops don't seem to care about us seeing them like the other guys. Wonder why? They stand there for a long minute and turn and leave without another word.

"Hey John!" I rise to my knees and go over and shake him. "Hey!" He shakes his head and his eyes slowly focus. "Mark?" "Yeah John, you, ok?" "I don't know, I think I've been dreaming." "This is a dream, right Mark?" "If this is a dream then we are both having the same one, a nightmare, but I think we are really in this parking lot, in this swamp and those guys are up to no good." John says "I think this is a dream, a bad one, pinch me" he says. I reach over and slap him hard twice, full hand and backhand. I hear chuckling in the shadows, it's my lunatic friend. He drops his head into his lap and begins to cry, loudly sobbing. "Hey, hey, I say I'm sorry you needed more than a pinch and I'm still pissed about my sneakers. "Calm down we have to think, whatever this it is we are in it together."

"That guy is bad," John says in a shaky voice.

"What guy?" "The one that asked me questions, lots of them."

"What did he do to you, John?" "He cut my hair, about blinded me, stuck something in my mouth, punched me in the gut and cut my finger!"

"Did he make you put your hands on a funny plate?"

"Yeah! He did that too."

"Was he mean?" "Oh, yeah, that guy is mean alright, and scary."

"We are in some deep shit here John."

A car starts, then another. The ugly voice in the shadows says to stay there and don't move. I've heard that before I think. Two cars pull nose to nose with us in the middle. All the lights they have are on us again. Can't see anything but glare, again.

The calm soothing voice is on the bullhorn. "You boys need to take a break and rest awhile. "I know what you need. I brought you some supplies. I'm going to leave a bag full of things that you need. Get something to eat and calm down, it's ok. There is drinking water and water to wash up with. Understand?"

Yes. Well, no, not at all but I didn't say it.

"And one more thing, and this is important – in one hour's time, you both are to leave. Go to the right out of the parking lot and walk that way. You can hitchhike I don't care, just be sure that both of you walk that way. Understand?"

I say "Yes."

He says it again, "Do you understand?"

He wants John to say yes. I give him a nudge.

"Yes, I understand" John says. "We are to walk that way."

"Point, please." John points to the right side of the road.

The voice says, "And you?"

"Me?"

"Yes, point, please."

I point to the right side of the road.

"I have to make sure that you both understand, in one hour you will both walk that way."

And he says it again, "Do you both understand?"

"Yes," I say, 'In one hour we will walk that way," and I point again to the right.

"Good, walk that way."

A car door opens and closes, then another. The last three vehicles pull out of the parking lot and they all turn to the right. They are in no apparent hurry and drive slowly away.

We are alone again, in the parking lot in the swamp.

Three

The tail lights of the last three cars slowly disappear down the road to the right. There is a lot of dust in the air, but a slight breeze floats it away.

John says "What just happened? What did those assholes want?" I don't say anything, I'm thinking. I'm thinking that my feet are cold. I'm looking at John and thinking about beating the shit out of him, taking back my sneakers and leaving him.

I am looking a little past him and I notice something in the gravel just over his right shoulder. A bag is on the ground and what is that other thing, a triangle? It looks like a tent, what is that? I get up, man I'm sore, I hurt in places I didn't even know I had. I feel way older than my fifteen years. I wonder if this is what it feels like to be old. I get up slowly like an old man and walk over for a better look. I see a long bag, like a baseball bag but longer and fatter. I nudge it with my barefoot and it's heavy. I walk a few steps over to the weird triangle thing; it is holding a bag of some kind. I give it a push and it sways.

As I explore the bag with my hands, I find a knob or some kind of thing at the bottom and twist it, nothing. There is a button in the middle of the knob, I push it and water spurts out. It's a water bag and there is writing on it, I can't make out what it says.

"John!" "Come here, I need your matches."

He comes over and is fumbling with the Marlboro pack trying to get out a twisted cigarette.

Good idea I think we might as well smoke em if we got em. He hands me one and strikes a match, we light up. I take the lit match from him and hold it up to see the writing on the bag - US Air Force.

Come to think of it, it has been a long time since we had anything to drink; just a passing thought seems to instantly transform into an urgent thirst. I sit down to get my face under the spicket, toss the cigarette aside, push the button and taste the water. Cold clean wonderful water, I drink until I have stop for air, and do again, & again. I get my fill and hold my head under the stream trying to wash the dirt and grit out of my hair and off my face and out of my eyes. I really want to take a bath.

I remember John and I'm just about to tell him about the water when he calls to me first.

"Mark! Come look!" "Look at all this stuff!"

I walk over a few steps and see that John has already unzipped the fat baseball bag and it looks like a lot of "stuff".

There are about half a dozen paper bags in the black bag and a pile of things around John. He is sitting Indian style on the ground. He has a Hershey's bar in one hand and a Pepsi in the other. He seems almost happy.

I know that I feel one hell of a lot better. I think we are both forgetting the strangeness – no, that's not the right way to say it, more like thankful there is no stress at the moment. And I'm thankful for the water bag and the bag of, what? Presents? That's kind of what it feels like, presents. Presents from who? Who would do all of those crazy things that just happened to us and leave presents for us?

John says, "Want a Pepsi?"

"Yeah."

"A candy bar?"

"Yeah."

"With or without nuts?"

"There are that many?"

"Yeah," he says, "I counted 20, ten of the plain ones and 10 with nuts, we are down to 18, I think."

I say, "Yeah, hand me a candy bar, I don't care which kind, and a Pepsi."

He does, and I notice that the Pepsi is cold, ice cold. I consumed the candy bar in four bites and the Pepsi in six gulps.

"What is all this stuff?" I say, as I sit down on the gravel next to him.

My feet are killing me and I'm not as happy as I was just a moment ago. There are a million things that we should talk about, need to talk about, but that's not the priority. Of course, the 'presents' are. The slight breeze I noticed before must be happening way up in the sky too, as the clouds are breaking up and a more than half-moon is providing some light. The light is still dim, but it's a big improvement.

At the same time, we both naturally grab two of the biggest paper bags. The tops are folded over and stapled, but neither one of us notice as we both ripped the bags to shreds. "Clothes, Sneakers!" John says. I find the same in my bag. "Socks!" I say "And sneakers!" I'm really interested in those. I wipe the stones off my feet and slide a sneaker on, it's a little big but that will work, yeah, so much better. "They are too small!" John says in the girliest voice I have ever heard out of him. "They are too small" he says again.

"Jesus John, calm down. Maybe they are my size and maybe these will fit you, try em."

I throw him the one I haven't put on, and kick off the other; it comes off easily and flies right to him.

"It fits!" John says.

"Good," I say "throw me your bag and the sneakers; I have a feeling they know our sizes, right down to the T." We trade bags – or I should say piles.

I slide it on & a perfect fit. I examine the other one more closely; it's a Ked, the kind with the red toe, the good ones.

John says, "What else is in the bag?"

I quickly tear through it to find the socks I mentioned before and one pair of new underwear. A pair of pants, 32-32, my size, & not just the cheap K Mart brand I'm used to, but the real Levis. There is also a t-shirt and a long sleeve shirt.

I'm saying this out loud and everything I say John says – "I got that too." John is back in the black bag, he says "This one's heavy, let's open it. "The bag is being ripped apart even as he is saying it. "Food!" More unwrapping. "A sub!"

Luckily it has already been cut in half so there is something for me to grab. I do like before with the water, having food right in front of me makes me suddenly ravenously hungry. After four giant bites right in a row, I grab one of the cold Pepsis that are next to John and wash it down.

"Holy shit that's good" John says and I agree.

"What else is in that bag?" We didn't notice before because we are both concentrating on the submarine sandwich.

"Chips!" It's a big bag of Lays potato chips. It's quickly ripped open and in seconds we are both crunching on potato chips.

I lean over and paw around where the ripped-up bag the sub came in and come up with a cardboard container of strawberries. "Yes!" I say, "I love strawberries!"

We both chow down on some strawberries and I notice that I am getting full already, I didn't eat that much, it seems weird I can normally eat a lot. I put what's left of my sandwich down. And I think to myself – don't trust John, remember the sneakers? I'm sure he will eat it if I don't, so I force myself to finish the sandwich.

"What else do we have?" I say as I glance up at John, who has finished his sandwich and about all of the strawberries. Damn, I think and grab the last two. I reach for a small bag and John does the same, I rip mine open and find two toothbrushes, a small tube of toothpaste, a bar of Ivory soap, two wash clothes and two bottles of what I would now know as hotel size bottles of shampoo. I tell John what I have, item by item as I discover them. "What is in your bag John?"

"Two canteens and two pieces of some kind of plastic I don't know what they are." He sounds disappointed that he didn't get a better "Present" "What do you mean plastic? Let me see." I recognize the plastic as collapsible cups, like the ones that came in my Cub Scout mess kit.

"They are cups" I tell him.

"Let's open the big bag," John says, then rips it open. Two very nice heavy denim jackets fall out.

"Take the one that fits you" I say, "I'm sure the other one will fit me just fine." He puts his jacket on and I do the same. Yep, perfect fit.

Only two bags left, John picks up the bigger of the two, and I take the other one.

John says "Alright! Cigarettes!" And sure enough, he has four packs of Marlboros. "What else in there?" He says, "Four packs of matches and a bag of, I don't know, I can't read it."

He hands me the package and it is kind of heavy, I squint and I'm able to read the writing - beef jerky. I never had it before and neither has he, but of course we'll keep it. My package feels light.

"Open the last one Mark, open it!".

"Ok," and I do.

In it are two baseball caps. One is an L.A. Dodgers cap and the other one is an Atlanta Braves baseball cap. I hand him the L.A. Dodgers cap and I keep the Braves cap.

And something else is at the bottom of the bag. I pull it out and stare at it. It's a stopwatch. Chills run up and down my spine, as I stare at it. It's running and the hands have that luminous glow of some watches of the day. The hands say thirty-five minutes have passed. "Twenty-five minutes," I say.

"What?"

"It is twenty-five minutes until we have to leave."

"Oh, hell no," John says, "I don't want any part of those crazies, I know that Omaha is to the left and that's the way I'm going. I'm going east on I 80. I want to go home."

"Yeah, me too John, I mean, I want to go home, but we can't go that way."

"Why can't we go that way?"

"John think about it, remember those two crazy, mean bastards that were asking us questions?"

"How can I forget them?"

"Well, they are down the road to the left, and their just hoping that we come that way."

"How do you know?"

"I'm telling you, it's true. I don't know how I know it, but I do. I can feel it deep in my bones."

John says, "I'm not going the way they want me to!"

"John do what you want, all I know is that in 25 minutes we need to be out of here - or they will come back for us."

"How do you know?"

"Damn it, John, I don't know what you want me to tell you; I'm going to wash up and put these clean clothes on. We don't have all the time in the world, we have what? Twenty-three minutes!"

It doesn't take me long to get undressed; I take off my new jacket, peel off my pants and my shirt, and that's all I have on. I don't say anything and John is quiet. A thought passes my mind; it would be nice if he is thinking about what I said. I find the washcloth, the bar of Ivory soap and the small bottle of shampoo. John says "I want to wash up too!" "Ok, I say get ready, hey throw me my old pants and shirt. I want to stand on them, my feet are sore enough, pal."

"Ok," he says sheepishly and he tosses me my dirty clothes. I put the pants that are already wet under the water bag and save the shirt for a towel. I start to wash up – really good, oh, my goodness, it feels good. I try to be quick, but it still takes about four or five minutes.

John's turn. I pick up my dirty dry shirt to dry off and put on my new clothes, then sit on my old shirt and put on my new socks and wonderful new sneakers. Everything fits perfectly. I feel a lot better with a full belly, a bath, clean clothes and comfortable sneakers. Even my head feels a little bit clearer. It seems like I can think better and I'm thinking – how did they know exactly what we needed? And get the right sizes? Do they care about us? Or, do they want something else? What could they want from us; we don't have anything except what they left us. How long have they been watching us? Are they watching now? Yes, I think they are, but how? I don't see anybody.

Have they been watching us ever since we crossed the Nebraska state line and that funny feeling set in? That kind of makes sense. I feel a need to move and decide to walk around the parking area and search for clues, maybe I can I can spot somebody watching. I put on my new Atlanta Braves baseball cap and the denim jacket and start walking toward the back side of the parking area. There is a wooden stairway leading down to the river or stream. I slowly descend the steps, walking carefully, still worried about snakes; I wish for the stick I had before & don't see one handy.

The steps are steep and seem to go on forever. I come out of the wood line and can see a river below, a big wide river. On the other side of the river, I see a bright light moving rapidly in my direction, I feel the ground rumble and I hear the long blast of a locomotive horn, a train roars by on the opposite side of the river. I can hear the click, click, click of the wheels on the rails. This is important information; I know that train tracks always lead to a city. Maybe we can get to the other side of the river and follow the tracks. Maybe walking the tracks would be a good idea. Maybe we can hobo-ride a train to the east.

About the same time, I wonder if there are boats and barges on this river; of course, there would be. I strain my eyes to see down to the bend of the river and I see a faint green light & maybe a red one behind it, I have been on boats before and I know that navigation lights are required to burn at night. It's a boat on this side of the shore. Is that them? The time! Holy shit, the time! I race up the steps, two at a time, forgetting about snakes. "John!"

"What?" he says. John is still messing around with the water; he doesn't even know that I left.

"Come on! We have to go!"

"I'm in no hurry."

"Well, you damn sure better be, if you're coming with me! The time! I run over to the watch; it's two minutes past the hour!" I pocket the watch.

John says "So what; fuck those people."

"You don't get it do you, John? These fuckers are going to kill us if we don't do as they say."

I need to move! I know it. I shake everything out of the black bag and check to make sure that it's empty. It is. Next, I pick up all the trash and wrappers, and toss them into the bag. The pile that's left, we are keeping. Two packs of cigarettes and two books of matches are going in my pocket, along with my toothbrush, toothpaste and the beef jerky. I'll take the canteen; yes, fill it up and take it. What else is there? Oh, those little plastic collapsible cups – I don't know what I am going to do with them, but I'll take them. And, that's it. Oh – get one of the packs of gum and half of the candy bars, eight each. And that's it. John can have the half bag of Lays chips and the two Pepsis.

John is taking his time drying off and hasn't said anything stupid in at least 2 minutes, until now–
"What are you doing?" he says.

"I'm going to fill this canteen and I'm out of here. Don't forget to fill yours."

"Wait for me" he says.

"No, I can't," I tell him "It's five minutes past time to leave, and this place is not safe. You should know that. You stay here and you're going to have company, the kind you don't want. John, we have lots to talk about, but we have to do it as we walk. I'll walk slowly. Hurry and catch up."

"But Mark, wait for me!"

"I told you, I'll walk slow, but I have to walk that way." I point to the right and start out.

Four

I'm still a little scared; but, not nearly as frightened as when we were with the police – or when we were first dumped in the swamp – or in the car with the crazy, possessed women – or in the Pontiac before that. I feel strangely good. I'm rested and comfortable in my new clothes, kind of energized, like a major second wind. I have to wonder if they drugged me – somehow; maybe in the food or water; or maybe, when they poked my finger or "cleaned my teeth".

I didn't taste anything bitter or nasty, everything was delicious. It couldn't have been downers, because I'm wide awake. Amphetamines, speed? I never tried that – but maybe they did, because I have all kinds of energy.

I have to remember the kind people I'm dealing with – the army, air force, or government. I think of the general; who would he be taking orders from? Maybe a higher ranking general? Or, maybe a senator, or… the President of the United States? I wish I could figure it out.

The swamp is back to its full night noise, and it's kind of soothing; I'm not scared of it anymore. I'm thinking – yes, there are snakes and things in the swamp, but the people we met tonight take the cake; compared to them, the swamp is nothing to be afraid of.

I am walking slowly and also wondering about John. Did he stay put, or turn and walk to the left– like he said he was going to. No way am I going back. He can do what he wants; my mind is definitely made up. I stop for a few seconds and listen, can't hear anything but swamp noise.

I think about calling to John and decide not to. I made it clear to him that I am going to slowly walk this way. I keep on trucking. No traffic at all, why did the man with the bull horn say we could hitchhike if we wanted to? Maybe he knew there would be no cars, because maybe he closed the road? I like the way I'm thinking – it seems that I am on the edge of making sense out of something that makes no sense. It's like having an answer on the tip of your tongue and not being able to spit it out.

I don't know why, I just seem to know certain things, like we better go the way were are told. Ok, keep moving – if I am right, he'll be along shortly. I'll count to one hundred and stop and call for him. Maybe if he hears me, he will hurry his ass along. "Hey John!" I holler down the road just as loud as I can.

"Mark, Mark" I hear him faintly. He must be alive and coming this way; that's good, but he didn't have any choice.

I have been walking slowly for about ten minutes or so; if he hustles, he should catch up in less than five. It doesn't take him that long. He comes at a fast walk.

"Hey," he says.

"Hello, it's good to see you. What took you so long?"

"I started to walk the other way and I got scared, I knew it would be the end of me if I kept walking. So, I turned around and hustled to catch up with you."

"How are you feeling?"

"Better, a lot better. I am full of energy and I thought about what you said; you're right, we have to keep going and see what happens."

"Did you bring your canteen?"

"Yeah, I did, and everything else I thought was useful."

"Good."

"It sure was nice to have a bath and some food" I say.

John says "And the clothes, how did they know the size of my feet?"

"I know John, a million questions and I can't think of a good answer to any of them."

John says, "Except one thing, they picked us. And they have been watching us for a while."

I say "Yeah."

John says "I think the black guys and the girls were a part of it."

"Yeah, I say, willingly or unwillingly."

"Right?"

"Right."

I'm so happy the old John is back and he seems to be thinking along the same line as me.

"So, the black guys led us to the girls, and the girls to them, in the swamp."

"Who are they?" John asks.

"Good question" I say. "You're not going like this, but I think they are the government, and they are not playing with us – they are experimenting on us."

"What do you mean" John asks.

"Well, I am wondering if we were given some kind of drug or something."
"Why are you wondering that?"

"Because of the way I'm feeling right now, I want to do as I am told and I want to hurry and get there as quick as I can. How about you? You feel the same thing?"

"Yes, and it's weird.'

"No kidding."

'Your head feel clearer?'

"Yeah."

"Are you full of energy?"

"Yeah."

"Scared like before?"

"No."

"See what I mean?"

"Hey," John says "if they are experimenting on us do you think they will kill us and cut us open to see whatever it is they are looking for?"

"I hope not John, but it's something creepy alright."

"Let's walk faster I want to get this over with, whatever it is" says John.

We walk faster, it's like we are being pulled along the road. Neither one of us says anything for a long time.

"Hey," I say to John "Why didn't they just give us a ride?"

"The possessed girl said that we are to come of our own free will. That makes sense and it doesn't; well, maybe they were just helping."

"Helping who? Why did she say we were to come of our own free will?"

We keep walking.

"Hey John."

"What," he says.

"You didn't overhear any names, did you?"

"Yeah, Ivan, I heard someone say Ivan; I think he is the mean prick that was asking me questions."

"Did you see any uniforms?"

"Yeah, I did, the cop uniforms."

"What else did you see?"

"I'm not sure; I have been scared all night."

"Mark I'm having a hard time talking, I mean I feel ok, but my mouth does not want to work."

I am thinking the same thing because I want to tell him about the river and the railroad tracks, but it seems like too much work.

"Stop," I manage to say. "Do you hear that?"

"What?"

"The frogs and the crickets quit making noise; it's not loud like before. Listen, nothing but quiet."

John says "I hear something."

My hearing has never been that great and I hear nothing. "What? What is it?" I say. All I hear is spooky quiet, why did all of the swamp things just shut up?

"No," John says, "I hear something, it's faint; wait, its music – like state fair or a field - days, a carnival kind of music. There must be a field - days or something going on. Can you hear it?"

About the same time, I hear the carnival notes and notice that the road is getting wider and the swamp is retreating back on both sides of the road. We are coming up on some kind of intersection, something bigger than just a country crossroad. I say, "Yeah, it's a carnival of some sort John."

John says "Let's go over there and see if we can get some work, make some money. They always need help manning the rides and booths, and we sure could use the money. When the carnival leaves, we can go with them and get out of this awful place."

I think about it for about one second, that's all. "No," I say, "I have a bad feeling about the carnival; I think there are more bad people and weird stuff over there."

"Why?" He shouts "You don't like my idea? Get some money and get out of this place?" He is getting angry with me; he doesn't feel my sense of dread about the carnival.

"Stop John, just stop walking – ok?" And we do. "Do you feel that?" "What?"

"The pull, I don't feel the pull anymore. Do you?"

"Yeah, you're right, I can definitely stop."

I say, "Let's think a minute, you want a smoke?"

"Yeah, sure," he says. We have some water from our canteens, light up a smoke, and sit down on the edge of the road.

"Why did the pull, the urgency to move, just stop? What was up with the police? I mean they were real, but they didn't act real."

"I know" John says "But, there were more than cops, you said there were some army guys, you said a general?"

"Since when does the army work with cops?"

John says, "I lied to them; I told them Father Ralph beat me and sexually abused me. I think they knew I was lying and they didn't care, how about that?"

"Oh yeah," I said. "I lied about my age, my name, and I don't even remember what else – but yeah, they knew and didn't care. Why? Do you think the regular cops are working with the army, or have been ordered to?"

"When we had that weird feeling on the bridge, that's when it started, right?'

"Right."

"Think about this – the black guys, maybe they were controlled, like mind control. I have seen something like that on Star Trek, the girls too, and what about the traffic? We haven't seen any cars – except the police, since we have been on this road."

"We hear carnival music and yet where are the cars?"

"People have to drive here, right?"

"I heard the general guy say something about 03:00, what time is that?"

John says, "3:00 am. "What time do you think it is now?"

I say, "Well it had just gotten dark when all of this started to happen, 7:00, 7:30? And, it's been what, two or three hours?"

John says "It can't be past 11:00, because the carnival would be shut down."

I check the stopwatch; it says one hour and forty-five minutes have passed. I say "That makes sense; it must be about 10:30."

"So, what do you think is going to happen at 3 am?"

John says, "I don't know but I still feel scared, something is way wrong here."

"I'm hip to that," I say, "Let's move." At least we seem to be thinking more clearly and we know that we can't just sit here.

It is still weirdly quiet, except the carnival music is getting clearer as we walk up a small hill, toward an intersection that we can now see is another bridge. We walk without saying anything until we are standing on a highway overpass looking down on two sets of double lanes. Are the highway lanes east and west, or north and south? I am thinking of the river to the right; if it is the Missouri, it runs mostly north and south… so, east should be to the right and west to the left. There is a road sign that says Omaha 24 to the left and a sign that says Des Moines 46 to the right.

There are four ramps tying this intersection with the main road; two off ramps and two on-ramps for each direction of travel. We are standing at the center of the bridge, staring down; we are looking for traffic, there is none. No cars in sight. We cross to the other side of the bridge and look the other way with the same intensity. No cars in sight. It is the same thing, spooky.

"Where are all the cars?"

The carnival music is louder and we can see the lights and hear the din of people talking and laughing, just over the ridge. "How can there be people laughing and having fun just over there – but, no people or cars in sight at a major intersection?"

"Fuck this!" John is whacking out again, but in a different way. "I'm going over there where it seems normal! I have had enough of this strange shit!" He starts walking toward the carnival noise.

"John wait!"

"No, Mark, you don't get it, I'm getting outta here! Come with me if you want, I'm splitting!"

I run to catch up with him. I want to explain why I think – no, I know – it's a bad idea to go there.

We both hear, "Sandy! Stop!"

I look up and I'm startled to see two young girls, about our age, standing in the road right in front of us.

Five

Strategic Air Command, Offutt Air Force Base Omaha, Nebraska.

General Walter Brannon sits alone at a plain grey metal desk, in a soundproof room, waiting for a call on the red phone. Three of the four walls are lined with deep pyramid shaped acoustic padding. The wall in front of him is of thick bullet and soundproof glass; beyond and below is a large room, not just any room, it is a state-of-the-art satellite communications center. It had recently been refurbished with banks of computers, most just slightly smaller than a one car garage.

They all have spinning tapes, dials, and blinking lights. Two officers with the highest security clearance are assigned to each of the eight huge banks of computers. Suspended in the air, high above the front of the room, are four giant television screens – each screen is ten feet tall and fifteen feet wide. What they display is the latest information of military importance. Highly secret information is displayed on the screens, such as the locations of US and Russian submarines – and that is just one screen.

All US Navy nuclear ballistic submarines are instructed to open their secret orders and maintain radio silence. Their positions are now only estimated. Another screen shows the location, altitude, and speed of eighteen individual B-52 squadrons. Three B-52's is considered the ideal number of aircraft – as at least one is likely to get through, and three would be the maximum loss. Each squadron consists of three B-52 bombers, all are loaded and fully armed with four nuclear missiles. Each missile contains four individually targetable warheads.

There are eight hundred and sixty-four nuclear missiles in the air and ready to fire. And, that's not counting the ICBMs, or the missiles on the submarines. All military personnel have been ordered to full alert status. All aircraft are to be either in the air or on ready standby.

All Navy ships and submarines have been ordered to sea. The known and estimated positions of all naval vessels in the world are shown other screens. The fourth screen is a map of the land mass of the world, but enlarged and emphasized are the maps of the Soviet Union and of the United States.

General Walt Brannon looks at the scene through the glass. He sees dozens of uniformed men working frantically at their stations. Men scurry about with papers and messages on the main floor below. Senior officers from all branches of service, Air Force, Navy, Marines, Army, and Coast Guard are standing with several clean-cut government men in black suits, at a high railing in the back of the room. All are gripping the railing with both hands. All are sweating and acting stressed.

General Brannon is looking through the glass, down into the situation room, taking it all in and accessing the situation. He needs an order, a presidential order; the red phone at his right hand is a direct line to the President of the United States. He stares at it and wills it to ring; it does not ring.

The scene below him is of military chaos. There is a flashing yellow light at the center of the front main wall, below the flashing yellow light are words, they say DEFCOM – 2. The military alert hasn't been at this high of a level since the Fall of 1962, with the Cuban missile crises. One more level and it goes to DEFCON – 1; that will mean war, not just another war, but an all-out nuclear war – and the destruction of the planet.

Generals are usually not squeamish about going to war, just the opposite; they normally would welcome the opportunity to show off their military skills. But in this case, they are very squeamish about going to war. They know that it is a war that cannot be won. The enemy is not just the Russians… if only it were that simple.

The general has to get up and pace. He is one of the few people who know the whole truth, the reason both countries are at their highest military alert levels. The truth is unbelievable, but true. The truth is code named – Operation Noah's Ark; and, if it doesn't work… well, he can't think that way; the project must work. But, will the Russians go along with the plan?

General Brannon knows that President Nixon is trying, really trying, to save the United States from destruction. Brannon believes in Nixon, who personally briefed him with the details and seriousness of the situation. Just twelve hours ago, Brannon had been summoned to the Oval Office to receive the unbelievable briefing and set of orders. Shortly after the meeting, President Nixon flew, nonstop, from Washington to Moscow.

General Secretary Brezhnev is facing the same problem in his country. Brezhnev has invited Nixon to push forward a previously scheduled summit by a day; and, has granted Nixon an immediately audience at the Kremlin. In the meantime, the Russian armed forces are also on their highest alert level. A very dangerous time. What if the Russian hotheads start launching?

The generals and men in black suits also know most of the truth about Operation Noah's Ark. That's why they are sweating, even though the room temperature is a constant 68 degrees.

The ringing phone startles General Brannon out of his thoughts; in three strides Brannon crosses the room; he picks up the phone on the second ring. The voice on the other end is familiar, from the nightly news. It is National Security Advisor Henry Kissinger, calling from Air Force One on a runway in Moscow Russia.

"Good evening, General," Kissinger says in his slow, deep and somewhat nasal voice.

"Good evening Mr. Kissinger, sir."

"General, we are using Air Force One as our hotel and headquarters while we are in Moscow. The president is getting ready for his meeting with Secretary Brezhnev; he will be with you in a moment and give you your orders. But, for now, I have been told to brief you on the situation as we know it, at this time."

"The "Others" have doubled their demand for healthy adolescents; from fifty to one hundred. That's one hundred from both Russia and the United States. The timetable for delivery has been pushed back by twenty-four hours. You will be given the location with enough advance time to ensure the cargo is delivered. There will be no hostilities toward the "Others;" and, there will be no civilian witnesses, or recordings, of this action."

"Yes sir, Mr. Kissinger, anything else?"

"No General, that's all I am to brief you on. Please hold the line, the president will be with you in a moment. Goodnight, General."

"Goodnight, Mr. Kissinger, sir."

Six

President Nixon comes on the line. He begins the way he always does, in strong clipped sentences.

"General Brandon?"

"Yes, sir."

"Stop with the yes sirs, for now Brandon. We are in a real fix, as are the Russians, the whole world in fact. Your mission is very complicated; and, if we succeed, no one can ever know. If we fail – well, no one will ever know that either. I'm going to spend as much time as needed on this call to explain everything, as I know it. I want you to feel free to ask questions. You need to know as much as I do."

"Yes, sir."

"You may call me Dick or Richard. If we are successful in our jobs, we will beat this thing; and then, we will get to live, along with the rest of the world."

"Sir, Richard, can you fill me in from the beginning?"

"The beginning, no, I can only guess at that, as we are talking about thousands of years. To put it bluntly, there are at least three species of aliens – we call them the "Others." They have been visiting Earth for their own reasons, and have been doing so for a very long time – Walter."

"They all want something, and are getting something from our planet. They want humans and human DNA. We discovered DNA in 1953 – I believe with their help. We have much to learn, but it seems very important. They also harvest minerals, plants, and compounds that are useful to them. The "Others" are concerned that the USA and the Soviet Union will engage in a nuclear war or unintentionally poison the planet with radiation. If that were to happen, their investment of thousands of years and their Earth mine of resources would disappear."

"This month alone, the Russians have "tested" eight nuclear devices. And, we have "tested" two devices this week, with two more tests set for later in the month. We have set off more than 450 nuclear weapons in our own country since 1945. Some of them were damn powerful and not good for our planet. These beings I'm telling you about do exist; and, they have a reason to be nervous about the health of our planet. This cannot continue. We won't have to go to war, at the rate we are testing; we will have poisoned the earth beyond repair in less than three years; and, what if there are more detonations besides just tests? Our otherworldly visitors are very real; and they're not at all kidding about squashing us like bugs and starting over."

"I know this shakes your faith in God, in everything. It shook me up, but now everything is crystal clear. It is my destiny to fulfill this fifty-year lease on the planet with the "Others;" there is no choice. It's too bad I won't be able to take credit for this in the next election; I could use the public relations help. I believe I'll need one more term to fully implement all of the conditions of this agreement. Can I count on your vote, Walter?"

"Absolutely, sir."

"Just kidding Walter, kind of; but I will do whatever it takes to win this next election – not just for me, but for our country. I need to clean up the mess that Johnson left. Ok, back to our situation. It has been made perfectly clear to Soviet General Secretary Brezhnev and to me, that we have seven days to reduce our nuclear arsenals and improve our dialog, to eliminate the chance of nuclear war. That was four days ago General, we have three days left to comply."

"Mr. President sir, what happens if you and Brezhnev can't come to an agreement?"

"At midnight on the seventh day, a plague will descend on Earth. The plague will leave 100 percent of all humans dead; and, the "Others" will start over again."

"Sir, Richard, help me understand; why are the kids are so important to them?"

"Three reasons I can think of Walter. First, they want cooperation between our government and themselves, cooperation between the Russian government and themselves; and; of course, a type of forced cooperation between the US and Russia. The two hundred adolescents are kind of an insurance policy for them, kind of an Adam and Eve, X 100. That's why I chose the code name Noah's Ark."

"How long have we known about them sir; I mean Richard?"

"I suspect that some, if not most leaders, have known about the "Others" over the centuries. But, almost none of them had the balls to write any of it down, except Harry Truman. Thank God for Harry; he left his presidential successors a very comprehensive and detailed notebook on the subject. Harry believed that President Roosevelt had extensive dealings with the "Others" during World War II, but, kept it a secret from him – that and the Manhattan project. It pissed Harry off, and he decided that no US president would be completely in the dark on this matter ever again. So, he wrote the notebook and more. Harry Truman's insight and genius initiated the Department of Defense and the Central Intelligence Agency."

"The agencies primary and undisclosed mission is – to cooperate with the "Others" and gather as much scientific knowledge as possible, while at the same time keeping the truth a secret and protecting the public as much as possible. President Truman signed a classified executive order, the National Security Act, and traded operational areas to the "Others" in exchange for technology. We also agreed to produce the food they eat from Earth. This still goes on to this day. It is a top-secret farming operation carried out at Area 51 and Los Alamos. Most of the technology we acquired is unusable as it requires telepathic input. We are still unable to use most of what they traded in 1947, but not for lack of trying. Oh, we try; for twenty-five years we have been trying to bridge the gap between alien technology and ours. The few things we have been able to reverse engineer are astounding. Would you believe, we are on the verge of transmitting vast amounts of information through wires made of glass? The different colors of the light spectrum transmit data. We are shrinking the size of computers by 50% a year, while doubling their processing power. This is what is going on Walter, all because of a brilliant deal made by President Truman."

"He wrote the notebook in August and September of 1947, right after the Roswell incident. I believe he had a rude awakening that Summer. Late in Harry Truman's presidency, he decided to collect information from the public regarding unidentified flying objects with the inception of Project Blue Book, that is – the one that is publicly official. Before that, there were other top-secret endeavors; Project Sign and Project Grudge were two such undertakings. None of the information from those two projects was ever made public. It is still highly classified."

"That is some of what is contained in Harry Truman's notebook. Every president since then has had access to the document and is expected to keep it up to date. The information scared President Eisenhower to death. As a brilliant general he knew when a battle couldn't be won. He was forced into signing another pact; one he didn't want to accept. The Presidential Alien Pact of February 1954, allowed for non-interference with the abduction of one thousand American citizens per year as test subjects for experiments; mostly, they were women and adolescents to be examined and supposedly returned. That's just about where we come in Walter. Oh, I should tell you Kennedy was aghast when he read the notebook and planned to reveal the information to the American public. That's the real reason Kennedy was killed in Dallas. And, a damned good reason we keep this secret. Do you understand?"

"Yes sir."

"Johnson didn't give a damn about anything except his own ass; and, here we are."

"I had heard about the notebook and was anxious to read it after my inauguration; from then on
I became an even a bigger supporter of NASA. I was the proud president to congratulate the crew of Apollo 11 on their successful lunar mission, and Apollo 13? Well, there is more to that story as well. I have pushed hard for funding something called the Space Shuttle. That's a reusable spacecraft that will blast off like a rocket and glide home with wings on its return. That technology is what's needed to economically put satellites in space and maybe even build the space station NASA is dreaming about. Oh, sorry General, let me get back to the point."

"The idea of Project Blue Book was to collect information on the "Others" and their activities with average American citizens. And at the same time, we were "officially" conducting investigations of unidentified flying objects; ultimately, we explained them as: weather balloons, military aircraft, lighting, auroras, stars, planets, and clouds, anything but the truth was to be told to the public. It proved to be a kind of a debunking mandate. The panic from Orson Wells broadcast of War of the Worlds influenced his decision to keep the project secret. I ordered the termination of Project Blue Book in 1969. The reason, too many questions were being asked by the public. Too much had been whitewashed, and the venture was becoming counterproductive. It was best to put Project Blue Book back into the Top-Secret realm."

"Mr. President, sir, may I ask why the "Others" would need us to herd these children along, I mean; they seem capable of doing that without our help."

"Walter, their reason as far as I can figure, is to demonstrate their powers to us and the Russians, and to force cooperation between our two superpowers. The scarier thing is that we know of at least one species, the Nordics we call them, has the power of mind control; they can control one or many, maybe even everyone on Earth at the same time. That's how they brought these 100 adolescences to the same area. The "Others" steered them to that part of the Midwest with mind control, on the children and on anybody else who needed to be moved in the right direction. The boys you met are the only ones we have been able to tag so far. If possible, get more of this group tagged, preferably all of them, the same way for our scientists to research. Didn't you wonder where people and cars were during our interrogation of the two young boys in the swamp, or at the intersection where they are at right now?"

"Yes, sir, I did."

"Well, that is them not us. What I am saying is that everyone on that road traveling in both directions had an urgent need to pull over or stop, or turn around. They might have remembered leaving the stove on at the house, maybe they had to use the bathroom or were worried about their car. Or they chose a different route, or stopped for coffee. I can tell you there were a lot of automotive breakdowns this evening. The point is they can do that, and they can crush our species like a bug any time they want to. And, that is what they are threatening to do."

"May I ask, why don't they just use their power to make us do what they want with the nuclear weapons?"

"That is a good question Walter, and not an easy one to answer. I can only make my best guess, and this is it, we can't fully understand their motives because the "Others" are so much more advanced, they have the power to cross galaxies in the blink of an eye. Time is different for them also, a hundred or a thousand years or certainly a day or a week they can bend around. Even our best scientists can't come close to figuring that one out."

"My point is they don't think like us, we can't even imagine their true motives. But I can guess, humans are their project, maybe we are like a church missionary to them. They want us to advance and succeed on our own but feel that from time to time we need to be pointed in the right direction or maybe trained like we would train a puppy. But they are willing to start all over again; they say that they have done it before. So, what has to be done is full cooperation from us and the Russians on their Noah's Ark insurance policy, and a real and binding agreement between the USA and the USSR limiting strategic arms. That's my end Walter; your end is to coordinate the harvest, as they call it, of the one hundred adolescences in the United States. All of these children have already been chosen by the "Others" and cannot be substituted."

"May I ask sir, why did I have to give control of the interrogations over to the Russians? And what is the purpose of those tests?"

"The tests weren't the "Others" doing, our top scientists, and the Russians as well, insisted on those tests to study what makes these adolescents unique enough to be Adams and Eves. National Security Advisor Henry Kissinger also insisted that the tests to be able to positively identify the individuals through fingerprints, and as our technology advances, we will find out what makes their DNA special, that's why the blood and saliva samples."

"What about the eye flash, Mr. President?"

"Our scientists think that a retinal scan will one day be a fast and very accurate way of identification. As for the Russians on your team, that was insisted on by the "Others" – as a way of forcing mutual cooperation between the Russians and us. There are also two American agents with the Soviet team, they are about as happy about it as you are. Let the agents be a part of your operation, but certainly, don't trust them and don't divulge any more than is necessary."

"Of course, Mr. President, they are Russian spies after all."

"Where are they now?"

"Fuming mad in the cafeteria, they are mad as hell that I would not let them into the satellite communication center."

"Good, as it should be. Walter, there are other people, some are in your communication center right now, who are not to be trusted. I should tell you why I chose you. I chose you because I know you to be a man of good charter and sound decisions. That's one reason and well, the truth is, I don't trust my Secretary of Defense, Kenneth Rushie; no, that is not entirely accurate, it's his senior associate Curtis Knapp."

"He's the one I don't trust. Knapp has been involved in some very underhanded ploys. That in itself wouldn't bother me; I have done it myself in the past. Authority and power are like a drink of Scotch to him, the more power he gets the drunker on it he becomes, and the more he wants. Walter, this man is ruthless and will do anything to achieve his own agenda. That's not the part that bothers me, what concerns me is that he obviously has some powerful dirt on his boss, Kenneth Rushie; I don't know what, but I'm sure it's one nasty skeleton. Regardless I would never stoop to his level; he is putting himself above the interest of our country. I would never do that, country above all; are you with me on that General?"

"Of course, sir."

"Ok – this guy Curtis Knapp is not to be trusted. He is pissed, pissed that I dared to personally assign this mission. Normally that would be Rushie's job, as laid out in the Truman notebook, and of course Knapp would have the mission – and the unquestioned power that goes with it. At the moment I trust our military with this, and you General, not the CIA, or the Department of Defense, and certainly not that little prick Curtis Knapp."

"You say that man is here sir?"

"Yes."

"Do you see Secretary Rushie on the platform?"

"Yes, I see him."

"There will be a man nearby, probably with his nose up Rushie's ass, maybe more than that. I think they are both queer. Do you see a man like that?"

"Yes."

"Be careful of him Walter, he is a snake and incredibly dangerous; I feel it in my gut, sometimes I just know things."

"Yes sir."

"Kind of like playing poker. Walter did you know that I put myself through college with the money I made playing poker in the Navy?"

"No sir."

"And I financed my first congressional campaign with the money I fleeced out of the intellectuals at college poker tables. Walter, hold tight, continue to track the boys you tagged. When I give you the location of the transfer, get your team there and obtain DNA samples from all of them. Also, secure and protect the perimeter, as Henry outlined. When I meet with Brezhnev it won't be like negotiating, we don't have to dance at all; what we must do is agree with the conditions set forth by the "Others." The Russians have known about the "Others" and their advanced technology for at least as long as us. The Russians are taking this very seriously, and I am also. The world won't continue with us in it if we don't do as they say. I know it, and Brezhnev knows it too. All we have to do is deactivate most of our nuclear weapons and limit our remaining weapons to two hundred each. That's it."

"That and delivery of the two hundred boys and girls for their insurance policy. That's the wild card, they could easily abduct them themselves but they don't want to. They want the Russians and us to witness the overwhelming power the visitors have and to realize signing and abiding by the contract is the only choice. The American side of Noah's Ark is your responsibly Walter, don't screw it up. The success of Noah's Ark both on the American and Russian side is a pre-condition of the contract. They get the gene pool they want, or there is no fifty-year contract. They will eliminate humans in seven days, no, three days from now."

"When will I have the location sir?"

"Mid to late afternoon Moscow time um, seven to ten hours is my best guess. At some point, we will receive visitors from another galaxy and we will sign a very binding agreement and swear to abide by the agreement as set forth by the "Others"."

"Fifty years."

"Sir?"

"Fifty years is the term of the contract. After that, a new generation will have to sign a new one. Well, more accurately, agree to terms of a new contract and secure another fifty-year lease on our planet. Did you know Walter, that no other sitting United States president has ever visited Moscow? And been invited inside the Kremlin, inside the General Secretary's chambers?"

"No sir, I did not."

"That gives me great hope, as it proves that Brezhnev is taking this seriously. If you need to get a hold of me, the number I gave you is the Air Force One switchboard. You may leave a message, or if I'm here I'll take the call. You know Walter, I have to wonder how long we have known about them, the Russians also, I mean how many fifty-year leases have there been already? Like I said, other than the Truman notebook I have found no other real reference of them. There is a motorcade waiting to take me to the Kremlin, and Cronkite is on the phone. He wants a statement for the press. I'll have to bullshit them with talk of the strategic arms limitation treaty, of course with no mention of the crisis we are facing. No one can ever know what happened to force the USA and the USSR to cooperate and reduce arms out of the blue, and to get it done in less than a week. We take that to our graves, Walter."

"Yes sir."

"I have to go and deal with the day. You know I should be exhausted but I'm not, in fact, I have never felt better or more alive or alert. I wonder if that's them. Scary, isn't it? What if the aliens are affecting the thoughts and bodies of the United States President and the General Secretary of the USSR? And what if they are influencing the thoughts and actions of everyone else in the world?"

"Shit."

"I have to go; I'll call you on a secure line in seven to ten hours. Good luck Walter."

"Good luck to you Mr. President." Click - the line disconnects.

Walter is alone with his thoughts in the secure room. He is thinking about the situation and what orders he needs to issue immediately. He is also thinking about the warning from Nixon about the secretary of defense and Curtis Knapp. Where did that come from? Was that a warning that the "Others" planted in Nixon's head?

Shit.

The general is looking through the window at the situation command center. He scans the platform and railing at the back of the room. He does not see Secretary Rushie, or his aid Curtis Knapp. Where did that little weasel go?

Seven

Kenneth says to Curtis, "It seems like nothing is happening for the moment. Let's go to the cafeteria and grab a bite to eat. I could use a glass of milk to settle my stomach."

Curtis nods and they walk off the platform and out of the secure situation room. Five minutes later they sit with their trays in the farthest corner of the cafeteria.

Kenneth only got what went easy on his stomach, cottage cheese, peaches, and a glass of milk. Curtis, the opposite with a bacon double cheeseburger, extra bacon, onion rings, and a chocolate milkshake; he has an appetite.

"You're going to kill yourself with all that cholesterol Curtis."

"Yeah, I'm going to kill myself, but not with a cheeseburger."

"Curtis, not that again, I thought you were past that. What about the two times you were hospitalized because of intentional overdoses when you were a teenager?"

"That's just the two you know, of old man; some asshole always seems to save me."

"Curtis, what happened to all that counseling I paid for? What about the four years of Harvard? What about this nice fat government job? Who did that for you Curtis?"

"You did, old man; you did it because you're a pervert and you want to keep it a secret. What were you thinking back then, thirty years ago? You think that you can take a pretty whore off the strip, buy her a house and give her twenty thousand dollars a year to be your private whore? Well, that's not so bad, the really bad part happened when you had the bright idea to pay her an additional twenty thousand to produce a son, your son me."

"It happened and she had me; then what? You didn't want anything to do with me, or her either. You cut her off. What was she supposed to do? You know what she did; she went back to whoring, drugging and drinking. To her credit, she kept me and somewhat took care of me. She did a hell of a lot more for me in those years than you did. Why did you pay all of that money for me to come into this world and then abandon me?"

"Curtis, we talked about this fifteen years ago, when I paid your hospital bills and got you into counseling. I told you how sorry I was and that I would spend the rest of my life trying to make it up to you."

"And what about my ma? You killed her!"

"I did not; she overdosed."

"No kidding; that was the only way out that you left her! Every since, I have thought about it and it sounds like a fine way to go. Join her; I'm tired of fighting it, and tired of all of the assholes and perverts in the world. Like you old man."

"Come on Curtis, we are involved in a situation that will change the world. Can't you get over it and work with me here?"

"I'd love to, but what can I do now? I have been castrated by that prick Nixon. What the hell is he doing bypassing the Department of Defense, when it clearly was created for this type of situation. Hell, this defines our mission statement to a tee. I am the one that should be in control here, not General Brandon."

"Be thankful that you are on the team and a part of this. It is vital to our country, and a top-secret assignment, you know."

"Yeah, I know Kenneth. That's why I'm as calm as I am; I know that I can still make a difference."

"What do you mean Curtis?"

"Never mind old man, you'll find out."

"Don't start your bullshit games with me again, Curtis; tell me what's on your mind."

"All right, give me a minute, I'm still thinking and I want to finish my cheeseburger."

They finish their meals in silence.

Curtis says "I know what happened to my sister."

"What the hell are you talking about now Curtis?"

"Mom's friend Denise told me about it, right after mom died. She had a baby girl first. You didn't want a daughter; so, you sold her to that whorehouse you used to visit in Thailand. Hell, you probably traded her for services, didn't you?"

"Now, Curtis, you don't know what you are talking about."

"Now, don't you start your bullshit games with me again, Kenneth. You never did tell her how sorry you were for what you did. Or, spend the rest of your life, or even a minute, trying to make it up to her. You just forgot about her, like she never existed. I know why too. It's because you like boys better, right? Like me, right?"

"Curtis."

"No, shut the fuck up and listen to me; I'm trying to tell you something; I know why I'm fucked up; it's because of you. I know why I tried to kill myself; because of you. And, I know what stopped me from doing it."

"What stopped you from doing it, Curtis?"

"Remember Dr. Myers who treated me for six years?"

"Of course, I remember him, a very smart man."

"Well, I told him one time. I had the perfect suicide in mind, a murder-suicide. Kill you slowly and painfully; then kill myself with the Valium that I've saved up, wash it down with a bottle of Jack Daniels. Do you know what he said?"

"No, I don't know what he said, but it should have been good for all the goddamn money I paid him."

He said "Ok; let's say you do that, then what? Yes, there will be one less asshole in the world, but you'll be gone too."

And, you know what else he said? He said, "The world won't miss a beat; it will just go on, without you in it. Yes, your father will be gone, but you will have no more influence over anything, ever again; because dead is forever."

"Somehow, that made perfect sense to me, and that's when I decided to get my grades up and ask you to get me into Harvard."

"Curtis, this isn't the time, and certainly not the place to be discussing that."

"Wrong again old man; this is the time and place to discuss it. Remember, the briefing we attended this afternoon?"

"Of course, Curtis how could I forget that? That was the most important meeting either one of us will ever attend."

"Remember the part of the briefing about the "Others" insisting on their genetic insurance policy, the project that the prick Nixon code-named Project Noah's Ark?"

"Goddamn it, Curtis, what are you getting at?"

"It's perfect."

"What's perfect?"

"All I have to do is put a monkey wrench in Nixon's little plan; make sure that the American delivery of the adolescents doesn't go smoothly."

"Goddamn you Curtis, I don't like the way you are talking."

"You know what, Kenneth? People suck, all people. I think the "Others" will be better off wiping us off the face of the earth and starting over. In fact, that's what I am going to do, make sure this goes wrong. I'm checking out, and the rest of the world is checking out with me. Like I said, it's perfect."

"Curtis, you can't do that!"

"Oh, but I will old man; and, you won't interfere with me, you've lived a hell of a good life. Fuck with me and I'll write a book about you and my "family." You've been fighting cancer for three years. Fuck it, just let it go, let it go with me. It's the perfect suicide; kill myself and every other asshole on the planet, and if my sister is still suffering in that hellhole, you left her in well, I'll be doing her a favor. Tell you what Kenneth, come to my room tonight and I'll give you what you want one last time."

Curtis gets up from the table and leans over to kiss his father on the ear.

Eight

Victor and Ivan are sitting alone in the opposite corner of the large cafeteria. They have been sitting for three hours. They are the invited Russian agents; invited to verify the American cooperation as mandated by the "Others". They argued passionately to be included in all aspects of the operation, including the secure situation room – But, General Brandon nixed that, saying that they were only allowed in the common areas of the base, but are to be included in all field operations. They are about to leave the base for the night and go into the city to spend the night at a place called Howard Johnsons. What luxury! As they are getting up to leave, two men sat down at the other far corner an older heavy man and a sharply dressed younger man.

"Let's not go just yet," said Ivan; "Maybe we can learn something from them. I'll get more coffee, you set up your directional microphone; let's see what they have to say."

"And pie Ivan, any kind, it's all delicious and abundant, not at all like back home." Victor gives Ivan a wink.

Ivan shakes his head and walks off.

Victor takes out his pen, unscrews the top and fiddles with it in his left hand for a moment; then, he places it on the table with the writing end pointing toward the two men seated across the room. What Victor has done is attach a small translucent wire, similar to a lightweight fishing line, from his left cufflink to the pen. The wire runs up his arm and across the top of his back to a recorder in a side pocket, then down his other arm to his cufflink, which has a small amplified speaker. Very simple, very inexpensive, and very Russian, but it works. Victor quickly establishes a signal.

Ivan comes back with coffee and two slices of pie; he places a cup of coffee and a piece of pie next to Victor.

Victor looks at it the coffee and says, "Shit, I have to pee so bad, I don't even want to look at any more coffee."

"Concentrate Victor, go fishing and see what you catch. After this, we must make our report."

"I hope we get something juicy, just like those knuckleheads want.'

"Careful what you say, Victor!"

"Oh, sorry Ivan; I've worked with you so long, sometimes I forget that you are a political officer. Come on Ivan, lighten up; I'm proud to be a part of this mission, we absolutely must succeed. If we fail, or I say something politically incorrect fuck it, what are they going to do to me? Put me in the coal mines in Death Valley Siberia? No, they can't because I'll be dead; and, so will every human on Earth, including my superior officers. Ivan, I have a family back home and I'm not quite ready to die; so, believe me, I am doing my best on this mission."

"Ok Comrade Victor. I understand; there is no need to report you."

"Quiet, they are talking again." Victor places his elbows on the table so that his cufflink is close to his ear, and Ivan does the same. They pretend, and appear, to be in an intense and intimate conservation; it is a ploy they have practiced many times. "Holy shit! This is good, Ivan. I only have two minutes of tape and I don't want to miss something important, or to run out of tape, shit."

"What are they saying?"

"Apparently, the aid is the illegitimate son of the Secretary of Defense, Kenneth Rushie. And, he's blackmailing him."

"Wow, this is incredible."

"I am going to take my chances and start the tape." Victor is whispering the jest of the conversation to his partner across the table. "The old man is a pervert. He paid a whore to have a son him; wow."

"The kid is pissed that the assignment went to Air Force SAC command and not to the Department of Defense. Rushie would have put him in charge of this mission. The kid had a sister and the old man, Kenneth, apparently sold her."

"The kid is strange; no, he is completely fucked up! The boy grew up in a whorehouse. The kid has a death wish, oh shit! He wants to sabotage the operation; he wants to kill himself and take the rest of the world with him! He is a pervert too! He is a father fucker!"

Victor and Ivan watch as Curtis stands and kisses his father on the ear.

From the small speaker in his cufflink, Victor hears a faint click; his small recorder is out of tape. He got lucky, as he nailed a perfect two minutes of tape. He got all of Curtis' threats. What's on the tape is more than a juicy tidbit. It is imperative that it be handed up the chain of command, all the way to the Kremlin, ASAP.

As soon as Kenneth and Curtis disappear into the corridor, Ivan says, "Tell me you got that!"

"I believe I did; but I can't check it here. Let's get out of here. Ivan, call our American handler, Captain Duffy, and check the status of the situation. If its calm, ask him for an escort out of the building. Have him order a car and driver to take us to our rooms."

"What are you going to do?"

"Take a leak, I'll be right back."

Three minutes later Victor is back at the table sipping cold coffee and thinking about what just happened.

Ivan returns and says, "Captain Duffy will be here in five minutes to personally escort us out of the facility. A car and driver will be waiting outside to take us into downtown Omaha."

Ivan was able to follow the conversation with Victors help and what he is trying to understand is just as unbelievable as everything else is on this mission. He is hopeful that he will receive the order to kill this pussy of a man, this trader to the world! Maybe there will be time to kill him slowly. No, can't think like that, better to let someone else do it, unless of course, he receives that order. Maybe his orders will be to play the tape for General Brandon. Would he have the balls to kill the little weasel? He is thinking that Brandon probably would, General Brandon seems to understand the importance of his mission. That would be good if the Americans would do it, much cleaner and, he and Victor would be able to see the mission to the end.

"Ivan? Are you ready to get out of here? Let's walk to the corridor and wait for Captain Duffy, he should be along any minute."

Ivan says, "Ok, how do you think our motherland team is making out?"

Victor thinks for a moment before answering and says, "Our leaders are very good at giving orders, but I'm not so sure that they will be good at following orders, even from them."

"That's my biggest worry, the motherland team; and, that lunatic Curtis Knapp is my biggest worry with the American team, for the moment."

"Here comes Captain Duffy."

"Good morning, men."

"Good morning, Captain."

"Your car and driver are waiting outside. When you need to return, call the number on the back of this card, it is the number to the base motor pool. Colonel Knight is in charge and has standing orders to take you anywhere you need to go, within restrictions of course."

"Of course, Captain. Thank you, shall we go?"

Together they walk a short way down the corridor, to a bank of elevators. Fully armed MPs stand at each elevator; both MPs snapped to attention and sharply saluted Captain Duffy.

"Main lobby please, Sergeant."

"Yes, sir!"

The MP picks up a black rotary phone and dials three numbers; he speaks a few words. Seconds later two more fully armed MPs appear.

Victor notices that the MPs are corporals, as they salute the sergeant.

The elevator arrives and the two corporals' step inside and inspect the cab. Satisfied that everything is in order, they each produce a key. Both men insert their keys into two identical control panels, at opposite corners of the cab. The elevator is designed to only operate with two key holders. The passengers cannot operate this elevator.

The corporal at the front of the cab salutes and says, "Ready for passengers, sir."

The sergeant talks to Captain Duffy, in a quiet voice. "You may board now sir."

Captain Duffy says, "Thank you, Sergeant" and gives a crisp salute.

The three of them board the elevator and the corporal in the front says, "On, 3, 2, 1." At one they both turn their keys, at the same time; they push some buttons and the elevator doors close. The cab starts to move upward.

Elevators have always made Victor uncomfortable. He thinks of them as the perfect killing zone, which they are. The KGB love to make hits in elevators. Victor has worked with the KGB many times, in many places around the world, to do just that. The target is cornered in an elevator, with nowhere to run, vulnerable to: poison gas, shotgun crossfire, electrocution, or even equipment malfunction where the cab takes a death drop into the basement.

To help ease his discomfort he studies the corporal across from him. In the Soviet Union the senior officer would have accompanied them in the elevator; after all, the senior officer would be held responsible if anything went wrong. Victor's eyes run down past the corporal's stripes to his sidearm, a 1911 Colt 45. Now that is a fine weapon, powerful and reliable like his beloved AK 47.

He looks at the M-16 slung over the corporal's right shoulder and thinks now, that is a piece of shit. Back home, in Russia, the Ministry of Propaganda is always broadcasting in public places like bus stops, train stations, and town squares. One broadcast he remembers played for years; it was about American soldiers in Vietnam, with M-16's and the ammunition they were issued. The ammunition was not made to withstand the wet, humid jungle weather; and the rifles constantly jammed. The men were forced to completely disassemble, clean and reassemble their rifles, while under fire, and half the time they had to do it in the dark. Many American servicemen died this way; and, the propaganda ministry thought it was funny and a fine example of American capitalist, greed, and arrogance.

There were always people that cheered and laughed at the broadcast. Victor was not one of them; soldiers' lives are not meant to be wasted like that, enough of that in the Great War. His father is among the dead, wasted Russian soldiers in that awful war.

The doors open and the three of them step out into the lobby. There is a golf cart waiting for them. The golf cart is the size of a Volga car back home, plenty of room for all of them. Captain Duffy speaks for the first time since entering the elevator, he says, "General Brandon has ordered all necessary personnel to attend a briefing at 10: 00; I trust that you will both be there?"

"Of course, Captain" Ivan says.

"I want you to know my job has been made much easier as you are both fluent in English, I don't have to hold your hands and translate everything that is said or happening. Also, I want you both to know that you are part of this effort. Russian or American, it doesn't matter at this point; I want your input. We have to work together because, as you know, we cannot fail in this mission. Tomorrow could be a long and stressful day. General Brandon has ordered all personnel involved in this project to get as much rest, sleep and food as possible during the next nine and a half hours. You're not ordered to do anything of course, but it is very good advice."

"Yes, Captain, I understand."

"Ivan, it is imperative that we know what is happing with the Soviet side of Noah's Ark. I know it goes against all of your natural instincts, ours too but, I want you to convey that General Brandon has ordered that you and Victor have access to all information, regarding the American side of Noah's Ark. Also, I want you to relay that we intend to stand down one level tomorrow at 10:00. We sincerely hope that your country will do the same, as we must start to de-escalate the military tension between our two countries. But we do have to draw a line somewhere, and that line is we can't allow either of you into the satellite situation room, a room that displays all of our world assets. That is one of the restricted areas that you cannot visit. You can't have our nuclear launch codes either."

That brought a rare smile to Ivan's face. "Of course, Captain Duffy, I will convey your concerns."

"Ivan, when you make your report, as I know you must – please ask for permission to update us on exactly what is happening with the Soviet end of the operation. I know that is unnatural and against all of your instincts, but remember, we feel the same way here. We are including you and Victor as much as we possibly can. Surely you understand we can't allow you to see our real-time maps of the world, with the strength and positions of all our assists, including our nuclear submarines?"

"For the record I have to say no, I do not understand. But yes, Captain Duffy I will do my best to make the case for cooperation."

"Thank you, Ivan, our countries need each other right now and we have to try to trust each other, at least in this matter."

The golf cart had been following a green line painted on the floor and now the line turned left. The scenery had changed from a concrete tunnel to a wide corridor with offices on both sides. There are a lot of personnel about and wide awake, even though the time is 12:30 am. Victor remembers this part; they are getting close to the entrance. There it is, two armed MPs and a sergeant guard the entrance way and watch their approach. The golf cart stops at a revolving door.

A sergeant approaches the cart and salutes Captain Duffy while saying, "Sergeant Rufus - motor pool, sir."

"Very good Sergeant, please take our guests anywhere they need to go."

"Yes sir."

Captain Duffy says, "Ivan, please think about what we talked about, we need to share information and de-escalate this situation."

"Of course, Captain, I will."

Duffy turns to Victor, in the back, and says "Victor, I understand that you have exceptional hearing and I'm sure you heard what Ivan and I were talking about; so, what I said goes for you as well."

"Yes, Captain, I thank you for your hospitality."

"Goodnight, men I mean good morning."

Nine

The car is a dark blue Ford Galaxy, with a small USAF stencil and numbers on both front fenders. Sergeant Rufus opens the rear door and Ivan gets in and slides across the seat to make room for Victor, but Victor says to the sergeant, "I would rather ride in the front, please." "Of course," says the sergeant as he opens the front door. Victor gets in and immediately starts inspecting the gauges and dashboard.

By the time Sergeant Rufus gets in, Victor is almost caressing and petting the car. The sergeant gives him a smile, Victor stops and sits up straight. "I admire this automobile" he says. The sergeant starts the car and says "This is as plain Jane as they come, buddy." Victor has to think about that one as they ride through the base without saying anything until they clear the last checkpoint.

"My orders are to take you to the Howard Johnsons on Dodge Street; would you like to stop anywhere on the way, maybe to get a bite to eat?" "Oh, no thank you," Ivan says "I am most anxious to get back to my room, we have spent more than three hours in the base cafeteria – so no, we are not hungry."

"I could use a pack of American cigarettes" Victor says. "Victor you can buy those in a machine at the lobby of the motel." "But they take coins, I have no American coins." "Here, buddy," the sergeant says, "I have some change, take these," he hands Victor two quarters; "That should be enough."

Victor has not smoked a cigarette in more than four years – since his 'accident' split his face and lips. He couldn't put a cigarette to his lips for years and when he could, the craving had passed; the craving is back now though.

"This is our exit," the sergeant says "I believe it will be three blocks on the right."

In the city, the bars and nightclubs have not yet closed. People are out and about, young people are hanging out – sitting on porches and cars, playing music, drinking beer and smoking cigarettes, or something.

The cars fascinate Victor – so big, and shiny, with so much chrome! He wants one; no, he wants two or three. This is only his second visit to America and he has been thinking – If we can pull this off, I'm not going back to Russia. The sign for Howard Johnson Motor Lodge is visible and he has to wonder what the "Motor Lodge" in the name stands for.

Ivan tells the driver, "We are in rooms 215 and 216, in the front." Agents never stay on the first floor. Sergeant Rufus parks; they thank him and get out.

Ivan has to be quick, he has fifteen minutes to shower, shave and change clothes. First things first Victor thinks, checking the tape is a priority as turning over a blank tape to the KGB wouldn't be a good idea.

Victor retrieves a small tape player from the false bottom of his suitcase. They go to the balcony and close the sliding glass door. Maybe it's not bugged out here. They listen to the entire tape – twice. They are both thinking the same thing, how the hell could the Americans be so stupid? In Russia any prominent member of the party, or a high-ranking general, would have been properly checked out – all the way back to his grandparents, and then some. No way this much dirt and a graveyard full of skeletons would have been overlooked. Ivan is running behind schedule now; so, Victor excuses himself and goes to his own room.

Victor's immediate plan is to take a long luxurious hot shower, then take a walk to find cigarettes and maybe a drink; he thinks maybe he'll just settle for some of that watery American beer. He needs something to wind down and he knows a bottle of Vodka is a bad idea. As much as he would like a bottle he is determined to resist, as Ivan would surely report him and he would promptly be shipped back to Moscow. Not at all what he has in mind.

The procedure at the moment is simply for Ivan to walk to the boulevard at the front of the motel, fifteen minutes after arriving. Someone from their team is always watching their rooms; a car will pull to the side and pick him up. That's when he will give his report to his superior. There is no need to be elusive, as the Americans know he is here – they invited him.

Ivan hurries down the steps and walks briskly to the main boulevard. He knows it has been at least 18 or 19 minutes since they arrived at the motel; maybe his superior won't say anything about it. A long-nosed, white Jaguar is cruising slowly down the boulevard and pulls to a stop where Ivan is standing; the driver motions for Ivan to get in.

"You're late! This is my third pass; you know how amateurish that is! I could have been easily been made by our enemies! How the hell did you ever make it to senior agent?"

"Apologies Comrade Nikolai; Victor insisted on checking the quality of the tape recording before submitting it to you."

"What's on the tape?"

"It is a conversation between American Secretary of Defense, Kenneth Rushie and his senior aide, Curtis Knapp."

"Well? Report Ivan!"

"It's easier to show you than it is to tell you." Ivan pulls the tape player from his pocket and turns it on.

Nikolai turns the car into a housing development that the Americans call a subdivision. Nikolai drives slowly and listens intently. The tape ends and he angles the car back toward Dodge Street. After a moment he says, "This man must be eliminated, chose your moment and take him out."

"With respect Comrade, what if we give a copy of the tape to the Americans; it is their problem after all."

"That is traitorous talk, Ivan! We give the Americans nothing!"

"Captain Duffy has asked for a full report on our progress in the motherland."

"I will authorize no such thing, Ivan, as far as I am concerned the Americans are enemies of my country and I will have no part in helping them! Is that what you want to do Ivan, help them?"

"Comrade Nikolai, as I understand my orders, I am to ensure the success of the American side of this project, does that not mean to help them?"

"You are an insubordinate ass, Ivan; my recommendation will be to replace you and Victor with agents of my choosing. Do you have anything else to report?"

"Yes, Comrade, the Americans have identified and tagged two boys."

"Huh! Two! We have tagged more than twenty! Our superiority is apparent! Did they attach a transponder?"

"Yes, Comrade."

"Do you have the frequency?"

"Yes, Comrade."

Ivan hands Nikolai a packet that contains a piece of paper, with the transmitter frequency, a cotton tip on a stick, two locks of hair, and one piece of blood doted gauze.

"This is complete with all of the samples we require?"

"Regretfully, no Comrade. One set is complete, but Victor's set is incomplete as the commanding officer felt Victor was being too rough on the boy, and took over himself."

"What did Victor collect?"

"The hair sample is all Victor was able to collect."

"Incompetent and inexcusable! How did you two clowns get chosen for this mission, when I myself volunteered?"

"Comrade Nikolai, I know now that we went about this the wrong way, all we have to do is ask for the samples."

"Comrade Ivan, you are ignorant like a cow, don't you know the samples they would give you will be switched, disinformation. They will give you samples from retards! The only way to know for sure that the samples come from the targeted group, is to get them yourself!" The Russian colonel calms himself for a moment, takes a deep breath and says, "Your mission is complete here Comrade Ivan, a car will pick up you and Victor at dawn. Be ready to travel, your next assignment will be in our motherland. I'm sure that I can find you both more suitable posts." With that, he pulls the car to the side and says, "Get out".

Ivan gets out and the colonel makes a wide U-turn. The white Jaguar is gone in seconds. Ivan grew up in communist Russia and is used to the arrogance of senior officers, but this guy takes the cake. Ivan is thinking that he has done everything right; he identified a major threat to the operation, befriended an American officer, produced most of his required samples, and obtained the frequency of the tracking devices that were placed in the boy's sneakers. All of this and the cocksucker is going to send him to Siberia! Shit, this is not going well; he has a lot to think about on his walk back to the Howard Johnsons.

Ten

Victor thoroughly enjoys his long shower with the endless hot water. It's not like that back home; either there is no hot water, or very little. If you live in government housing, it's somebody's job to monitor water usage. A two-minute maximum is the rule, after that the water is turned off. It's always a pleasant surprise for him to have plentiful hot water. He hurries to get dressed and get outside – he has never had the chance to explore America on his own. He is anxious to examine some American automobiles and spend some of his money. He has one hundred $100 dollar bills, a hundred $50 dollar bills, and a hundred $ 20-dollar bills – all in the false bottom of his suitcase.

Victor closes the door and stands at the railing for a moment. He is studying the cars in the parking lot and deciding which ones to inspect more closely. He is also trying to figure out where his watchers are. He can't spot them so he makes his way down the stairs to a car that caught his eye.

He does not yet know the brand name of the car, but he can see that it is a big car with two doors. He decides that the big American two-door cars have a sexy look and the chrome on this one is abundant and shining, even at night. He bends down for a closer look at the grill and notices a red, white, and blue emblem in the center. That's as it should be, any country should be proud to manufacture this automobile.

He stands up and reads PLYMOUTH across the hood. At the center of the hood, an ornament decorates the top center and has three numbers on it 440 maybe that is the engine size?

Victor remembers a time when he crossed the English Channel. He became involved in a conversation about cars with an American businessman, who was a car enthusiast and a collector of cars. They became so engrossed in their conservation that the trip across the channel seemed to take no time at all. He gained a lot of knowledge about American cars from that man…what did he say about how to tell the year of manufacture? The tail lights, the year is stamped or embedded into the tail light lens.

He gets up and walks toward the rear of the car to look at the tail light lens. On the fender a chrome emblem catches his eye, it says Satellite GTX. Victor looks into the window and is astonished by what he sees – two white seats in the front with beautiful stitching, and chrome everywhere – across the top of the windshield, down the roof pillars all the way across the top sides and around the rear window! And more chrome in the shifter console. What a beauty! He wants one, no he wants two or three! He walks to the back of the car and finds the rear bumper; it is also chrome and shining like a mirror; he looks at the tail light lens and there are even chrome strips on the lens. He is impressed and he hasn't even heard it run yet. He looks at the date stamp, it says "67".

He stands up and looks around again, he can feel his watchers watching him, but he still cannot make out where they are. Across the street is a sign that says Stop & Shop open 24 hrs. Victor crosses the street and enters the store; he takes only a few steps before he has to stand still in the center of the store. He is momentarily overwhelmed by the vast selection of goods in the store.

A pleasant young black man, with wild hair sticking straight up and out like a puffball is working behind the counter. He says "Can I help you find anything, sir?"
"Well yes, I am thinking about some American beer and cigarettes, and maybe a small bottle of Vodka."

"I can help you out with the beer and cigarettes, but the Vodka, no way man; we don't sell it."

Victor says nothing and after a moment the young man comes out from behind the counter and walks to the beer cooler. "Here man, let me help you out." He grabs a six-pack of Budweiser beer from the cooler and hands it to Victor. "You can't get a beer any more American than this, man." He turns back to the cooler and comes out with two large cans of Colt 45, he hands them to Victor and says "This is the closest thing there is to Vodka in a beer, man. Oh, you want cigarettes you probably want Marlboros. Kools are my thing. How many packs do you want?"

"Two please, he notices when the man turns around that the tag on his shirt says "Berry".

"Ok, here are some matches and oh, you're going to need one of these."

"One of what?"

"A church key man!" He is laughing as he is ringing up the sale, that's $3.83, my man."

"I have a twenty-dollar bill."

"That will work, man. $16.17 is your change."

"No, you have been most helpful, you may keep the change."

"Wow man, this shit has never happened to me before, it takes me a whole eight-hour shift to make fifteen or sixteen bucks. You're a strange cat, but you can come back and see me anytime!"

This is one of the tricks that Victor learned in Noragrad, the fake American city in Russia established for training of agents. Establish friendly contacts whenever possible.

"Hey, you want me to get Vodka for you tomorrow?"

"Thank you no, goodbye."

"Goodbye cool cat and thank you!"

Victor steps out onto the sidewalk carrying a heavy brown bag and almost collides with Ivan who is walking at a fast pace down the sidewalk.

"Ivan!"

"Victor!"

"We must talk. Not in our rooms certainly, hold on I have a thought."

Victor steps back into the store to talk with the young black man with the kinky hair.

"I need a place to talk with my friend and have our drink, we require privacy, do you know of such a place?"

"Sure man, there is a picnic table out back, it's our break area and it's fenced in to keep the bums out. Come on, let me show you."

Victor gives Ivan a slight nod of his head and Ivan knows to follow him, they have worked together a long time.

Ivan steps inside and together they walk past the restroom and a storage area. At the end of the hall is a green door, the clerk Berry holds it open for them and says, "The door locks automatically. Be sure to keep this wedge in it like this," and he shows them the piece of 2x4 that serves this purpose. The break area is as Berry described; it has a white wooden fence surrounding a small well-kept area with a picnic table in the center. Berry says, "My boss comes in at six, I trust that y'all will split by then, right?"

"We require only fifteen minutes."

"Ok, pick up after yourselves, all right? No beer cans or butts laying around, my boss freaks about that kind of stuff. He's the one that built the fence, made the picnic table, and planted the flowers and rosebushes; this is his hangout."

"Mr. Berry, may I have a moment with my friend, please?"

"Sure man," with that he goes back inside and places the wedge in the door.

"Why were you walking Ivan? What did the colonel say?"

"What's in the bag, Victor? Did you purchase Vodka?"

"No Ivan, just some American beer." Victor fishes out the two cans of Colt 45 and hands one to Ivan. "The clerk said this is the closest thing to Vodka there is in a beer."

With that they both pull the newfangled tabs off the cans and take a long drink. Ivan says "I thought American beer would taste better than this, it tastes like Russian beer, like fermented piss."

"Just drink it, Ivan, I have more beer of a better quality; now please tell me what happened."

"The colonel is not pleased with our progress, in fact, he is angry beyond belief."

"What? How can that be?"

"Come on Victor you know how vicious and unreasonable our officers can be. Well, Colonel Nikolai is pissed beyond reason; crying like a baby that's had its favorite toy taken away, and bitching like a whore that has not been paid. He is furious that he wasn't chosen to be in field for this mission. I believe he wants the mission to fail; it has to be, he does not like our success. We have our very own version of a Curtis Knapp to deal with."

"Damn it Ivan, spit it out, what happened?"

Ivan takes a long pull off the can and stares at the label for a second. He says, "Victor do you remember what you said about the coal mines in Death Valley?"

"Yes."

"Well, I believe that will be our next assignment. Nikolai has ordered us off of this mission; we are to begin our trip home at dawn."

Victor doesn't say anything, he reaches into the bag and pulls out two bottles of Budweiser and opens them with his new church key. He hands a bottle to Ivan.

They both tip up the smaller brown bottles and slam down the beers without stopping. "Ahh, that's better, said Ivan. I could get used to these."

Victor opens two more beers and sets one on the table in front of Ivan, while he tightly grips the other one. He looks Ivan right in the eye and says in a low voice, "I'm not going back Ivan."

"I know Victor, I have known for some time now."

"And you Ivan, what are your thoughts?"

"This thing that we recently learned about with the "Others" well, I have always wondered about something like that. Now that we are involved in this mission, the most important thing in the world, literally, is that we stay and see it to a successful conclusion. I mean Victor, what are the alternatives? Let that jackass of a man, my "superior officer" fuck this up?"

"Then what? You already said it, Victor; they can't send us to Siberia because we will be dead before we get there, and so will my wife and daughter."

Victor says "Fuck me to tears, do you have a plan?"

"I do. I have been thinking hard on my walk back."

"The way I see it, we have no choice but to tell Captain Duffy everything we know; hopefully, we can tell it again to General Brandon. We must convince them that we are valuable assets to the operation, that we cannot be replaced."

"Ivan this is not like you, to willfully disobey orders, it's a death sentence for us if Nikolai or his men catch us."

"And it is a death sentence for my country, my family and everybody else in the world if I don't."

"So, are you going to call Captain Duffy and ask for transportation?"

"Yes, Captain Duffy only, he must be aware that this is an emergency pick up; we could be followed, chased, or shot at."

"No better place to call from then here." Victor says.

"Yes, but in a moment, first we must make our plan. We could make our break from here, right now."

"No, Ivan no, I must have the green money in my suitcase."

"I've had the same thought, Victor. You do know that the money is counterfeit, don't you?"

"Of course, I know that, Ivan. There have been many jokes and rumors about that over the years. Enemy currency supports our agents and missions abroad, and a good part of our economy as well; so what if it's counterfeit, it spends just fine."

"I agree; so, it's settled. We have to go back to our motel; I suggest a flash pick up in ninety minutes. What do you think Victor?"

"Our superiors appear to be stupid most of the time, but they are hard to deceive. It's possible there are assassins waiting to take us out right now, in the street, in the parking lot, or in our rooms."

"Shit."

"Yes Ivan, shit."

Victor says, "It is to our advantage to make the call now and set events in motion. We will have to take our chances on getting back to our motel rooms, agreed?"

"Agreed."

They both stand and finish their beers. Victor throws the cans and the bottles into a trash can and says "Let me handle the clerk, you make the phone call." A slight nod means "agreed" and they enter the store.

Berry is engaged with a customer. It almost sounds like an argument, but he can see that the customer is counting out change, paying for a pack of cigarettes. The money and the cigarettes are exchanged and the man has one more thing to say. "Tell the rag head owner of this joint that 62 cents for a pack of cigarettes is robbery! It ought to be illegal!" The customer leaves and Berry looks up and sees Victor. He says "It's the city man, some strange shit happens here."

"Yes, I know" Victor says.

"How did you like the beer?"

"The brown bottles are very good; the cans, not so good."

"Maybe it's an acquired taste. I grew up drinking that shit because it's cheap and strong."

"Berry, I would like for you to purchase Vodka for me tomorrow, any brand just a small bottle." He hands Berry a twenty-dollar bill. "You may keep the change."

"Far out man!"

"Excuse me?"

"Never mind, that's a deal."

"My friend needs to make a phone call."

"There is a pay phone on the corner, you need some dimes?"

"No, we would prefer to make the phone call from here."

"It's not long distance, is it? Last month this chick comes in with her tits hanging out, all flirty and shit she asks to make a phone call. I say sure, and you know what? The little bitch called Los Angeles! When my boss got the bill, he came unglued he made me pay for it. Six dollars and twenty cents! Fucking bitch!"

"I do believe that this will be a local call, but here," he hands Berry another twenty-dollar bill. "This should cover a two-minute phone call."

Berry takes the twenty-dollar bill and reaches under counter for the phone and places it on the top of the counter, he says "It has a really long cord."

Ivan has been quietly watching Victor work, but now he steps forward and takes the phone. He dials the number to the base and the phone is answered on the first ring, "Sergeant Davis speaking, how may I direct your call?" "This is Ivan, I need to speak with Captain Duffy most urgently, code 911." Sergeant Davis says "Please hold the line."

Code 911 is known only to a very few, and it means "Top Priority," find the person and put the call through, immediately. Fifteen seconds later Captain Duffy is on the line, if he was sleeping there is no indication of it in his voice.

"Ivan, what can I do for you?"

"We need to return to the base immediately."

"Ivan, I told you to call the motor pool."

"Captain Duffy, this is most serious; we have information of the upmost importance to share with you."

"Ok, Ivan, I'll send a car."

"Captain Duffy, I must inform you that we have not been authorized to share this information; in fact, it is highly likely that our agency will try to stop us, do you understand Captain?"

"I understand Ivan, what are your thoughts?"

"Send a car to our motel in ninety minutes, a quick snatch and run, if you can send Sergeant Rufus that would be good."

"03:15?"

"Yes, perfect."

"I will see to it Ivan, goodbye."

"Goodbye Captain."

Ivan places the phone back on the counter and says, "I thank you for the use of your phone." He looks at Victor and gives a slight nod; it's time to leave. They walk out the door and into the street half expecting shots to ring out, they don't.

Victor is still carrying the brown bag with two beers and two packs of cigarettes; he remembers that he has not even tried a Marlboro because of the excitement with Ivan and he thinks it's a damn good time to try one. He fishes out a pack while crossing the street, he offers one to Ivan and he takes it; they stop at the edge of the Howard Johnsons parking lot to light up.

They are both thinking the same thing; they could be in the crosshairs of a high-powered rifle, and this could be it for them. Victor strikes the match, his hands only a little bit shaky. They take a puff and Victor nods toward the shiny yellow car, he says "I am going to own two or three automobiles just like that."

"Why do you need two or three Victor?"

"Because I can use the parts and drive one forever!"

That broke the tension for a moment and they keep walking. "Victor, our biggest risk will be in our rooms."

"I know Ivan." They are quiet for a moment, Victor says, "In ten minutes if everything is all right, I will give one rap on the wall, you do the same."

"Agreed, and when Sergeant Rufus shows up, we bolt as fast as we can to the car."

"Right, good luck."

"Yes, to both of us."

As they climb the stairs they began to banter for the benefit of any listeners, about how awful the American beer is and the cigarettes too, awful. They throw their butts into the parking lot and Ivan says "I am most anxious to return home and get out of this awful place."

"As am I Ivan, it will be good to get back home, goodnight."

"Goodnight Victor, and remember we must be up and ready to travel by 6 am."

"I'll be ready Ivan, now I must get some rest."

They both enter their rooms and close the doors.

Eleven

The girl in front of me is wearing a skimpy shirt and jeans; she is soaked with sweat and barefoot. She stops right in front of me and stares at me hard. I asked her "What are you running from?"

"They're after us" she says.

The girl behind her steps out from the shadow. She didn't look much better, well she did, but they are still both a sweaty, dirty, barefoot mess. "They were going to give us a job at one of the midway booths, but we found out that's not what they had in mind for us; we have to keep moving."

They start walking again, fast.

"The girl from behind speaks up, "They jumped in their car to chase us down, but it wouldn't start. None of the cars in the parking lot would start. There were cars with their hoods up everywhere with guy's messing with the engines trying to figure out what was wrong, and it was weird. We ran a long way before I realized we should have taken two of the kid's bikes that were lying around, and now I am worried about it. If those two big guys' have the same thought, and they surely will, they'll catch us."

John says, "What big guys? And, how big are they?"

"The guys at the carnival they think they own us, and they are big, they look like WWF wrestlers."

John and I both say "Shit" at the same time.

The prettier girl with the sweat plastered red hair speeds up and is now out front; she calls over her shoulder, "We have to get off this bridge!""

"Hey! Don't go straight, there is nothing but miles of scary swamp, we just came from that way, you don't want to go there."

"Which way then?"

Mark speaks up, "To the right is Omaha, to the left is a place called De Moines; I say go left across the river, there's a railroad track that runs along the river, that is our best bet for finding a place to rest."

The girls break into a run. The brown-haired girl says, "They are close, I can feel them!"

"Wait for us at the railroad tracks, we'll cover for you!"

John says "What the hell are you talking about?"

"We can't let the girls get kidnapped."
"And how in the hell are we supposed to stop two grown men that are built like professional wrestlers?"

We are off the bridge now and the girls are flat out running, as fast as they can they can. They are taking the left ramp toward Des Moines.

To the right is a drainage ditch with fist size and bigger crushed drainage rocks. "Let's hold up a minute John."

I step off the road, I am looking for another big stick like I had before. And, like magic, I find one that is just the right size, smaller than a baseball bat, but a fatter than a broomstick, "Perfect" I say. John is busy making a pile of fist-size throwing rocks. Without us saying a word about making a plan we just did it; we had a plan, an ambush. In ten more seconds, we are ready with our pitiful arsenal.

We hear them coming, the guy in the back is calling for the guy in front to slow down, but he is having none of it. "I'm going to get those bitches!" We can see the front WWF wrestler guy; he looks like one too. He is big, not the fat kind of big the other kind of big, the muscles kind. He is pumping a shiny new ten-speed hard and going fast.

We are watching from the shadows of the ditch and can now see the second wrestler on a bike. He is on a Sting Ray type bike, with high handlebars and a banana seat. The bike is far too small for him, and he is having a hard time riding it.

John says "They are too far apart. Shit. Too late to move, let the ten-speed guy pass and I'll bean him in the back; you take Monkey Boy on the banana seat."

He is right. That is the way it has to be, there is no more time or choices.

Ten-speed guy says "I see the little bitches!" And, he pours on the coal, widening the gap between them even more; a little downgrade is also helping his speed. He passes us without even knowing we are there. "Now John, now." I say.

"No not yet." Two more seconds pass before John throws his rock. It is a high arching lob, about like a pop fly; it stays airborne for at least four or five seconds, but amazingly it finds its target and beans ten-speed guy in the center of his back. It is the worse bicycle wipeout I have ever seen. The ten-speed guy arches his back and stands up, a bad idea when you are doing 25 or 30 MPH on a bicycle. Bike and dude flip and roll more times than I can count and when he stops rolling, he isn't moving.

Monkey Boy sees the wipeout, but not the rock that hit him as he is looking straight ahead. "Tony! What the hell, Tony!" He is just about on top of us now. John and I both stand up and fire our rocks; my rock missed, but John's rock hits him on the hand wrapped around the handlebar grip. He skids the bike to a stop as he's probably done thousands of times before, when he was a younger ape, but now we are in his sights. He throws the bike aside and takes a stance like a football linebacker, crouched low with feet wide. We throw again, but both miss; he charges like a bull, focusing straight on John. John scrambles to get out of the way, but it is too late; the monkey bull has tackled John and already delivered the first wicked punch.

As Monkey Boy is drawing back for another punch, I am ready, it's almost perfect. He is lower than me and I'm on the higher ground, in a perfect position for the ax – a railroad hammer-type swing with my stick in a wide arc, with all my strength. The stick connects with his collarbone and both snap. The fight goes right out of him; he rolls over and is clutching his shoulder and moaning. He's done, but, John's not. John is on his chest, punching his face four, five, or six times. I pull John off. "Enough John! Look at him! He's bleeding from his lips, nose, and hands."

He is rocking and trying to put his shoulder back together.

"He's done! Come on, let's check the other one."

John kicks him three more times.

"Enough! Come on!"

"The bastard was going to do worse to me," John says.

Yeah, you're right, but he's done now; we won, we have to check the other one."

We run down the road to where the other big bastard is laying. He's not looking so good, he has the road rash bad, all down one side of his face. He is curled up, bleeding and moaning. "He's still alive," John says. "Don't kick him, John!" I know he is about to do it. "I can't believe we just did that, what a crazy damn night! Now what?"

John says "Listen," the music stopped and something else. I see the headlights of a car coming out of the swamp, and more on the Interstate highway. "Shit, we have to move this big bastard."

"Fuck em' let him get run over."

"Damn John, what got into you?"

"This night I guess, I'm tired of being scared, it felt good to kick their ass."

"Well, we can't let him get splattered on the road; help me move him to the side."

We grab him by the arms start to drag him to the side, he comes fully awake and is trying to get up. John kicks him in the ribs.

"No, John come on stop, don't hit him anymore he's not going to come after us tonight."

I say to the big guy with the beard "There is traffic coming we are just trying to get you out of the road. Just get to the side and stay there, all right?"

"Take his money" John says; "I'll throw the bikes in the weeds."

Good idea, I turn out his pockets, a few papers, some change, some keys, and a pocket knife. I tell him to take off his shirt, he does and I use the knife to cut it into strips to tie his hands behind his back and his feet together. I tell him to roll over or I'm going to let John kick him more, he does and I can see a long wallet with a chain that goes up to a belt loop, I'm still amped up and I yank it hard ripping off the belt loop. I pocket the wallet without even opening it.

"Let's get the other one."

We walk back and empty Monkey Boy's pockets, just as I am snatching the long wallet off his belt loop John says, "Car!"

We duck down and let the car pass. "Let's get out of here!"

"Hold on, I have to tie this guy up." I say to the man with the broken shoulder, "I can see that you are hurt so I'm not going to tie your hands behind your back. "I'm going to tie your feet and your left hand to this bush, don't make me regret it, one hour is all we need, understand?"

"Ye-yes" he says.

As Monkey Boy is drawing back for another punch, I am ready, it's almost perfect. He is lower than me and I'm on the higher ground, in a perfect position for the ax – a railroad hammer-type swing with my stick in a wide arc, with all my strength. The stick connects with his collarbone and both snap. The fight goes right out of him; he rolls over and is clutching his shoulder and moaning. He's done, but, John's not. John is on his chest, punching his face four, five, or six times. I pull John off. "Enough John! Look at him! He's bleeding from his lips, nose, and hands."

He is rocking and trying to put his shoulder back together.

"He's done! Come on, let's check the other one."

John kicks him three more times.

"Enough! Come on!"

"The bastard was going to do worse to me," John says.

Yeah, you're right, but he's done now; we won, we have to check the other one."

We run down the road to where the other big bastard is laying. He's not looking so good, he has the road rash bad, all down one side of his face. He is curled up, bleeding and moaning. "He's still alive," John says. "Don't kick him, John!" I know he is about to do it. "I can't believe we just did that, what a crazy damn night! Now what?"

John says "Listen," the music stopped and something else. I see the headlights of a car coming out of the swamp, and more on the Interstate highway. "Shit, we have to move this big bastard."

"Fuck em' let him get run over."

"Damn John, what got into you?"

"This night I guess, I'm tired of being scared, it felt good to kick their ass."

"Well, we can't let him get splattered on the road; help me move him to the side."

We grab him by the arms start to drag him to the side, he comes fully awake and is trying to get up. John kicks him in the ribs.

"No, John come on stop, don't hit him anymore he's not going to come after us tonight."

I say to the big guy with the beard "There is traffic coming we are just trying to get you out of the road. Just get to the side and stay there, all right?"

"Take his money" John says; "I'll throw the bikes in the weeds."

Good idea, I turn out his pockets, a few papers, some change, some keys, and a pocket knife. I tell him to take off his shirt, he does and I use the knife to cut it into strips to tie his hands behind his back and his feet together. I tell him to roll over or I'm going to let John kick him more, he does and I can see a long wallet with a chain that goes up to a belt loop, I'm still amped up and I yank it hard ripping off the belt loop. I pocket the wallet without even opening it.

"Let's get the other one."

We walk back and empty Monkey Boy's pockets, just as I am snatching the long wallet off his belt loop John says, "Car!"

We duck down and let the car pass. "Let's get out of here!"

"Hold on, I have to tie this guy up." I say to the man with the broken shoulder, "I can see that you are hurt so I'm not going to tie your hands behind your back. "I'm going to tie your feet and your left hand to this bush, don't make me regret it, one hour is all we need, understand?"

"Ye-yes" he says.

I get up and catch up with John.

Now there are a lot of cars, on the interstate road, coming from the swamp, but mostly coming from behind us, from the direction of the carnival.

"John, let's take the ramp west and try hitchhiking, the boss of those guys is going to be in one of those cars, he'll want to talk with us guaranteed. We'll make off like we are going to Colorado and we haven't seen the girls."

"Alright," John says, "But we tell him we did see two bikes going into the swamp, that might buy us a few minutes."

"Good idea" I say, "But we don't say a word about the wrestler guys, we haven't seen them."

"All right that's a plan."

We run the last bit to get on the ramp and start thumbing to every car that passes.

It does not take long; a shiny black Cadillac pulls to a stop on the side of the road in front of us. Two big, the fat kind of big, cigar smoking men get out and come over to us. The fat man in the passenger seat walks right up to John. He is standing close, just about nose to nose; he says "What happened to your eye boy?"

Shit, I forgot all about that. I guess I wouldn't have if I was the one with the shiner, damn I hope he makes up something good.

"I asked you boy, what happened to your fucking eye?"

"Faggots."

Both men stiffen right up at the word.

"No, not you. You wouldn't believe the number of faggots I have run into in the last three days; the last one was about two hours ago."

"Go on boy."

"Well, it was on this road and John points to the traffic on the interstate, we were on I 80, I don't know how we got off the 80 but we did. We asked everybody that picked us up to take us to I 80."

"Boy, I asked you what the fuck happened to your eye, you better spit it out or I'm going to dot your other eye!"

John says "Well, our last ride, I was sitting in the front seat with another pervert and he grabs my hand and puts it on his crouch, he tells me to play with it, but I didn't. I reached down and grabbed his balls and squeezed, hard. Well, he came unglued; he came right out of his seat and started punching me. Nobody was driving the car anymore and the stupid bastard crashed his car into the guardrail and then we went into a ditch. I took a punch and then cracked my head on the metal dashboard, that might have given me the black eye, my head still hurts."

"Hey, Frankie, you hear that, the kid had him by the balls!" They both have a good laugh.

"And you have been here ever since?"

"Yes sir, and it's been strange ever since."

"What do you mean by that?"

"Well, the pervert got his car running and was able to get it out of the ditch, then nothing; I mean no more cars for hours, until just now, it's strange."

"Hum, it's been a strange night all right. What did you do after the pervert?"

"We heard carnival music and we're going to walk that way, but it got too scary down there." John points toward the intersection of the swamp and the bridge. "We were down there and all of the frogs and crickets quit making noise, we got scared and came back up here, in the open."

"Did you see anyone on the road down there?"

"No sir, but Mark said he thought he saw two bicycles."

The fat man turns and takes a step toward me; he gets right in my face, like he was with John.

"Well, boy, how about it?"

I remembered the two trucker-type wallets that are sticking up in my back pockets. I think shit, if he sees those were done.

"Well, boy?" He gives me a shove. I stagger backward, a step or two trying my best not to fall or turn. I don't want him to see my back and the wallets.

"Speak up. What did you see?"

"I didn't see much sir. It's pretty dark out here, but what caught my attention was the clicking noise that a ten-speed makes. I heard a bike and when I looked, I could just make out a bike, then another one behind it, two bikes going into the woods."

"Were they men or women?"

"I couldn't tell; they were too far away."

"Just two bicycles, you're sure that there weren't more?"

"Two is all I noticed, sir."

The other fat man standing at the side of the car says "Let's take them with us, Joey."

The boss Joey thinks for a second and says "No, I don't want them knowing my business." He turns back to us and says, "Where the hell do you boys think you're going?"

"We're going to Colorado, sir."

"Maybe you'll get lucky and be gone by the time I get back. You'll see a sign for route 80, about ten miles down the road. Joey turns and says, "Let's go, Frankie."

The two big men get into the Cadillac and Frankie reverses down the ramp. The car is gone, down the swamp road. John and I look at each other, and without a word, we start walking, fast down the ramp. We had taken only a few paces when a shiny Chevy, butternut yellow car with two white stripes on the hood, stopped. I knew what kind of car it was because I like them; it's a 1969 Chevrolet Chevelle, nice. The driver is an older guy with white hair and John Lennon style glasses. He leans across the passenger seat rolls down the window and says, "You boys want a ride? I'm going all the way to Denver."

John and I look at each other, and I know that we are both having the same thought. Ever since we came out of the swamp, we have had this connection, like a brain string connection. We can't just leave the girls, but if this ride had come along an hour before, we would no doubt be so out of here.

"Well, what do you guys think?"

John says, "No we have gone far enough, we are tired, cold and hungry; we are going home."

"Suit yourselves guy's, it's probably a good decision; it's a cold cruel world out there."

"Yeah, we are finding that out."

He rolls up the window and does a cool burn out. Definitely cool, but damn we just turned down a ride to Denver. We watched the car and our ride to Denver, go with some regret; rides like that don't come along that often, they are rare indeed.

I can't help but say, "Damn, a ride to Denver in a super nice Chevy and the guy seemed cool too."

"Yeah, I'm hip to that." John says. We continue walking down the ramp and cars are streaming by. We're not hitchhiking, but I thought we would have had a ride by now. Oh, that's right we did, shit.

"Hey John, that was a good damn story you told about the pervert and the crash. I was believing you myself but damn, you threw me a curve ball, you put it right on me."

"I had to Mark that was the only way to sell the story."

My God, I think that's so adult. What happened to John? He wasn't like this two hours ago; he seems so much older now. I want to look into a mirror, really bad. I feel like an adult, I am even swearing in my thoughts like an adult; shit, how did I know that?

"Holy shit Mark, look at all of the cars; it's a fucking traffic jam!"

Wow, he's right. Where we were standing less than an hour ago was a deserted road, with no cars in sight. Now, it's jammed with traffic cars everywhere. Cars coming from the direction of the carnival, and they are all driving crazy. They are honking their horns, weaving back and forth, passing any way they can, and driving fast and stupid like they are on a racetrack but, they are far from professional drivers.

John says "Shit, how are we going to get across the road?"

"Let's walk down toward the swamp, then cut across and double back."

"Yeah, we are going to have to. How long before the two men in the black Caddy come back this way?"

"I don't think it will take them long and, it won't be good if they catch us; they will make us go with them and will beat the truth out of us."

"Your right Mark. There's a gap, let's cross now."

Now we are on the interstate ramp going toward De Moines. A big bridge is close and another bridge after that. The cars to our left are all trying to get the hell out of there. I say to John, "I wonder what scared all of these people so bad."

"I don't know Mark, but keep an eye on our back; I don't want to get run over by these crazy bastards."

About the time John says that, we hear a loud triple crash; bam, bam, bam.

"What the hell?" Brake lights come on, every car on the ramp stops. Horns blare and people are out of their cars yelling obscenities at the cars stopped in front of them.

"This ain't good John, let's get out of here."

John says "You know, I'm getting tired of running; in fact, I'm tired, period."

"Yeah, I know, me too. Let's get across this bridge; I'm sure we can find a good place to rest somewhere down by the railroad tracks."

"What about the girls? Think they will be waiting for us?"

"Oh yeah, where else are they going to go? Besides, they will want to know if we got those two big gorillas off their ass."

"All right, let's go."

We break into a slow run, we are tired. We pass dozens of stopped cars and agitated drivers shaking their fists and shouting. We see the problem, two cars sideswiped each other and crashed into both sides of the bridge pillars. The cars are sideways in the road and blocking traffic.

A green Ford has a crumpled nose and its engine is steaming. A big white Plymouth has a smashed fender that has crumpled into its front tire and flattened it. We pass the wreck and hear a guy yelling, "Move that fucking car or I'll move it for you!" I turn around and can see that the guy means it. He pushes the skinny driver aside, gets in the Plymouth and starts driving it across the bridge. Well, kind of driving it anyway; the car is moving, but making God-awful screeching noises. The blown tire is thumping and the car is driving kind of sideways, but it is moving. The cars behind quickly move through the gap and scream by the slow-moving Plymouth that stops directly in front of us. We stop too, partly because we are badly winded and partly because we don't need any more strange shit in the middle of this bridge, with the Missouri river far below. The guy isn't interested in us though, his ride is coming up, a big United Van Lines moving truck. The truck slows almost to a stop; the guy jumps on the truck's running board and climbs into the cab, then the truck is gone.

John sits down and I do too, we are beat bad and having a hard time breathing. A minute or two passes and I notice the traffic has cleared. Very few cars are moving across the bridge now. I say to John "We have to go; we stick out like a sore thumb out here in the open; you ready?"

"I guess, but no more running, I can't take it."

"It's not far now, let's get moving." We stand up and start to walk, and it's painful. I am about to say something, but John says it first. "Shit, I hurt everywhere, my feet are killing me and I can hardly move."

"I feel the same way buddy." Oh, shit John says, "That's another bridge up there!"

"We don't have to cross that one John, the railroad below is where we are going; we need to get off this bridge, start looking for a path down to the tracks."

We are almost off the bridge and John says, "There's a path right there."

We walk a little more and I can see he is right, there is a path, but it leads to the river not to the railroad. I stop and lean over the side for a better view, "Look John." He does and we both see the same thing, the path winds down to the river. "It's a fishing spot, John."

"Yeah, I see."

"There should be a path just like that going down to the tracks." We are finally off the river bridge and coming up on the next one. "It's been too long" I say to John, "That big black Caddy has to be close; we have to get off this road, right now!"

We are about to jump into the bushes when we hear, "Hey over here!" It's one of the girls, only twenty more feet; we stagger the last few feet and climb over a guardrail. They had both been waiting for us, and I immediately have the impression that they aren't dumb. The brown-haired girl says, "Follow me and be careful where you step; don't crush any plants or break any branches. We can't leave a trail, understand?"

We do, we follow her about twenty feet to a hideaway they had made. I didn't see it first, obviously, that was the idea. She pushes aside two bushes, except they are not bushes, they are broken pine branches stuck in the ground for cover. She goes through the gap and says, "Step sideways trough here." We do and we are in a clearing about fifteen feet square. They had stomped down or pulled up all of the brush and used it for a natural looking wall of forest green. On all four sides are broken pine branches stuck in the ground, in two alternating rows. The result was a well-concealed hidey hole.

They had been busy and were using their heads too. John and I didn't say it, but we are both impressed, "Where's your friend," John asks.

"Betty is covering our tracks; she will be along in a minute."

Betty is busy sprinkling dry dirt over some muddy footprints we left at the guardrail and backing slowly into our temporary hideout. She is using a pine branch to sweep away any signs of our passing and sprinkling dry leaves and pine needles where she thought they were needed.

John and I collapse on the ground, exhausted and temporally unable to move or speak. It is not long before the girl named Betty comes into our little clearing. You guys look like shit." she says in the sweetest voice in the world.

"No worse than you the first time we saw you." I say.

"Hi, I'm Sandy," the brown - haired girl says; "and, this is Betty."

"I'm Mark, and this is John."

After the introductions are out of the way, Sandy says, "God, we are so thirsty, please tell us that you have something to drink."

John hands Sandy his canteen and she hands it right to Betty. Betty takes a long drink and hands the canteen back to Sandy; she hesitates a long time and Betty says, "Sandy's funny about drinking after other people unless, of course, its whiskey."

Sandy says "Everybody knows that alcohol kills germs."

"Hey" I say, "I think I have a cup," I check my pocket. It's still there, two of them, the little collapsible cups. I take off the top and shake it open, "Its magic." I say, "You have a cup."

Sandy takes it and gives me a sweet smile. Sandy drinks six or eight small cups and hands the canteen back to Betty. In the meantime,

John and I have been sharing my canteen of water. Betty asks, "How about something to eat?"

"You girls are in luck," I say. "How about some Hershey's bars?" I toss them the seven chocolate bars that I had in the outside pocket of my denim jacket, I hope they're not melted, and they aren't. John does the same thing.

The girls pounce on those, quickly eating four each.

Sandy says, "I hate to ask, but do you have anything else besides candy?"

"Well," I say "Kind of, is this something you would eat?" I toss the package of beef jerky to Sandy.

She glances at it for a second and hands it to Betty. "What is this stuff, Betty?" I'm listening because I don't even know.

Betty knows what it is, she is the daughter of a hunter and woodsman, and she says, "It's persevered dry meat. Very tough and hard to eat, but good for you. Eat it slowly, there's no other choice. Jerky is some tough stuff." She opens it, takes a piece and passes the bag around. We are all slowly eating our first piece of beef jerky.

Sandy says, "What's on the bottom of this cup?"

"I have no idea."

"Do you have a match?"

Betty says, "No, Jesus, No. Don't light a match, we are trying to hide, not to be found! Christ, somebody check the road."

John says, "I'll check." He crawls a few feet up the hill to the road, John checks out the road in both directions and calls back, "Clear, some traffic but clear."

Ok, Sandy says, "Can I have a match, please?"

"Come here, we'll keep it low, what are you trying to see?"

"I want to see what's on the bottom of this cup."

I strike a match and cup it in my hands. Sandy holds the cup over the light and she studies it, turning it around slowly. "It's a dollar bill; no, it's more than that, let's break it open."

Betty has a pile of rocks from clearing the area. "Let me have it" she says. She takes the cup from Sandy and breaks it open; she pulls out the bill and looks at it. "It's a fifty!"

"How did you get a cup with a fifty-dollar bill in it?"

"It's a long story," I say.

John calls out, "There is a car stopped at the river bridge; it's the black Caddy!"

Betty calls out to John, in a not so loud voice, "Make sure that you stay out of sight, what are they doing?"

"I think they went over the guardrail."

There is a three-way chorus of "Shit".

Betty crawls up to where John is to see for herself. "Anything?"

"No, I haven't seen them since they went over the guardrail."

"You didn't step anywhere around here, did you?"

"I'm not stupid," John says.

"Sorry, I had to ask." We see a fat man crossing the headlight beams, in ten more seconds the car starts to move forward.

"Let's get back. You go first," Betty says.

John crawls down the hill to our little base. Betty does some quick housekeeping, as she slowly backs away. She gets to the group and makes the down signal and shush sign. These are four kids that know how to be quiet, for once.

Since we have been here, car lights have been flashing through the trees; the headlights, and the not so far away river bridge, provides some light for us. Now, it's getting brighter, as the black Cadillac moves slowly forward with its high beams on. We hear the car's tires crunching on the shoulder gravel. We are down and quiet; but my heart is hammering so loudly in my ears, it seems that the whole world should be able to hear it.

The car stops directly in front of the path. A door opens and closes, then another one.

Twelve

Curtis and his dad are provided luxury suits in the residential area of the base. To make his stay more comfortable, Curtis had quite a few personal belongings shipped from his apartment in Washington D.C. to the Strategic Air Command base in Nebraska. He assigned a junior aide the task of shipping his possessions – one of the benefits of having a high-ranking government job.

Curtis brought a Hi-Fi stereo, with most of his album collection. He also brought posters of Jimmy Hendrix, Janice Joplin and one of his favorites, the Beatles Abby Road poster – the one with Paul McCarthy walking barefoot across Abby Road, He also brought his favorite down pillow, a silk screen from the orient that his father gave him, a water pipe with a good lid of Vietnamese reefer, and a few other items.

Soldiers over there call the weed, Greenie Meanie; Curtis likes it, but not as well as the Thai stick that his father used to bring him from Thailand. Kenneth can't, or won't, go to most of those Asian countries anymore because of the war, and the fact that it is not going well, not at all. The last time Kenneth was in Saigon he brought Curtis home a present of a kilo of the Mean Green weed and he told him to make it last, because he wouldn't be going back there any time soon.

Curtis is surprised that Kenneth hasn't shown up by now; he's never turned down that offer in the past. He tapes his three new posters to the wall; he has a bunch of them. Curtis buys them by the dozen so he can make any room, his room. It makes him feel comfortable; it's an anti-anxiety trick that Dr. Myers taught him.

Curtis goes to the refrigerator and gets some ice to make a drink, then he thinks fuck it, might as well have a Budweiser, time to get mellow, wasted anyway. He is thinking about what album to put on and the Abby Road poster catches his eye. Perfect, he puts the platter on the turntable and drops the needle on the first track. The Beatles start to sing "Come Together;" he likes it ok, but the weird tracks on Sergeant Pepper are better, maybe he'll play that one next.

Beer, bourbon, and weed will have to work tonight, because he is determined not to take any Valium. The Valium makes him crash hard and long – he must be present and sharp at the 10 am meeting. He loads up his water pipe; he has been thinking of the water pipe lately as his mean green smoking machine, he smiles at the thought.

After two or three big hits, he feels much better. He reaches for the beer, it's empty. The bourbon glass is empty also. Wow, it must be some good weed; he doesn't even remember drinking the drinks. Well, one more of everything should do it. The stereo is making that click, click, click sound at the end of an album; he gets up and flips the album over.

Here Comes the Sun comes through the speakers, a little too bright and cheery but ok, another reload on the smoking machine and another bourbon. He is about there, relaxed, mellow and wasted.

Curtis is listing to the Beatles singing "You Never Give Me Your Money," and he's thinking that is not true of his dad. Kenneth has given him lots of money and he has spent a lot, but the old man insisted on him putting one thousand dollars a month into stocks of his choosing, DuPont, Boeing, Hughes, and Remington. All of the stocks have been producing huge returns, because of the government contracts that Kenneth approved. At this rate, he will be a millionaire in just a few more years.

He doesn't have it that bad. He knows that he has it better than most; he has money, a good government job and the power that comes with a high government position. He wonders why he can't stop thinking about suicide. He doesn't know why he's always had the thought, or why he can't shake it off. He remembers Dr. Myers saying, "If you keep trying you are going to succeed, then what? You'll be dead. You have to stop thinking about it."

But Curtis can't stop thinking about it, especially now with the perfect opportunity to take the whole world with him, it's like a huge turn on for him. Curtis is right where he wants to be in his mind, he is buzzed peaceful and happy. He is thinking, I'll call Dr. Myers in the morning, he can help me to shake it off. I'll tell the old man that I changed my mind. He drifts off to sleep.

Thirteen

Kenneth can't remember the last time he was so pissed off never, he thinks. That ungrateful little bastard, I should have left him in that whorehouse, or let the little fucker kill himself a long time ago and I wouldn't have this problem now. On one hand, he has this whiney little bastard of a son and on the other hand is every human in the world. It's a no-brainer; Curtis has to go. But what is the best way to do it? Maybe get him locked away in an asylum? No time for that, and it wouldn't work anyway. He is smart and could probably convince the authorities that he is normal. Or, he could spill the beans. That is too risky. He is thinking that Curtis needs to go away forever.

Maybe put him in prison? He is sure he could get Nixon to issue an executive order that would lock him away forever in Guantanamo Bay, Cuba. But Nixon has his hands full with Russia at the moment and can't be bothered. He could have him killed, maybe that is the best answer. First things first, Kenneth thinks; he picks up his briefcase and goes to the desk. The first thing is to fire Curtis, as of tomorrow morning, when he can make it official. Curtis will no longer be the second in command at the Department of Defense, in fact, he will be unemployed.

Kenneth places a piece of his Department of Defense stationery on the desk and stares at the blank page for a moment; he is thinking how to best write Curtis' dismissal. Kenneth wants – no, he needs a drink. He had put the booze down three years ago, because his doctors told him that alcohol could kill him with his medical condition and the medication he takes. Fuck it, three years on the wagon is long enough. The mini bar in the refrigerator is well stocked with three small bottles of most everything a drinker could want. Scotch was his favorite poison in the past, so he makes a double scotch on the rocks and takes a sip, too strong it will be better when the ice melts a bit.

Back to the desk, he knows how he is going to start and finish the termination letter insubordination, dereliction of duty, and unexcused absences; that will be enough. He writes a stinging dismissal letter. Finished with the letter he tries the drink again. Perfect, damn he has missed the Scotch; it is about gone already so he freshens it up with the last small bottle. Next, he needs to change his will. How is the best way to do that and make sure that it's legal? Going to have to call that Jewish lawyer of his, but its 01:45 in the morning.

Fuck em, he has paid that sleazy bastard enough money over the years, and done him enough favors. Now he needs a favor; he needs legal advice, right now.

Kenneth finishes his glass. Shit, that was the last of the scotch. Well, there is still Jack Daniels and Jim Beam. He settles on Jim Beam, good stuff without the coal taste. He makes a double and collects his thoughts for the call; he dials the number.

He is going to wake the bastard up for sure, but Kenneth doesn't give a flying shit. He dials the number from his rolodex, and a sleepy very grumpy man answers.

"It's two in the morning, what the fuck do you want?"

"It's Kenneth Rushie and I need some legal advice; go take a shower or make coffee, I'll call you back in ten minutes."

"Kenneth, oh, well; all right, give me a few minutes." Saul hangs up the phone and goes into the bathroom.

Kenneth makes his notes for the phone call; he doesn't want to forget any important questions. He finishes the Jim Beam and as he gets up to get the last bottle, he staggers and almost falls down. He steadies himself on the wall for a few seconds, and the wave of dizziness passes. Damn, he thinks, I used to drink this shit all day and all night, and function just fine. I must be becoming a lightweight, just this last little bottle of Jim Beam, and then I'll stop. He makes his way into the kitchen, fills the glass with lots of ice and the last shot of good bourbon. He is thinking he will let the ice melt to mellow the taste and sip it slowly; it would be better for him not to slam booze like he did in the old days.

Kenneth dials Saul's number again and Saul answers on the seconded ring. "Kenneth, what's so important?"

"My will Saul. I want to change it, and I want it done right now. What is the best way to do that?"

"The best way would be for you to come into my office."

"Saul, you're in Washington and I'm in Nebraska. So, as I said, what is the best way to do it?"

"Do you have your wishes written out? Of course, that's the first thing... make a rough draft, it needs to say that it's either an amendment and modification to the existing will, or that your wish is to nullify the old will, and replace it with one dated today."

"I think a new one, Saul."

"Ok, use that phase in the opening nullify and replace, or if you wish to change the will, start with 'this is an amendment to my existing will on file.' Got that?"

"Yes, ok I got that, what else?"

"Write your wishes and be sure to have it notarized; that shouldn't be a problem for a man in your position, you can summon anyone, any time day or night, like me. After it is signed, dated and notarized, mail it to me. That will be good enough in the interim, but of course I will professionally write it up and express mail it for a signature. Mail it back to me and it's done; and legally airtight."

"Saul, that will take days, I want it done now, today."

"What's the matter Kenneth, you planning on dying tonight?"

"Not if I can help it Saul, but if I do, I don't want that mistake I used to consider a son to get a dime out of me."

"Ok, Kenneth, that's your business, just be sure to have it notarized and get the papers in the mail to me immediately."

"Ok Saul, anything else?"

"Yes, in case you don't finish it completely, or can't get it notarized in the middle of the night, it wouldn't hurt to put your thumbprint near your signature. Initial below the print and include the date and time."

"Is there anything else Kenneth?"

"No that's it. Wait, there is something else; I don't want to see a bill for this little consultation, understand?"

"Of course, Kenneth, if there is nothing else, I'm going back to bed; goodnight."

"Goodnight Saul, and thank you."

Saul smiles to himself, other than getting up in the middle of the night, that was easy. Kenneth is a very smart man; he should have already known all the things he told him, seems like common sense to him. He liked the last part he threw in about the thumbprint; it does give a degree of legitimacy but, basically, he pulled that one out of his ass, being a lawyer is all about the art of bullshit.

Kenneth is starting to realize that he feels drunk not the pleasant kind he expected, but the –I don't feel so good kind of drunk. His mind is made up about Curtis and he is not going to change it. He must finish what he started out to do, and that is to fire Curtis and change his will. He doesn't want to do anything except lay down in bed, but he didn't get to his position by not doing the work or by procrastinating until tomorrow.

Kenneth thinks I'll just keep it simple no need to rewrite the whole thing right now, just change Curtis' benefit from everything to nothing. Ok, he thinks, I'll just make an amendment, a modification, he writes a few paragraphs excluding Curtis and leaving any assets to the American Cancer Society, he dates and signs it. The thumbprint idea that Saul gave him is sharp and smart, that will have to work for now because he is in no shape to summon a notary.

He takes the ink barrel out of a cheap disposable pen, cuts off the tip and smears ink on a scrap piece of paper. He rolls his thumb in the ink and tries two test prints, they are smeared, two more tries and the impression is perfect. He makes his print on the document, initials, dates and time stamps it, as Saul told him. Done, he thinks. He is trying to read what he wrote, but the lines keep blurring, it's going to have to be good enough for now.

He carefully places the termination letter and the modification to his will in his briefcase and locks it. Kenneth is trying to make his way to bed, but is having trouble walking straight; he zigs to the side, stopping to lean on the wall for a few seconds, and then tries for the bed again. He zags successfully to the bed and plops down, fully clothed. Suddenly he feels hot. He is sweating and very uncomfortable in his clothes.

He thinks, I have to get undressed and turn the air on. It seems like too much effort, but he makes his mind up to do it. He sits up and gets out of his shirt and tie, and with an effort, he peels out of his pants and underwear too. He is lying on the bed naked, except for his socks. It's better and then it's not. The room starts to spin; he is hot again, sweating. The A/C he thinks, I must turn on the A/C. With a tremendous effort he gets out of bed. He doesn't even try to walk; he crawls the short distance to the window unit. He punches the A/C button and turns the dial to maximum cool.

It's not better. He feels worse with every second. Oh my God he thinks, I'm going to throw up. He crab crawls as fast as he can toward the bathroom; the friction of the carpet against his knees takes the skin right off. He, of course, notices the added pain and has a flash thought. The last time I had carpet burn on my knees, I was young and having a hell of a good time not now though he thinks, and he begins to vomit just short of the toilet.

He can't even hold himself up on all fours anymore; he's lying on the bathroom floor, curled up and holding his stomach. He is curled in a fetal position, on a slimy tile floor. He thinks why isn't this passing? Then he knows; he is having a heart attack, because now the pain is in his chest and he can't breathe. He rolls on to his back and the pain stops everything stops.

The last thing he notices is a large brown stain on the ceiling, he wonders why the stain has never been repaired and painted. Kenneth Rushie; Director of the Department of Defense is dead.

Fourteen

"I'm telling you, those little bitches are long gone, Joey. How the fuck did we let this happen?

Fuck, go down there and see if you can find any trace of them."

The one called Frankie clicks on a powerful flashlight and shines it over the guardrail and down the hill, back to the spot just the other side of the guardrail.

"Frankie, get your ass down there and look!"

"Damn it Joey, give me a minute, I'm thinking."

"That would be a fucking first."

"Something is wrong here, Joey."

"What do you mean?"

"Look, no footprints; hundreds of people must use this path in the course of a month. Sneaky little bitches – it's them, it has to be. I'm going to check it out." Frankie goes over the guardrail and takes a few steps, concentrating on the path. It doesn't take long, after five or six paces he finds footprints, lots of them going down the hill. He stops and shines the light slowly in all directions. "They had to go down the hill." he says.

"Get your ass down there and look for them!"

"Joey, it has to be a quarter of a mile down the hill and back up again. I'm old and fat, just like you – and, what the fuck do we pay Muscle Mike and Crazy Tony for? It's their job, where the hell are they?"

"Maybe they went after them."

"Think Joey, they were on bicycles; they would have had to ditch them somewhere around here."

"Check the brush for the bikes, Frankie."

Frankie slowly sweeps both sides of the path with the light, then the roadside brush, walking a good way up and down the road.

"Check the other side of the road, Frankie."

Frankie spends a few minutes checking the other side of the brush alongside the road. "Nothing boss. Those bikes should stick out like a sore thumb, they're not here."

"Fuck Frankie, you know what this means, don't you? It means that we'll have to break camp and get the hell out of here. If those girls tell the cops that we have been running a whorehouse, with underage captive girls, we'll never get out of jail. I think we should cut and run back to Florida."

Frankie says, "Let's go back to camp and call Uncle Louie in Florida, maybe Mike or Tony checked in with him."

"I doubt it, it's not like there's a pay phone on every corner around here, but yeah all right; we'll do that and get the lumpers to start breaking down. We'll get a few men to come back with us to take another look for the bitches. It certainly would be best if we could find them. Damn it all to hell, where the fuck did Muscle Mike and Crazy Tony go?"

"I don't know, maybe we should drive really slow on the way back. I'll check the sides of the road for them, or the bikes."

"Ok, that's all we can do here, let's go."

They get into the Cadillac make a U-turn and drive slowly over the river, back into Nebraska.

"Holy shit, that was close!" John says. "He was right on top of us, twice."

Sandy says, "Betty did a good job with our shelter."

"With our shelter yes, but boy did I make a mistake erasing all the footprints, I outsmarted myself and that guy Frankie is a whole lot smarter than he looks."

Mark says, "Let's get down to the tracks, we can jump a fright and put this place behind us."

"I have been thinking about that," Betty says. "You are forgetting that we are barefoot, walking or running on the road is one thing, but the tracks are nothing but crushed sharp rocks – no way we can walk on that."

"Hey John, you didn't bring my old sneakers, did you?"

"No, I left them in the swamp."

"Shit."

"We have to think of something," says Betty.

For some reason, I am thinking of WWII stories. Maybe because it seems like the carnies, cops, Army and Air Force are after us? Shit, it seems like a genuine life-threatening situation, because it is. I remember old films where men, women and children were walking barefoot in the snow, with nothing but rags on their feet. "That's it," I say.

"What's it?"

"Rags. John and I are each wearing two shirts; we'll take off a shirt, cut it, and wrap your feet with the cloth."

John says, that's a good idea, let's do it."

We peal out of our denim jackets and our long sleeve shirts. I take out my new knife and cut the sleeves off. I cut the sleeves lengthwise; that gives us four strips for wrapping, and I cut the two shirts in half. John folds them into four pads and wraps Sandy's feet; I do Betty's. It came out pretty good, as we kept the material on the bottom for cushion. We weren't worried freezing cold weather, just some foot protection.

Sandy says, "Thank you, I'm so glad we met the two of you."

"Yeah," Betty says, "Same here, we need to move."

"Hold on a minute, I want to ask you something well, more than one thing but, how did the two of you wind up here? Did you run away? Why?"

Sandy says, "It was like a dream. I had a strong feeling; no – that's not the right way to say it. The feeling was more like an irresistible urge, a need to travel west. I couldn't shake it. I was scared; I have never done anything like this before. I counted all of my money, sixty-two dollars including change. I decided to take a Greyhound west, in the morning, when cousin Betty called; and, she was having exactly the same problem."

"Wait, you're cousins?'

"Yes, Betty says. "Sandy is my Yankee cousin."

"Where are you from Sandy?"

"I'm from Baldwinsville, New York."

"Wow," John says, "That's just west of Syracuse, that's where we are from! How about you Betty, where are you from?"

"Chamblee, Georgia. Well, Baldwinsville a long time ago when I was little; my dad's job at General Motors transferred him to the Georgia assembly, plant in 1960."

"So, you two had the same urge, or pull, to travel west at the same time?"

"Yes, Sandy and I decided to meet at the Greyhound bus station in Chicago, and we did; then we bought tickets to Omaha."

"What about you two?"

John says, "Yes, the same urge or pull, but we hitchhiked."

"It's weird." Sandy says, "What are we in to?"

"I don't know," I say. "But I think we are about to find out."

"Why do the carnie guys want you so badly, what did you do to them?"

"We escaped," Betty says. "They had plans for us that weren't in our best interest; they wanted to get us hooked on heroin and then use us as prostitutes. They joked about how many times they could sell us as virgins. The big guy, Joey, said his record was a hundred and seventeen."

"We were locked in a trailer with eight or ten other girls, and about the time it got dark, something strange happened. There was this buzzing noise. Loud, but more like in my ears than in the distance. I'm sure that everybody at the carnival heard it. It put everyone except Sandy and me in a trance. The door on the trailer was locked, but it popped open and we went outside. Everyone was like sleepwalking, not saying anything but moving around with their eyes wide open and glazed over. It seemed like a good time to run like hell, and we did."

"Think, Anything else strange?"

"Isn't that strange enough? The buzzing and the zombie-like people?"

"I mean, did anybody tell you to walk or run this way?"

Sandy says, "The door popping wide open was strange; I mean, it was locked six different ways. But no, nobody told us to come this way, it's just the way we went I don't know why."

Betty says, "You heard them; they're going to get more men and come back. Man, we got to go!"

"All right," Sandy says, "Let's try out our new peasant shoes."

"Hey," John says, "That's the best we can do for you, right now; we'll get you both some shoes tomorrow. We have money now; that fifty plus, whatever is in the wallets that we took off the wrestler gorillas – the ones we got off your ass."

"You guys did that?"

"Yeah, we kicked their asses."

"That's how you got that black eye, John? I've been meaning to ask you about that."

Betty is on her feet, brushing off the dirt and the leaves, "Let's go!"

"One check of the road first," John says, and he is off and crawling up the bank. After a few seconds, he scrambles back down. "Clear, we can go."

The four of us leave the relative safety of the blind, for the path then, the tracks and more strangeness to come.

The path down the hill is twisting and steep; it quickly becomes almost pitch black. Betty, who is out front, has stopped to let us catch up, "Best if we stay together," she whispers as she takes my hand. John and Sandy are right beside us; and, I can see that they are hand in hand also. We continue down the hill in silence for a few minutes. We are approaching the bottom of the hill and the tracks.

"Shh, look," Betty says. We do and we can see the flickering light of a campfire to the right, across the tracks. "A hobo camp," she says.

"Angle left," I say, "That's the way we need to go, north." We are almost out of the woods. The track is right in front of us, and it's a little brighter for lack of tree cover.

John says, "There's a road alongside the tracks; we don't have to walk on the rocks."

I tell him, "It's called a right of way, to give the track workers easy access to the track." We are holding up at the base of the hill. We can see the hobo camp easily; it's in a clearing on the other side, not far away at all.

There are four of them. Two are walking around the fire, tending to it; two are sitting on something, slouched back, with cans in their hands, probably beer.

"We have to get by without them seeing us."

"We might have to angle through the woods," Betty says.

Sandy says, "I don't like that idea at all."

"We might have to."

No sooner than Betty says that, the sound of a locomotive horn begins blasting in the distance.

"Here comes our cover," John says. And we all sit down on the path to wait.

It doesn't take long, in less than a minute we hear the train horn blowing for a road crossing, it is much closer now. Soon we can see its headlight and hear the rumble of the powerful engines, it is going northbound, perfect. The air and the ground rumbles as the train approaches, the power of the engines is amazing to me.

Sandy says, "We can't jump on that; it's moving way too fast."

"We have to find the train yard; we can get on a train when it's stopped or moving slowly."

The train is on top of us. The engines roar by and we break from cover walking fast and north of the right of way. The night is full of sounds from the train. Air hoses hiss, wheels click on the joints, and everything rumbles. The track and the road bend to the right; we are safely out of sight of the hobo camp. I slow to a walk, everyone else does too; we are all tired.

The train of cars keeps rolling by. I wonder how long it can be. The last railroad car rolls by, it's a caboose and standing at the rear platform is a man, who is called a brakeman, for whatever reason. He sees us and waves, he has a lantern that he is swinging back and forth, like he's trying to tell us something. The train and the noise fade in the distance, but we can still see the swinging lantern.

Sandy stops and sits down on the ground. "I can't go anymore; my legs are like rubber and I'm so tired, I can't move."

John sits down next to her and says, "Let's take a break and have some water."

Two more tired kids plop down on the ground, beside Sandy and John.

We pass the canteen around and everyone has a drink, except Sandy. "Oh yeah, I forgot," I say
and reach into my pocket for the other plastic cup. I flick it open and hand it to Sandy; she drinks her fill and hands the cup back to me.

"Hey, let me see that cup," Betty says. She looks at it in the pale moonlight, without saying anything, then walks over to the rail and smashes it open with an old railroad spike. A round piece of plastic with transistor wires and a small battery fall out of the broken cup. Betty looks at it for a moment then passes it around for all of us to see. "Any ideas," she asks.

"Yeah," John says. "I know what it is. It's a transmitter; they are tracking us like caribou."

"Shit, smash it," Sandy says.

"No," I say. "Let's put it on a southbound train, or a car, a riverboat, a truck, anything not going our way."

"Ok, all right," agreement all around.

Betty says, in her sweet southern voice, although it's not so sweet at the moment. "I think it's time you guys tell us what the hell is going on. I mean, what happened tonight; and, how you got a cup with a fifty-dollar bill in it and another cup with a transmitter? Just the facts sir, like the guy on Dragnet says." She is trying to lighten it up a little bit.

"You start John," I say.

John tells them about the Pontiac with the four black men, about the bridge and the first part about the wild ride in the Plymouth Road Runner with the four beautiful women.

I jump in and tell them about the police chase. We leave out a lot though, John only says they threw his sneakers out the window.

Betty can sense we're not telling the whole truth about what happened in the car, and she says so.

"All right we won't sugar coat it." We tell the truth about what happened in the car. Our new girls listened intently to our story about the possessed women. I think they believe us. The part about the swamp I let John tell, because I didn't want to embarrass him. The part about the police brought a lot of questions from both Sandy and Betty; and, I say, "Just let us get through this and you can ask questions later, we need to get going again."

The girls are quiet as we finish the police story, the part about the presents, and our walk up to the bridge, where we found them.

Betty says, "Last week I wouldn't have believed a word of that story; it's hard to now, but I believe you are both telling the truth."

"How about you Sandy, do you believe us?"

"I sure do. This pull thing that you mentioned well, I know that's real and so does Betty."

"Can you go a little more Sandy?"

"Yes, I think so; maybe another piece of that dried beef to munch on as we walk?"

"Sure," I pass the bag around and we get up slowly; I don't know how much more any of us can take.

Up ahead, another track branches off to the right. I am walking on the track searching for something – I don't know what; and, the rest are walking on the right of way. I am looking down at the new rails that branch to the right, I know it is called a switch. I know, because my dad works in a shop for the railroad and his friend, Dick, is a brakeman.

I grew up around the railroad, and have heard endless railroad stories. The switch is what they call "lined for the straight;" the rails that narrow down to points are open, allowing the train's wheels to pass over and continue down the main. The story post is green; it's like a stop-go sign, green for the main, and red for the siding.

Two longer ties stick out at the end of the switch. A heavy lever is attached, that's how they "throw the switch"; there's a big padlock that locks the lever down. I know what I am searching for – the key. Uncle Dick has a bunch of them on his key ring; big, brass, oversized keys. He told me that with those keys he could open any door on the railroad.

I move some rocks near the switch lock. And damn, if I didn't find just what I was searching for! A brass switch key! I pick it up; I'm amazed, not only that is there, but that I knew it was there. I didn't notice John or the girls watching me from the side, so I'm startled when Betty says, "What did you find Mark?"

"The key to the railroad" I say. I walk over and hand her the key; she looks at it and passes it around.

John hands the key back to me and asks, "This opens any door on the railroad?"

"All of the switches for sure, and probably some buildings too." I say.

Sandy says, "There are more of those switches up ahead."

"That's good, it means that we are coming into a yard. We'll stay on the main and should see some buildings soon."

"Train!" Sandy says.

Fifteen

Joey drives the Cadillac across the bridge; when he comes to the intersection he stops, and asks Frankie which way they should go.

"Go back toward our base," he says. "I've had about enough of this night; drive slow and I'll look for the assholes."

Joey grunts and turns right; he is driving slowly with the high beams on. The road and the shoulders are brightly lit.

"What the fuck," Frankie says. "Up ahead on your side do you see that bush moving?"

"Yeah," Joey angles the car onto the shoulder, on the wrong side of the road, so that the bushes are flooded with light.

Frankie is already out of the car and standing over Muscle Mike.

"What the hell is this shit? Those two girls kick your ass?"

"No, two boys, big boys, they ambushed us."

"Big boys my ass! That scrawny little blond kid and that long-haired hippie punk; you've got to be kidding me! What the fuck, you're not even tied up!"

"I am too! My feet are tied my left hand is tied to this bush; and, I can't move my right arm or shoulder, something's broke, it hurts like a son of a bitch."

"I'm about in the mood to finish beating you to death, you worthless piece of shit! You got me out running all over the place doing your job!"

Joey says, "Damn Frankie, calm down; it's usually my job to do the screaming and yelling. Untie him. Where is Crazy Tony?"

"I saw him wipe out on the bike he was riding, a little bit down the road, that way." He nods his head in the direction of the swamp.

"Put him in the car Frankie, and back it up to give me light, I'll look for Tony."

Muscle Mike is whimpering and almost crying, he is in so much pain. He tells Frankie that it hurts like all holy hell, and Frankie tells him that he really doesn't give a shit.

"Get in the car wimp."

"Hey, Frankie give me that flashlight. This side of the road, right Mike?"

"Yeah, I think so."

"All right, let's find the son of a bitch. I'm not at all happy with either of you, damn it all to hell!"

Joey starts checking the ditch and the brush, back in the direction of the swamp.

Frankie gets behind the wheel and backs the car up slowly.

It doesn't take long for Joey to find Crazy Tony.

"Shit Frankie, come here; the son of a bitch looks like he is dead!"

Frankie gets the headlights on where Joey is standing and puts the car in park.

Joey is kneeling down holding Crazy Tony's wrist. Joey says, "He is warm and has a pulse."

"Humph, did you try kicking him in the ribs?" With that, Frankie draws back his foot and kicks him a good one in the ribs.

"Ow shit, no more!" Crazy Tony is awake.

"See that? The lazy bastard was sleeping!"

"I wasn't sleeping, I was unconscious! Untie me."

Frankie clicks open a switchblade and says, "I ought to do us both a favor and slit your throat." Frankie is still for a moment and appears to be thinking about it – then, he cuts Crazy Tony's hands and feet free.

Frankie offers his hand and tells Tony to get up.

Crazy Tony says, "I don't know if I can." He takes Frankie's hand, and Frankie pulls him up.

"Damn, he says, you look like shit. That road about peeled your face clean off. Aw, what the fuck; maybe it will be an improvement on your ugly ass."

"I hurt boss."

"All right," Frankie says in a nicer voice, "Get in the car. Can you make it or do you need a hand?"

"I'll try it." Tony manages to stagger to the car and gets in the back seat next to Muscle Mike – who is not looking so muscular at the moment.

"What the fuck are we going to do Frankie?"

"I don't know about Joey, but I'm done; me and my rig are going back to Florida. You can buy out my half, I'll sell it cheap."

"Don't talk like that Frankie; we have been together for what, twenty-five years?"

"You don't get it, Joey. I had a genuine Come to Jesus moment back there. I felt like I was dead and everyone else was too, but we were still walking. Everybody that was there must know it too, they have to. You have to know what I'm talking about, you were there Joey. I was paralyzed, helpless. I didn't like it; it is a sign from God. I must atone for my sins and stop sinning, right now. Don't you just know it, Joey?"

"Damn Frankie, I need a drink. Let's get these two sorry assholes back to camp; we can talk in Dr. Quack's trailer."

Joey gets in behind the wheel and Frankie settles into the front passenger seat. Muscle Mike says, "Take me to the hospital, I'm hurt, bad."

It's Joey's turn to snap. "You're more stupid than you look! You want me to waste time going to the hospital? And then what, answer a bunch of questions maybe from cops? And, pay an outrageous hospital bill? You've lost your fucking mind. You're damn lucky that I am taking you to Doctor Quack."

"But he's a veterinarian. What does he know about setting a broken shoulder on a man?"

"You're more an animal than a man, so shut up; we're almost there."

Joey turns onto a gravel road; ahead, on the left, is the back side of their little traveling carnival. On the right, is freshly planted corn. The carnival's not in one individual town, but between three – the idea being, to service all three towns at once.

"I told you to stick to the mill towns Joey, what the fuck are we doing way out here in the middle of nowhere?'

"I told you before Frankie, we have always had a loyal following with the migrants; they are always willing to pay our price and, they're never a problem."

"Well, at least you had the sense to stay out of the Southern Bible Belt, like I told you. Our luck would have certainly run out, long before now, if we tried to work that part of the country."

Lights are on in most of the trailers and every light seems to be on inside Doctor Quack's trailer. The Quack himself is sitting on the doorstep with two cans of beer at his side. The Cadillac pulls to a stop and Dr. Quack gets up and walks over to the rear passenger door, opens it and helps Muscle Mike out. Somehow, he just knew that more patients would be arriving.

With Mike's whining about his shoulder, it doesn't take long for Dr. Quack to figure out that Muscle Mike probably has a broken collarbone.

Crazy Tony has his old fire and cockiness back. He is already out of the car and demanding the Quack fix his face.

Dr. Quack looks Tony up and down; he says, "Shit boy, you're a mess. Go clean yourself up, take a hot shower and shave, the best you can. Any gravel you can pick out of your face, I won't have to cut out."

"Just patch me up Doc. I need to get back and find those bitches and the punks that did this to me; I can't wait to pound them into pulp."

"Tony, I'm not your mother or your nursemaid; you have to clean yourself up – besides Mike is hurt worse than you are, and he is my first customer. Go on, and use the antibiotic soap that I left on your step."

Crazy Tony reluctantly walks toward the small trailer that he shares with Muscle Mike.

"Come on Mike, let's get you inside, the good news is, this won't take long. You know, you're not my first customer; I've been swamped, nonstop."

Frankie says, "What has been happening around here, Doc?"

"I don't know what happened to cause this night. I know I felt pretty strange myself, but of my patients, two were cross-eyed. On each of them, I put a patch over one eye and told them their eyes would straighten out in a few days."

"Will it?"

"Hell, I don't know, it's all I knew to do or say."

"Four patients complained of terrible ringing in their ears tinnitus, which I have myself."

"What did you do for them?"

"I gave them sleeping pills and told them it would be better in the morning."

"Will it?"

"I don't know, but I can't wait to try it myself."

Joey says, "What else Doc?"

"You're not going to like this Joey but, when I went to give the girls their evening injections, every one of them refused it. They said they are done with that shit. They don't seem like airheads anymore, and they all look beautiful. They are waiting to see you; they want to be paid."

"Fuck, their trailer is locked?"

"Nope, all the locks are broken; doors and windows both."

"You mean they could have just left?"

"Yes, they could have, but like I said, they are waiting to be paid."

"Oh shit, what a night, Frankie. I'm starting to think you may be right; it just might be time to quit this shit. I need a drink Doc."

"Help yourself, you know where it is. Joey, I need your belt; Mike, I want you to sit in this chair."

Joey downed one shot and has another one poured.

The Doc says, "Joey, bring the bottle; I think we all need a shot. And, I wasn't kidding about your belt. The Doc takes a long swig off the bottle and hands it to Muscle Mike. "Here, you're going to need this."

"But I don't drink," Mike says.

"You do like I say now Mike. We're going to take this belt and put it under your armpit; Frank and Joey are going to hold the belt, while you and I ease that bone back in place."

"How is that going to work?"

"They're going to hold the belt tight; you're going to raise your ass up, about four inches off the chair; and then, you'll sit down, real fast. Your own weight will be enough to set your bone; I'll ease the bone back in place with the tension."

"Oh, hell no!"

"Mike, it will work. It's about the same thing that a hospital would do for you, and it will be over within a few seconds."

Mike takes a deep breath and a sip of whiskey, them and hands the bottle to Frankie.

"I just swore it off," Frankie says, "Let's get this over with."

Joey's belt is perfect for the job; it's a handmade Amish, heavy leather belt. Doc slips the belt under Tony's arm and centers it. "All right, all you men have to do is hold steady; Mike and I will do the adjustment. And, for God's sake, don't york up on the belt, we can't move the bone too far, got it?"

The Quack places both hands on the top of Muscle Mike's shoulder and tells him to raise his ass up on the seat.

"You don't want to do this twice Mike; so, do what I tell you."

"When I say three drop your ass; you do it. Joey and Frank, you two hold steady, and I'll get the bone positioned right. Ready? One, Two, Three!"

The shoulder crunches and Mike lets out a low moan, he's gone pale and beads of sweat have popped out on his forehead.

"Better?"

"It's too soon to tell," Mike says, "But, I think so. How long will this take to heal?"

"About a year," Doc says, "if you don't injure it again. It's going to be your weak spot forever, and, I forgot to tell you the bad news, putting the bone back in will hurt like hell, but it's over now; we did it."

"Fuck!" Mike says, "I can't do this anymore. I'm done. I'm going back to Florida."

"That makes two of us," Doc says, "I'm pulling out for Florida at first light. You can ride with me Mike. Here, let's put this sling on your arm for now; we may have to body wrap that arm later."

Frankie says, "I'll travel with you Doc, my mind is made up."

"What the fuck? Is everybody abandoning me? The season is just getting started!"

"Come on Joey, you know it too. If we stick around something else bad is going to happen, maybe jail or worse. I'm telling you, that could have been God talking to us; I'm taking the hint and getting out. I'll be leaving at first light."

"Come with us; we can always go back to trucking for a while. We already own the equipment and we've been drivers before. At least this time, we will be owners and operators, we'll be our own boss."

Joey says, "Shit, I think this is the first time in my life I have ever had trouble making up my mind. I don't want to walk away from my hustle, but I damn sure don't want to go back to jail, or be damned, shit."

Crazy Tony burst through the door, looking true to his name. His hair is wet and sticking up, he has clean clothes on and is holding a white towel to his face; the towel has considerable blood on it. "Let's go," he says, "I got the Impala running, it started right up; I can't figure out why it wouldn't start before. That bugs me, but not as much as what those little assholes did to my face! Those little pricks are going be sorry they ever messed with me!"

The doc says, "Tony let me have a look at your face."

"It's good enough" Tony says. "I picked a half a pound of rocks out of my face, and now I'm going to take a pound of flesh out of their asses! The fuckers took my wallet to, ah man; I'm going to get them!"

"Calm down," Joey says, "We're not going after them, this year's tour is over. We are packing it in and going back to Florida."

"Not me! What about the girls?"

"Doc tells me that our girls just want to be paid and go on their way. That's what I'm going to do, pay them. The two young girls that ran let them go; forget about them, they're gone."

"I'm not forgetting anything! Come on Mike, let's go."

"I can't go with you Tony; you don't know the pain I'm in. It hurts to move; it hurts like hell, period. I'm going back to Uncle Louie's. I have to heal up; the doc said it might take a year."

"Nobody hurts me, or my little brother, like this and gets away with it. I'm going to hunt them down and make them pay. Maybe I'll scalp the punks like the Indians did. And, if you don't want the girls, I'll find a use for them!" Tony goes out the door and slams it behind him. Five seconds later they hear the Impala start and leave.

Joey says, "Frankie, spread the word, pack it up we're leaving."

Sixteen

In the distance ahead is a southbound locomotive; we can see its headlight but haven't heard its horn, it seems to be going slow or standing still.

"I think we can move up a little more." I say, "He can't see us from there, we have all those side tracks to duck into when the train gets close. We'll stay in the shadows and move up; all right?"

"We have to do something," Sandy says, "I have to stop sometime soon."

That's enough discussion. Our group moves to the far-left side of the right of way, and slowly we make our way forward.

After about five minutes John holds up his hand to stop. "Are we getting closer or he is he moving?"

We all look around, there is a ditch full of water on our left and the next track siding is almost straight across from us.

"No choice I say, we have to cross. Shit, we should have done it sooner. If they're moving, they are looking down the tracks, let's hope the train isn't moving. We have to get across, but we do it low, on all fours; it will look more like dogs or deer are crossing, not people. Ready? Go low and fast." The four of us scamper across in less than five seconds, and automatically, dive into the shadows on the siding track.

We hear the engine moving slowly toward us; it's getting brighter from the headlight. The pitch of the engine changes from a low rumble, to a hard pull. As it comes into sight, we see thick black diesel exhaust pouring from the top of three engines, and it's steadily picking up speed. The boxcars the train is pulling are different than the ones we'd seen before; they are all black and open at the top, and something is piled high inside each of them. John asks, "What is all that stuff?"

"Coal," Betty says. "It's a coal train and it's going to a power plant. I've seen them before; there's a big, coal-fired power plant just north of Atlanta. Quick, Mark, throw that thing from the cup in there." I take it out of my pocket and hand it to John. "You do it," I say. "Your aim is way better than mine tonight." He takes it and walks several steps toward the moving train; he waits a few seconds, timing his shot, then lobs it into one of the open cars of coal.

Perfect shot, two points.

"The stopwatch Mark, throw it in too."

I don't say it, but I don't want to. For some reason, I like the watch, but I know that Betty is right. I promise myself to get another one someday and make it a real pocket watch. I walk up to where John is and hand him the stopwatch; he lobs it in the second to last coal car. The last car, the caboose, goes by and again standing on the platform at the railing is a man; he sees us and waves, and we wave back. And like the last one, he swings his lantern back and forth.

The two girls are by our side and Betty asks, "What do you think he is trying to tell us?" John says, "I think he is trying to tell us to keep going; my gut says that the railroad guys are going to help us." "That feels right" I say, and everybody agrees.

We cross the track, back to the dirt and gravel road and walk some more. We can see a building ahead on the left; on the right are lots of switches and tracks, all lined with boxcars, coal cars, tankers, and engines as far as we can see.

Sandy says, "We have to find a place to rest, or I should say, sleep." "And a bathroom," Betty adds. John and I don't say anything; what can we say to that?

A big square building comes into sight; it is old but well-built with a lot of craftsmanship, a fancy slate roof, stone walls, and arched windows. "I bet that is the old passenger station, they probably still use it for offices or something; let's see if my key opens the door."

We walk the last few feet and climb three steps up to a platform where in the old day's passengers would board their trains.

John and Sandy are both looking in windows, while Betty and I walk up to the front door. It has the same kind of big padlock as the switches; my key fits right in and opens the lock. We enter the dark building; someone finds the light switch, and turns on the lights.

Straight ahead is the original ticket window, from the days when this was a passenger station. The frosted window has an arch and the word TICKETS is embedded in the glass. I touch it, it feels like a washboard, bumpy lines all the way up; it's thick too, it must weigh a ton; no doubt about it, it's a beautiful piece of glass, probably a hundred years old or more. That's it though – no booth behind the window, just the original wall set up as a display.

John and Sandy are already rifling through the desks. "Hey! You can't make a mess; we don't want someone to call the cops; come on be cool about it! We can't stay here long anyway. Those railroad guys come in first thing in the morning, and that's not long from now."

"I'm thinking that we need to find a caboose out there to crash in."

"I'm glad you're thinking, Mark; we don't need anybody else after us. Hey! There's a phone! I'm going to call my daddy! He'll straighten this mess out, and get us out of here!" She is already headed for the phone.

"Betty No!"

"Why not? Daddy will be on the next plane to Omaha and I know what he will bring, a 357, a 45, a pair of 38's, and all the ammunition he can fit in the suitcase. The only way he'll bring a toothbrush is if ma helps him pack."

I am concerned beyond all logical reason. It should make sense to call her father, or someone, anybody that could help us out of this mess, but it doesn't. My gut feeling, which I just developed a few hours ago, says this is a bad, bad idea.

"Betty think, you don't want to involve your father. It won't help; it might make it worse. Hell, if he brings all those guns, he is bound to find somebody to shoot. Remember what we told you about the army, air force, cops and Russians? Well, they all have guns, lots of them; and, they'll shoot back! Do you want to get your daddy killed?"

"My daddy could take care of those carnie assholes!"

"Oh yeah, the carnie assholes too, I'm sure that your daddy could take care of them, but they are not even our biggest problem."

"They were our only problem, before we meet the two of you!"

I look Betty in the eyes, put my hands on her shoulders and pull her close. In a soft voice, because I want this to be private and don't want anyone else to hear. I say, "Betty, how did you get here? Remember the pull? The pull that you in Georgia and your cousin Sandy in New York both experienced, at the same time. That fact that you both decided to meet at the Greyhound bus station in Chicago, and buy tickets to Omaha? The carnie guys that John and I took care of for you? Are those the guys that you left the bus station with? Seems like you would know better than that; Why did you do it?"

"I'll tell you why, it's because of you. I am meant for you; and Sandy is meant for John. I think somehow, we knew that you and John would find us.

One more thing, you and Sandy saw a door, locked six different ways, pop open and let you out. And, what was that buzzing sound in your ears? The people walking around like zombies, in a trance? How about the cars that would not start? Why did you run straight to John and me? You know why; kind of, it just has to be. I don't think any of us have a choice, maybe no control at all. I believe that whoever, or whatever, is doing this could turn us into those wide-eyed, buzzing zombies that you described. Do what you want Betty; and if Sandy wants to go with you well, that's her choice. But I have to tell you, I think you are going to get your dad in trouble, or maybe even killed, if you call him."

"Hey, what's going on over there? Look what I found!" It's Sandy, she is holding up a mostly full pint bottle of bourbon. Betty says, "Sandy, you share that, I don't want you getting slammed on it." "Ok," she takes a swig and passes the bottle to John; he takes a swig and coughs a few times. "Damn," he says, "I'm glad I only took a small sip of that shit."

I ask "What kind is it?"

John is reading the bottle as he is walking over to me. "Wild Turkey, yuk; you try it. What's up with you and Betty?"

"She is thinking about calling her dad."

"I don't know what to say well yeah, I do. That is not a good idea; it doesn't sound right, or feel right. I'll leave you two alone. Here, try some of this." He hands me the bottle.

"Thanks, why don't you look around John and see if you can find some work boots, anything is better than what they have."

"Ok, I'll do that. And Betty, go with your gut feelings. Just all of a sudden tonight, I feel things, like deep in my gut like Mark said he did. I bet you have it too; we need to trust our instincts."

"Thanks, John you may be right but man, but I can't even tell you how bad I want to call my daddy!" Betty tears up and turns away.

"I'm going to look for a caboose."

"You want me to go with you?"

"No, keep an eye on the girls; give me a minute will ya?"

"Sure." John is walking toward the far corner; he stops and turns around. "Hey Mark, the wallets, let's check the wallets."

"All right, go find Sandy and we can look together."

John is calling for Sandy, "Where did you go?"

"What?"

"Oh, she's in the bathroom."

"That reminds me," Betty says, "I'll be right back, excuse me."

My eyes fall on a desk sitting alone against the wall, next to it is a big clunky machine. I sit down at the desk and take the two long leather wallets out of my pockets and look at the outside of them. They are inlaid with tool work; one has hunting designs, and the other has trucks.

The big clunky machine catches my interest. I have to stand up for a better look. It has a large cylinder at the top, with gears on the ends. There are wires going from the machine into the wall and a pile of blank white paper sitting next to it. I touch the cylinder and it's wet with ink.

"Hey," John surprises me from behind. "What's in the wallets?"

"I didn't look," I say. "I was waiting for you, they are right there on the table, you open them."

He opens one and takes out the cash, "Eighty bucks! Cool!" He opens the other one and takes out the cash. "Seventy bucks. What's that altogether, $150, right?"
He looks deeper and pulls out two driver's licenses, Tony Gambino and Michael Gambino, both from Gibsonton, Florida.

"Think they're brothers?"

"Probably," I say. "Too bad they don't put pictures on driver's licenses."

"Yeah, but we know which one is which. The Tony guy is the one that took the bad wipeout on the bike; the other one, with the busted shoulder, must be Mike."

John says, "Let's split the money up; we should all have some money in our pockets."

Wow, I think that's not like John.

He says, "Betty should keep the fifty from the cup; here you take fifty, and we'll give Sandy fifty."

"Yeah, that's a good idea. We don't know what is going to happen."

"That's for sure. Hey Mark, here comes Betty."

Betty says, "Didn't you say you had a toothbrush, Mark? Can I borrow it?"

"Sure," I take the toothbrush and the small tube of toothpaste out of my pocket and hand it to her.

"What about Sandy?" John asks "Here she can use mine."

"I told you she's funny about that."

"Hey, I heard that," Sandy says, "Just get John's, I'll use it."

"Hey," John says, "Check the closet by the bathroom, there are some old work boots and coveralls in there if you want to use them."

"Ok, we will," Betty says. She is looking deep into my eyes, holding the two toothbrushes, not moving toward the bathroom.

"I'm going to look for a caboose; you guys be ready to travel when I get back, ok?"

"Yeah, no problem, we'll be ready."

"Hey Betty, do you know what kind of machine this is?"

"Sure, I do, it's called a telefax. You put your letter, or whatever, in here and it spins and sends the letter through the telephone line to another machine just like it – anywhere in the world."

"Come on, no way. I can't believe that a letter can be sent through a telephone line."

"Sure, Betty says. "My mom works at the airport she uses them all the time. I've seen them work."

"Wow, I say. That's still hard to believe. I'm going out, wish me luck."

"Good luck Mark, be careful, and hurry back."

I go out the door and back to the right of way, which is more of a road now. Ahead to the right are long siding tracks filled with train cars. I count the tracks that I can see, seventeen.

I have to stand still and think. No way can I walk up and down all these tracks looking for my caboose. I'm not going that way, or the way I came, so that leaves straight ahead. In the distance, I hear train engines rumbling and the sound of cars being coupled together. I walk as fast as I can. I just know what I am looking for is on the seventeenth track. I pass tracks eight, nine, and ten. Up ahead, on track seventeen, all the way at the back, I see a light. By the time I get to tracks twelve and thirteen, I can see that track seventeen looks like it has all cabooses coupled together; and, lights are on inside the last caboose. That's it; I know this is what I am looking for.

I get to the seventeenth track and step in-between the cars. On my right side are cars after cars of tankers; on my left are all cabooses. Some old and some new, but they all just have so much character, they are way cool. I feel like I could live in one forever. The thought strikes me, if these cars were moving, this would be a scary, dangerous place; there isn't even much room to walk between cars without touching them. I am there, at the last caboose; I climb three steps and walk in the door, like I'm home.

There are two teenage boys sitting at a small table playing cards. The one closest to the door looks up and says with a smile and a funny laugh "Geez, it's about time, we have been waiting for you; tell me that you have three more with you."

"I do."

"Well, where are they?"

"They are waiting at the station for me to find a caboose."

"Go get them, we have been traveling for two days and we're beat; Louise and Christine are sound asleep – and, we want to join them."

"Do you know where we are going?"

The other guy says, "Kind of. Our new friend Pete, the railroad guy, told us to expect four more… and, that it's his mission to get us to where we need to go; he promised he will get us there. This caboose will roll north at about nine in the morning; we are to pick up more railroad cars in a place called Woodstock and then go east for a few hours. Go get your crew; we can talk when you get back."

"Right, we'll be right back."

I hurry back to the station, as fast as my weary legs and sore feet will go.

Back at the station, my old friend John and our two new friends, (girlfriends?) are sitting at the desk nearest, the door, waiting for me.

Betty and Sandy are wearing men's work boots and they each are draped with a coarse wool blanket.

"Hi," Betty says "You found it, didn't you? You found a caboose with other kids just like us, right?"

"Right," I say, "How do we know these things?"

Sandy says, "Two boys and two girls right?"

"What else do we just know?" Betty asks.

John speaks up, "There are more, lots more. We are to join a large group of kids just like us, runaways for no good reason, kids traveling hundreds or even thousands of miles to get here well, not right here, but close. The place we are going to; they are going there also."

Sandy says, "What could be the reason for teenagers, like us, to all be traveling to the same place?"

"We have no choice but to find out." I say.

"Agreed?"

Everyone agrees.

"Are we ready to go to the caboose?"

Everyone says they are ready, and we leave the old passenger station. Outside the air is a lot chiller, not freezing, but cold enough to see our breath. I'm glad to see the blankets on the girls.

"How are the boots working" I ask?

"Way better," they both say at once. "We had to stuff them with newspaper and they feel clunky, but so much better than nothing, or our peasant shoes, no offense."

"That's ok; we did what we had to do."

"Tell us about the other teenagers." Sandy says."

"Not much to tell." I say. "Two boys playing cards at a table and two girls sleeping in bunks."

"What did they say?"

"Geez, took you long enough, we have been waiting."

"What else?"

"Well, they knew that four more teenagers were coming, they asked where the rest were, I told them you were at the station; and, they said go and get them."

"That's it?"

"That's it."

"How far is it?" John asks

"There, see the light down that track? That's our caboose, are you ready to meet our new friends?"

"That's another thing I just know," John says, "that they will be our friends, for life."

"Yeah, I know." Everybody says.

We step off the road and onto an uneven stone ballast, between the tracks. The girls are having trouble walking and take our hands.

Sandy says "Betty; you still have the bottle, right?"

"Yes, we'll pass it around when we get in there; I hope they have something to eat."

"All I want to do is sleep," John says.

"I'm excited to be here; it feels like a miracle that we all have made it."

We are at the steps of the caboose. John hops up first and helps Sandy up the steps. I go next and help Betty. We stop on the platform and look at each other, for the briefest of seconds; then, almost all at once, we go through the door.

Inside, it's warm and it smells like suppertime.

Two teenage girls I can't help but notice that they are beautiful are fussing over a kerosene stove.

"Hi welcome, I'm Christine." She steps forward to shake everyone's hand.

"Louise," the other girl says, and she does the same.

"We are trying to warm up the chicken dinners that our new friend, Pete the brakeman, bought for all of us. It's hard to reheat box dinners on this stove, how do you like our solution?" The girls had stacked up railroad spikes like Lincoln logs, with the dinners on top, allowing them to heat slowly without burning the paper boxes.

The two boys' step over and introduce themselves. "Walt," says the first one. "Brownie," says the kid with the funny laugh. And we shake hands all around.

"My God that smells great," Sandy says, "It smells like I cooked it myself."

"A guy named Colonel Sanders cooked it. Help yourselves; there is a box for each of you and a cooler of soft drinks in the corner, against the wall."

"Hey, any of you guys have a cigarette?"

John hands him his open pack and says, "Keep them."

"Ok," Louise says, "Clear off the table and let our guests have a bite to eat. Christine and I will make your beds; Pete brought four thin mattresses, blankets and pillows." We need to crash; somehow, we just know that tomorrow is going to be a big day."

Our group sits at the table and digs into our delicious boxed dinners.

Christine asks, "So, where are you guys from?"

We tell her and return the question.

"Louise and I are from Boulder, Colorado."

Walt says – "Las Vegas, Nevada; we moved around a lot, but now we are just kind of stuck there. My mom was a dancer, but I think she got too old, and maybe too fat, for those types of clubs. Now she's just an overworked and underpaid waitress; she's very unhappy and I was trying to help her."

Louise says, "Tell them about what happened to you, Walt."

Well," he says, "I learned how to steal cars. I couldn't stand to see my mom so poor. But I got caught and sent to reform school. Two days ago, there was this buzzing noise and every door just popped open. I walked right past the guards, to the outside. I had this strong compulsion to travel east, to Omaha. I went to the rail yard in Las Vegas and hopped an eastbound train. Brownie was in the boxcar and also going to Omaha. That's when I knew we were into some strange shit. When we got to the Omaha rail yard, Louise and Christine were waiting for us."

"And you, Brownie, where are you from?"

"Salinas, California. Kind of the same thing, I mean no buzzing, but I couldn't help myself from traveling to Omaha. I was alone until I met Walt. I mean, that's not like me at all, but it seems all right now. I was lucky, I knew that a train went east every day, carrying California produce; that part was easy for me."

Christine says, "Louise and I are cousins. We were together last weekend and, at the same time, we both said out loud that we needed to go to Omaha; we looked at each other, and just started planning it. It was easy for us because our parents are rich. We each had about five hundred dollars; so, we bought bus tickets to Omaha and hired a cab to bring us to the railroad yard. Somehow, we just knew that we were to meet Walt and Brownie at the railroad station, then and continue on somewhere; right Louise?"

"Right cousin, everybody settle down its almost two in the morning, we can talk tomorrow."

"Here," Betty says. "Everybody take a swig of this." She passes the bottle around. When it came back around, there was only a little bit left and Sandy has the last of it.

"I'm glad that's gone," Betty says.

"Geez, are you kidding?" Brownie says. "These railroad guys have bottles stashed everywhere. Here, I've got another one." He passes around a half-full pint of Jack Daniels.

Weariness hits everyone like a ton of bricks. It's all I can do to take my glasses off and make it to my bedroll; the light goes out and I feel Betty snuggling up tight to my back. It feels good, and about five seconds later, I am fast asleep.

Seventeen

After Ivan is satisfied that they're no assassins in his room, he lies on the bed and closes his eyes. He is sick at the thought of abandoning his country, and worried about his wife and daughter. He has already made up his mind to disobey orders; and worse, to defect to an enemy camp. The way he sees it, he has no choice – he must tell the Americans they have a lunatic, traitor on their hands; and that, his superior officer has no intention of cooperating. The problem, he thinks, is that Nikolai doesn't believe the story about the "Others". He thinks it is disinformation a complete lie to trick Russia into surrendering its strength. If that's what Nikolai thinks, how many other senior officers feel the same way? Shit, this could be a huge problem. It's not simply disinformation, it's not a bluff. Ivan knows this is real and that the fate of the world is literally at stake.

Has it been ten minutes? It must be close; Ivan gets off the bed and listens at the wall. He can hear a TV playing is that good, or bad? Ivan sits with his back to the wall and listens. About a minute passes and he hears a thump on the wall; he uses the palm of his hand to return the thump, not too hard, and just once.

After Victor checks his room and finds no assassins or threats, he comes to the conclusion that Nikolai may be overstepping his authority. What is most likely happening, he thinks, is a power struggle between Brezhnev and the Stalinist faction, which is still powerful. The faction includes many generals who want to keep their jobs, and their lives. Victor is sure there are many in Russia who would never believe a situation such as this could be real. They would fight to the end of other men's lives to prove they are right, that it is a trick by the USA. People like Nikolai would never surrender their strength for a trick! Yes, that is what is happening, he is sure of it. If Nikolai thought he could get away with killing two senior agents, he would. Instead, he is doing the next best thing, getting them out of the way in the safest way he knows how.

Victor and Ivan have both been decommissioned; and worse, they've been tried, convicted, and sentenced to a slow death, in Siberia.

Eighteen

02:00 SAC COMMAND.

General Brandon is resting in his quarters, on the verge of sleeping and wakefulness. His phone rings, and he's instantly alert. "Yes?"

It's Captain Duffy. "There has been a development General. Our two Russian agents want to come in, unauthorized. They claim to have information that is vital to our operation, information they have been ordered not to share."

"Do they want to defect?"

"Yes, although I don't believe that's the main intention, at least not in Ivan's case. We know that political officers are brainwashed from the time they quit sucking milk to be fiercely loyal to the Communist party."

"What about Victor?"

"Sergeant Rufus informed me that Victor is very interested in American cars; it's Rufus' impression that Victor is a likely defector."

"Is there anything else?"

"Ivan asked for a 03:15 flash pick up. He also asked for Sergeant Rufus to be their driver, he is the sergeant who delivered them to the Howard Johnsons."

"I see, report to my office immediately; the two of us and Colonel Knight will finalize the procedure." Click.

Captain Duffy stares at the receiver for a minute; it's not unusual for General Brandon to be abrupt, that doesn't bother him. He's thinking, he ought to give Sergeant Rufus a heads up. Before leaving for the general's office, Captain Duffy calls the motor pool. He knows that Sergeant Rufus and his buddies have been working on a

1968 Chevy Impala. He gets Sergeant Rufus on the line and asks him if the Impala is up to a short run. "Is the thing somewhat stock and not too loud?"

"The sergeant smiles and says the Impala is a police interceptor, with a 396 engine; it has cop exhaust and it is no louder than any other cop car."

"We may need it, Sergeant, get it ready and standby close to a phone."

"Yes, sir." Click.

Somehow, Sergeant Rufus knew from the time he first met the Russians, that he hadn't seen the last of them; he expected something like this tonight.

The Impala is still in the fleet, but Supply Sergeant Gillfus has been reluctant to put a dime's worth of maintenance into the '68. "Too old," he says. That's when Rufus started calling him, "The parts Nazi." That prick has the radial tires that Rufus has been asking for locked up in a cage, almost as secure as the weapons in the arsenal. Those tires would be nice; they are supposed to add a layer of suspension and improve handling immensely, with just a tire change. "The Hell with it," he says out loud. All he can do is bring the old Chevy into the shop, check the fluids air up the leaking tires, and add maybe five gallons of aviation fuel. I have to be careful about that he thinks; don't want to melt the pistons out with too much octane.

02:15 General Brandon's office

General Brandon, Colonel Knight, and Captain Duffy are sitting in the general's office. Their chairs are pulled up close to the desk and there's a carafe of coffee, with three steaming cups, on a silver tray.

The general starts out by outlining the mission at hand. "Bring in the agents." He continues by informing them, he has officers watching the Russian's rooms at the Howard Johnsons. They report a heavy Soviet presence; but the agents have not left their rooms recently, and there has been no unusual activity. "To sum it up, we must assume that the Russian watchers will not hesitate to kill their agents, rather than have them defect to our base. With that said, we also have to assume that whatever the Russian agents have to tell us is of great value to our mission and, as you men know, we cannot fail in our mission. What I don't want, is to draw attention from either the police or civilians. Colonel Knight your thoughts please."

Colonel Knight reaches in his briefcase and pulls out his notes. "Sir, I suggest a convoy of ten to twelve vehicles rolling down the Interstate, it's not uncommon or unusual in this area. We time it so the extraction car can be inserted into the center of the convoy, and safely escorted to base."

"I like it, Colonel. Transfer the agents into an armored personnel carrier at the first opportunity. I have ordered three helicopters for air cover, and extraction if needed last resort only understood?"

"Yes sir."

"Captain Duffy, please let me have your thoughts."

"Sir, the Russians have asked for Sergeant Rufus, the driver they know. I assigned Rufus for their original transportation and still recommend him for this job. That leaves the extraction car. I believe it should blend in with the city, and be powerful if power is needed. I suggest the oldest car in our fleet, a 1968 Chevrolet Impala. The men love that car and maintain it on their own time. Before I came to this meeting, I asked Sergeant Rufus if the car is ready for a short run and how loud is it? He assured me that it is ready and no louder than any other police car."

General Brandon says, "I leave that up to Colonel Knight and you."

"Colonel Knight?"

"Yes, I am aware of the car. I am the one that ordered Sergeant Gillfus not to rotate it out of stock this year; normally that happens after four years of service, but I concur it is the best vehicle for this assignment."

"Bring them in, and bring them immediately to my upper office; I want to hear what they have to say. Colonel Knight, see to your convoy; Captain Duffy, brief Sergeant Rufus; 03:15 is the time of the pickup, and I want it on the dot. Any questions?"

There are none.

"See to it men. You don't have much time; dismissed."

The two officers leave the general's upper office and board a waiting golf cart. The colonel instructs the driver, "To the assembly area Corporal."

"Captain, I have already dispatched an advance scout team. We know that from the motel, it is only three blocks to the interstate. What is needed is a predetermined insertion point, a wide spot on the interstate, with a mile marker. I'll let you know as soon as I have the location. Get a secure radio in that car and use channel 43."

The golf cart exits the bunker complex and turns left. Ahead, at the parade ground assembly area, are a mix of jeeps and light-armored trucks, with about thirty men milling about.

"That's it, Captain, my convoy leaves immediately; we have to pass through the city and get turned around to be in the right place, at the right time. Hold down the fort here Captain, stand by the radio and give instructions to Sergeant Rufus."

The colonel gets out and starts barking orders to get underway.

Captain Duffy says to the cart driver, "Take me to the parts cage, just as fast as this thing will go."

The vehicle maintenance facility isn't far and is lit up like daytime; most of the bay doors are open and maintenance men are everywhere working on equipment. It looks more like noon than 02:30.

The corporal drives the golf cart through an open door and across the shop floor to the parts counter, on the opposite wall.

There are six men standing in line, most are filling out required requisition forms. When they see the captain, they all straighten up and salute, some with the forms in their right hands – very incorrect, but not a problem at the moment.

Captain Duffy returns a brief salute and hurries to the counter.

"I need a phone Sergeant, now."

The sergeant hands him the counter phone and Duffy quickly dials the radio communication center. "This is Captain Duffy, listen carefully. I need a secure radio installed in a car immediately; make sure it gets the secure channel 43. Forget the requisition form Sergeant; you have five minutes to get it down to motor pool maintenance and five minutes to install it."

"What?"

"Sergeant Gillfus, what bay is Sergeant Rufus in?"

"He's in bay 36 with that old Impala; I tried to tell him…."

Captain Duffy holds up his hand, a signal for the parts Nazi to stop talking; his attention is on the phone. "Bay 36 Sergeant, that car needs to be rolling in ten minutes with the secure radio in it, move it!"

The captain hangs up and quickly walks back to the golf cart. "Bay 36 Corporal," he says.

The corporal knows where it is, all the guys do; it's the one bay they are allowed to use to work on their personal vehicles.

Captain Duffy wipes the sweat off his brow; it's not like him to be sweating.

Nineteen

Ivan is lying in bed wondering how extensive the surveillance is inside his room. He is sure the room is wired for audio and that the phone is monitored. There could be a video camera somewhere but if there is, there is probably only one. Hidden cameras are possible but unlikely.

More likely, there would be a peephole in either the ceiling or wall, maybe in the mirror at the sink. Yes, he thinks that is the Russian way, cheap labor intensive, but effective.

The thing is, if he is seen taking the money out of the suitcase, he is done. The way he sees it he has three options – leave the suitcase, and the money here (not a good option), risk being seen removing the three bundles of American money, or take the suitcase with him when he leaves. Hum, that's a tough one. The timing, they have to count on the Americans getting the timing perfect. As always, when Ivan thinks hard enough, he comes up with a plan of action. That's it, the timing. He had set his watch exactly with base time when he was there; at 03:14 and thirty seconds, he will bolt up from a presumably sound sleep and snatch the cash from the false bottom of the suitcase.

Maybe that will take 15 seconds, and in another 15 he will be out the door and down the stairs, carrying only his shoes. It will be 03:15 exactly when he gets to the bottom of the stairs. That's it; that's what he is going to do. He has to hope that Sergeant Rufus will be there, with perfect timing.

Victor is thinking along the same lines. He has come to the conclusion that the peephole is in the mirror; probably the whole damn thing is a two-way mirror, with an agent in a chair watching his every move. That's ok thinks, as long as I have a plan and he does; he is not at all confused about what he has to do.

The first part is easy. All he has to do is act like any other Russian would in an American motel room. Turn the T.V. on and keep switching channels. Turning the heat on high would be another natural thing for a Russian would do. He goes to the window unit and plays with the temperature controls twice. Only he isn't turning the heat up, he's turning the A/C on to maximum cool, even though is not hot in the room, in fact, it's quite cool. The next part of his plan he doesn't mind at all, it involves another hot shower.

Victor starts his plan by placing his suitcase on the left side of the vanity sink, right in front of where he believes his watcher is. He opens the suitcase and naturally, the top of the case hides the bottom from view. Next, he checks his teeth in the mirror and takes out his toothbrush and tooth powder. He brushes his teeth and inspects them again. Teeth are clean; he runs a hand over his face and neck checking for beard stubble. He gets out his razor, soap and shaving brush and begins to lather up. And then, as if as on impulse, he peals out of his shirt and pants and jumps in the shower without closing the bathroom door.

He is quick about his shower this time; he gets out and leaves the shower running at full blast on hot. Steam is pouring from the bathroom into the cool room. He is hoping the agent on the other side wasn't smart enough to wax the mirror, he certainly would have; there's only one way to find out. Victor gets down on his belly and looks up at the mirror, it's steamed over. He quickly retrieves the three bundles of cash and places them under a towel; perfect! Plan "B" wasn't good.

He wipes off the mirror, shaves, and dresses. Agents are expected to sleep fully clothed while on assignment, in case they have to make a fast exit. A trip to the bathroom and he has almost seventeen thousand American dollars in his pocket. Now he is ready a fast exit and that will happen at 03:14. All he has to do is wait 30 long minutes.

Twenty

Nikolai is furious; it seems to him that his country's strength is being lost on the chessboard of international politics. That fool Nixon is outsmarting Soviet Secretary General Brezhnev with a brilliant ploy. It makes him sick to his stomach, literally; he stops the car and opens the door just in time to avoid making a mess in the Jaguar. After a short fit of dry heaves and coughing, he wipes off his face and looks at himself in the rearview mirror. He looks like shit and he knows it.

Ahead on the right, is a big yellow sign with black letters. Joe's Waffle & Coffee House open 24 hours. That's what he needs he thinks, some food in his stomach. He parks and goes straight to the restroom to wash up. He gets a good look at himself and tries to remember when the last time he ate anything? Or slept? Three days. He has been taking too many of the army's Victory Pills. Ok, he thinks. I'll get some food and lie down for a few minutes; there is still work that needs to be done tonight.

Nikolai has two men on surveillance duty, watching Ivan and Victor through two-way mirrors. One will be promoted to his right-hand man. The other will be fired, in his favorite way killed, blown to bits in an explosion that will be blamed on the Americans. It will be the agent watching Ivan who will be promoted. Gennady and Nikolai will attend the 010:00 meeting and complete the assignment.

Nikolai's superior officer, has been screaming for a progress report. So far, Nikolai has been making off like Ivan hasn't left the base or reported. It's best when you can blame problems on a dead man. The icing on the cake will be the microcassette tape he has in his pocket; its dynamite. It can, and will, be used to blackmail the U.S. Director of Defense, and Nikolai will take credit for bringing the information in. With a successful conclusion to this mission, and the fact that the old generals have been dying off like flies, Nikolai believes he will finally make the rank of general. It has been his goal since childhood. He has been passed over enough times, and this is his chance.

First things first, soldiers must eat and rest at every opportunity; he can't believe that he made the mistake of not doing either during the past three days. He ordered food like he was starving; he wasn't, and his eyes proved to be far bigger than his stomach. He leaves the restaurant carrying a heavy box of leftovers that he intends to force himself to eat, a funny thought for a Russian that had a childhood of hunger and starvation, along with rest of his countrymen.

His stomach feels better, but his whole body is exhausted and reluctant to move. It's all he can do to shift the car and drive back to the Grand Hotel, for a short rest. Back at his room, Nikolai decides it is easier and more time efficient to skip the rest and pop three more amphetamine pills from his bottle. He doesn't swallow the pills, he chews them; he used to hate the taste, but now he enjoys the bitterness; plus, the effect is quicker too. He grabs a shave and packs his briefcase with the tools he will need.

Nikolai thought of the explosives well in advance. He had American C-4 plastic explosives sewn into the trim of each agent's suitcase; the idea being, to blame the explosion on the Americans. Perfect. He packs his briefcase with an American made radio-controlled detonator, his 9mm Makarov pistol, and three spare eight round clips. The explosion / execution was planned for 04:00; now it will happen whenever he can get there. The thought of the explosion gives him a pleasant chill up his spine. He has always loved to blow things up.

Nikolai drives back to the Howard Johnsons and parks across the street, in front of a donut shop. There is a telephone booth on the corner. He needs to call Gennady and tell him to evacuate, now. He walks to the phone booth and digs out an American dime. He dials Gennady's room. This is going to work out just as he planned; he feels great again.

Twenty-One

Sergeant Rufus turns left off the interstate and onto Dodge Street at 03:10; three blocks to go and two traffic lights to consider. The first thing is to get through the traffic lights and within sight of the Howard Johnsons; then, park on the street and concentrate on the timing. Sergeant Rufus pulls to the curb and turns off the headlights less than fifty yards from the Howard Johnsons; they have a clear line of sight of rooms 215 & 216. He takes a deep breath and looks around, almost no traffic; the only activity is a few people milling around a donut shop and a man in a phone booth, up ahead on the left. Rufus picks up the microphone of the secure radio and calls in his position to the rolling command. Colonel Knight acknowledges and informs Rufus that he is to intercept the convoy on Interstate 80, at mile marker 33 west.

Sergeant Rufus studies the Timex on his left wrist, 03:13:30. He has to get into the parking lot, turn around, and drive like a grandpa doing it. He decides on 45 seconds, his eyes don't leave the Timex until it ticks to 03:14:15.

He turns on the headlights and drops the car in drive at the 15-second mark, then eases the big Chevy onto the street. The man at the phone booth has hung up the phone and is staring at him; more specifically, he is staring at the sky-blue air force vehicle with duct tape on the front fenders where the identification numbers should be.

Sergeant Rufus signals, and slowly turns into the parking lot. He lines up on an empty parking spot nearest the stairwell, and backs in. He glances at his Timex, 03:15 exactly. The rear door opens and Ivan jumps in, three seconds later Victor jumps in the front passenger door. "Go!" they both say at once.

"Ah, shit" Ivan says, as Nikolai and the white Jaguar pulls into the parking lot and angles to a stop in front of the Impala. Sergeant Rufus floors the car, it leaps forward and spins the lighter Jaguar out of the way. The sergeant expertly fishtails the big block Chevy out of the parking lot and onto the street.

The Jag does not follow them, Nikolai wants a bit of distance between them when he pushes the detonator. He hopes like hell they have the suitcases with them. He pushes the American made radio detonator and an explosion equal to four hand grenades rips through the top corner of the motel, raining debris on the white jag. Shit, he thinks, not what he had in mind. Rage and furry are always just below Nikolai's surface, now an anger he has never known before boils. His plan is ruined and he has been humiliated and outsmarted; that has never happened before. He bangs the car into gear and chases the receding tail lights in the distance. His intention is to kill Victor and Ivan, regardless of the consequences.

"So much for not attracting attention" Sergeant Rufus says, "You boys were supposed to go out with a bang."

With the interstate in sight, a black and white police cruiser comes out of nowhere and is trying to catch up with the Impala, its one bubble gum light is flashing and its siren is screaming. The sergeant bears right onto the interstate and the cop follows. Behind the police car, a white Jaguar is quickly gaining ground.

Victor says, "Please show me the power of this automobile."

"Looks like I have to, hold on." Sergeant Rufus puts the pedal to the metal.

Victor's eyes are wide open, staring straight ahead; he is not afraid, but excited. He has always thought intelligence work should be like this, good overcoming evil and in the best interest of his country. If it happens to be in the best interest of the world, all the better. He has been chased before, but not like this, this time he can make a difference. He is thinking the engine of this car is amazing; it doesn't stop winding, up and up. He glances at the speedometer, but he can't see the red needle.

In the back seat, Victor has a clear view of the red needle; he has been watching it steadily climb from 90 to 100, 110, and 120. The red needle is buried out of sight in the right-hand side of the instrument panel. Sergeant Rufus is concreting on the road and the car, he is more or less in the center of the two-lane highway, but the car is starting to get that high speed, squirrely feeling. It would be a good time to have those new radial tires. Handle it, he thinks.

The car will go faster, but that's as far as Rufus is willing to push it. He backs off and the Impala holds the road steady again. He is also trying to read the mile markers in the dim light; he can't do it, and he says so. "The mile markers, call them out!"

"Mile number 30!" Victor says. Both Ivan and Victor are intensely watching the right side of the road for the markers.

Sergeant Rufus is thinking about timing again. At 120 mph he is making a mile every 30 seconds and he knows that he will need at least a mile to bring this iron sled to a stop; he backs all the way off the gas. "Mile 31!" The sergeant glances at the speedometer; it is at 120 and slowly dropping. wonders why he has seen no traffic, and then he realizes that they blocked the road for him; probably just before the ramp he took to get on this interstate. There are two sets of headlights behind him, and he knows who they are.

"Mile 32!"

Ahead Rufus can see the flashing yellow lights of the convoy on the shoulder of the highway; he touches the brakes and holds them for three seconds. The Impala responds by shaking violently, with a terrible rumbling noise coming from the wheels. The car was all over the road for those three seconds, and when he lets off the brakes, the car is down to 90 mph. Another touch of the brakes, and less severe shaking, and the car is down to a manageable 75.

Victor says; "Please tell me why the automobile shook so much when braking."

"Well," Sergeant Rufus says, "This car goes like hell, but it stops like shit."

Victor is looking at him; he is not satisfied with the explanation.

"This car was made to be a police interceptor. A complete police package, well almost, the bean counting accountants decided to save a few dollars and not pay for the new disc brakes. They downgraded the brakes to the old fashion drum style because it was cheaper."

"Oh, now I understand, it is the same way in my country."

Ivan speaks up from the back seat; "Please tell me, what is the plan?"

"You men are to transfer to a secure truck, right about now. The brass went all out on this one; you even have air cover; you're going to make it."

Armed MPs are lined up beside the parked vehicles; one is standing in the middle of the road, waving them forward. There are six trucks and six jeeps, some of them armored. Another MP in the road is pointing to the last truck, an armored personnel carrier; Sergeant Rufus pulls to a smooth stop beside it. The doors are opened by MP's and the now defected agents are whisked into the waiting truck. The convoy immediately starts moving and the truck carrying Victor and Ivan inserts itself into the middle. Sergeant Rufus follows the truck.

The police car and the white Jaguar have caught up with the rear of the convoy. As soon as Nikolai sees the military convoy, he knows he is in deep trouble. Not only have his agents successfully defected right under his nose, but he is also on a one-way road with the American police and no exit in sight. Not good considering this car was probably seen at the Howard Johnsons after the explosion, and it attracted some attention, had to. Damn.

Nikolai pulls to the side and opens the hood of the car. He is hoping that by pretending to have car trouble he can go unnoticed for a few minutes. Two more police cars go by at a fast clip, then two more, and more after that. The convoy must be moving since all of the flashing lights have disappeared around a curve in the road. The next traffic he sees is normal eighteen wheelers and civilian cars; they must have re-opened the road; time to go. He gets back into the Jag and drives at normal speed, in the wrong direction; he needs to get back to the city. Finally, a road sign tells him that there is an exit ahead, Johnsons Ferry Road, one mile.

Nikolai gets turned around and drives as fast as he dares back to Omaha; he avoids Dodge Street and exits just past downtown. He knows there's an industrial area along the river and that's where he is going. His plan is to dump the car, with the keys in it, and walk back to the Grand Hotel. With some luck a degenerate will steal it. What the thief won't know is, that the car he's stealing is red hot; and with a little more luck, that thief will be answering some very tough questions from the police. There is a perfect place ahead, an old decaying building with a faded sign, it says Heavy Metal Lead Works, and across the street is a large, rundown apartment building, perfect. He parks in front of the apartment building and rolls down the windows. Next, he takes the detonator out of his briefcase and places it under the seat. He decides to leave the case and pockets the Makarov pistol and spare clips. He has a ten or twelve block walk through some tough neighborhoods before getting back to the Grand Hotel; maybe some American punks will mess with him. He hopes so,
he is in the mood.

Twenty-Two

Victor and Ivan are sitting across from each other on hard bench seats. They are sandwiched between two silent MPs. The lighting is a soft red light. Battle red is what they call it in the Soviet army. Victor catches Ivan's eye and it's not fear he sees, its worry. Ivan is seriously worried about the safety of his family; Nikolai could order reprisals immediately. His only hope is to destroy Nikolai's creditability and career, and to do it fast.

Victor has been a subordinate colleague for years and, somewhere along the way, they became friends. They know each other well and can tell what the other is thinking, just by looking into the eyes. He knows that Victor is thinking the same thing.

Colonel Knight is on the radio with General Brandon, the general is already aware of the explosion at the motel and he anticipates the police wanting answers. Colonel Knight is told to bring his convoy in – all but the last two trucks, they are to stop and block the gate. General Brandon tells him that Captain Duffy is to deal with police. "The mayor and chief of police will be given the 'national security' speech, and I will convince them to call the incident a gas explosion, even if I have to get Nixon on the line to do it."

Captain Duffy is standing at the gate with fifteen soldiers, armed with M-16's, when the column comes into sight. He gives a nod to the gateman and the gate opens. Six jeeps and four trucks pass through the gate and one 1968 Chevrolet Impala. The last two trucks stop just shy of the gate, and the eight police cars behind them also stop. Eight agitated police officers are out of their cars and clamoring for answers.

Captain Duffy gives them an answer; it will only be explained to the mayor of Omaha and the chief of police. Only the two of them are invited to General Brandon's office for an explanation. They are to be brought to the upper cafeteria upon arrival and will be personally escort to the general's office. Captain Duffy excuses himself; he doesn't want to miss the debriefing.

160

Twenty-Three

Colonel Knight personally escorts Victor and Ivan to the general's upper office. The general is at his desk in a freshly pressed uniform; he is on the phone and motions to them to have a seat. "Mr. Mayor, he says, I am afraid I can't tell you anything unless you and the chief agree to a very binding confidently agreement, stating that you won't repeat what I tell you; it truly is a matter of national security."

"What?"

"No, Mr. Mayor, it is a take it or leave it proposition." He hangs up the phone.

"All right gentleman, explain yourselves."

There is a light knock at the door, the general says, "Come" and Captain Duffy enters.

"Glad you could make it Captain, have a seat, we are just getting started."

"Now, who would like to go first?"

Ivan speaks up and says, "My commanding officer, Colonel Nikolai is very much unpleased with my report."

"Go on."

"He did not like the idea of sharing information; in fact, he called it traitorous talk."

"What else?"

"We were to collect duplicate samples of hair, blood, and saliva for our own research in the new field of DNA technology. I got all of mine from the long-haired kid, but Victor failed to get all of his samples, as you took over."

"Colonel Nikolai was furious and ordered us off the assignment and back to Russia. I believe Death Valley in Siberia is what he has in mind for us, but I miscalculated. He wants us dead and out of the way; I know that now."

"There is something else, what is it?"

"General Brandon, we made a tape. The tape reveals a very blackmailable senior government member, and a traitor."

"Do you have the tape?"

"Sadly no, I turned it over with my report to Colonel Nikolai. He was not impressed and called me an ignorant cow for suggesting making the Americans aware of it; now I know he intends to take credit for the tape and blackmail the official. I am also convinced that his intention is to insert himself into the operation and the 10:00 meeting."

Victor says, "Excuse me, sir, I would like to thank you for bringing us in, and apparently just in time. I would like to prove our value to you. I have a copy of the tape Ivan told you about."

Ivan says, "Victor, you made a copy?"

"Yes Ivan, when I played the tape the second time, I was making a copy. The quality may be poor, as I used my back up recorder to capture the tape you gave to Nikolai. Victor reaches in his pocket and pulls out the microcassette; he places it on General Brandon's desk. I didn't bring a machine to play it back; I trust you can find a way."

General Brandon picks up the phone and calls the computer specialist on duty. "This is General Brandon, send your best man to my upper office immediately." He abruptly hangs up the phone.

"Did you learn anything about what is going on in Russia?"

"Yes, Colonel Nikolai laughed when I told him that your team had only tagged two, he said that they have tagged more than twenty. I fear this could be a significant problem as travel is much more difficult in my country than yours, especially for teenagers with no travel documents. Also, with the high alert level even experienced agents, such as Victor and myself, would have a difficult time crossing the country unnoticed. I am very worried that my country will not comply with the demands, and there are the problems we face here."

"What else can you tell me?"

"Sir, I am so happy Victor made a copy, if you could listen to the tape, you will see what we are up against, a lunatic on the Russian side and a lunatic or two on the American side."

There is a knock on the door. "Come," the general says.

The door opens and a young sergeant with large teardrop glasses enters and salutes.

"Sergeant, I need to play this tape."

"It should be no problem, sir; it looks to be a standard size." The sergeant starts to leave with the tape in his hand.

"Sergeant!"

"That tape stays right here in my sight; just bring a machine to play the tape! Hell, I don't care if you have bring two or three machines to get one to work, just do it on the double Sergeant!"

The sergeant salutes and leaves at double time.

When the door closes the general asks for a summary of what's on the tape.

Victor replies, "Sir, first let me tell how the tape came to be made. As you know, we spent several hours in the cafeteria; and, to tell you the truth, your decision to not allow us in the situation room was sound. Ivan had a hidden camera and I had a hidden tape recorder. We were about to leave when two men entered the cafeteria and sat down with their trays in the far corner; an older man and a well-dressed younger man. We decided to listen to what they were saying; I call it fishing."

"Wait, you had a microphone capable of listening to their conversation across the room?"

"Yes, sir, I will show you. Victor takes out his pen; one click pen, two clicks microphone. I attach this thin wire from my left cufflink, the wire runs up to a recorder under my left armpit. I have to reach into my shirt to turn the recorder on, and there are only two minutes of tape. Another wire runs across my shoulder and down my right arm, to a small speaker in my right cufflink for listening."

"Please hand me the equipment, Victor."

He hands over the cufflinks and the pen.

"Are you carrying any other spy equipment, Victor?"

"Just lockpicks and a sharp blade in my belt."

"May I have them, please?"

"Yes, sir." Victor takes off his belt and lays it on the general's desk, along with his pick set.

"And you Ivan, what equipment are you carrying?"

"The same in my belt, sir; and, a camera with pictures of your base and of the two men we are discussing. I did not turn them over to Nikolai; he was pissing me off, as you would say." Ivan takes off his belt and retrieves the camera from a secret pocket in his jacket; he places them on the desk.

"Colonel Knight, who is in charge of photo analyses at the aerial reconnaissance unit?"

"That would be Captain Munice, sir; he has a picture of a golf ball on his office wall that was taken at eighty thousand feet, at Mach two. You can read the name on the golf ball in that picture."

"Good. I want this film processed immediately."

"May I use your phone, sir?'

"Of course."

The colonel makes a brief phone call and sits back down.

Ivan asks, "Sir, may I be permitted to be present when the film is devolved? It is one of my specialties."

"Ivan, there is top secret information all over that room. No, I'm sorry Ivan, I can't allow that. Now, I have to ask you, is there anything else?"

"Yes, I should tell you that I was able to ascertain the frequency of the tracking device that was installed in the boys' sneakers. Nikolai has the frequency. Also, there could be something that I am not aware of, in our clothes or shoes. General, I suggest replacing our clothes and shoes."

"All right, when we are done here, that will be taken care of and a room will be provided so that you both can get some rest. Now tell me about my American lunatics."

It's Ivan that speaks. "Sir, your very blackmailable lunatic is the Director of Defense, Kenneth Rushie and the lunatic that intends to sabotage your mission is Curtis Knapp, Rushie's second in command."

General Walter Brandon has heard of people having the experience of their hair standing up on the back of their necks, as a warning or premonition. This is the first time he's had that sensation – every hair on his body is prickly. And President Nixon knew it! How does Nixon know that Curtis Knapp is a very real danger? Why does he strongly believe the defecting Russian agents are telling him the truth?

Again, the general picks up the phone; this time he calls base security. He orders Director Rushie and Deputy Director Knapp to be taken to separate interrogation rooms in the brig. He is about to call the computer specialist and ask about the tape player, when there is a light knock on the door. "Come," he says.

The specialist with the teardrop glasses enters rolling a cart of equipment. "Sir, I believe this machine will work. I also brought an amplifier and speakers to enhance the sound; it should be ready to go. Would you like me to insert the tape?"

"No Sergeant; Stand by in the hall, ten paces down the hallway. Dismissed." He gives a nod to Victor and says, "Victor, play the tape."

Victor waits for the sergeant to exit and close the door, then he stands up and starts the tape.

Assistant Director Knapp's voice comes through the amplified speakers loud and clear. "You know what, Kenneth? People suck, all people. I think the "Others" will be better off wiping us from the face of the earth and starting over. In fact, that's what I am going to do, make sure this plan goes wrong. I'm checking out, and the rest of the world is checking out with me, it's perfect."

"Curtis, you can't do that!"

The general, colonel, and captain are all listening intently, at the edge of their seats.

The tape ends with a click and Colonel Knight can't help saying "Holy shit"!

Captain Duffy says, "Ivan, do you swear this is on the up and up? That it's not some kind of diversion or false information?"

Ivan says, "I swear we made this recording in your lower cafeteria three hours ago."

"And you Victor, is this tape the real thing?"

"It is sir."

General Brandon is about to say something when his phone rings. "Yes? I see. I want it investigated as a crime scene. Take Curtis Knapp to the brig. Treat him as a prisoner. Tell him he is the subject of a murder investigation. I'm sending Colonel Knight to take charge." Click.

"Men, the Director of Defense, Kenneth Rushie, was found dead in his room. Colonel Knight, get me some answers regarding his death. I want to know how he died, when he died, and if this piece of scum Curtis Knapp is responsible. Captain Duffy, see that these men are outfitted with what they need and take them to their quarters. I have to ask that the two of you stay in your rooms; in fact, I insist on it. Captain Duffy post guards, I have had enough surprises for one night. Dismissed."

The general sits alone holding the bridge of his nose for a minute, collecting his thoughts. The only one he reports to is the president himself. It's been long enough and the president needs to be aware of the director's death and know that his instinct is right about Deputy Director Curtis Knapp. He sincerely hopes that things in Russia are not as bad as Ivan fears. General Brandon leaves his upper office, for the secure bunker complex and his red phone.

Twenty-Four

Even the general has to be escorted in the secure elevator; he doesn't mind, he has always been impressed with the security on SAC bases. Inviting known Russian spies into the heart of the base is a scenario he never would have believed, even last week. And now, he feels like he can trust the Russian agents. It's a real head scratcher, and a sign that President Nixon is convinced that what he was told, is real. For Nixon to allow Russian spies in an SAC base he has to believe it's true. In military circles, Nixon is not known for being weak or stupid.

Before entering his office, General Brandon goes to the computerized command center for an update. Colonel Richardson is in charge and has not left the command center in more than thirty-six hours; there are deep dark circles under his eyes, and he needs a shave. "What is our current status, Colonel?"

"Sir, we still have eighteen B'52 strike squadrons in the air. Most have been airborne for more than thirty hours; all have been refueled twice, and will need another refueling within four hours. One bomber had to be replaced while in formation, because of an overheated engine; another returned to base with smoke aboard, it has also been replaced. Operation Over Cap is still fully operational sir."

"How are the crews holding up?"

"Fine sir. The flight crews are on a four-hour rotation and, except the few mechanical problems that I told you about, there are no other complications."

"Any update on our naval position assets?"

"Sir if the Navy knows, they're not telling us."

"Where are our young subjects now?'

"They are in a rail yard, just north of Council Bluffs, Iowa; they're currently stationary."

"I see. Colonel, I don't foresee much action for the next few hours, I want you to get some rest. I need you to be extra sharp tomorrow, report to the lower conference room at 09:30."

"Yes sir."

The colonel salutes the general and informs the second in command, another colonel in the satellite communication center, that he is now in command. Colonel Richardson is grateful for the break, he needs it, but would never admit it.

The general sits down at an empty console and takes off his cap. He closes his eyes and squeezes the bridge of his nose. For some reason, he is thinking of the Excedrin moments, T.V. commercials; this would definitely be an Excedrin moment.

General Brandon has to prepare for the phone call. His report is not as good as he would like it to be, but overall, things are more or less on track on his end. It's the other end, the Russian end, that concerns him. If Ivan and Victor are worried about it, that means he should worry about it too. His gut says it's not going well over there. The general slowly gets up and looks at the situation boards again. There are two flashing yellow lights on the maps, that weren't there a moment before. One is in central Iowa and the other is in south-central Poland.

The flashing yellow lights are the locations where the one hundred young people are supposed to be… in how long? In less than twenty-four hours? Did the date and time get pushed back again? Why has he had no word on the other ninety-eight teenagers that he is responsible for? It's time for him to report, and hopefully get some answers of his own. Now he has a phone call to make. There is a pad of paper and a pencil at the control console he is sitting at; he slides them over and starts ticking off his thoughts. Quickly, there are ten points on the paper; he thinks that ought to be enough for a lively conversation, he is ready.

The general enters a code on the door to the empty reception area and enters. Ahead and to the left is Master Sergeant Thompson's desk. Sergeant Thompson is a woman and his choice for his personal secretary. She is extremely efficient and her presence definitely brightens the place up. It looks normal here; there are flowers on her desk and other pleasant female touches. She has put a crocheted afghan over the back of the couch, and there are handmade lace doilies on the coffee table. She said her grandmother made them just for this reception area. Very comfortable for an office 100 feet underground.

Another eight-digit code, and the general is in his soundproof office. At his desk, he arranges his notes in front of him, and the red phone on his right. He reviews his earlier notes and tears out the pages. He places the Air Force One phone number on top. Next, he prioritizes his list in order of importance; it's tough because all of the points are important. Well, it's something he must do, he has been thinking about it for hours. It's a lengthy list, but he learned long ago the importance of a prioritized list for a successful phone conversation. With that task completed, he dials a ten-digit number. After a tone, he dials another ten-digit number. After a series of clicks and beeps, a clear voice comes on the line. "Air Force One Switchboard, Captain Taylor speaking, how may I direct your call?"

"This is General Brandon, Omaha Strategic Air Command; I need to speak to the president."

"He is expecting your call sir, I am putting you through."

"Walter!"

"Good Christ Walter, what a mess I have here; you're not going to believe the shit the Russians are pulling. Brezhnev and his inner circle are trying hard to make this work, but everyone else in this god forsaken country is about as friendly as a mound of fire ants. You first Walter, tell me what is going on."

"I need to report that you are absolutely right about Curtis Knapp. I also need to tell you that our two Russian agents have defected to my base."

"Hold on Walter, what happened to prove me right?"

"Last night the agents made a two-minute tape recording of a conversation between Director of Defense Kenneth Rushie and his second in command Curtis Knapp."

"Wait, Walter, they had recording equipment on them?"

"Yes sir, and a camera."

"Well, I guess they wouldn't be very good fucking spies if they didn't pull that kind of shit, go on."

"What they captured on tape was a conversation of Knapp telling Rushie that he was going to sabotage the mission. Apparently, he has always had a fantasy about suicide and sees this as an opportunity to sabotage the operation and commit a perfect suicide – taking out the rest of the world with him."

"And why didn't the director have his little ass arrested?"

"Curtis is his illegitimate son and Rushie is a world class pervert. Curtis threatened to expose Rushie if he didn't go along with Curtis' plan. I ordered them both to be taken into custody and brought to separate rooms. Director Rushie was found dead in his room, on the bathroom floor. Curtis is in custody."

"Good Christ Almighty! That little weasel killed him for the director's post! If that bastard wants to die, I want you to throw him a rope; let him put himself out of my misery."

"Sir?"

"I'm serious Walter, the time to kill a snake is when he raises his head up, and he raised his head. If he doesn't have the balls to do it. I have a cell with his name on it in Leavenworth. Do you know the prisoners there have been carrying the same pile of rocks back and forth, across the exercise yard, for a hundred and forty years? Well, I'll put an extra rock there with his name on it; he can carry that rock until the day he dies and when he does, he will be buried with it on his fucking chest!"

"You are acting Director of Defense, as of now Walter. We will make it official once we get out of this mess; but for now, you'll have to wear two hats. I will be glad to have you in that position, as you understand the needs of your men and your country. You are going to help me get out of this Vietnam mess also. The Russians are backing down, but the North Vietnamese are not. Even if we win this war, we will have another South Korea on our hands. Another worthless country, sucking on our tit and draining our economy. And if these anti-pollution, the next ice age is coming, worthless, hippie fucks have their way, all of our goddamn jobs will be over there, where we spilled our blood and spent our money, for ungrateful bastards that hate us. Fuck that Walter, God help America if we can't keep that from happening. Sorry, Walter, I'm having a rough day, the first thing we have to do is make it to next week. What else do I need to know about?"

"Sir, our Russian spies are not authorized to share that tape with us; they were ordered off the assignment. In fact, seconds after we picked them up, their motel rooms were blown to bits by their commanding officer, Colonel Nikolai. They were meant to be killed in the explosion and replaced. I would like for the agents Ivan and Victor to be officially assigned to this mission from their top brass. This Colonel Nikolai is a clear and present danger to us and seems to be very unstable."

"I've got news for you Walter, about half of the Russian population is unstable. In fact, they are about batshit crazy. Thirty armed men stormed the Kremlin trying their best to kill Brezhnev and me. It didn't work; the unsuccessful assassins are dead now, but they shot the hell out of the place. I spent three hours with Brezhnev and his interpreter, Viktor Sukhodrev, in Brezhnev's bunker. Actually, it wasn't so bad, we worked out a lot of details. Brezhnev invoked

Stalin's law on the nation – basically, anyone that speaks or acts suspiciously is to be arrested or shot on sight. That seems to be working; these people know how to respect that kind of an order."

"I had a phone call just a few minutes ago, it seems that things have calmed down. All Soviets are cooperating. The young adults that have been into custody are being escorted to South Central Poland, to a town called Slovak. The entire town is welcoming the young people as guests; they are treating them like gold. I expect the same thing will happen in your town, New Canton, Iowa."

"I believe the "Others" have taken care of some of our problems. These townspeople will do anything to protect the youngsters in their care. That's the "Others" interjecting thoughts into the minds of the populace. I am confident that with a little help from them, this is going to work. You have the location, Walter. At 02:00 you will need to shut down all road and air traffic within a thirty-mile radius of that town. All the people inside of that radius are to stay put. Try not to be too visible. Use the local police, and make off like a fugitive is being contained. Air Force One is still the safest place for me. Brezhnev and his interrupter are coming for a conference in one hour. After that, I'm going to catch some sleep. I'm beat to death; whatever energy I had, has done wore off."

"I will convince Brezhnev to leave Ivan and Victor on the case, and to recall Nikolai; I will see to that. Set things in motion Walter; and, next time we talk I want complete details on Kenneth Rushie's death. Keep Curtis locked up, and I am serious about throwing the little prick a rope."

Twenty-Five

At 07:30, brakeman Pete enters the caboose carrying two brown paper bags. He flicks the door with his foot and it slams shut. "Good morning boys and girls! Rise and shine, it's time to ride the rails! Come on, I brought you some breakfast, it's not much, but when we get to Woodstock, Large Marge is going to bring the good stuff. She has a real restaurant and is anxious to help; she is also a hell of a good cook. Did anybody hear me? Wake your asses up!"

Eight separate groans means that all eight of us heard. Louise is the first one up and goes into the tiny bathroom that Walt calls 'the head.' Christine is the next one up and she goes to the bathroom door and says, "Hurry up Louise, I have to go."

Betty wiggles to a sitting position and gives me a spank on the butt, "Wake up sleepy head."

I don't know why, but I liked that; and, when I sat up and looked at her, I had to laugh.

"What?"

"Your hair, it's a mess." Her brownish-red hair is plastered to her face on one side and sticking straight up and out on the other. Again, that earned me another spank on the butt, and it is her turn to laugh. I wasn't about to tell her that I liked the spanks on the butt, but I did.

Brakeman Pete has stacked the deck of cards, wiped off the table with a rag from his pocket and set the table with paper bowls, plastic cups, a box of disposable utensils and two boxes of Wheaties cereal. He also brought two gallons of milk, a jar of peanut butter, and two loaves of white bread.
"Come on grab a bite to eat."

The boys are all making their way to the table, and the girls are milling around the small bathroom.

Pete says, "You girls are lucky there's a head on this caboose. It's the only caboose in the fleet with one; and, if rumor control is right, they won't buy anymore, cabooses are going to be phased out."

"Geez, I have to pee too," Brownie says.

Pete jerks his thumb at the door and says, "They all come with two urinals front and back, for the men anyway."

Brownie goes out the door and, one by one, all the boys follow his lead.

There is only room for four at the small, bolted down picnic table; our entire group, except Sandy, grabs a bowl of cereal and we sit on the floor, since we were the last to come to this rolling shelter.

"Ok," Pete says, "We are going to do some switching, that's moving cars around. When we couple and uncouple the caboose, there's going to be a jolt, so hang on and be ready. This is what's going to happen, we are going to couple to the lead caboose and pull this whole string of cabooses out and drop you on a siding. Then, we have to put the string of cabooses back. The next time we couple to you, we'll be on our way. I'm going to be in the engine on this trip, there's normally another brakeman that rides in the caboose and watches the train."

"Harry the Lush was on today's schedule. Two things about Harry one, he is a bad drunk and two, he has a big mouth. I don't trust him with this and neither does Joe, our engineer. This is what we did, we made him a deal; all he has to do is hang out for the day at Murphy's Trackside Bar & Grill and drink. Joe and I will pay his bar tab and make sure he gets his days' pay. He didn't have to think about it long."

"This is what you need to know, his job is to keep an eye on the train and to look out for "hot boxes" that would be a failed wheel bearing or a dragging brake. You young men are going to do that for me."

Brownie says, "How are we supposed to know if a brake is dragging?"

"That's easy. All you have to do is look out the window, or stand on the platform, and watch the cars; more specifically, watch the wheels of the cars, especially when going around curves, that will be your best view. If you see smoke, then something is hot; that's a "hot box."

"Ok, what do we do if we see one?"

"Now listen to what I tell you, it's important." Pete takes off a boxy two-way radio that is strapped to his shoulder, like a big purse; it says Motorola on the microphone. "This is set to channel four, that's our frequency; don't mess with it; and, don't say a word on it."

"Why not?"

"Because you will be broadcasting on an open frequency and all the towers in the system will be listening and recording all radio traffic. Here, put this on and don't let anybody play around with it."

"Ok, but how do I let you know if there is a problem?"

"I want you to key the mike like this," Pete pushes the button on the microphone and says "Be right there, Joe."

"That's a four," comes back over the radio.

"Ok, but don't say anything. Hold the mike open outside, where there's lots of noise; do it three times and we'll know to stop the train. Got it?"

Brownie says, "Oh, yeah man that's my kind of job!"

Christine has been listening and says "Brownie, I want to help."

"Great! We'll watch the train cars from the platform and watch the world go by."

"All right," Pete says, "Just be careful, fall between the rails and you will be splattered like a skunk in the road."

Walt and Louise heard the end of the conversation and Walt speaks up, "Hey Pete, I want to ride in the engine." "Me too," Louise says.

"Let me check with Joe on that. Remember what I said about hanging on, we are going to be moving in a few minutes. I have some work to do; I'll be back as soon as we have built our train. We'll be rolling soon." With that Pete goes down the stairs and climbs up and over the tanker car on the next siding.

Brownie, Christine, Walt and Louise are standing on the platform looking strangely happy.

Brownie says "Christine, I'm tripped out that you were looking for me in the Omaha train yard, and you found me. Are you sure that you and Louise found the right two boys? I mean I think we all know that we are not the only ones going to this thing, meeting, event, or whatever it is. It's pulling teenagers like us like a magnet. Are you sure Walt and I are the ones you are looking for?"

Christine says, "Come here;" She takes Brownie in her arms and gives him a quick kiss and a fierce hug. "You, see? Like a magnet; yes, I'm sure. Have you noticed Walt and Louise? They already act like an old married couple. How about you Louise, are you sure?"

"Oh, yes, I'm sure." she says. She too gives Walt a quick kiss and a wink.

Walt stops at the table where John and Mark are sitting drinking milk. He tells us that "This is going to turn out to be the best thing that will ever happen to us in our whole lives" He just knows it. Not only that, it is somehow going to get him off the hook for stealing cars. "We are all lucky to meet these beautiful girls, one for each of us. I'm epically lucky, I have Louise and I'm going to marry her. I heard there is a town in north Georgia, called Dahlonega, that will marry any young couple if you tell them that the girl is 'in the family way;' yep, that's what I am going to do."

Louise says, "Walt! That's how you ask me to marry you? What if I say no?"

"You won't."

"I won't; I mean, I do want to marry you; the sooner the better." Louise tilts her head towards the back of the caboose and Walt gets the message. "Later," he says; and the happy couple walk to the platform at the back of the caboose.

"Hey, Mark," John says, "You know he's right?"

"He's right about what John?"
"About marrying these girls. We might as well think of them as women. I mean, I'm nuts about Sandy, I feel like I love her, I mean it. It's weird, I feel so much older and smarter, different in just one day. It's like I'm not fifteen anymore; I feel like a grown man, and I want to marry Sandy."

"I know what you mean John, I have never gotten an 'A' in any class, I could barely read or spell. Now, this morning, I'm reading a book on the shelf, "Railroad Maintenance of Way," written in 1926. It's about railroad tracks. It sounds boring, right? It would have been yesterday; I wouldn't have touched it. Today, in ten minutes I read a lot of complicated stuff and understood it. Like, a tangent of track is a straight piece of track. Did you know that one rail is higher than the other in curves? Curves are banked like a racetrack. The inside rails on curves, wear out quicker than the straight track. The track crews pull the worn rail out and turn it around, to wear the other side. It saves the railroad money."

"There is all kinds of stuff that I find fascinating now. Like the gauge of the tracks from the inside of a rail to inside rail is 56 ½ inches. And, the faster the train goes, the closer the ties have to be and the rail itself needs to be heavier. The rail is rated by how much it weighs every three feet; like a 105-rated rail weighs 105 pounds per yard, and it is bolted together every 33 feet. That's old fashion rail; now, it's used for sidings and low-speed track, there's even a handwritten note inside the book about that. I think I can spell everything I just said, I couldn't do that last week. It's like I'm getting smarter by the second."

"You know," John says, "I'm not at all scared anymore. In fact, I'm happy; happy I met Sandy. And, I'm going to do just what Walt said, take her to that town in Georgia, and marry her." John glances back toward the bunk that Sandy had crawled into, the one recently vacated by Walt and Louise. Betty is sitting on the bunk talking to her cousin, Sandy. John has been glancing back the whole time that we've been sitting here; and, he seems to be worried about her.

"You think she is sick?" he asks me.

"I'm not sure; could it be the whiskey she drank? Maybe, you should go check on her."

Betty stands up, says a few more words to her cousin, then comes back to the table and sits close to me.

"Be right back." John says, and he goes to the bunk that Sandy is laying on. "What's up Sandy? You don't feel good?"

"No, my stomach is queasy and my head hurts; but I'll be all right in a few minutes."

"I'm going to make you a peanut butter sandwich and bring you a cup of milk.

"John, I really don't…."

"Quiet." he says, "You'll do as I say this time. Who knows, we may not have another chance to eat again, for a while."

With that, John goes to the table and fixes two slices of bread with light peanut butter and folds them over so that they will be easier to eat.

Betty hands him a roll of course brown paper towels that she had found and says "She wouldn't eat for me John, what did you say to her?"

"I told her that she would do as I say."

For some reason Betty found that extremely funny and couldn't stop laughing, it's contagious and we all catch the laugh.

Betty wipes her eyes and pours a Dixie cup full of milk and hands it to John. "See if she will drink this, she hates milk."

John carries Sandy's breakfast to the bunk and says, "Sit up."

Sandy clearly doesn't want to, but she does. "I must look terrible" she says.

"No, you look beautiful, drink this."

"John, I don't," she sighs and without another word drinks the small cup of milk.

"What did you do Sandy? Find more whiskey? Or stash some of the bottle you found? Did you get up to drink all by yourself? What are you trying to do, kill yourself?"

"Maybe, John, my mother sells real estate houses, and land. When I was a little girl, I was always with my mom when she was working. She wanted me quiet or sleeping most all the time, so she mixed wine with my grape juice, a lot of it. I drank a bunch of wine before I was even four years old. Wine doesn't mix very well with milk, that's why I don't like milk."

"You didn't have wine last night, here; get this in your belly."

"Sandy, do you remember what we were talking about when we were walking, the part about just knowing stuff? Well, the way I see it, we are in a genuine life-threatening situation and we may not live through it."

"Yes, John, I feel that way too. Maybe that's why I don't care that, and I the fact that I feel like nobody loves me. Well maybe Betty, but she lives a thousand miles away."

Sandy starts to cry. John puts both hands on her shoulders and looks her straight in the eyes. "Hey, I care about you and know that I want to spend the rest of my life with you, however long that is."

Walt and Louise share a sweet kiss on the rear platform. When they break apart Walt looks up, something catches his eye. He is staring at something.

"Hello Walt," Louise says.

Walt doesn't say anything. He climbs down and starts walking toward a line of wrecked boxcars, three tracks away, and to the left. The same noise that we heard all night and morning is closer and louder than ever. It sounds like metallic thunder, echoing. The caboose jolts and catches everybody by surprise, even though it shouldn't have. The caboose jolts again, and starts moving forward.

"Walt! Get back on the train, we're moving!" There's a note of panic in Louise's voice – the thought of losing Walt terrifies her; she just knows this young man is the love of her life. Walt doesn't seem worried about missing his train; he runs a short distance and hops aboard the rolling caboose.

It doesn't take long until we are backing up on a different track. Pete appears and does something underneath; he unlocks the connection at the front of the caboose. He looks up and says, "Everybody ok?"

"Yeah," Brownie says, "We're all here."

"Good." Pete says, "When we get going, keep an eye out like we talked about, but don't worry too much about the hot box thing, that almost never happens. I've only seen it twice. You have Harry's radio. If I want to call you, you'll hear me say, 6833 Harry? That's our train number 6833. Say yeah, and muffle it, you know what I mean?"

"Sure Pete, I'll use background noise like you told me."

"All right, we're going to try not to say anything at all; it's only 46 miles to Woodstock and we'll be there in a little over an hour." Pete climbs up on the ladder of the caboose in front of us, and we hear him say over the radio that Brownie is carrying, "Go ahead slow 6833. Be right back." he says, as the string of cabooses pulls away.

Everybody is moving around, restless and maybe a little bit anxious. Brownie and Christine have climbed down and are walking around. Sandy has gotten up and gone into the bathroom, and John is cleaning up – putting the trash in a brown paper sack and folding blankets. Walt, Louise, Mark, and Betty are on the front platform talking and waiting for the train to return.

Brownie stops and looks up. "Look at that sky Christine, look how blue it is. What a perfect day."
"It is a perfect day." Christine says. "It's my first morning with you. I loved snuggling with you last night; I want that every night, forever." "Me too," Brownie says – and they embrace for a long moment. Christine breaks away and says, "did you hear that?"

"Hear what?" "Shh, it sounds like a cat crying." They stand still for a moment and, sure enough, a cat is crying. They cross two tracks and stand at the edge of the woods listening. They hear the cat loud and clear now. Christine says, "Down there." Brownie hands her the radio and goes down the bank to where the sound is coming from, a drainage culvert.

"Stay there Christine, I'll get it. kitty, kitty, kitty." A gray fluff ball of a cat comes right to Brownie and lets him pick it up. He gives the cat a few pets then holds it at arm's length to look at the belly. "It's a girl cat, not a kitten, but not an old cat either; she seems like a sweet kitty."

"Bring her up, I want to see." Brownie brings the cat up and hands her to Christine. The cat snuggles right in and hides her head in the nook of Christine's arm, purring and crying at the same time. "Just one." Christine says, "No kittens? You better go look to make sure. We don't want to take momma away from her kittens."

"I looked at the cat Christine, if she was a momma suckling kittens her chest would be, well you know; she's not, but I'll go look. We couldn't do that to kittens, could we?" He gives her a wink and goes back down the hill. He looks and listens, does the kitty call, listens and looks some more, until he is satisfied there no kittens. He didn't think there would be anyway.

Brownie comes up the hill to find Christine sitting on a rail rocking the cat in her arms and talking to it. She is telling it how pretty she is, and that everything is going to be all right. Every time she says something to the cat, she says 'Ging or Gink.'

"Did you name that cat already?"

"No, I'm talking to it."

"Why are you calling it stink?"

"You might think I'm a little weird Brownie, but I'll tell you. When I was a little girl there were always a lot of cats and kittens around, and I loved to play with them. I made up two words that cats understand; it was like magic to me. It still is, and the words still work. When I say "Ging" it can mean a lot of things, but mostly it means I love you and everything is going to be all right. "Gink" is more like a question. Like did you have a good day? Or are you hungry?"

"Well, pick one and you have a name for the cat. How about Gray Kitty, it sounds better."

"Ok, she is a fluffy gray kitty, you like that name, Gray Kitty?"

The cat answers with a funny meow that sounds a lot like, yes.

"The thing about "Ging," or Gray Kitty, and all the other cats in the world, is they won't come when you call them, unless they want to. It's like they are in a cat union or something. That's why I like dogs. Come on, the cat either comes or it doesn't; we can't chase it, we have to get back."

"All right, watch this." She puts the cat down, takes Brownie by the hand, and together they step over the tracks and make their way to the rear steps of the caboose, without looking back. When they stop the little gray kitty is right there with them, brushing up against Christine's leg. "Good girl," she says, "Ging." Christine picks up the rescued cat and places her on the platform. The cat quickly runs inside and hides under a bunk.

Walt sees them climb aboard and says, "Hey, Brownie, come here. I want to tell you something." "You go ahead," Christine says, "I have to get the kitty some milk."

Walt says, "This could be good, but I'm going to need some help with this idea and I want to share it with everyone here."

"What Walt, What's your idea?"

"Did any of you notice that line of wrecked box cars back there, three tracks over from where we spent the night?" Everybody is listening; the boys say "no," and the girls don't say anything.

"Well, they're old junk wooden boxcars. I'd love to drop a match on them and burn off all the wood, then come back with cutting torches and cut up all the steel. I could sell it to a scrap yard; there is more than $2,000 in scrap steel there, easy."

Louise isn't quiet anymore. "Walt! That's illegal! I think you are smart, but I want you to think about something that won't land you in jail! You light a fire like that, and the police and fire department will be out here in no time. And what about selling it? Won't the scrap yards know that it is stolen material?"

"Hold on Louise, I know that the scrap yards would call the cops if you brought in rails or tie plates. Hell, thieves would steal all the tracks in America, and there wouldn't be any railroads left. But who said anything about stealing? I want to do it the right way, if I could just figure out how to do it."

Louise says, "I'll help you, Walt. We'll do it together. I already have some ideas – like get the fire department to do it for us. They do that kind of stuff for practice. I didn't tell you, but my dad is a very good businessman. He owns four car dealerships in the Denver area. I know I can talk him into helping, especially if we are married."

Brownie has been watching the tracks while listening. "Here comes Pete," he says. And sure enough, a boxcar is rolling toward us with Pete on the ladder. We can hear Pete talking on the radio Brownie is carrying. "Ease it down Joe; 30, 20, 10." The train slows to a crawl and gently makes the connection. "Hold up Joe," Pete says, into his radio. He jumps down and hooks up an airline. "Is everybody still with us?"

"Yeah," Walt says, "What did the engineer say about us riding in the engine?" "Great news Walt, you and your girl can ride up front, you'll probably have to stand up for the whole trip though." "Fucking "A;" Let's go."

"Listen," Pete says. We just found out that we'll have a layover, of about an hour or two, in Woodstock. There's another train coming with more fright; it's going eastbound and we have to take it."

"I told ya, Large Marge, is bringing us breakfast. I can call her Large Marge, because she doesn't mind; she is super sweet and will be bringing us great food to eat. I also want to tell you, there is a church straight across the track, from the siding we are going to use. There's a thrift store in the basement, and the little store has plenty of clothes, jackets, and shoes. You girls look like you need to do a little shopping. It's cheap; I'll give you some money when we get there."

Betty says "Thank you, that's great. I can't wait, but I think we have enough money, right girls?"

All the girls start talking at once. Pete holds up his hand to get them to stop chattering. "When you hear the horn blast two times, that means we are about to move. Be careful getting back here."

Pete helps Louise down and the three of them walk toward the front. Walt has never been so excited in his life. As they go up the steps to the engine, Walt can feel the power rumbling in the handrails and at his feet, all up and down his spine and in his ears, the beat of the engine reverberates.

Joe, the engineer has a big belly and is wearing the typical railroad outfit, bib dungaree overhauls and the blue pinstripe engineer's cap. "Welcome aboard," he says with a smile. "I was hoping for some company on this trip. My wife and I both had the same dream, the night before last. We dreamed that God was telling us to build an ark. But it wasn't an ark and wasn't about animals either. We talked about it in the morning; we couldn't make sense of it, but knew it was important. Anyway, yesterday at work, Pete told me about his vision, that we had to transport young adults to New Canton, Iowa; that it is God's will; and boom, that was it! I knew it. I think you youngsters are going to be all right. It seems like a lot of people have had the same strong feeling about helping you, in any way they can."

Over the radio we hear Pete, "Go ahead slow 6833."

Walt says, "Can I drive the train?" "Pay attention," Joe says, "to what I do and how I do it; and you can run it a little just not right now we're in the yard."

"Watch. Two long blasts on the horn means that we're releasing the brakes and getting ready to move. Little lady, this is the air horn; pull it twice, two longs." Louise doses and she is beaming almost as much as Walt.

"Now watch, this lever is power." Joe kicks it up one notch and the engine picks up, but we are still not moving. "The lever below it is for the air brakes. Now I release the brakes slowly – like this, and the train won't lurch and slam. Do everything nice and slow, and easy, that's the way to do it." The train starts to ease forward and Joe says,

"We are going to keep it at right about 5 mph because we have to go through the switch where Pete is standing. The track is in bad shape right there, so there is a 5-mph limit."

The train rolls past Pete and, sure enough, the engine and all the cars behind it rock and clank through the switch. After about a minute Pete says over the radio, "That will do Joe," another few seconds and he says "Ease it on back 6833".

"I need three short blasts on the horn, please." Walt does it this time.

Joe does the same trick with the power and the brake and the train rolls back to where Pete is standing at the switch. Pete climbs aboard and says, "We're good Joe."
Again, the train creeps forward and Joe tells Walt, "I always start out like this, you add power slowly," he kicks it up a notch. Joe gives them the 'shh' sign and speaks into his radio, "6833 leaving the yard, northbound at 08:44."

"10-4, 6833" comes back over the radio.

Joe kicks it up another notch. The speedometer is a long black and white ruler encased in the panel. It has a big red pointer under the numbers and is pointing to 17 mph.

Walt and Louise are looking out the windshield at the track ahead. They are almost out of the yard when Walt spots a dirty brown 1963 Chevrolet Impala parked on the side, kind of tucked into some bushes. He can't help thinking how easy it would be for him to hotwire that car; this one looks beat and would only bring a hundred bucks or so. He and his buddies could have that thing cut up in about an hour, that's why he knows about cutting metal and scrap steel.

Joe kicks the engine up another notch.

Twenty-Six

It wasn't long after Crazy Tony left the carnival that he found the railroad yard. He had driven around as much as he could, but his body hurt so much, he wasn't able to look as hard as he should have. He decided to just find a place to park and lay down across the seat. It was hard for him to get comfortable, but weariness took over and he fell into an uneasy sleep.

Crazy Tony hadn't been awake long, and he was actually more sore than last night. His head hurt, his face ached, and his ribs are killing him. Damn, he is thinking, I should have just gone back to Florida with the crew. He counted the money he'd stolen from his brother's clown cookie jar; he has one hundred and nine dollars. He figures he can still catch up with them, just travel east and angle south after a while. Call Uncle Louie. Yeah, that's what I'm going to do. That and get a bite to eat.

Tony gets out of the car to stretch and take a leak, preparing for a day of driving. He gets back in the car and starts it. For the 100th time, he wonders why in the world the car it wouldn't start last night. What the hell was wrong with it? He is about to put it in gear and hit the road but decides to watch a freight train pass first. He has loved trains as far back as he can remember; he grew up with toy trains and model railroads.

When his dad and uncles get together, there are always stories about the old days. Stories about the carnivals and circuses that crossed the country on the rails. Not at all like his little outfit, beating the roads in old, worn-out trucks; hell, those trucks aren't fit to go around the block and are certainly not safe to cross the country. Miles and miles of road; the mountains are the worst, scary. Even though everyone acts like it doesn't bother them, it has to be in the back of their minds that the son of a bitch's engine or clutch may not make it up a steep grade. Then you have to worry about the brakes, transmission, tires and everything else going down the mountain. That's why he insisted on bringing his own car this time; he has had enough of those death trap trucks.

It's like he is missing a lifestyle he never had. The old people always talk like the good old days were the best. They probably were, not having to drive those ratty trucks arriving on a train, to a town that usually welcomed them with a parade. That's it, he thinks. The towns used to look forward to their appearance and were grateful for the entertainment. Their kind has always been a different breed once accepted, now shunned.

Another thing that makes the old railroad way seem so attractive, is not dealing with those damn weigh-station cops at every state line. Sometimes you can get around them, but not always, and those weigh station cops can be real ball busters. "Enough" he thinks, and drops the Chevy in reverse. He gets turned around; he knows the way out of the yard, is back the way he came last night. Crazy Tony floors the Impala, fishtailing to the right and throwing up dual rooster tails of dirt and gravel.

Tony glances over at the train, just as the caboose passes, what he sees causes him to whip his head around. The little bastards! That's them! The blond punk and the little redhead are standing at the railing, on the back of the caboose.

Twenty-Seven

Nikolai is trying to think the situation trough, and is having a hard time coming up with a plan of action. No doubt his superiors already know about the motel explosion and, most likely, about Victor and Ivan defecting to an American base. It's standard procedure to have spies watching spies, whenever possible. That means that he will most likely be recalled, and treated as a failure and a criminal. He won't be able to talk his way out of this one and his uncle wouldn't dare try to help him.

Fuck!

He never minded doing the arresting; never in a million years did he imagine that he would be the one being arrested. He must save face and somehow complete his mission without authorization, and that will make him no better than Ivan and Victor. This is not good, he has never failed at a mission, but one failure is enough to end his career, and his life.

Options and assets, he thinks. He is remembering his training. First, consider the options, at the moment there are only two, report or don't report. There are consequences for each action. Think. If he allows himself to be taken into custody, there will be no options; he will be a prisoner. That leaves only one other option. Going rouge, continuing the operation without authorization or support; but he'll be doing it in the best interest of his country.

The ideal thing to do would be to deliver the children to his motherland to increase his countries superior genetic stock, but that's not going to happen without support. That again leaves only one option. Kill as many of the children as he can; kill all of them, that would be best. That's what he is going to do, kill the little bastards and he will be a hero; it should be easy.

Without thinking about it, he has been automatically making his way toward the Grand Hotel from the moment he ditched the car. The only assets he has are in his in his room, in the suitcase; he needs that suitcase. He has to hope his comrades in the KGB aren't there waiting for him, they will be there shortly, if they are not there already. How long has it been since the explosion? He looks at his watch, just under an hour; it's going to be close. He picks up his pace.

Dodge Street is now in sight, about ten blocks to the right and he will be there. He realizes he is marching at double time and must be a funny sight, he doesn't care. Nikolai has never been a nervous type but he is now, for good reason. He can't help thinking about all the men and women he sent to the gulags. He laughed at their pleas for mercy and never thought of them again, until now. He knows his pleas will fall on ears as deaf as his once were.

Dodge Street would be considered the main drag in American slang. The slang terms and words have always confused him; even though he has tried very hard to master the English language. The slang, and the fact that he can never completely hide his Russian accent or looks, means he has never mastered the language. That is the reason he chooses to remain silent whenever possible.

It may not be possible now. Just after turning right onto Dodge Street, he encounters the last drunken stages of a block party; there seems to be hundreds of people in the street, on front porches, and sitting in or on cars. They are not quiet. Some are arguing loudly, on the verge of fighting, some are sitting in circles on the grass, and the rest are passed out. At least three different kinds of annoying music assault his ears. He's going to have to walk right through the middle of it.

He has definitely changed his mind about wanting to fight; he doesn't need or want the trouble it would bring, and he can't waste the time. He is about alongside the arguing young men, when they notice him and turn their attention to Nikolai.

"Hey Hank, look at the eyebrows on this cat."

"He only has one Nick, and it's a giant fucker."

'Why don't you trim that thing, old dude? Can't find your hedge clippers?"

"Let's do him a favor and trim it for him, Nick."

"All right, come on guys, hold him down and I'll trim the hairy bastard." Nick clicks open a pocket knife and two more of his buddies come over to share in the excitement.

Nikolai had stopped and is standing perfectly still with his legs spread, eyeballs directly on the long-haired, grungy looking one called Hank. He doesn't have a chance, but Nikolai has already decided to let him live.

When the four young men take a step forward, Nikolai does also. He slowly pulls out his Makarov pistol, and the four men stop dead in their tracks. Nikolai steps forward again and places the pistol's muzzle right between the eyes of the one called Hank.

With his free hand, Nikolai reaches around the back of Hank's head and pushes head and muzzle together hard, not for long, but long enough to convey the point and to leave a mark. He takes one step back and treats the other three to one second in his sights, he chambers a round and a 9mm bullet clangs onto the street. Maybe they are smart enough to know, he is not kidding and there is a round in the chamber.

He gives them a slight nod of his head, and a flick of the gun. They get the message and start backing up. Still watching them he bends down and picks up the bullet from the ground, he may need it. He takes two steps backward, then five paces. He turns again looking for threats, there are none. The music has been turned off and most of the people have disappeared.

He watches for a few seconds. He really wants to shoot out a porch light, just to let them know that they are dealing with an accomplished marksman. But he can't risk the trouble, it would bring the cops. In other parts of the world, he would be the cop and he would be shooting out kneecaps, not even thinking about porch lights.

He picks up his pace again and crosses the street for good measure. Except for him, the street seems empty. The residential area and the punks are far behind, and now the buildings are getting taller. The street lights are all working and on; also, the storefronts and building lobbies are brightly lit, making it impossible to stay in the shadows, not good.

He is visible and vulnerable out in the open like this, but has no choice, he must continue. He picks up his pace again, just short of running. He needs to get that suitcase; without it, he can't succeed.
His mind is racing with thoughts, but there is no different plan. He is operating on instinct and getting close to the Grand Hotel, it is in sight.

He stops to compose himself and wipe off the sweat in the only shadow he can find, an alley between buildings. He crouches low and scans the area. No apparent danger, but the KBG are good and wouldn't be seen, if they are here. No choice, Nikolai crosses the street and forces himself to walk at a normal pace.

He is just going to have to walk in the front door, get to his room on the second floor, and then what? Leave with his suitcase. How can he do that? To take a taxi from the front of the hotel would leave a giant breadcrumb, not a good idea. He keeps walking. Ahead a yellow cab pulls to the curb in front of a place called 7-11. That's it; he must hire this cab. For once tonight, his timing is good; he reaches the cab just as the driver comes out of the store with a cup of coffee.

The driver stops and looks at Nikolai suspiciously. Taxi drivers have to be on guard in this city, there have been many robberies, and a murder just two weeks ago. "What can I do for you, pal?"

"I would like to hire this taxi."

"Do you have money?"

"Yes."

"Let's see it."

Nikolai reaches in his pocket and pulls out a thick wad of cash, all big bills; he peels off a fifty and hands it to the driver.

The driver takes the fifty, his eyes still on the wad of money. Nikolai puts it away.

"Where do you need to go?"

"To the airport."

"Ok, jump in."

"We must first go to that hotel," he points toward the Grand. "I need my baggage."

"That's a problem, Buddy. I can drop you off, but I would have to go to the end of the taxi line; the cab at the door gets the fare. I can't jump the line without getting fired, and I need this shitty job pal." With a groan, he hands Nikolai back his money and opens the door.

"Wait," Nikolai adds two more fifties and hands the driver $150. He has his attention. "Enjoy your coffee, I will walk to the Hotel and exit the side door on that street he points and says, "What is the name of that street?"

"That's West Street."

"Be there in ten minutes and I will give you another one hundred dollars, just for a ride to the airport."

The driver pockets the money and nods his head once, "Ten minutes" he says.

"Ten minutes." Nikolai repeats and he turns and walks off at a fast pace. Two blocks to go, then up and down a flight of stairs; it might take more like fifteen minutes, but he wants that cab to be there when he comes out. He has confidence the driver will be there. He'll wait a few minutes, greed is universal; but on the other hand, so is thievery; he could simply keep the $150 and do nothing. Well, if it comes to that he will take a taxi from the front, there are two of them waiting for fares. A deep breath and he pushes through the revolving doors, he has already decided that if they are waiting for him he will accept his fate, if not; he will push on with determination.

The lobby is deserted, except the clerk at the front desk who seems completely engrossed in a book; he didn't even glance away from it when Nikolai came into the lobby. Straight ahead is the elevator with its doors standing open. It wasn't his original plan, to use the elevator, but it's the easy way up and sometimes, easy counts. The ride up one flight didn't take long. Nikolai is torn between holding his gun, or putting his hands up. In the end, he did neither; he just stood still.

The elevator doors open and the hall is quiet and deserted. His room, 214, is two doors down and across the hall. Ten long strides and he is there. A quick examination of the door shows it hasn't been tampered with; it appears to be safe, move.

He goes through the door and straight to his suitcase, under the bed. He quickly checks the contents he can see; everything seems to be, as it should. He clicks it closed and scans the room, nothing except a box of leftovers from Joe's; he'll leave it for the maid, it will be her tip.

Nikolai is out the door, down the stairs and standing on West Street seconds later. He made good time; it didn't take as long as he feared. He scans the street, no sign of the yellow taxi; surely it's been ten minutes. This is the first time he's been still in hours, and he doesn't like it. The need to move is embedded in his mind.

He strolls twenty paces down the sidewalk, then turns, and walks back. The sky is brightening and there is an increase in vehicle traffic. He is not the only one on the sidewalk anymore, people are going to work. The old white-haired bastard must have decided to keep the money in hand and do nothing. No choice, he'll have to get a cab from the front; it will work if he changes cabs a few times. Nikolai had just given up on his hired cab when a familiar voice said, "Hey, buddy." Nikolai is startled; the cab has pulled alongside him without him noticing its approach. A bad sign, he is not as sharp as he needs to be.

"Are you getting in or not?"

Nikolai doesn't lose another second; he tosses in the suitcase and climbs into the backseat.

The driver has the cab in park and is half turned around in his seat looking at Nikolai.

"Go!"

"Not until we get something straight pal. I know you are up to something no good. Now, I might not care what you do, as long as I am well paid. This is my problem, and yours, I'm on parole pal; two years into it and about to get off. There is no way I'm fucking that up for you, or anybody else. I can't be involved in anything that might draw the cops; if they ask me questions, I have to answer them. I can't lie, they catch me in a lie and they can violate my parole and send me back for another three to five. That's not happening; do you understand what I am telling you?"

"I understand. I assure you; you're just taking a fare to the airport, doing your job, nothing illegal about it. You may answer any questions about me truthfully; however, if you could delay such answers for 24 hours, I would very much appreciate it."

"My shift ends at 7:00 and tomorrow is my day off; I could go fishing for the day and not be around to answer any questions."

Nikolai peels off three hundreds and hands it to the driver. He can respect the man's position; he is handling the situation well.

"That buys twelve hours pal. I could spend the night the night out of town, stay in a nice motel, and eat and drink well, but that's expensive."

Nikolai peels off five more bills; he doesn't even look to see if they are fifties or hundreds. "May we go now?"

"Yeah, you bought a ride to the airport and a twenty-four hour vacation for me." He drops the arm of the meter box to start the fare and pulls away from the curb.

Nikolai uses the opportunity to remove everything from his suitcase and to access the compartment underneath. The bundled green money is all there; $42,000, the last time he counted. Very well, but that's not what he's after. In the side pocket is a two-page dossier, a summary of a semi-deep cover asset, in the Omaha area.

Internal Security Report –28/08/1955; last update 27/01/ 67
Nadia Basov DOB 03/03/1942; Leningrad

There is a handwritten notation under the date and place of birth, requesting its confirmation. A one-page report is the second page of the dossier.

Apparently, the deputy director had the same doubts as Nikolai – How the hell did she survive as an infant, when the city was under siege by the Germans for 872 days? For over two and a half years, Leningrad suffered constant shelling – no food or supplies entered the city. One-third of the population died of starvation and disease, and many more died from bombs and artillery.

The Germans were very efficient. They didn't waste their shells or bombs; they would time their barrages to mornings and evenings when people that had jobs to go to were on the streets. The Germans got the results they were after as Nadia's mother is killed in that manner sometime in the summer of 1943.

The report went on to say that there was no official birth certificate for Nadia but that was not unusual, given the time and place. The investigator found four of her mother's coworkers, who claimed to have helped the child survive on breast milk – any woman's breast milk. They worked at the morgue and had access to plenty of young women who had lost their children, but still had the milk of life to give. The women also tried to look after Nadia's brother, Yuri, DOB 27/09/1936.

When the siege finally ended in late January 1944, Yuri was literally on death's doorstep, he was living and dying in the overwhelmed city morgue. In January 1952 Yuri had the misfortunate job of sterilizing a surgeon's operating room at night. Normally this would have been considered a good job for a 17 year-old, but in this case the surgeon, Vladimir, had at one time treated Joseph Stalin. All of Stalin's former doctors were arrested; along with their families and employees. Most were sentenced to life in prison, or executed. Yuri got off easy with a twenty-year sentence.

Nadia's father, Boris, was captured by the German Army in 1943 and liberated by the Soviet Army in April of 1945. He was sentenced to hard labor for life, in Siberia for the crime of allowing himself to be captured.

Thirteen-year-old Nadia spent every morning and afternoon in the local director's office lobby hoping for an appointment, to plead for her father's and brother's release.

The director was aware of her the first day. He had been told to be on the lookout for young teens with 'the right stuff.' He waited for a week to see if Nadia would be persistent; she was. He ordered a report on her; when he received the report two weeks later, she was still waiting. He notified the KGB.

The KGB had an assignment in mind, and made Nadia an offer. Her father and brother would be released and she could spend a week with them, at a fancy dacha by the sea. But, she would be required to swear an oath of secrecy and forever go away on an important assignment. Communication by letters would be allowed every three months.

She agreed.

After more than two years of intensive training at Noragrad Spy School, Nadia had mastered the required English and art of spy craft. She was secretly placed in America as the daughter of Mr. & Mrs. Dickman, of Stanton Island, USA. Three years later the family moved to Omaha, Nebraska where Nadia attended college at Nebraska University.

Nadia, now Jane Dickman, studied art and graduated with honors in the spring of 1962. In 1963 she took a job with Nebraska University and still works there. Her "mother" and "father" have both been called on for two assignments, the last one during the fall of 1963. Nadia had as of yet, never been called upon. Nadia's code phase was "Your aunt has been called home; I will pray for her."

An address and phone number, that's all the information Nikolai had, and that information was exceedingly hard to get.

"Hey buddy, which airline?"

"Excuse me?"

"Are you flying on Eastern or American?"

The question confuses Nikolai, but he doesn't show it. "I'll let you know where to drop me off, just drive."

The sun is fully up and it's a bright morning. On both sides of the road are aircraft hangers, with big and small planes scattered about. "There!" Nikolai says, and points, "There at the telephones." There are two telephone booths, side by side, on the corner of a parking lot. The sign over the building said Airport Inn. Gennady had secured two rooms here, days ago, as a backup rendezvous site. The key to room 33 is one of Nikolai's assets.

"That's six dollars and fifty cents, pal."

Nikolai doesn't have any small money, so he hands the cabby another large bill.

There is no change.

"Thanks, you stay out of trouble buddy; I don't want to see you on the news."

Nikolai says. "Good fishing to you." and gets out with his bag.

"Hey," the driver says, "A day spent fishing is never a wasted day!"

"Wait! I need coins for the telephone."

The white-haired driver digs in his pocket and hands Nikolai his spare change.

"Your change sir." He laughs and drives away.

Nikolai deposits the ten-cent piece and dials the number he has memorized.

"Hello?"

"Is this Jane Dickman?"

"It is."

"Your Aunt has been called home; I will pray for her."

"I see, perhaps we should meet?"

"Yes, the Airport Inn, room 33."

"I will need one hour to get there."

"Very well."

They both disconnect at the same time.

There are several Airport Inn business cards stuck in the molding of the booth. Nikolai studies one and dials the number on the card.

"Airport Inn."

"Room 33, please."

Gennady answers on the first ring.

"I am here. Is there room service at this motel?"

"No, but there is a diner next door, it opened at 05:00."

"Good; go there and get me food. I want meat and potatoes, not breakfast junk. I'll be in my room. Oh, bring coffee and pastries."

"Yes, Comrade, it is good to hear from you."

Twenty-Eight

General Brandon leaves the lower complex with the intention of personally gathering as much information as possible on Kenneth Rushie's death. He also intends to pay the weasel, Curtis Knapp, a visit. There is a golf cart waiting for him at the top of the secure elevator.

"Guest housing Corporal," he notices the name tag sewn on the corporal's chest; it says Benson.

The electric golf cart moves at about the speed of a slow jog and makes the general think that's what I should be doing, jogging. He hasn't worked out in days; well, no time for that now and he has to manage on an hour and a half of light sleep. When the cart exits the main complex, he breaths deep the wonderful, cool, fresh morning air. The sky to the east is brightening and birds are chirping, sunrise is not far off.

The guest quarters look like any other modern motel, a long wing at the back and two smaller wings on each side. The smaller wings are the fanciest; the wing on the right side contains the rooms used by Director Rushie and his assistant Curtis.

Is Curtis really Rushie's son? Could what was said on the tape be true? If so, no wonder the kid is fucked up. The rooms used by Kenneth Rushie and Curtis Knapp are crawling with personnel. On the opposite side, are the rooms assigned to Ivan and Victor. There are two jeeps parked and two MPs on patrol. The cart stops in front of a cluster of officers. They all face him and salute.

"Good morning, General."

"Good morning, men, where can I find Colonel Knight?"

"He is in room four, sir."

"Very good, what can you tell me about the Director's death?"

"The doctor and his team left about five minutes ago. He said he will have a preliminary report in two hours; a full toxicology report could take as long as forty-eight hours. No apparent signs of a struggle, or apparent wounds. He feels that it is either natural causes or poisoning; he needs tests to confirm either way."

"Is there anything else Sergeant?"

"Yes sir, Curtis' room is unusual in a few ways, for example, he hung posters on the walls, brought his own stereo and had a bag of marijuana and a smoking pipe out in the open."

"What about Rushie's room?"

"Nine empty bottles of various kinds of liquor. It looks like he was writing. He became violently ill and died in the bathroom, just short of the toilet. That's all I can tell you, sir, except that Colonel Knight had the director's locked briefcase opened. He is in room four reviewing the contents, everyone has been ordered out of the room."

The general walks past two saluting MPs and into room number four. The colonel is sitting with an open briefcase, it is split half in two, with the hinges and clasps cut off. The contents of the briefcase are separated into three piles. Colonel Knight appears to be in deep thought reading a piece of paper, he didn't notice the general come in.

"Good morning, Colonel, please, remain seated."

General Brandon takes a seat across the table and asks, "What do we have here Colonel?"

"Good morning, sir." He hands the general one of the three piles. "This is his daily report and recommendations concerning this operation, all favorable. Director Rushie is very supportive of your command decisions."

He hands him a single piece of paper. "This is a very sharp dismissal letter concerning Curtis Knapp, unfiled and with today's date." He slides the last pile, the largest, across the table. "This appears to be a revision of his will, leaving nothing to Curtis. Again, unfiled with today's date, it gets progressively sloppy. I believe he was progressively getting drunker as he was writing. We found nine empty shot bottles in the trash; the bottles were sent for testing."

"Was there anything else in the trash?"

"There are several crumpled up writing attempts and one paper covered with ink and what are presumably his fingerprints. We think he talked to someone, possibly a lawyer that suggested the fingerprint as an absolute proof of the signer's authenticity. The technicians are checking the phone records now."

"What did the doctor say?"

"The doc is very interested in the director's prescription bottles, there are quite a few, he took all of them. It could be either natural causes or poisoning; he said nicotine poisoning would look like this. Rushie's vomit, blood, and tissue will have to be analyzed; as well as the liquor bottles and pills, before he can say for sure; he said the tests will tell the story. He needs a full autopsy and the laboratory results to rule on a cause of death."

"How long will that take?"

"He will begin the autopsy immediately. But the laboratory testing will take forty-eight hours or more if the testing is done here, or four to six hours if the tests are done at the FBI's forensic lab in Quantico, Virginia. I have an F-4 and pilot standing by for the run, with your permission sir."

"Granted, do it. Carry on Colonel; leave no stone unturned. I need your report at 08:30, you don't have to type it, an oral report will be fine; and, I want that jet in the air the minute the doc has all the samples he wants analyzed. I should tell you, the president made me the acting director of defense, with Director Rushie's death. I intend to use the position to see that those samples are expedited. I'll see you at 08:30, good day Colonel."

Without another word, General Brandon makes his way to the golf cart and gets in. "Building maintenance Corporal."

"Which one sir? Bunker maintenance or ground maintenance?"

"Ground maintenance will be fine." He would just as soon spend a little more time outdoors, and ground maintenance would have a better selection of rope to choose from. Ten minutes later, Walter is back in the golf cart with an eight-foot length of nylon rope. Not exactly what he was looking for, apparently hemp rope is no longer available well, it will serve the purpose. "Corporal, take me to Freedom Park."

Freedom Park is a good-sized picnic area, just outside the secondary entrance to the bunker. It was intentionally placed there to give fresh air and sunshine starved personnel an occasional glimpse of the outside world. The sun has risen over the horizon, on the airfield side of the base. The corporal stopped the cart at a picnic table, under an Oak tree with small, bright green leaves. "Will this do sir?"

"This will be fine Corporal; I want you to go to the upper cafeteria and get us some breakfast. Sergeant Dwayne Washington should be on duty ask for him; he's from Alabama and makes the best damn biscuits I ever had. Tell him this order is for me. I want ten of those biscuits, a bucket of his sausage gravy, four western omelets, eight buttered slices of toasts, and a gallon of coffee. Do you have it, Corporal?"

"Yes sir."

"Good. Tell him to put it in a field kit, to keep it warm and bring it here. Don't forget cups and utensils." The general gets out of the cart, carrying his rope, and sits at the picnic table.

Corporal Benson doesn't pull away immediately, he is eyeing the rope the general has and the Oak tree with the big branches that he is sitting under. The corporal thinks, don't speak to a general, unless spoken to. He looks away and drives off to the bunker entrance and the upper cafeteria.

The words that President Nixon spoke, "Throw the little prick a rope." have been echoing in the general's head. It brought back a memory from his youth. He had been on a two-week summer camping trip with his boy scout troop. It was called a Jamboree, with troops from several states attending.

One evening, he and his buddy, Frank, were trying to fashion a hangman's noose like the kind they had seen in western movies. They weren't having much luck; they couldn't get it to look right. Jimmy, a friend they had recently made, stopped by their campsite and laughed at their attempts. Jimmy was a country boy, from a small town in a different state, and he knew how to make a hangman's noose, the right way. Jimmy showed Walter and Frank the way his grandfather taught him to do it; and he made a perfect hangman's noose.

We were just making our own kind of fun and tied it to a branch. It looked like the real thing, because it was the real thing. The next morning when the Scout Master saw it, he had a royal fit. He made us take it down and for the rest of the trip Frank and I had latrine duty. We had to push a wheelbarrow of lime around the camp and put two shovelfuls down each hole, twice a day, morning and evening. We never mentioned Jimmy.

The general finished the job and was admiring his work; perfect, a far cry from his first attempt, all those years ago. Corporal Benson returned with breakfast and when he sees the noose that the general is holding, he jumps out of the cart. "General! What are you doing? Um, I mean, I thought…" he stammers, "Sorry, sir."

"Relax Benson; did you get Washington's biscuits?"

"Yes, sir, fresh out of the oven, he said your timing was perfect." He really set you up, sir."

"Good, bring that field kit over here."

The corporal places a large insulated, metal container on the picnic table and opens it.

"Don't be bashful Benson, dig in and relax, we're just two men having breakfast in a park."

The two men load up their plates with some of everything that is in the kit, gravy over everything on the general's plate.

"He gave me two gallons of coffee sir; he said it holds two gallons; you take two gallons. He said it is a cook's sin to send out a field kit that isn't full."

"That sounds like Washington, and it makes sense."

"Sir, as long as we are just two men having breakfast in a park I have to ask, why the hangman's noose?"

"That's classified. Outstanding breakfast; wouldn't you agree, Corporal?"

"I think it's the best I ever had sir; I had no idea biscuits could be so good."

"Where are you from Benson?"

"Detroit, sir."

The general nods his head. "Are you planning on working for one of the big car companies when you get out of the service?"

"I hope not sir; I mean, I would rather not."

"What are you going to do, make a career out of the Air Force?"

"Well, maybe ten years, sir. I recently decided to let the Air Force teach me a trade that I can make a good living at. I want to be an electrical engineer."

"You haven't always wanted to be an electrical engineer?"

"Oh, no sir. When I graduated from high school – I made a list of things that I wanted to do, and didn't want to do. I didn't have much on the want to do side. I knew I didn't want to get drafted into the Marine Corps like my neighbor Ron Betts; he went to Vietnam and he didn't come back home. I didn't want to be drafted, or work for GM, like the rest of the neighborhood. A whole lot of what I didn't want, helped me make up my mind to join the Air Force. Does that make any sense to you general?"

"It makes perfect sense to me son; knowing what you don't want, is just as important as knowing what you do want."

They finish Washington's delicious breakfast in silence.

Benson stands and places the dirty dishes in the bottom of the field kit. There is a place for them; it is a well-designed unit. Benson again looks at the noose and can't help himself from asking. "Why are there so many coils? Wouldn't one or two work just as well?"

"That's a good question Benson; and, there's a good reason for that many coils, exactly thirteen and a half. That's twelve for the jury, one for the judge, and a half a chance for the poor bastard swinging from the end of the rope. We have one more stop to make Corporal, put that rope in the field kit and take me to the brig."

The administrative building is a large four-story structure that houses not only the courts and legal offices; it also has secure cells in the underground brig. Corporal Benson stops the cart at the front entrance and turns toward the general. "I'm sorry sir; I don't know where the brig is." "That's probably a good thing Benson; it's around back, follow the road to the right and down the hill."

The hill turns out to be a steeply angled ramp. As the road continues underground, it is choked off by a manned security checkpoint. From the bulletproof booth gate, a guard straightens up, salutes the general, and nods to his partner to open the gate.

"Sergeant, I want you to call the holding cell area; I need an escort to take me to prisoner Curtis Knapp."

"Yes sir." The sergeant salutes again and takes two steps to a phone on the wall; he speaks a few words into the phone and hangs up. "Level four sir, Orange Level. Sergeant Lang will be your escort; and, he will be waiting for you at the first orange door."

The general nods and gives a flick of his hand as a signal to move on. They drive down a spiral
past the green, blue, and yellow levels. The level and color changes to orange and sure enough, Sergeant Lang is waiting for them, at the first orange door.

"Pull right up to the door Corporal."

"Sergeant Lang, take me to prisoner Knapp. Corporal, bring the field kit."

It takes Benson some time to get through the door that Sergeant Lang is holding open for him. "Sir," he says, "I think I should strap this on my back."

"That won't be necessary Corporal; Sergeant, give him a hand."

Sergeant Lang takes one handle and says, "It's not far sir, follow me." They pass through a lobby and a heavy steel door, down a hallway, and through one more steel door. "Knapp is in the second cell, on the left, sir."

"Curtis Knapp, we have never been introduced, but I know who you are; and, you should know who I am."

"Of course, you're General Brandon."

"I'm going to come right to the point Knapp. I am in possession of an audio tape with you and your father, that was recorded last night in the cafeteria. Now, I don't care if you want to kill yourself, but taking the rest of the world with you, no. You take nobody but yourself.

"Perhaps I'm not being clear enough. Corporal, place that field kit in front of Knapp's cell and make sure he can reach it."

"You will find everything that you need in there for a morning of clear thought."

"Can I have my Valium, please?"

"No. You do this with a clear head."

"Do what?"

"Make decisions, open the field kit."

Curtis opens the kit and sees the coiled noose on the top.

"The rope is my gift to you; I crafted the hangman's noose myself, just for you Curtis. If you had anything to do with Director Rushie's death; I suggest you use it. The president told me that if you were involved, he will see to it that you spend the rest of your days making little rocks out of big rocks, in Leavenworth Penitentiary."

"But I didn't have anything to do with his death, other than making him mad."

"That you certainly did Knapp. There is breakfast enough for three men in that kit, and I wanted to make sure that you had a fitting last meal, if that's the course you choose. One more thing Knapp, if you try to use the utensils, rope or anything else I was nice enough to bring you against the guards well, Sergeant Lang has my permission to make you wish that you had used the rope. Understand?"

Curtis says, "Yes," in a choked voice.

"Sergeant Lang, clear this block. I want Knapp to have complete solitude until the evening meal."

Twenty-Nine

Engine 6833 rolls into the Woodstock, Iowa rail yard; for a small town, the rail yard is big. It also has a river port access, for moving grain and goods anywhere in the world. They can see grain cars with grain falling from their bottom bellies to a conveyer belt that transfers it up and over to the hold of a cargo ship. The grain is falling off the conveyor belt like a golden waterfall into the ships hold.

Walt asks, "Is that corn? Where is it going?"

Joe, the engineer answers, "Yes, it's corn; last fall's crop; you wouldn't believe how much corn is stored in silos around here. And, you won't believe this, the corn is all going to Russia; they have some kind of a deal with our government, regarding the sale of the corn. A lot of it goes out that way, but for the life of me, I sure can't figure out why we would help feed the enemy."

Joe brings the engine to a slow roll and Pete jumps off. The engine and the cars roll on until Pete's voice comes over the radio and says, "That will do 6833, ease it on back." The train reverses through a switch and is now on a side track. They see Pete bend over and throw the switch, and Joe stops the train.

Pete climbs aboard and says, "Come on youngsters, we have to walk to the back and spot the caboose; this track dead-ends just about where I want to drop it, and it's not a good day to run it off the tracks. Come on." Pete climbs down the ladder and is followed by Walt and Louise.

"How many cars does it take to make a train, Walt asks?"

"Anywhere from one to a hundred, or more, as long as you keep adding engines, at the front, in the middle, or even all the way in the back; we call those engines pushers. A train can be a mile long, or even longer. Right now, we have eleven empty grain cars and eight loaded propane cars. We drop the empty grain cars, and on the way back, we pick up however many loaded grain cars they have for us. The propane cars go to our next stop in New Canton. There's no natural gas pipeline out there in the middle of nowhere and the farms use a lot of the stuff."

This time, walking alongside the track is much easier than when the track is perched high on a bed of rocks. Walking alongside of a track like that is walking on a steep hill, sideways. This track seems to have sunk into the ground. The cross ties that must be there are invisible because of the dirt, muck, and grass that covers them.

Mark, Betty, John, Sandy, Brownie, and Christine are standing at the railing on the front platform talking excitably. Pete calls out, in his loud manly voice "Hey, everyone all right?" They all stop talking and say almost as one, "Yeah!"

Sandy says, "Are we there?" Before she even finishes, Brownie says, "No hot boxes, Pete. I watched, and I didn't say anything into the radio, is that all right? Louise! How was it to ride in the engine? I want to ride in the engine. Can I Pete, can I?" "Hold on here, you two get up there." Walt motions for Louise to go first and then follows her.

"You guys stay put; I have to walk back a little further." Really, Pete just needs to go to the other end of the caboose, but it's easier to walk the track a little more, than to go through a bunch of teenagers. Pete climbs the rear platform, leans on the railing and takes a couple of deep breaths. "Ok, everything is fine so far, and it's only another forty miles to New Canton."

"Hey, Brownie, is everyone on board?" "Yeah! I didn't know you were back there. Pete." "Tell everyone to hold on, we're moving. Ease it on back 6833."

The caboose barely jolts, as it begins to slowly roll down the sidetrack. On the right, are large warehouse-type buildings, with tall fat silos above another side track. On the left side, green and red farm equipment, of all types, are lined up in rows. After that, it's flat open fields of young corn plants on each side. Around a slight curve, a large brick church, with high steeple comes into view. There is a break in the corn plants, as the backyard of the church is a manicured lawn all the way to the track. There is a car and a pickup truck parked on the lawn near the track.

"See that big red Lincoln Continental up there? That's Large Marge, I bet that trunk is full of good stuff to eat." There are three older ladies standing beside the open trunk, smiling and waving. The pickup truck's tailgate is down and we can see boxes piled high in the bed. When the caboose is about even with the Lincoln, Pete says into the radio, "That will do Joe; set em." That's the signal for Joe to set the brakes, and come on back for something to eat.

Eight young men and women climb down along, with Pete the brakeman. Christine tells Gray Kitty to stay, and she sits like an obedient dog. Marge is standing at the trunk of her car; she opens the coolers and takes out a wicker basket that holds paper plates and utensils. "Come on everyone" she says, "This is going to be cafeteria style. What we have here is a basic, greasy spoon breakfast. Eggs, bacon, sausage, home fries, and toast; there's also milk, juice, and coffee to drink. Come on, don't stand there and let this get cold!"

Brakeman Pete is the first in line, and he takes a plate from the basket. "I'll show y'all how to do this. Marge, let me have some of that that cheesy egg thing you have there, some bacon, sausage, and home fries." Marge is spooning it up, just as fast as Pete is speaking. "There you go, honey," she says, as she slaps toast on top of everything, "Next!" Brownie is the only one ready with a plate, "Same" he says. And, one by one, they all get the same plateful.

The eight young travelers sit on blankets that are laid out on the ground, and dig into their food. It's a funny thing; every one of them had cereal and milk just a few hours earlier, but the whole group is ravenously hungry. Maybe because everything on their plates looks, smells, and tastes so good.

Betty says, "I wonder why she said something about a "greasy spoon", it doesn't taste greasy." Sandy answers her question. "It's because she cooked it right, the oil was hot enough; at a lower temperature, the oil would have a chance to soak in and make it yucky. See how the potatoes are brown and crunchy? It's because the cook knows what she is doing."

John says, "You cook Sandy?" "Oh, yes, I love to cook, but I sometimes have a hard time eating."
"Well, I can't wait to try your cooking," He gives her hug. Louise says, "Look how close those two have become; isn't that sweet?" "Are you kidding Christine says, look at us, we are not eight people, we are four couples." For some reason that made perfect sense and the four couple's kiss.

"Hi, I'm Marge, you can call me Large Marge, everyone else does. In fact that's the name of my restaurant, Large Marge's Roadside Café. My husband Stan is doing the cooking at the moment, but let me tell you, he runs the kitchen exactly the way I say. I'm the boss of the kitchen, and he's the boss of everything else, she gives the girls a wink."

"Let me tell you a little story. Stan and I have been setting our alarm clock for 3:00 am for years, that's the time we need to get up to have the café open and ready for customers at 5:00 am. This morning, at 3:00, we both sat straight up and were wide awake. "Wow" Stan said. "What a dream I just had. We have to help them, to feed them, that's our job." The young travelers I say. Yes!" As we talked, we realized that we all had exactly the same dream, but it was more like a commandment from God.

The phone rings, and it's our friend Pete, he called to tell us about his vision and we knew what we had to do. It wasn't just me and Stan that had a vision. Pete and his Julie, Joe and his wife Barbra, we all had the same dream. These two ladies standing with me are June and Velma, they also had the same dream, or a version of it.

"So, it's like this," Marge said, "Joe and Pete's job is to get you to where you have to be; Stan's and my job is to make sure that you don't go hungry; and June and Velma's job is to make sure that you all are clean, have enough suitable clothes, and are not cold. I'll let everyone else tell their stories. If anyone wants seconds, now is the time."

Christine says, "I need milk for my kitty; I think she will eat whatever we give her." Large Marge says, "I saw that cat sitting on the railing; she will be pretty once you get her brushed out."

"I don't have a brush."

"That's ok, we'll get you whatever you need; and, I'll fix the cat a feast right now. What's her name?"

"Gray Kitty."

"All right, I have to run in a few minutes, but I'll be back. June, Velma go ahead.

June says, "The same thing happened to me the night before last except of course, my vision was to make sure that a lot of young adults had suitable clothing, maybe a hundred of them. How? Why? I don't know, but I do know it's my mission; and, I gladly accept it. There are just two things that we needed and don't have at our store, underwear and that many socks. I was thinking about that when Velma called. I'll let Velma tell the rest."

"Thank you, June. Let me start by saying this is powerful; powerful in the same way that God is good. Whatever task you children have been chosen to fulfill; it is good. But I have to warn you, there is evil in the world too. My warning is this, there will be an evil force, maybe the devil himself, that will try to stop you from reaching your goal. Please be aware of it, and be careful."

Velma's comments have an impact on everyone sitting on the blankets. It makes sense and we all know she is right.

"Back to underwear and socks, I picked June up and we went to K-Mart. Between us, we had eighty dollars to spend and we thought that would be enough; but the funny thing was when we got to that department, there was a sign saying that all undergarments and socks were buy one get two free; today only! We spent less than thirty dollars and got two baskets full!"

"On the way to the church clothing store, we were talking about our inventory of clothes. We were worried that we wouldn't have enough; and, the question of shoes really had us stumped. Then another miracle or two happened. When we got to Cradle and Beyond, that's the name of our little church boutique there was a lot of traffic. Cars, most of them with Nebraska plates, were lined up in front of our little store, dropping off donations. Almost all of the people were strangers to us. They were working together, unloading cars, and neatly stacking the boxes against the wall."

"A man came over and introduced himself as Mr. Edsel. He said he owned a chain of shoe stores, called Best Buy Shoes, and that he brought a donation, a pickup truck full of new shoes and boots. He left the truck and said he would be back next week to get it."

"Make good use of them and God bless," that's all he said. "It's that Ford right there, so when your done eating go over and pick out a pair of shoes or boots. There's more, but I'll give you a few minutes to let all of that soak in. June and I are going to have a bite of this breakfast."

Velma joins Pete, Joe, June, and Marge at the trunk of the Lincoln leaving the teens alone to talk that one through. After a moment, Walt says "About half of us have already been exposed to some kind of evil. Well, five out of eight, if you count my cell doors popping open, but that didn't seem evil to me.

Of the other half, no evil at all. Christine and Louise, are rich kids - no offense, and they had no problem getting here. Brownie and I had nothing but good luck getting here. Betty and Sandy were almost enslaved in a carnival sideshow oh yeah, that sounds evil enough. And the thought of the evil or possessed cops and army guys that John and Mark encountered gives me the creeps."

"But with good too" Sandy says. "Our doors popped open and let us out of that place. That was good and so was meeting John and Mark.

That is better than good; they saved us. And then what? We fall in love with them, in less than a day? That seems good."

"Remember I told you that I was in reform school. "Walt said. "Well, that's basically like jail; and when I walked through the open doors, it was like I was invisible. I was invisible because nobody noticed me or tried to stop me. I didn't feel scared, more like I was in a trance or sleepwalking. I walked with a definite direction, somewhere in my mind. I walked to the rail yard and got into a boxcar, like I knew what I was doing. That's when I met Brownie; he was in that boxcar waiting for me. How did he know that I was coming? There were hundreds of boxcars there, how did I know which boxcar to get into? My point is it's weird all right, but more like it was meant to be; not evil, right Brownie?"

"Yeah, it was meant to be. I was expecting you, and even knew your name was Walt, before you got there. Nothing seemed evil to me; but I sure had a compulsion to get on that train and that particular boxcar. I think it was the only car that didn't have a full load. I'll tell you what I didn't expect – that two beautiful girls would hunt us down in the Omaha rail yard to join us in our journey; wherever that leads us. It feels like we're living a Twilight Zone episode."

"What do you think Christine?"

"I believe everything we have told each other is true. Remember when Louise and I told you that, at the same time, we both said that we needed to go to Omaha? That wasn't evil. It was a good kind of compulsion; but it was a command that we both obeyed, without hesitation or really any question. We were just going to do it and we did. I'm not sorry about the decision, are you Louise?"

"Not at all, whatever we are up against, it isn't all bad; and meeting Walt is my destiny, whatever happens. I believe it more every minute. That's my point, do we all agree that whatever happens to us is destiny, may preordained before we were even born?"

"Maybe." Mark says, "That sounds right."

"I'll give you an example" Christine says. "Louise and I didn't know we had to find Walt and Brownie in the rail yard until we got there. And when we got there, I knew Brownie was my man and Louise knew Walt was her man; and, before we even met them, we knew their names. That's a good kind of weird and it guided us right to them. I have been to church enough times to believe in the forces of God and Satan; and their continuous work against each other. But we are together now, the eight of us; and we are going to look out for each other, and protect each other, right?"

Seven of us say, "Right," all except Betty, who is preoccupied with a man raking at the edge of the church property; she is staring at him.

"Betty, what is it?" "Is that man a danger to us?" Mark asks. "Why didn't I notice him before?"

"He has been there, kind-of in the shadows. It looks like he is clearing the woods; he's been throwing all the brush he cuts into that pit. I think he's harmless, because of something my grandma says that keeps popping into my head. It goes like this, Bless his heart the boy ain't right".

"What does that mean Betty?"

"Well, it's a southern thing; I guess if you bless someone's heart first, it's ok to say something bad about them. He looks like he belongs here though; and, I think the church ladies would have run him off if he didn't belong here, right?"

"Here comes June and Velma, let's ask them."

"Are you ready to get sized up for shoes? Mr. Edsil left one of those metal foot gauges in the cab of the truck; we might as well get the sizes right. Anybody ever used one of those things before?"

"Oh, yes" Louise says, "Christine and I love to shop for shoes."

"Good, you size em up, ready?"

"Mrs. June," Betty says, "Is the man over there all right? I mean, is it ok for him to be here?"

June follows Betty's glance and says, "Dennis? Why yes, he may be a card or two short of a full deck, but he's harmless. This whole part of the church's rear lawn was wild scrub brush just four years ago. About that time, someone took him to a golf course to see if the game might help him focus. The game of golf didn't, but the beautiful green, manicured grass captured his imagination."

"That's when Dennis got in his head that it is his mission in life to "clear the land." He wants this piece of land to look like the golf course he saw. Never mind that It's railroad property, but they don't seem to care, or at least no one has ever said anything."

"The whole town knows about his project, and it's been very good therapy for him. He is allowed to use the church's tools and maintenance shed, and he does every day. In the spring, we take up a collection for his grass seed fund. He plants the seeds, one by one, using a tool he made – a board with nails sticking through it, to make holes for the seeds. He doesn't say much, but he did say one thing that you need to know about."

"What's that June?"

"Well, remember I told you that he is a few cards short of a full deck? Well, that's not quite true; he might have a full deck with some jokers and wildcards threw in. He can sense things that others can't. For example, the weather, he can predict next week's weather better than the weatherman on T.V. But of course, he won't watch T.V. He's afraid the people on the screen can see him; that's not true about radio though. He collects the old fashion kind of wooden radios and somehow, he knows how to restore them to perfect working condition, he taught himself how to do it."

"When Dennis says tornadoes will be in the area, we listen, because he has never been wrong about that. Normally, all the dogs in town are with him as he clears brush, or plants grass seed. The dogs run and play with him all day; the dog's even help by carrying sticks in their mouths and dropping them in his burn pile. He must have told them to stay away today; those dogs will do anything he says. There are a lot more examples like that and, that brings me to my point."

"Dennis was carrying donated boxes downstairs when we came in. He put down the box he was carrying and looked me right in the eye, which is highly unusual for him; he took my hand and led me into an empty office. It took some time for him to get out what he wanted to say, but I encouraged him and did not rush him. This is what he said." "You clothe them. I burn everything they are now wearing."

"Now, when you think about the unusual day that we are all having, it only makes sense that we should take him seriously. So, as we pass his burn pit, on the way to Cradle and Beyond, I want you to throw in your outer clothes, including your hats and your jackets. On the way back, everything that you are now wearing gets tossed in, understand? Good, now let's get some boots."

John says, "Boots? No sneakers?"

"All I saw were boots and hiking shoes; there could be some there, buried at the bottom, let's look."

Velma says, "I'll fold the blankets and pick up. Go ahead when you get done, I want that entire load of boots on the caboose, you are meant to take them with you."

Betty and Sandy are the first ones at the open tailgate of the pickup truck. "Wow" Sandy says, "There are a bunch here, we're going to have to sort and stack the boxes, just to see what we have."

Eight pairs of hands made short work of sorting the boxes by, size and by the Men's / Woman's tags. John is not happy about not finding any sneakers; I'm interested in two of the heaviest boxes that I had handled. What I find inside are, heavy men's work boots, the kind with the steel toe. I like them; they are made of thick reddish-brown leather and are very tough looking."

Louise had already done everyone's sizes, except mine, she calls me over to the truck's cab. "Bring them with you" she says, "Maybe you'll get lucky."

My size, 9½, is exactly what my top box is. A perfect fit. I am pleased, as I laced them up. I can't understand why John is still bitching about giving up his sneakers. "John," I say "Get a pair like these. For one thing, the boots lace up, so there not coming off your feet unless you take them off. Think what Monkey Boy would have looked like if you had kicked him wearing a pair of these, with the steel toes." That changed his tune; and, after he had laced up his boots he agreed, they are perfect. Funny thing is that everyone even the girls, picked work boots over the hiking shoes.

Sandy and Betty are really happy about their boots. "I can't wait to throw these old boots from the railroad station into that fire pit" Sandy say's, and Betty agrees.

Large Marge and Pete the Brakeman walk up to the truck. Marge asks "Did everybody get enough to eat? Well, I think you did because nobody came back for seconds. I have to go; I'm going to bring back bagged lunches for everyone and a box of 9 lives for Christine's cat. I got to run; I'll be back in an hour. Bye."

One by one, everyone says bye to Marge and thanks her for the food that was really quite outstanding. Marge doses the fat lady waddle back to her Lincoln and drives away.

"Ok," Pete says, "Joe and I have to do some switching. I'm going to drop the caboose and I want you all to be on it and be ready to go in an hour. We need to be in New Canton at 1:00 pm to be on schedule. Get what you need from the church thrift store, it sounds like there's been plenty of donations probably just for you, like the boots. They have a gymnasium down in the church basement that has both boy's and girl's locker rooms, with showers. All right, get on with it, I have to go."

Pete turns away and goes to the grain car ahead and unhooks it from the caboose. He climbs the ladder of the grain car and we can hear him say into his radio "Go ahead slow, 6833;" Pete gives a wave and turns around. The train rolls away, leaving the caboose behind.

Christine starts putting boxes back into the truck and the rest of us joined in to help. Walt is putting the last of the ninety-two boxes in when Velma appears. She says, "I'm going to back the truck up to the caboose. Everybody make a chain and pass the boxes of boots in, it won't take long; you boys grab the blankets, I want you to take those too. The bag of trash comes with us too."

She's right, it doesn't take long. Velma takes her place in the driver's seat and June gets in the passenger side; the rest of us climb into the back. The boys are on one side of the pickup's bed, the girls are on the other. Velma eases the truck up the side yard and stops the truck so that the truck's bed is parallel to the burn pile. Eight bundles are tossed in, along with a bag of trash, and eight crushed shoe boxes.

Dennis has a downcast manner. His green John Deer cap is pulled all the way down, covering the whole top of his face. He stopped raking and is holding his head up just enough to watch the items drop into his fire pit. The Ford continues up the lawn and along the side of the brick church. It bumps over a curb and turns left, then left again into the main entrance.

There is a United States Postal truck; the mailman unloading still more boxes. Velma parks next to the mail truck and talks to the mailman through the open window, "Hey Carl, what do ya' have for us?" "A bunch of packages, from all over the country Velma; all express one-day delivery. I don't see that very often, especially not with so many packages. I need signatures for these Velma; just a second, there are a few more in the back." With the packages unloaded and signed for, Carl says he is way behind schedule. He excuses himself and drives away, leaving yet another pile of boxes stacked up against the wall.

June says, "All right, everyone grab a box or two and carry them downstairs; we're going to use the gymnasium to open and sort all of these boxes."

"Good idea June; we can have the boys bring in all the other donations and us girls can start sorting." Christine says, "Look, six boxes from Levi Strauss!"

June says, "Don't start opening them here! I'm already afraid of the mess we are going to make, let's take them to the gym." June holds the arched wooden door open. Velma picks up the first box and says, "Follow me." She goes through the door and down a staircase on the right. At the bottom of the stairs to the right there is a set of double swinging doors leading into the gym.

Christine and Louise immediately start tearing open the Levi Strauss boxes. That brought on a Christmas morning-like feeling and everybody joined in, opening the remaining boxes. There are a bunch of boxes from Fruit of the Loom and Avon. There are piles of jeans, denim jackets, and shirts. There are also T-shirts, underwear, socks and a wide variety of crazy stuff in the Avon boxes. Another two long boxes are from the commissioner of baseball, Mr. Bowie Kuhn Park Avenue New York City. Those are the boxes I open and find four official baseball caps, from all the major league teams.

Velma says "My goodness, look at all this stuff! Plus, there must be a hundred boxes in our store that we haven't even opened yet!" Her voice is shaky, with maybe a note of panic, when she says; "I feel that you must take it all with you."

Betty comes over to her side and says, "Velma you have done your part for this cause. We are not meant to take it all, just what we need. I promise you, Velma, the rest of the group that we are to meet are being taken care of by other good Americans, just like you and June."

"But how can you know that for sure?"

"Just like you knew for sure that we were coming."

"But all this stuff, it's so much."

"It's for your store Velma; it's to help you continue to do the good work that you've been doing. Anyway, we're not going to need purses or makeup kits. Besides, I want my shower and we are fast running out of time."

"Ok, Betty, one thing though, I want everyone to at least pass by the donated boxes and if something feels right, take it with you."

"You're getting the hang of this Velma, where are the showers?"

"Girls' locker rooms are to the right; boys' are to the left. I stocked them with soap, shampoo, and towels."

"Thanks, I'll use the towel, but I have to try some of this Avon soap and shampoo. We're definitely ready for a shower."

The couples kiss and go to their separate locker rooms. Fifteen minutes later the boys come out together, looking much better than they did a short time ago. They are all carrying everything they were wearing in tied-up T-shirt balls.

Walt says, "June, Velma, I have been thinking. I think we should take the Levi and Fruit of the Loom boxes, along with the hats; that way, there will be something to go with the boots. I don't want to regret not taking them."

"Now you are getting the hang of it Walt," Velma says. "You might as well take them all to the truck now; you know the girls will be awhile."

When the boy's come back they are all wearing their favorite team's baseball caps. They are just in time to see their women coming out, giggling and laughing carrying their old clothes tied up in their towels. They are radiant and beautiful young women.

When they get to where the boxes are Louise says, "I see you boys came up with the same thought as we did; but why didn't you take the Avon box too?"

"Betty said it was too much stuff, but we changed our minds, take it. Leave out those two big purses, they are for June and Velma. Hurry back we are going to pass through the store like Velma suggested."

"Better make it quick" June says. "We have less than ten minutes to get back."

Betty is the last one to pass down the aisles of donations, nobody else had the urge to open or inspect any of the boxes. Betty went straight to a small box and opened it. Inside were eight beautiful silver St. Christopher medallions, on heavy chains. "Better take those," June says. Betty nods and follows the rest of the group up the stairs.

Mark says, "We are going to have to either sit on the boxes or walk, what do you girls think?" "I think we did enough walking yesterday," Sandy says, "lets ride." Velma drives slow and easy over the curb and down the lawn. Again, she positions the bed of the truck, so that it is parallel to Dennis's burn pile, he is nowhere in sight.

John asks, "Do you still have the wallets, Mark?" "Yeah. The wallets, Monkey Boy's keys, his pocket knife, and my switch key. I don't mind burning the wallets and everything else, but not the money or the switch key, we may need them. Is that all right?" Betty answers "Of course, we can't burn money and I think the switch key will be ok, but that's it. I mean is anyone else carrying anything that is more than an hour old?"

"Not any more" Christine says, and she tosses in her towel into the burn pit. "Not anymore," Louise says," and her bundle goes in. The same thing is repeated six more times, along with a few extra items from Mark.

Pete is waiting for them on the rear platform of the caboose, when they pull up. "I see you decided to bring the rest of the boots; why not, it can't hurt. Marge came by and dropped off four bags of groceries, she wished you the best and said she had to go; Stan is making a mess out of her kitchen."

June says, "A few more things need to go with them Pete." "No problem, pass up whatever you have." With that done, Pete gets down and says to Christine, "You and Brownie can ride in the engine if you want; Joe says it's all right."

Brownie looks at Christine and says "No thanks. I need to do the brakeman job like before; and, I think it's best if we all stick together for now." "Suit yourself; the radio is on the table, next stop New Canton." Pete says goodbye to June and Velma, then excuses himself to go to the engine. As he turns to leave, he tells the group "Five minutes, we'll be rolling in five minutes." The church ladies get real tight hugs and sincere thanks from all eight, after that we all boarded our caboose.

Brownie says, "I need to go to the front platform; I need to watch the train." Brownie and Christine walk holding hands to the front platform. Grey Kitty comes out from under a bunk; she stretches, and follows Christine.

"Hey, there's Dennis," John says. And sure enough, Dennis is coming from the maintenance shed, pushing a wheelbarrow. He stops at the fire pit and takes something out of the wheelbarrow. It's a five-gallon metal can of gasoline; he is pouring all of it into the pit.

Walt calls across the caboose "Hey, are you guys seeing this? That's a lot of gas, too much." When Dennis finishes emptying the can he puts the empty one it back in his wheelbarrow, and gets another full one. "Hey! That's too much!" Brownie yells.

Dennis continues to pour the gas until he is satisfied in his own mind that it's enough. He moves the cans and the wheelbarrow to the other side of his cleared lawn. Eight young pairs of eyes are on him as he gets down on his knees and is doing something that we can't see.

We hear Pete's voice come over the radio; "Go ahead slow, 6833." The caboose jolts and slowly starts to move forward.

When Dennis stands up, he is holding a sawed-off mop handle with a rag tied around one end. Nobody can figure out what to hell he's doing; until he lights the gas-soaked end. He stands there for a second holding the flaming mop handle like a spear, he is concentrating on his shot like a hunter of old days gone by. He takes three running steps and heaves it toward the pit. It is a perfect shot. The flash is first, flowed by a blast of heat, and then a terrific boom. There is an instant thirty-foot fire and a fireball cloud, shaped like a mushroom climbing high above. Dennis is standing up straight with his face to the sky, he is smiling.

Thirty

Nadia hasn't forgotten her Russian childhood, her adolescence, or her training. In fact, she still has nightmares about that bleak depressing place. She could not have known at the time, that the three weeks she spent in the area director's office was the smartest thing she could have done. It changed her life in an impossible way she could have never imagined. She gained loving adoptive parents and the lifestyle of a privileged American young adult. For that she is grateful.

Nadia remembers how proud she was to secure both her father's and her brother's release from prison. The week they spent together at the resort on the Black Sea is her fondest memory of Russia. During one of their many walks on the rocky shoreline, her father whispered a secret in her ear. When both he and Boris write to her, if all is well, they will always use an even numbered date and include an even number of pages. A two-page letter, dated 2/2/64 would mean all is well. If a three-page letter were to arrive with an odd date, 1/1/68, it would mean – all is not well.

In the past two years, there have been eight one-page letters, all with odd dates. All is not well with her father and brother of that, she is sure. The dilemma she faces now, is that she feels more loyalty to America than to Russia; the place that is still mistreating her family.

Nadia does have an option. Her loving stepfather, Harry Dickman, had long ago set her up with an alternate identity in the name of Janice Dunn. He had told her that it is always best to use the same initials as your real name. It buys a faction of a second, between the first stroke of the pen and the correct name to write.

Harry also made sure that Janice Dunn had a cabin in Montana, completely stocked with supplies. The only drawback is that it's inaccessible during the winter months. He also provided money in many different forms, bank accounts, cash, bearer bonds, and gold and silver coins. The little Volkswagen "Thing" that she drives should be able to make it there now in late May. Nadia has everything she needs to plunge into a new identity and life; but she doesn't want to give up the life she has in Omaha. That leaves one choice, and that is to see what the communist bastard wants.

8:15 am

Nadia knocks on door number 33 at the Airport Inn. Nikolai answers the door before she even finishes knocking; he had been impatiently pacing. He opens the door but does not immediately let her in, he studies her. Nadia's appearance and demeanor pleases Nikolai. She does not appear to have fallen for the trappings of America. Her hair looks like she cuts it herself and there is no attempt to color the, more than a few grey strands. Nadia's blouse, jeans, and boots are all of working-man quality and everything is stained with paint splatters.

"Which vehicle did you arrive in?"

"The white Volkswagen," she answers.

"That little piece of German junk; that's a goddamn Nazi staff car! Get in here!" He steps aside and lets her in. "Why the hell are you driving a German staff car?"

"Comrade Colonel, I understand the vehicle; I have studied it and am very familiar with its working components. I can work on it myself and I have confidence that I can always keep it running. I always carry tools and spare parts. I do not care to rely on anyone else for my needs; also, I am not comfortable with the newer cars they are too complicated."

"It may not be large enough; do you have access to a larger vehicle?"

"Comrade Colonel, as you know anything can be acquired with American currency. I can retrieve the funds if you wish and secure a larger vehicle by the end of the day."

"You should have anticipated that need well in advance agent; your failure to do so is sloppy and shows a lack of advance thinking! Amateurs, everywhere I look!"

Gennady is sitting at the small desk wearing headphones that are connected to a case on the floor and a wire in the wall. A map of the area, with a notebook, is on the desk and a pen in his right hand.

"Gennady! Stand up! Let our guest sit; she needs to make a list. What is their position?"

"Unchanged Comrade; they are still stationary in what appears to be a rail yard in Council Bluff, Iowa." Gennady flips the notebook to a fresh page and stands up, he leaves the pen.

Nadia takes his place and picks up the pen. "What do you require Comrade?"

"I am interested in contacts and weapons. Do you have access to a network of Mother of Russia patriots? What is the status of your immediately accessible weapons arsenal? Where is it located? Contacts, I want contacts! They need to be called in; they are needed."

"My stepparents would sometimes pass orders to me, Comrade; other than that, I only know the code phrase that indicates a contact in need. I have no knowledge of other working cells. Our primary mission is to maintain a safe house for agents and to photograph aircraft as they approach and depart the air base.'

"The weapons Nadia, what about the weapons?"

"Small arms and ammunition, also I have three rocket-propelled grenade launchers, a case of grenades, and a small package of plastic explosive."

"AK 47's?"

"Yes, Comrade, I have many of them."

"Good, I want the grenades, the grenade launchers, the plastic explosive, three AK's and plenty of ammunition, and bring some 9mm rounds."

"Is there anything else you require Comrade?

Yes. Three backpacks, tactical vests, if you have them, and enough food and water for three days. Write it down and don't forget anything. I have already asked you once agent where are the weapons located? How long will it take to retrieve these items?"

"Apologies Comrade; my stepparents and now I maintain a small working farm for operations. I will show you on this map. There is a town called Parish, it is fifty miles west of here, in farm country."

"Damn, north would have been more convenient. How much time will it take for you to retrieve these items and return?"

"It will take slightly more than two hours to obtain and return."

Again, Nikolai is impressed with her; she did not pin herself down to a specific time, she left a window of time she may need, smart. "Comrade Nadia, time is of the essence right now; get these items and return within two hours, you may take a pastry with you."

"Thank you no; Comrade I only eat, when necessary, I will hurry back." She stands and exits without another word.

Ok, Nadia thinks I still have the option to run, but what has been asked of her is not too much. If she can extract herself after this mission, she is confident he would never give up her identity.

Proceed.

Thirty-One

10:00 Meeting; Offutt Air Force Base, Upper Office.

There are only five people present at the 10:00 meeting: General Brandon, Colonel Knight, Captain Duffy, Ivan, and Victor. General Brandon starts the meeting. "Gentlemen, as you know, the director of defense should be here with us, but he is not because he is dead. Kenneth Rushie's second in command Deputy Director Curtis Knapp is jailed, as he may have had something to do with Rushie's death. I should know more details at any moment. The situation in Russia is tense and still unpredictable. There was an attempted coup against Brezhnev; it was put down."

"After the gunfire stopped, amazingly, there now seems to be 100% cooperation on their end. Our agents are present at the assigned site in central Poland, and report that eighty of their one hundred children are there. From the flyover information we have on our New Canton, Iowa site – we can see that a tent city has been erected, apparently by the townspeople. There are more than thirty tents erected on a slight hill, just outside of town. We couldn't get an exact count, but we believe the count to be similar to what the Russians have."

"I have decided that I want no interference in the town of New Canton. I am convinced the "Others" will not let anything interfere with their abduction of the one hundred children. What I witnessed on the swamp road convinced me of that. It is their guiding hand that quelled a serious situation in Russia and individually brought each of the children to the assigned places. I am convinced armed troops in the area would be a bad idea. However, that does not mean I want to be unprepared."

"Capitan Duffy, do you own a good suit?"

"I do sir."

"Good, as of right now you are the acting Deputy Director of Defense. I will prepare the paperwork and a letter of introduction. I want you to go to New Canton and have a sit-down talk with their Chief of Police. Don't hide any details and answer his questions. Make it clear to him that he runs the show in his town, unless serious unforeseen conditions arise, in which case, you will be in charge of decisions regarding the operation. Bring a secure radio and drive your own car; you will be our eyes and ears in that town."

"Yes sir."

"I want you to befriend that officer, stay at his side and make sure he believes that you're not there to step on his toes. Colonel Knight your thoughts, please."

"General Brandon, as I see the objective and the present situation; your plan is sound. I agree our military options are limited." Colonel Knight pulls a map out of his briefcase. "May I use your desk General?"

"Of course, Colonel, I asked for your thoughts, l want to hear them."

When he spreads the map out it is obvious that he has been studying it, because it is covered with markings from different colored pencils. A red X on the map marks the tent city in New Canton. There are also four aerial photos clipped to each of the four corners of the map. This is the site of the delivery, at 03:00 tomorrow morning.

"That time still stands, correct sir?"

"Yes, at this moment Colonel, keep in mind this is a constantly changing situation. I am scheduled for another phone call with President Nixon, from Moscow this afternoon and another one this evening; but yes, 03:00 tomorrow morning still stands."

The colonel nods and points to the red X. "That's the tent city; the pencil dot just above it is the only likely point for a large hovering craft to land. It is the crest of a hill planted with young corn; the corn is three to five inches in height and not much of an obstacle. The main road through New Canton, a town of 1,200 people, is Route 11 and is a half a mile south of the site."

"The road parallels the railroad tracks, and a half a mile east, north-south power lines cross the track and the road, here where the yellow circles are. The power lines are a weak point, I don't like. There is a company access road that runs right underneath the lines and a lot of cover to hide in the wooded easements on each side. The green circles on route 11 are the only crossroads in town, there are four of them; they are basically roads into farm country. The blue X's are the first roads they intersect with. In a different situation; that's where I would place choke points. Do we leave these points to fate; General?"

"Correct Colonel, to fate. A strong military presence is not an option; we are not fighting an army. Your Russian counterpart Colonel Nikolai; he is a nasty unknown. I will find out soon if he has been apprehended or is loose and considered to be a threat to this mission by the Russians."

"Victor, what are your thoughts on this?"

"Sir, it would be best if he were dead, but I fear he is not."

Colonel Knight says "I suggest twelve transport Huey's standing by on base along with at least six attack choppers; all manned with combat veterans. That will allow for a workable extraction plan. With luck, we will have the hundred children safe, along with the requested DNA samples. We must find out why these children are special. And of course, bring a successful conclusion to this mission. They are bringing them back, right General?"

"If they don't Colonel, they will be the lucky ones, the only survivors on Earth or I should say from Earth. President Nixon and Brezhnev must comply with their demands; there is no choice; well, not a good one. Ivan, Victor, how do you see the operation, particularly Colonel Nikolai?"

Ivan goes first. "The colonel's assessment and your judgment are sound. Captain Duffy's instinct and quick action saved our lives; we are of course, most grateful. We can certainly give insight to Nikolai's thought process. May I use your map, Colonel?"

"Of course."

Ivan stands and studies the map, his finger lands on the north-south power lines. "Sir, this is my assessment; Nikolai is senior KGB and he would know best how to elude his own kind. My guess is, that he did. It is drilled into all of us from, our first day of training, to have a backup plan and a backup after that; that is the way we think, like chess players. So, assuming he hasn't been captured, he would have a loyal subordinate establish a backup rendezvous point. Not downtown; I would say near the airport, where he would have many locations to choose from, and the benefit of cover in plain sight. It is possible that he somehow gained access to one of our most secret operations, the name translates roughly to Operation Homecoming deep cover sleeper agents. I fear this because, it could cause great damage to your country and our mission. I believe his backup plan would be to disrupt this mission, and most likely, to kill the children as to deny America of their superior genetic stock."

The general says, "Go on Ivan; you have my attention."

"Sir, it is my observation that Nikolai is showing the effects of long-term amphetamine abuse. The last time I time I saw him, he looked as if he hadn't slept in days, and his demeanor was – unstable, I can't think of the right word, but not right in the head. The attempt on our lives and the fact that Victor and I have defected to your base are known at our highest government levels. He knows that he is considered a failure; his personality will refuse to accept that and he will want to redeem himself. He has always been ruthless and cunning, but he is also now desperate and drug-crazed; very dangerous."

"Victor, I would like to hear your input, please."

"Sir, I agree with Ivan's assessment, and I can add a few things. First, I say again he believes that we are being fooled into weakness; he is convinced the story about "The Others" is complete nonsense. He is, however, a believer in genetic superiority, he thinks the weak and undesirables should be eliminated. Only the strong and intelligent should be allowed to propagate; he believes in genetic stock. Therefore, he would like to capture the children and return them to Russia, but with no support that would be impossible. His mind would automatically conclude to kill the children, as to deny superior breeding stock to the Americans, that's his plan."

"What else can you add to that? I want to know more about the Russian "sleeper agents."

"Sir, Ivan and I are being honest about that, we couldn't tell you more if we wanted to; it is a closely guarded secret; thankfully, I believe above Nikolai's rank and status."

"Except for safe houses" Ivan adds. "He would know of many mid-level safe houses and they would have the basic military supplies he needs. But I would be surprised if he had the access numbers and the required code phase to activate a sleeper."

"I still want to know more about these "sleeper agents;" tell me everything that the both of you know about them."

Victor says, "Sir, I can only tell you what I heard while drinking vodka with other agents, that had loose tongues with their drinks. The sleepers are chosen young; the ideal age for recruitment is around fourteen. That gives them about two years of training and they are inserted in the USA at the age of sixteen. The candidates are chosen by the KGB. They must be motivated, by not just love for their country, but also with unveiled threats against their families. An example would be a family member's release from prison, with a good lifetime job. Another thing that would be promised, would be apartment housing for their loved ones left behind. Deep cover agents know a violation of their oath would result in unpleasant things, for the ones that are left behind like a return to prison, or worse. I can't tell you where they are General, but I assure you they do exist."

"What would be the missions of these sleeper agents?"

Basic day to day activities, would be to photograph aircraft and bases. They would also be expected to obtain jobs in government or with government contractors, with universities, or possibly with utilities - such as the railroad, power companies, or oil companies and report on their activities. Those are the kinds of positions you will find them in, sir. And with that, I can never return home; and neither can you, Ivan."

Ivan says, "Sir, I would like to request political asylum for myself and my family."

"When this is over gentleman, I will have two priorities first, to root out these sleeper agents, and second, to make sure that you men and your families are safe in my country. Ok, I know you men can add more, so let's have it."

Victor speaks, "Sir, when Ivan was looking at the map, I saw that he had his finger on a specific point. It is my guess his finger is on the north-south power lines. The north side of the power lines, that's where Nikolai will be."

Ivan says, "Very good Victor, now tell the general why we know that."

"Nikolai has always admired and studied General Zhukov. As you men may know, he was the general in charge of the Stalingrad defenses, at a time when everything looked lost. Ruthless sacrifice and bold planning were required. Nikolai tries to think like that great general; in fact, it has always been his life's ambition to become a general."

Victor stands without asking and joins Ivan at the map. Ivan still has his finger on the power lines. "He will approach from behind, from the north; not only is it the high ground, it is in his nature. With his mind demented even more than usual, he will think of himself as doing hero's work very dangerous to our mission." With that, Victor sits back down.

Ivan says, "Remember I told you that I gave Nikolai the frequency of the tracking device? He will have no problem finding the town. I'm afraid that's all the information we can offer; please consider Victor and I are the ones best suited to take him out." Ivan takes his seat.

The room is quiet for a long minute.

"God damn it all to hell!" It is Colonel Knight. "My hands are tied, and the only thing for me to do is to stand by the evacuation helicopters, damn!" He slaps his legs and stands up, clearly frustrated.

The general says, "I understand Colonel, but that's exactly what I want you to do; take charge of the evacuation. It is my intention to play the cards that are dealt, and you two Russians are cards that are in my hand; they are cards that are meant to be played. Ivan and Victor are to neutralize the threat of Nikolai. I need your plan please, either of you."

Victor again gets up and looks at the map without asking for permission. "There," he says, "We need to be inserted there." His finger is on a yellow circle on the north side of town. "The yellow circles are where the power lines cross, the first intersecting roads. Nikolai will have a map identical to this, and he will reach the same conclusion. Colonel Knight is correct in not liking the power lines. It is the weakest point, and also the high ground."

"Ivan?"

"I agree that will be his approach; an encircling move. Your orders General?"

"I don't like any of this, but I have to go with my instincts. My instinct is to trust the Russians to take care of their own problem, and of course ours also. I want everyone here to know the rationale of my decision. The "Others" insisted on cooperation between our two countries and I believe Victor and Ivan are sincere in their desire to bring this mission to a successful conclusion. Colonel Knight, organize the helicopter squadron. All men assigned to the helicopter squadron are to rest all day and go on duty at 12:00. Captain Duffy, see to it that Victor and Ivan have everything they ask for; use Sergeant Rufus and the 68 Impala to insert them at the point they chose; then, make your way to New Canton. Colonel Knight, meet me in my lower office at 15:00. Good luck men, dismissed."

Thirty-Two

General Brandon is alone in his office when his phone rings it's his secretary, Sergeant Thompson. "Good morning, General, several telefaxes have arrived to your attention. Sir, one is from Senate Majority Leader Mike Mansfield; he wants to know when you can be in Washington to begin Senate confirmation hearings on your appointment to secretary of defense. Congratulations on your appointment, sir; I trust you will need my services in Washington?"

"Of course, Sergeant Thompson I will insist on it. What else?"

"Joint Chiefs of Staff Admiral Moorer is asking for a phone call to his secure line in Pearl Harbor."

"What else Sergeant?"

"General Westmoreland has somehow caught wind of what is going on, and wants to be included in the loop."

"Is there anything else, Sergeant?"

"There is a long list of phone messages for you. Would you like me to read them to you now?"

"No, that's enough for now; I will be down there in about an hour. Please call motor pool and arrange transportation for me, golf cart only; I want Corporal Benson assigned to the duty."

"Yes sir."

Click, - he disconnects.

The general makes a two-sided list. On one side are the main points and questions for his phone call with President Nixon; on the other side are questions for Curtis Knapp. He can't get his mind around the Knapp situation; it just doesn't make sense, not at all. Next, he calls the medical center and asks to speak with Dr. Bishop; he is the one responsible for the autopsy on Kenneth Rushie. When Dr.

Bishop comes on the line, the general immediately asks "Do you have any details on Director Rushie's death?"

"Yes, General. I can safely say the cause of Director Rushie's death is due to a ruptured aortic aneurysm. He also had other conditions that justify the medications he was taking. I just got off the phone with the lab in Quantico. They found no poison in his blood, the pill bottles, or the empty liquor bottles. His blood alcohol level was 1.6, he died drunk sir."

"Thank you doctor, that's what I needed to know."

There is a light knock on the door.

He says, "Come." A nervous private comes in, clutching a briefcase with both hands.

"Colonel Knight told me to bring this to you; he told me not to drop it."

"Put it on the desk private, that will be all."

The private carefully places it on the desk, salutes, and quickly leaves.

The general unties the string that is holding the case together and removes the papers. The colonel had the locks removed, and the silk interior had been slit on all sides to check for anything that may have been hidden. After reviewing the contents for the second time General Brandon places the Positive Operational Review on his desk. He puts the ink smudged, sloppy attempt at a last will and testament and Curtis' dismissal letter back in the case. The general then uses the string to tie the two halves of the case back together again. He just finished the knot, when there is another knock on the door. He picks up the case and goes out the door.

General Brandon steps into the hall. He gets in the golf cart and says, "Take me to the brig Corporal, Orange Level."

Make that Freedom Park, Benson; I need some fresh air."

When they get to Freedom Park it is crowded with personnel. I don't want to disturb these people Benson, go to the athletic fields. Once there the general says, "Come on Benson, let's walk a lap; normally I would jog, but I'm not dressed for it."

About halfway around the track, General Brandon says, "There is an upgrade scheduled to the base, starting next month. We are going to add a new runway, and modernize and lengthen another. It is going to involve a lot of runway lighting and beacons. I am willing to arrange for your transfer to electrical engineering for this project. You should know Benson, the man in charge of this project is Colonel Mc Cray and he is a hard ass. He will delight in busting your hump. You can count on digging ditches and pulling cable. Every dirty job he can think of, just for you. If you survive the project, and the summer, you will be on your way to becoming an electrical engineer."

"Yes sir; absolutely, thank you."

"Glad to do it Benson, thank you for your service; now I need to get on with my day, let's go."

Again, they stop at the brig choke point barricade that leads to the underground brig facility. A different sergeant salutes and approaches the general. "How may I help you, sir?"

"I need an escort to meet me at the Orange Level."

"Yes sir." He gives a nod to the corporal in the bulletproof guard shack, and the gate opens. Sergeant Lang is waiting at the orange door when they arrive.

"No one has checked on him, sir. I can't tell you the status of prisoner Knapp, sir."

"I want to check his status now."

Sergeant Lang is the first through the cell block door. "Prisoner Knapp step back; now!"
He approaches Knapp's cell with his nightstick drawn, and is ready to use it. "Where's the rope, Knapp?"

"The rope and everything else are in the container."

"Everything is in there Knapp, the utensils too?"

"Yes sir, in the container."

Sergeant Lang pulls the field kit a few feet back. "Sir, do you want me to shake him down?"

"That won't be necessary Sergeant; privacy, please."

"I will be watching sir." With that, he closes the cell block door; Benson never steps across the threshold.

The general sits on the field kit and says, "You didn't like my rope, Knapp?

"I honestly don't know what came over me General. It's like I was truly possessed by the devil. Not that I ever believed that stuff, but I'm starting to. Something had a hold of my mind and was making me say awful things to my father; and worse, I meant them. That's gone now, sir. I don't feel any of that anger. I wouldn't normally act like that; it was like something was in my body and brain."

"I am so grateful that my father coming into my life when I was fifteen. He pulled me up. I didn't care that he was a pervert; maybe I am too, but I don't want to be. Yes, I am an asshole but try to understand how hard I had to work just finish high school, let alone Harvard. I couldn't even spell general; I earned my job at the Department of Defense."

"You may have Knapp; that is one of the things we have to talk about. I need your resignation,
now." He hands him a clipboard and a pen, "Write it."

Knapp does as he is told; he dates and signs the resignation, and hands it back.

"I want to know more about the conversation in the cafeteria. Exactly, when did you decide to sabotage this mission, and why?"

"It was just at that moment sir; when we were ordering our food. I had a chill run up my spine, and my mind wasn't my own anymore. I immensely enjoyed torturing the old man. His frustration and anger were like candy to me. Just the thought of being a part of the end of the world gave me the best high I ever had; do you understand?"

"No Knapp, I don't."

"I feel awful about the old man's death, but I didn't kill him, sir."

"The autopsy results aren't final yet, but Doctor Bishop is confident that the death was due to natural causes."

"Can I go?"

"No, Knapp, you are a guest of this brig, until I determine all danger is past. You aren't going anywhere in the meantime. I'm going to leave you with something to think about. He slides Kenneth Rushie's briefcase close to the bars. Apparently, you were a few breaths away from being fired and disinherited; you may do as you wish with these papers."

The general stands and says, "Goodbye Knapp."

"Thank you for the breakfast, sir; it woke me up in more than one way."

"Stay out of trouble Knapp. It looks to me like you're a wealthy young man with a future. A future brighter than it would have been; there is no future in being dead Knapp."

Thirty-Three

Nadia made it to the farm in only forty minutes. The farm is only about thirty miles from the motel, as the Airport Inn is on the west side of Omaha; she didn't tell Nikolai that. She has some time and she needs it. The first thing she does is go into the kitchen and open a few drawers. She finds the two items she is looking for, a Phillips head screwdriver and a sharp knife.

On both sides of the cabinet is ordinary white painted molding. She knows that two inches from the top and bottom and in the middle, are screws covered by putty and paint. She digs out the putty and removes the screws holding the molding. Next, she unlatches the hidden window locks.

When the cabinet is pulled back, a hole in the wall with a steep set of stairs is revealed. You can't call it an old fashion root cellar, as it's deeper than most of them, and not made from field stone. The walls and the ceiling are concrete, with many steel beams to support the thick layer of earth above. There is far more inventory than she told Nikolai, everything from mortar launchers to machine guns, as well as the basic 'beans, guns & bullets' that form a survival hoard, anywhere in the world.

Nadia only selects only what has been asked for; she already knows that weight and transport of these items is a major consideration. The rocket-propelled grenade launchers are of a two-part paratrooper model. Each steel base is fourteen pounds and the fragmentation grenade rounds weigh over two pounds each. She retrieves three launchers and nine light grenades and carries them to the small car; already more than sixty pounds, and that's close to the maximum weight that one solder can carry; and, none of the three of them are at optimum fitness. She carries the rest of the required items to the Volkswagen and goes back to secure the cabinet taking care to re-putty and repaint the molding, making the hidden room again, very hard to find.

If the Americans were looking for an underground room, they would use ground penetrating radar to cover every square inch of the concrete and wooden floor; they wouldn't find it. If the Russians were to look for it, they would use a dozen men with hammers tapping and dragging the hammers over every square inch of the floor and the walls, listening for the hollow sound a void makes.

The Russians would find the hollow behind the cabinet in less than an hour; but overall, it is an excellently hidden cache. Next, she fuels the Volkswagen from a farm supply tank, and checks the oil and the tires. She drives to the barn and removes a heavy toolbox and the canvas convertible top. There are items in the barn that she needs and she needs all the space the little car has to offer.

In the barn, she retrieves the items she ordered from an American auto parts mail order company. J.C. Whitney. Nadia is not as unprepared as she led Nikolai to believe; there are plenty of large trucks on the farm.

The farmland is leased to a neighboring farm now, but in the days her stepparents worked it, many trucks were required. There are Ford and Chevrolet pickup trucks around, as well as large flatbed and some dump trucks. She instinctively knows, the more weapons she brings, the less her chances will be to get out alive. Besides, she likes her Volkswagen "Thing."

J.C. Whitney offered an accessory called a four-post luggage rack. She bought that as well as a wicker basket, designed to be strapped down to the rack. She had bolted the four bases to the floor pan when the package arrived. It only took a few minutes to install the square posts and the top rack, securing it with clips and pins. She drags a step ladder over and straps the wicker basket to the center of the rack.

Next, she secures two 8' lengths of PVC pipe to each side of the rack. Each end of the pipes is fitted with a threaded cap. She copied the idea from the maintenance trucks at the university. They store small pipes inside a large pipe, great idea. It also works well for grenade launchers and rifles.

The stepladder goes in the back and she drives to the porch and uses it to load the vehicle. The last thing for her to do is to go to her dad's workshop and get three fishing poles and two floppy fishing hats, complete with fishing hooks on the brims. With the fishing poles lashed to the sides of the rack it will look more like they are on a respectable camping trip; not a mass murder expedition.

Thirty-Four

Shortly after ten o'clock, Gennady loses the transponder signal from the boys' sneakers. He glances over to Nikolai. He appears to be sleeping fully clothed, except for his shoes, on the top of the bed. He hasn't been acting right lately. His decision to take out Victor and Ivan and insert himself into the operation was risky; then disastrous.

He is still loyal to his colonel, but hopes that Nikolai can regain his wits. Gennady knows it would be best to think of a good suggestion to the problem, before he wakes the boss. At the moment it's better to let him rest; for more than one reason. He studies the map; they have been traveling north and still could be.

The problem is Woodstock is a rail junction, with an intersecting east-west rail line. It's also a river port, so they could be traveling by boat or rail north or east. He doesn't think they would go back to the south, the way they came, and the west maybe, but it seems like they would have stayed on that side of the river, if they intended to travel west. He keeps coming back to the east rail line; they were on a train and probably still are.

It's time to take some initiative. Gennady gets out the yellow pages and starts going through the pages one by one. Anything can be had in America with currency and the yellow pages. It doesn't take long to come to aviation. He is at an airport and nearby there are a half a dozen charter services and flight schools. It could work, but he needs a good cover story; and, what exactly is he looking for?

He starts scribbling notes in his notebook - city - county - hotels - tents - military base? City gets a line drawn through it; what's going to happen isn't going to happen in a city. The county gets circled, that makes sense. Hotels gets a line drawn through it, there won't be any large hotels in the middle of farmland. That gives him an idea; he writes farmland then neglected and overgrown farmland; he circles neglected and overgrown farmland.

Tents get a circle, as tents would be the ideal way to temporarily house a hundred teenagers in the middle of nowhere. Military base gets a line drawn through it, as when this started the two known children were only a few miles from the largest military base in the region. He looks at his notes and writes the circled words, country, farmland, tents. He adds train with a circle and boat with a line through it a bit of a gamble on that one, but so is the direction of travel he chose - east.

That's what he needs to look for from a low flying plane; a cluster of tents in country farmland. It is too early in the spring to have many campers about, if he finds a cluster of tents, that's got to be them. They will probably be near the railroad tracks, and probably east of Woodstock.

Able Charter Service is the first listing in the yellow pages; he dials and a gruff older sounding man answers. "Able Charter," is all he says.

In his smoothest American tone, Gennady inquiries about a two-hour charter.

"It depends on the type of equipment, number of passenger's, weight, and where you are going. What do you need?"

"I have in mind a two-hour flight; I would like to go north and east; I think maybe following the railroad tracks. I am looking for neglected and slightly overgrown farmland that hasn't been worked for a few years; that would mean that there is maybe a better opportunity to buy more land at a better price. Do you think that is something we could observe from the air?"

"Of course, that should be easy to spot; young scrub brush and saplings in large squares of unplanted land."

"My company has silos near the Woodstock rail line. That would make the transportation of grain economical; so, that is the area I want to search. A small plane would work as it would be only me traveling, no luggage. Would today be convenient?"

"Be here at noon no, 11:45. That way we will be in the air at noon. It will be four hundred dollars cash in advance, no checks. Is that acceptable?"

"Very good, may I have the address, please?"

"1958 Airport Road. You will see a Piper Aircraft Sales and Service establishment, three doors down from that you'll see Able Charter. If you get to the main airport, you went too far. I need your name for my flight records."

"Gennady Bujak; I'll see you at 11:45"

"11:45 Very good, see you then."

Gennady goes to his suitcase and retrieves the necessary funds. He scribbles a note to his colonel, explaining that he went for supplies and would return by 3:00 pm with Nadia; ready for the mission.

Nikolai begins to snore loudly; that's good Gennady thinks; he is sleeping soundly. He unplugs the phone, picks up his notebook, and goes out the door. He locks it and hangs the "Do not disturb" sign on the doorknob. He hopes no one will disturb the boss; that wouldn't be a good thing.

It hasn't been quite two hours yet; so, he has some time to kill before Nadia is due back. He walks to the front of the motel, where the restaurant is located, and looks in through a window. It is almost deserted; it's that slow time between breakfast and lunch. A newspaper box to his right catches his eye. "Historic Strategic Arms Limitation Summit underway in Moscow" is the headline showing in the display window. He deposits the necessary coins, pulls out a copy and goes inside.

The aroma of coffee, fried bacon and old grease inside the restaurant instantly assaults his senses. His eyes go straight to the rack of many different varieties of pie displayed under a clear plastic dome. He takes a seat at the counter and begins to read the front page.

According to the paper, the summit is going exceedingly well. A signed treaty reducing the nuclear arsenal of both countries is expected, as soon as the next day. He is just wondering how much of the story to believe when the waitress startles him.

"Do you need coffee, honey?" The waitress has large curls in unnaturally red hair. The name tag across her large bosom says, Naomi. She is holding a coffee pot in one hand and a large heavy mug in the other hand, ready to pour.

"Yes, please."

"What else can I get ya?"

"A slice of pie from the top of the rack, it looks good."

"You mean the Boston cream pie?"

"Yes, please."

"Ok, what else would you like?"

"I would like a BLT sandwich, but there is never enough bacon on them to suit me; could you make it with triple crispy bacon?"

"Of course, but I will have to charge you for two sides of bacon; you still want it?"

"Yes, make the sandwich to go with a large Coca-Cola."

She places the wedge of pie on a plate and serves it. "You're not from around here are you honey?"

"Germany, sweetie, I am here on business."

"Must be corn business, because that's all there is around here. Enjoy your pie; it will be a few minutes on the sandwich."

Gennady had just finished his delicious pie and coffee when the waitress, with the big red curls, returns with his sandwich in a brown paper bag and a large Styrofoam cup of Coca-Cola.

"You knocked that pie out in a hurry, it must have been good."

"Outstanding, thank you. What is the bill?"

"Let's see," she says, as she starts scribbling on a guest check. "That comes to five dollars and eight cents; the cook gave you lots of crispy bacon, just like you asked for."

He pulls out a ten-dollar bill and places it on the counter. "Many thanks," he says.

She smiles and says, "Do come back anytime honey."

Gennady sits on the bench, outside of room 33, and takes two bites of his mostly bacon sandwich. Damn, that's good he thinks; bacon is the best food in the world. The paper says the treaty will limit the number of missiles and launch sites of each country; it will also provide a protocol for communication when tense situations arise. A direct line will be established between Moscow and Washington to de-escalate situations. There will always be an available phone line between both high commands. If this is true, it will be a great thing. Nobody wants a nuclear war; well, almost nobody.

He can't help thinking something that's been in the back of his mind all day; that Nikolai is working without authorization. Maybe Nikolai is doing exactly the wrong thing. Perhaps he should check in with command by calling the number with the Washington D.C. area code, that he was required to memorize many years ago; he has never used it. He didn't know it at the time, but he now knows, it is a secure hotline to the Russian embassy.

After finishing the sandwich and the front-page newspaper article, Gennady walks to the road and circles the parking lot. He is uneasy, something does not feel right. That's it he thinks, he has never questioned an order, or a mission. This is the first time calling the

Washington phone number has ever crossed his mind. Is it necessary? He asks himself. As he is looking at the phone booths, in the corner of the parking lot, and considering making the call when the white Volkswagen, "Thing," Nadia behind the wheel, pulls in and stops in front of room number 33.

Without even realizing it, his mind has snapped back into mission mode. Gennady climbs into the passenger seat and simply says, "1958 Airport Road, it has to be back the way you came." In less than two minutes, Gennady says, "There," and points to a Piper Aircraft sign on the right. Once in the parking lot, he directs her to the third building down, Able Charter.

Gennady tears out a page from his notebook; "We require these items" he says.

Nadia looks at the list – boots with sizes, warm dark jackets with hats and socks.

He asks her, "Do you have enough currency?"

"Yes, Comrade, I have enough."

"Good, I want you to return here at 2:30 pm; do not go to the motel or disturb Nikolai." With that Gennady gets out and goes inside the Able Charter building.

Nadia thinks it will be a funny thing; an unlocked and very open automobile in a Sears parking lot, loaded with weapons and explosives. Americans are never suspicious of such things; in the Soviet Union, everything is suspect.

Thirty-Five

The decision has been made; things are in motion. Tonight, it will happen. General Brandon is in his lower office watching the big board and waiting for the phone call from President Nixon. The Russian agents are charged with a mission that the best and most experienced American two-man team should have been assigned. Why did he do that? He can justify it now, or if he ever has to.

Hell, if this goes wrong, he'll never have to justify his decision to anyone. What is bothering the general is the way he came to the conclusion to use Ivan and Victor. His mind never considered other alternatives. That's not the way he commands. Normally every option is on the table; not this time. The order to send Ivan and Victor came out of his mind and mouth like he was a puppet. The worst part is, he knows why. It is exactly what the "Others" want. Its ok he thinks; it's ok. He pulls out the bottom drawer and a bottle of scotch; he pours a tall drink.

Colonel Knight attended to the details of the evacuation, and took the general's advice; he retired to his quarters for a rest.

Captain Duffy brings more than just a suit. A coat and tie are fine for meeting with the police chief but after that, he wants to blend in, not stick out like a sore thumb. He packs jeans, T-shirts, checkered flannel long sleeve shirts and work boots. While studying the maps and aerial photographs, he noticed a small stream that runs along the ridge north of town then bends to follow the tracks, probably all the way to the river. He brings his fishing pole, a great way to scout the area; there might even be some trout in that stream.

Colonel Knight assigned Sergeant Rufus the duty of transporting Ivan and Victor to the first road north of New Canton, that intersects with the power lines. The shop is Rufus' first stop, and then on to the quartermasters to get his spies geared up. The "68" Impala is in the shop getting the new radial tires. The Parts Nazi, Sergeant Gillfus, looked at the requisition form signed by Colonel Knight and said, "It will be a few hours."

Rufus wishes he had a picture of Gillfus's face when he said, "Thirty minutes, I need the car in thirty minutes; you can check with the colonel if you like." It is perfect.

When Rufus lets the Russians in on his feud, his joke on Gillfus, Victor roared with laughter until he had a coughing fit. It lightened up Ivan's mood also.

"It's going to be all right!" It is Victor. "I know it! Up until yesterday, I was miserable, just like Nikolai. I know now, I just have to kill that prick. Then it will be all right."

Thirty-Six

Captain Robert Duffy found Chief Sullivan on the old passenger station platform. Sullivan said, "I'm not at all surprised that you are here. In fact, I have been expecting someone like you to show up." Sullivan looks Duffy up and down and says, "My gut feeling is that we will work well together; I hope it's not wrong. One thing though Duffy, you have to lose the suit."

"I know, here comes the train; I'm going to step back out of the way and let you handle this, there is more we need to talk about."

The mood in the caboose is more than quiet as the train slowed, it is almost somber. Brownie and Christine are sitting on the front platform, each with an arm around the other. Christine's other arm is holding the Gray Kitty and she is talking to it.

Walt and Louise are doing the same thing on the rear platform. The two other couples, John and Sandy and Mark and Betty have been talking at the lunch table, but no words have been spoken for a while.

"I'm scared," Betty says, "This is so weird." "Me too," it is Sandy. "I mean I wasn't scared, but I am now. I think we are there." "It's ok," John says, as he takes Sandy's hand. The train stops. Eight young men and women rise as four couples and step off the caboose for the last time.

There are only three people on the platform, Pete the Brakeman, a policeman, and a woman. Pete introduces them as Chief Pat Sullivan, and his wife Carol.

Carol speaks first. "If you look across the tracks you will see a tent city set up for one hundred young men and women. Volunteers are about finished building the outhouses, but I want you to know there are bathrooms here at the station. You are welcome to use the facilities at our community church; we use the one church to serve all faiths around here; it is half a mile up the road. There are showers in the bathrooms; of course, it will be unlocked."

"Food and drink are in that big army tent in the center; that's like headquarters. There are town ladies in there that will help you with whatever you need. Tractors and hay wagons are our transportation. Around here kids start driving them at around eight years old. They are easy to drive; use them if you want, just don't try to drive fast; slow and easy, all right? I better let my husband speak but first; everyone say your name, that way we are not strangers anymore." They all say their names. "Good; go ahead, Pat."

"All right, there is not much to say. Every one of you knows that you are meant to be here and everyone in this town knows that we are meant to support you; in any way possible. One more thing, I am the police chief in this town and I will protect you from any harm; I promise."

Sandy says, "Look Betty, that beat up brown car over there. It's that guy from the carnival! Shit, he is still after us!"

Carol says, "If all of you would climb into the hay wagon, I'll give you a ride over there."

"Tell that Policeman."

"You tell him, Betty."

"Ok," Betty says "Now would be a good time."

"Excuse me sir;" Betty says, and she makes the sign to come closer. He bends down. She cups her hand and whispers in his ear. "Excuse me, sir; that man over there in the brown car, he has been after me and my cousin, Sandy. He wants to make us sideshow girls for his carnival; he had us locked up in a trailer. It's prostitution that he had in mind for us. There were other girls there, I think all hooked on drugs. We escaped and he wants us back. We are very afraid of him and what he will do to us if he catches us. Can you make him go away? Maybe arrest him?"

"I see him; don't point. Go ahead and join the rest of your gang. I'll take care of him, don't worry."

Pat Sullivan had a niece mixed up in that kind of thing. She was murdered two years ago in a back alley on the dark side of Omaha. His sister has never gotten over the loss; or himself for that matter. Pat is not a small guy, or a guy you would want to mess with when he is mad. What this girl Betty just told him makes him more than steaming, screaming mad; he wants this guy's hide.

He glances toward the brown car and it's gone. Pat Sullivan's adrenaline and all his sense are sharpened. It's an old familiar feeling, he is on a search and destroy mission. This time it's his hometown and this guy is messing with children he has sworn to protect. The guy doesn't know it yet, but he is messing with the wrong man. Pat waits a few seconds to let the kids climb aboard the hay wagon. He takes quick long strides toward his 1970 Ford Galaxy police cruiser. Captain Duffy had been watching from the shadows, observing everything. He reaches the passenger door of the cruiser at the same time as Chief Sullivan. Captain Duff asks, "Trouble?"

"Did you see that brown Chevy at the corner?"

"Yes, I noticed it."

"That guy is stalking two of our girls, its trouble for him."

The Galaxy fires up and leaps forward, just short of burning rubber. After making a right turn at the corner Chief Sullivan floors the Ford and in no time flat, they are doing better than one hundred miles an hour.

Crazy Tony had just made up his mind to give up on the girls and go back to Florida. He would have been better off if he had made the decision ten minutes sooner. A police car is right on his ass, flashing red light and siren going. He is getting pulled over, for what? He didn't do anything and he is not even speeding. He pulls the Chevy to the shoulder and stops the car.

Chief Sullivan opens his door but he doesn't get out. He picks up the microphone and flips a switch from radio to the bullhorn. "Driver! Step out of the car and walk slowly to the front of my patrol car."

Crazy Tony gets out and takes two steps toward the cruiser, and he stops.

"You better move it, boy!"

Crazy Tony just realizes that he still has the cheap blue barrel 38 special tucked in the front of his pants. He is thinking that he should have ditched it, or at least put it under the seat. He is not too bright, no choice now but to do what the officer says. He walks slowly to the front of the car.

"Hands on the hood!"

He does as he is told. He is bent over with his hands on the hood.

"Spread those legs boy! You're under arrest!"

Crazy Tony asks, "What did I do wrong? What am I being arrested for?"

"Suspicion of being an asshole! Now, I don't want to hear any lip out of you or I'll take you right to jail!"

"But, I..."

That's all it took for Chief Sullivan to grab the back of his scruffy hair and slam Tony's face on the hood of the patrol car. For good measure, he rotates Toney's face three times like he is waxing the car with his face. Chief Sullivan stops long enough to handcuff his hands behind his back. He squeezes the cuffs just as tight as he can make them.

"Let's see, where were we? Oh yeah, right here." His hand goes inside Tony's belt and grips the handle of the stub nose 38. "This is nice," Sullivan says, "I'm very tempted to do the world a favor. I would hate for a creep like you to reproduce." He roughly jams the barrel of the 38 deep. He loosens Tony's belt. "Better angle this way," he says. "I might even get a three for one. What do you think Captain Duffy? He shot his own balls off pulling a gun on me."

"My orders are not to interfere with how you run your town, or step on your toes. I will back you up whatever you decide."

Sullivan thinks for a few seconds then removes the pistol and hands it to Captain Duffy.

"I forgot to ask you creep; do you have a permit to carry a pistol in the great state of Iowa?"

"No."

"How about a driver's license? I didn't find a wallet."

"My wallet was stolen yesterday."

"This is getting better all the time, Captain." With that, he takes Tony's handcuffed hands and pulls straight up with all of his strength. Tony stands immediately, but not fast enough to avoid both shoulders being dislocated.

Tony howls in pain.

"Come on," The chief more than half drags Tony to the passenger side, rear door. "Let me help you in." He puts one hand on top of Tony's head like a concerned police officer and says, "Watch your head." Tony is about halfway in the car when Sullivan's right knee comes up into Tony's rib cage. The ribs that were only cracked are now broken, and the undamaged ribs are now damaged. Tony is splayed out on the back seat coughing on his own blood and wincing at the pain in his ribs, wrists, and shoulders every time he coughs or moves. For some reason he can't get the image of the shiny white hood out of his mind, then the shiny white hood with red swirls.

The pace for the ride back to town is much slower than the ride out. They ignore the moans from the back seat.

"Hey chief, that stream that runs along the ridge, any trout in it?"

"Oh yeah, it's loaded with rainbow; been fishing it since I was a kid, why?"

"I brought my pole; I would like to try my luck."

"You can't miss buddy, tell you what; let me put this punk away and I'll join you. Follow the stream up the hill until you come to a small pool. There is a nice big oak tree there with a flat rock under it. That's my spot, I'll meet you there in an hour, where's your car?"
"It's up there at the front of the station."

"That you're Pontiac?"

"Yes."

"That's a sharp car, I like it."

"It's a 1970 Bonneville Deluxe; I was going to trade it in the first of the year, but I like it better than the new ones. While I was at the dealership I noticed a convertible, just like that one on the used car lot. I bought it and couldn't be happier with my purchase. These cars look nice and drive like a dream. I plan to keep them."

Sullivan drops him off at his car, "See ya' in an hour."

Captain Duffy changes into more presentable country like clothes in the station restroom. He grabs his pole and a light backpack out of the trunk. He walks the tracks passing all of the activity on the left; he observes but doesn't speak to anyone.

He stops at the place where the stream crosses under the tracks and baits his hook with a red Canadian night crawler. It is the perfect bait; all fish love them. The third cast produces a medium size rainbow. He releases it and continues upstream to the place Sullivan told him about. It looks like a perfect fishing hole. It has a good view of a slightly sloping, freshly planted, corn field with a wooded ridge behind it.

Captain Duffy sits behind the oak tree and takes a small pair of Zeiss binoculars out of his pack. He stays low and moves to a better position. He slowly scans the ridge and the wooded area this side of the power lines. Ivan and Victor should be up there by now; he can't see them, but that's because they don't want to be seen. It's the out-of-control Russian colonel that he is worried about. Where is he? Did everybody guess wrong about his intentions and his approach?

Duffy comes out of the cover, re-baits his hook and is about to make his first cast when he hears, then sees, Sullivan splashing up the center of the stream. He seems to have all the gear, waders, fishing vest, small backpack, a wicker fish basket, and his pole.

Sullivan sees Duffy and ask's, "Any luck?"

"Some, very nice spot, thanks for sharing it with me."

"No problem. Thanks for your help with the creep."

"You're welcome, got him locked up, ok?"

"Yeah, I put him in the courthouse holding cell. I have one of those old fashion sheriff offices, the kind with two cells on the far wall. He is much safer at the courthouse than he would be if I had to look at him."

"Good thinking Chief, lets fish. Should we keep what we catch?"

"Oh, Hell Ya! I have everything I need to fry them perfect and delicious; I'm going to fry them up on one of those campfires over there. I need to find that girl named Betty and her cousin and tell them they never have to worry about that punk again; he's going away for at least three to five, maybe more."

Thirty-Seven

Gennady opens the door to Able Charter and finds himself in a long hallway with an open door at the far end. Both sides of the hall are lined with pictures, all the way down. Some World War II shots catch his eye and he stops to examine them. There are pictures of B-17's in formation and pictures of B-17's on the ground, the flight crew, and the ground crews are posing together for the shot. There are similar pictures of P-51's in formation, high above a squadron of B-17's, definitely a combat mission. Also, there are a few framed newspaper articles, he does not read them; there is business at the end of the hall. He knocks on the doorframe.

"Come in, Mr. Bujack?"

"Yes, please call me Gennady and I'm sorry, I didn't get your name."

"Junior, just call me Junior everybody else does, my real name is Horace. I like Junior better. Look, I laid out a rough flight plan." He points to a piece of tracing paper overlaying an area map, the flight plan penciled in. "It's only going to take about an hour to cover this area, if you want to see more you call the path, ok?"

"If it's less than two hours, you may still keep the full amount."

"All right, that reminds me, did you bring the cash Mr. Bujack?"

"I did." Gennady takes out eight fifty-dollar bills, folded in half, and drops them on the desk
between an open can of Budweiser and a half full square bottle of brown liquor.

Junior sees him staring at the whiskey bottle and says, "I never drink the hard stuff before noon. But, it's almost noon." With that, he takes a silver flask out of a drawer and fills it. "Let me take a leak and I'll be ready; you might want to hit the can to buddy. The plane is out back. I'll be out in a minute."

"Put your belt on if you want, it's worthless in a crash, but if we hit a downdraft, it will save your neck from being broke on the ceiling." Junior picks up the microphone and calls the tower, "Able- 14, requesting clearance to depart." A reply is immediate.

"You have about three minutes to get clear Junior, traffic is incoming."

"Thanks, Jack, I'm taking her up." Junior lines the Piper Cub up with the center of the runway. He holds the brakes while increasing the engines RPM's. At almost full throttle, he releases the brakes and the plane gathers speed and lifts off.

"I figure we'll stay low for this trip, under 5,000 feet. Maybe well under. If we fly too high, we won't spot the telltale signs we talked about; too low and we won't see much either. We are at 2,000 feet, heading north and a touch east. That's the Missouri River and the railroad track next to it is the one you mentioned. Give me a minute and I'll get right over it and follow the tracks. It will be a few minutes before we get to farmland, and there will be lots of it."

"Did you fly in the war?"

"Yeah, big ones and little ones, but I don't like to talk about it."

They fly on without speaking until Junior says, "Hey, do you know what a negative G is?"

"No, what's a negative G?"

Junior pushes the small plane into a steep dive. "See the way your ass wants to come up out of the seat? That's a negative G." He gives it full throttle and pulls back on the yoke and the Piper Cub pulls up out of the dive. "That's a positive G, a weak one I admit. Now, if I had a jet well, you would really know about positive G's."

"You know, I never did get to fly one of them jets; they didn't come into service until after the war. I guess if I had stuck with the Army Air Corps, they would have given me one, but I would have been flying in another war, Korea. The way I figure it is a man can only be lucky so many times. I believe I used all of my war luck up; so, I passed and got out of the service."

"When jet airplanes started coming into civilian service, nobody would let me fly one. They said I needed schooling, training and some kind of certificate. Fuck that! I could jump in one of those machines and fly circles around the young punks. It still pisses me off though, what's this world coming to? Hey, there's your east-west track; you want to follow it or continue north for a while?"

"Let's follow it east, and then we'll go north, and double back."

"That looks like one right there."

"Where?"

"Off to the left, 10:00. See that? That's just what you are looking for, a bit more overgrown; it might have been sitting five or six years, the little trees aren't so little. Let's go down and buzz it."

After the view from above and three low passes, Gennady and Junior both have a good feel for what they are looking at. It looks to be fifty or sixty acres, with an old farmhouse and a barn with half a roof. There are several rough outbuildings and the dirt road leading to the farm is choked with brush and not so young trees. Nobody has set foot on this farm for years. Gennady takes out a notebook and writes the details.

"Do you know the name of the blacktop road?" He points.

"That's county route 38, we look to be eight to nine miles northeast of Woodstock. I'll give you the map quadrants when we get back, seen enough?"

"Yes, I would like to follow the tracks east, please."

"You got it", the plane climbs and turns SE. Junior reaches in the door pocket and pulls out a large silver flask, "Drink," he asks?

"Don't mind if I do." Gennady says, using an American phase he recently picked up. They both take a long pull from the flask.

"Tennessee whiskey," Junior says, "What do you think?"

"Very different from what I am used to; I thank you for sharing it with me."

"You're welcome, more?"

"I don't want to consume all of your whiskey."

"Don't worry I have more, drink up."

Gennady takes another long pull on the flask and says, "Can we go higher, please? I would like a good view."

"Of course, you're the paying customer." He laughs as he throttles the plane up.

Gennady asks "Do you have a pair of binoculars?"

"Ya, reach around behind you, they are in a case." Gennady finds the case and begins to scan left to right, paying particular attention to the track below. Movement is the first thing that catches his eye, maybe six miles ahead on the north side of the track. What initially catches his eye is, the movement of a yellow backhoe; and, now he can see a red dump truck and hay wagons moving around and tents; lots of tents are set up. As the plane gets closer, he can see activity, a lot of people are moving around and judging from the way they move, they look young. He lets Junior fly over it without saying anything, until they are well past the gathering. Gennady instructs Junior to fly north and lose some altitude.

The farmland below has many areas that fit the search requirements; he takes careful notes and asks a lot of questions. Gennady is starting to think he came up with a good idea in spotting undervalued land from the air, he is thinking about using this information for his own benefit; does that make him a capitalist now? He has to wonder if the high command, at the Kremlin, ever thought of it. Maybe they do it with spy satellites now. Or maybe they never thought of it at all.

"I would like to angle south and east, and maintain this altitude, please."

There are two more farms to check out before they again reach the railroad tracks. "We can head back now." Gennady says, "I would like to follow the tracks again, west."

"No problem, Mister, how about another drink?" Gennady accepts and Junior finishes what is left in the flask. "Hey, would you mind giving me a refill? There is a bottle behind you in the same spot where you found the binoculars."

Gennady refills the flask, he doesn't mind, the less Junior remembers about this flight the better.

"There, that town up there, what is all of the activity?"

"Damned if I know, it looks like maybe they are going to have one of them rock concerts, like the one they had a few years ago in New York."

Gennady looks hard at the scene below. He notices, there is no stage, no big trucks carrying equipment, and not enough people. He doesn't say so, but it's not a rock concert; it's the group of children he is looking for.

"Need another pass?"

"No, make your best time back to the airport, please."

Junior angles the plane southwest. The little Piper Cub lands and Junior eases it back, in its spot. After chocking the wheels and giving the plane a quick walk around inspection, Junior says, "That's enough work for one day. I'm going to do some paperwork, get your map quadrants and go to the bar. Care to join me?"

"No, but I do have an hour to kill before my ride arrives."

"That's fine, come on in and we'll have a drink. Come on, this time we have ice!"

Junior provides Gennady with map quadrants for every entry in his notebook. The whiskey flows and the war stories pour out of Junior.

Gennady had met many combat veterans who either chain smoked or drank to excess, sometimes both. At 2:20 pm, Gennady stands and thanks Junior for the flight and the drinks.

"Any time buddy; you know if we look a little further north and east, we will find plenty of land, at a better price."

"Yes, but the transport of the grain is an expensive headache. That's why I want to stick closer to the tracks and the silos."

"Very good sir, thank you and goodbye. Come back anytime."

Thirty-Eight

Nadia parks in the same parking place as before; in front of the Able Charter sign; it is 2:10. She had plenty of time to complete her assignment. There was enough time to enjoy a lunch special at the mall. The mall's Chinese's restaurant had her favorite, cashew chicken with a side of hot and sour soup.

She had first tried hot and sour soup, on the advice of a colleague who brought her some when she was trying to recover from a severe bout of the flu. She hadn't been able to keep anything down for days and was weak as a kitten. The soup was delicious; she held it down and immediately felt better. Today is a good day to get some of that energy in her. She feels better, but just can't figure a way out of this mess. She intends to keep her eyes open and to weigh all of the alternates.

"What is all of this?" It is Gennady. He is looking at the packed car with all the bags and boxes, there is nowhere to sit.

"It is every item requested of me. You can wiggle in; perhaps Comrade Nikolai and you can do a better job of packing."

"Very well, back to the motel Nadia, I sincerely hope the colonel is rested and in better spirits."

The door to room 33 is wide open and the television is playing loudly. Gennady motions for Nadia to stay back while he enters. Nikolai is standing at the mirror in his underwear shaving; when he sees Gennady, he actuality smiles.

"I hope you brought me fresh clothes."

"Yes, Comrade Colonel. Nadia has been securing supplies all day. In fact, we may have too much, there is no room in the vehicle to sit."

"Bring me my change of clothes please, and we will lighten the load. I have decided this will simply be an overnight mission, not a three-day excursion. We will need only one day of supplies. Have you eaten?"

"I have had some food, Comrade Colonel."

"Go to the restaurant and get us three good meals with Coca-Cola. Also, go to the office and pay for another week on these rooms; we will use them to store our excess equipment. First, bring me my clothes."

Gennady instructs Nadia to go to the restaurant and get the three meals; and, after a second thought, he adds, get six bottles of Coca-Cola and a large black coffee also. "I will walk up front with you; I need to pay our room bill."

When Nadia comes out of the restaurant carrying a large cardboard box, Gennady is waiting for her. "Can I carry that for you?"

"No, com –" she stops herself from saying 'comrade' in public, just in time; she is out of practice.

"I would like to speak to you about the corn business; you should be knowledgeable in that area." He pulls out his notebook.

"Yes, my parents operated a farm, as you know."

"Yes, I am curious; our country has an existing agreement with the Americans, regarding corn exports. How do we benefit from having agents poised as corn farmers?"

Nadia smiles and tells him, "Since the very first days of the treaty com –" she stops and looks around. "Comrade Khrushchev ordered a 10% overload on all departing ships. We add 10% off the books, now 20% is required."

"And the transport ships; they aren't already fully loaded?"

"Yes, they simply travel overloaded."

"Ah, I see. My earlier flight was very successful, I reacquired our targets. My cover story is that I am looking for neglected and abandoned farmlands; I found six in just an hour. How can they be abandoned? It's good land, why wouldn't somebody work it? The government wouldn't just take it over?"

"The farms usually become abandoned because of a death in the family, and no family member is willing to step up and do the hard work of farming. If the taxes go unpaid, the government will take it over, but they won't work the land, it will be sold to the highest bidder at auction."

"Is the water good in these towns?"

"There is good groundwater in this entire area but, you have to drill to get it. She taps the notebook with her finger; find one of these with good deep wells and you will always have a crop."

The conversation stops as they enter room number 33. The T.V. volume is turned down and Nikolai turns the desk sideways and places a chair on both sides. The bedside table light is removed and placed at the foot of the bed, near the desk. Nikolai says "We will have to make due using these for tables. Let me help you with that," he takes the box from Nadia and places a Styrofoam container at each place. "What did you bring us?"

"It's the blue plate special; today its meatloaf, mashed potatoes, and of course corn, there is also cornbread and peaches."

"Everybody eat up! It might be a long night." Nikolai looks Gennady in the eye. "I checked the transponder signal, there is no signal. Why am I not worried about that?"

Gennady tells him about his charter flight and the gathering he had found. He identified it on the map, as a town called New Canton. He slides the map across the desk.

Nikolai asks a lot of questions and Gennady lets him come to the obvious conclusion on his own. He will take advantage of the power line road and find camouflage in the south side of the wooded area. It will be a perfect place to finalize his plan of attack.

Nikolai studies the map, makes notations in his book and finishes his meal. He asks, "Are we ready?"

"Please, bring the supplies in; leave the weapons and ammunition. We will take only what we need, I'll clean up."

Gennady raises a thick eyebrow, but he doesn't say anything. He nods to Nadia, and together they go about the task.

Nikolai cleans up and returns the furniture to its original positions. He next proceeds to sort the items as they are carried in, he uses both beds. "Everything on this bed can be repacked in the vehicle, where are the weapons, Nadia?"

"Comrade Colonel, it would be easier to show you than to tell you; please, look."

At the door, she points to the pipes on the roof rack. "The weapons and most of the requested ammunition are stored in the pipes."

"And the fishing poles Nadia?"

"They are our cover; we are going fishing."

Nikolai laughs so hard he has to sit down. "Come he says, close the door. I want you both to know that I no longer wish to be a general. I'm going to skip that and move up to a director's position, maybe even Chief Marshal. Gennady will serve our Motherland well, as a general. And you Nadia, the knowledge, wisdom and the American experience you have gained makes you a most valuable asset to the Soviet Union. I will see to it that you receive the rank of full colonel with the responsibility of implementing training programs at our American compound. I believe we are ready; we must be in place well before nightfall."

Nadia feels her heart stop. Returning to Russia is the last thing she wants. She smiles and says, seemingly sincerely, "That would be an honor, Comrade Colonel." Inwardly she's sick, there has to be a way out of this. She can't see it at the moment, but she must find a way.

The repacked Volkswagen now has three uncluttered seats, not quiet plenty of room, but certainly better. When they are settled Nadia hands them the floppy fishing hats and cheap aviator style sunglasses. Her own sunglasses are sparkly pink with star-shaped lenses. A Cincinnati Reds baseball cap completes the appearance she had planned.

After twenty minutes on Interstate 80 east, they exit and proceed north at a slower pace. Talking while on the interstate is impossible because of the wind and the screaming of the little engine.

Nikolai asks, "How much further Nadia?"

"It is twelve miles to a town called Hampton. From there, we turn east on County Route 38, it will be six miles to the power lines and about four miles on the access road, before we come to the point you indicated on the map."

"Very well, concealment will be important and this white vehicle stands out. I should have told you to get some green paint to break up the silhouette. There is a hatchet and some rope with our supplies. When we get to wooded cover, we will lash some greenery to this "Thing.""

Thirty-Nine

General Brandon has grown tired of waiting for the red phone to ring. He flips back to the first page of his notebook and dials the numbers to connect with Air Force One. After a series of clicks, a clear voice comes on the line, "Air Force One, Captain Taylor speaking."

"This is General Brandon, is the president available?"

"I will check sir; I was told to put you through to Mr. Kissinger when you called. Stand by one."

Two more clicks and an extension is ringing.

Captain Taylor says, "When Secretary Kissinger disconnects, stay on the line and I will make sure that you are transferred to the president, or I will be right back with you, sir."

In the same nasally voice the general heard before, Kissinger says; "Kissinger."

"Good morning, Secretary Kissinger, General Brandon here."

Secretary Kissinger speaks slowly and precisely. "General, I am to inform you of a change of plans. At the conclusion of the official signing of the Anti-Ballistic Missile Treaty, the president intends to fly to Berlin. Cronkite, Brinkley, Huntley, you name the reporter; they're all in Berlin, screaming for a press conference."

"He is going to give them one. It will be a victory speech and a very strong campaign speech, at the same time. It is a perfect opportunity, for more than one reason. It will also provide a window of opportunity for the president to secretly visit your base, and that's what he is going to do. Anyone and everyone especially the children that are a part of this, are to be present for a very private speech he intends to give. He will fly to Berlin, and then to Omaha, when he is supposedly sleeping in comfort. He then has to fly back to Berlin, and back to Moscow again, on Air Force One. The conference isn't scheduled to wrap up until the 29th. It is going to be difficult, especially on him. I think he is ready for your call, yes; his secretary just informed me that he is ready. Shalom General."

"Walter!" Nixon sounds genuinely glad to be on the phone with General Brandon. "Did Henry tell you about my plan to visit your base?"

"Yes sir, you want everyone involved assembled; but Secretary Kissinger didn't give me the details."

"Well, the devil is always in the details, isn't it Walter? It's going to be a little tricky, as I am coming in secret. I'll tell you the details in a minute, first I must ask; how are things proceeding on your end?"

"I am still worried about the out-of-control Russian colonel. I have tasked Ivan and Victor with taking him out. They are in place and have an ambush planned for when he arrives."

"Are all of the children present?"

"Sir, the last report I had from my captain on the ground was that the police chief's wife is mothering the kids and keeping count. Her count is ninety-two, with eight more due on the westbound freight train at any minute. The report indicates a smooth operation."

"Good, good. Aside from a rocky start, the Russians are behaving quite well. Our agents report that all are present, with no complications, at the central Poland site. I have every confidence the same will be true with your site, in Iowa. My Russian trip is not scheduled to conclude until the 29th; but, most all of our business will be finished with the signing of the Anti-Ballistic Missile Treaty. I asked Brezhnev if he would agree to a 24-hour break, with the pretense of high-level meetings and a press conference in Berlin. He agreed. Now the trick will be to get from Berlin to Omaha and back, fast and unnoticed. I have four, new, fully armed Phantom F-4's waiting to escort me to your base. I believe you know my personal pilot and commander of this mission, General Chuck Yeager."

"Yes, sir, I served with him the 363ed. I am the one that shared a half a kill with him on a 109. He has rarely spoken to me since. He didn't like the idea of half a kill, he thought that it should have all been his."

"Well, Walter, big balls come with a big ego, you know that."

"Yes sir, I see it every day."

"Yeager is the pilot I chose because, in my eyes, he is the best. Non-stop at better than 1,400 miles per hour, certainly cuts down on travel time; and I feel perfectly safe with him. I'm going to tell you something Walter, I get a kick out of those things. Almost nobody knows it, but I ride in those fuckers every chance I get. You know the feeling, straight up to 45,000 feet in a minute. It's a perk I love more than my bowling alley. The next best thing is, the revenge I get on my enemies. This office is great for that; fucking actors."

"Excuse me, sir?"

"Why can't they keep their big mouths shut? That pretty boy, the blue-eyed prick Paul Newman, made my shit-list with his stupid comments. The little prick is going to have a tax problem next year; I guarantee it; him and a bunch of other assholes. You know, I bet one of those acting pricks will run for president one day, and win."

"The American people know they have a strong leader in me, Walter. That clown Mc Govern doesn't have a chance. Watch the country speak in November. I wouldn't be surprised if I won every single state. Well, maybe not Massachusetts; those Kennedy cocksuckers have that state wrapped around their crooked fingers. They bribe and cheat at every opportunity, but I don't blame them for that; if you're not cheating, you're not trying. I learned that a long time ago. And, I damn sure try Walter.

"Your Russian agents, Ivan and Victor are in the clear. They are fully authorized to continue the mission and to remove Nikolai, permanently. All right, mission first; Walter, it absolutely must succeed. Secondly, I want these kids 100% taken care of, anything they need; ok?"

"Yes, sir."

"Now, when they arrive at your base, I want their families notified that they are safe. Make off like they stumbled into a top-secret military operation; that's not far from the truth anyway. Tell them that they're being debriefed and will phone within a few hours. Arrangements will be made to get them home as soon as possible, but they are not allowed to talk about what they have seen."

"Yes sir, anything else?"

"Have you decided to stay on as my secretary of defense?"

"I am honored by the offer sir, but I respectfully decline. I would like to call it a career, end it on a high note and retire."

"I understand, and have the highest respect for you General Brandon. I will see that you get one more star before your retirement. It will make the pension checks you earned a little bigger and you will also be paid for your time as secretary of defense. That brings me to another item. I have another job for you Walter; it will only require two or three days a month at full-time G-15 pay; along with many other perks. Are you interested?"

"Of course, sir, I would like to hear the details."

"Ok, let me start like this, General Chuck Yeager is going to be the only one present at the meeting tomorrow that wasn't directly involved in this operation. I have a reason for this. Yeager and your self are to be mentors to all one hundred of our kids. It will be a ten-year project, initiated by a classified executive order and funded by the National Security Administration. I will tie this to the Truman notebook. Anyone that has the authorization to open the file will leave it alone. In reality, it represents a few man hours and equipment costs. It is a minimal cost; peanuts in the national security budget. It's a can of worms, nobody in their right mind would care to open. Teach them to fly; that's what I have in mind. You and Chuck will certainly have their attention for a few hours at a time. What do you think Walter? Want to sign up for the best part-time job in the world? Your thoughts please Walter."

"Mr. President; I know the correct response as a general but I would like to ask for permission to speak with you as a civilian, as I soon will be."

"Absolutely Walter, speak your mind."

"I want a seaplane; I have always wanted one. With that, I can give my students flight time, land on lakes, fish off the wings, and fly to another one. In the summer we will do the Alaskan lakes; I'll give my students something to remember."

"Funny, Yeager said almost the same thing, except he wanted jet time with his students. Congratulations, you both just had a hundred kids. Any equipment either of you request, base privileges, maintenance, fuel, any and all costs, will be covered by the NSA. Are we good on that General?"

"One thing sir, I would like that plane to be in my name, but not the expenses."

Nixon laughs. "Good God Walter; you sound like a politician now; agreed, let's move on."

"I got a letter from President Truman this morning, can you believe that? He wasn't sure he would still be alive on this date; so, he enlisted the aid of the Postmaster General. He said that he knew the date May 26th, 1972 would be important to America. Every Postmaster General since 1948, has been charged with the safekeeping of the letter and the responsibility of delivering it to the sitting president on this day, no matter where I am. The fact that I am in Moscow, certainly made it difficult on our Postmaster. He had to make use of the diplomatic pouch and enlist the aid of our ambassador to Russia. The Postmaster and my ambassador delivered it to me just an hour ago, on Air Force One."

"President Truman wanted the sitting president to know that his thoughts were with me and that he is confident that I'll make the right decisions for America. Little did he know, the president would be me; Richard Nixon. I do admire him; I know now that he was a great president, but that son of a bitch always hated me."

"He also asked the sitting president to keep his notebook updated. He wanted me to send a letter to a future president if I had a similar premonition. He said this is the only detail he left out of his notebook. He ended the letter with; please keep America safe. He wished me success with whatever dilemma I am dealing with. That's it. When this is over, I am going to invite him to the White House. He deserves to see his updated notebook. President Truman did more for America than the American people ever knew, or will know. He never got the respect he deserved. I have to wonder if I'll wind up the same way. I know damn well the Democrats, and some Republicans too, would love to crucify me if they ever get the chance. Big day ahead of me, Walter, I have to get ready to go back to the Kremlin for the signing of the Strategic Arms Limitation Treaty. I'll see you soon Walter."

"Thank you, sir, I look forward to it."

"Anything you need, anything at all; I want you to call Captain Taylor at the switchboard and he will find the right person to resolve your issues. Good luck General."

"Good luck Mr. President"

Forty

Carol stops the tractor at the edge of the tent city, next to a yellow backhoe. A clean-cut young man jumps off the backhoe and helps the girls down. "Hello, I'm Pear;" he says it loud enough for everybody to hear.

Sandy says, "Pear, that's your name?"

"Yah, Pear like an apple; only I'm a Pear."

"That's a funny name; how did you get that?"

"When I was a little guy, I loved pears; hell, I still do. Anyway, my ma started calling me Pear, and it stuck."

Walt asks, "What's with the backhoe?"

"Sand, if I put a scoop of sand on the floor of your tent, it will be a lot smoother. How many tents do you want? I have a big one left, or you can have two smaller ones; whatever you want."

Mark says, "The big one please, we would like to stick together."

"You got it; makes it easier anyway. Let me make your sand pad and I'll be right back with your tent and sleeping bags." The young man with the strange name dumps and smooths the sand. He drives away toward the red dump truck.

Carol says, "Does anyone want a ride up to the church?"

"No thank you," Louise, says, "We all had a shower this morning at the Woodstock church."

"All right, get your tent set up and get settled; I'll be right back; I need to do a firewood run. Now don't forget, anything you want to eat or drink is at the big army tent in the center. You should all wander around a bit anyway. You're not going to believe the amount of stuff that's up there."

"Are the boots we brought there?" Louise asks.

"Every group brought a donation; along with most everyone else in this county. The boots and the Levies were your group's donation, along with Marge's care packages. You will have to look."

Betty says, "The St. Christopher's metals! I meant to show them to you on the train, but Dennis and his giant bonfire made me forget all about the medals. They are meant for us! Come on Mark, we have to go look for them."

"What about the tent? I have to help. And didn't we say that we were going to stick together?"

Walt says, "We're not going to need nine people to put up a tent. Take Sandy and John with you, we'll just make that the minimum; at least half our group is together at all times. Hell, everybody here is in the same boat we're in anyway."

"Hold on," Sandy says, "I want to talk to that Pear guy. He seems so confident and happy; it's like he's got stuff all figured out."

Brownie says; "What do you mean, figured out?"

"It's like he's on his way to something big, maybe like a politician or an important businessman."

Walt says, "We're all on our way to something big; and you won't have to wait long, here he comes."

The Gray Kitty jumps out of Christine's arms and goes to inspect the sand pad.

Pear stops the backhoe at the edge of the pad, lowers the bucket and climbs down. "This won't take long, less than five minutes; I've done a million of them." He shakes the tent out of a long bag and hands it to Brownie. "Here, you guys stretch out the four corners and I will stake it; we'll throw the poles up, and we're done."

"This is your business, tents and sleeping bags?"

"Yah, well, a lot more than that; I sell and rent anything to do with camping or fishing. It's finally starting to take off. Last fall, I was able to buy the boat I have always wanted. It was a hard road getting to the point of actually making a profit. When I first started, I had long hair and a beard. Nobody took me seriously. The equipment came back late, or not at all. Then I got smart, I shaved got a haircut and insisted on a deposit or collateral, like the title to a motorcycle or car. After that my equipment always came back, and I was making a profit."

"What do you call it, I mean what's the name of your business?"

"Pears Camping and Fishing Equipment, rent, buy, sell or trade."

Sandy says, "Yuk" and there are seven more yuks and groans.

"You have to come up with a better name than that," Sandy says.

"Like what?"

"Well, what do you like to do?"

"I like to camp and fish, that's kind of how the whole thing got started."

"What do you like to fish for?"

"Well, it used to be trout, no boat required; but now that I have a boat, I use it every chance I get; so, bass fishing is my thing now."

Louise says, "That's it! Bass Pro Shop! That's the name for your business."

"Hey, I like that! I'm going to use it; it's perfect! Thanks, guys. I have one more group to set up, I'll see you around. Best of luck with whatever is happening, I have to tell you; it's all good vibrations. I'll check back, goodbye for now."

Betty grabs Sandy by the arm and says "Come on, bring John with you." The three of them start to walk toward the center army tent. "What am I going to do? I guess Betty is my girlfriend now so, it's my first "Yes ma'am to Betty; it will certainly not be my last.

We definitely blended in with the rest of the gathering. It seems like we belong here. Nobody pays us much attention, a few smile or wave, but they seem to be doing the same thing as our group, sticking together.

Most of the campsites have campfires going, and some are cooking on them; they have apparently been here longer than us. On the flatter side of the field, a serious four-man game of Frisbee is going on. Near the frisbee players, a game of lawn darts called "jarts" occupies four girl players. I have to wonder if they are a "group," they probably are.

The door flaps to the army tent are tied back, creating a large square opening. The first thing we see is a blackboard. It says dinner will be delivered to the sites between 5:30 pm - 6:00 pm, and to please help ourselves to whatever we want in the tent. Betty scans the room until she sees what she is looking for. "There are the boots, the Levi's, and the box of St. Christopher metals!" She hands necklaces to Mark, John, and Sandy, and says to them, "Put them on." Sandy put it on, but John said he didn't want to wear any jewelry. He said; "I'll keep it in my pocket, all right?"

Mark says "I want to keep mine in my pocket, too."

"That's fine; I'm just glad we have them; they are meant for us. Anything else in here we need?"

"No, let's get back," Christine says. "I just want to be still in one place for a while."

"Hold on," Sandy says, "We're going to need blankets and pillows, and maybe a bunch more. I want to be comfortable, don't you?"

John says to Sandy, "Make me a shopping list and I'll come back with Walt; I know he won't mind driving one of those tractors. We'll load up and nobody has to carry anything. Come on let's get back, we'll walk fast."

Outside the shadows are getting long.

"Hey girls, Betty, Sandy, wait." It's Pat Sullivan, the town chief of police. "I've been looking for you; I need to tell you; we have the creep you pointed out locked up. He had an unregistered handgun, that's good for three to five years in this state; you don't have to worry about him anymore. He's going down for at least that long, I promise you." "Hey, would you like some delicious fresh fried rainbow trout? Captain Duffy is about done frying it up; come on have a bite to eat and meet some new friends."

"Betty, what do you think?"

Betty is looking at their campsite and not seeing any of her friends there. "No, thank you; I'll pass on the fish, there's no one at our campsite, we need to see what's going on."

Everyone in the group by the campfire is looking at her.

"We'll talk later, I'm sure. We have to check this out, bye for now. Come on!" The four teenagers, now young adults, break into a run. When they reach their campsite, it is deserted.

"Where the hell did, they go?" There is no sign of their friends, nothing but meowing from inside the tent.

Sandy unzips the tent and lets Gray Kitty out.

Betty says; "What did you do that for? Christine is going to have a fit if you lose that cat."

"Gray Kitty won't go far, look." The gray cat ran to a patch of sunshine and laid down. "See? She doesn't want to be alone anymore."

John says, "Look, here comes a tractor. It's Carol and our crew!"

Carol angles the tractor so that the wagon stops in front of the tent. Brownie and Walt start dropping good size rocks off the far side of the wagon. "We got these from the stream, over there; Pear insisted on rock rings around the campfires, even if we are in the middle of a cornfield."

"Need any help?" Mark asks. "Yeah," it's Walt. "Help the girls down and grab the picnic table."

John and Mark help Christine and Louise down from the wagon; then, the four boys lift the picnic table down then climb back up for the rest of the gear and firewood. Every provision is thought of. There are coolers full of drinks, blankets, pillows, a Coleman lantern, and a box of snacks.

"Ok," Carol says, "I'll be back in a while with your dinner, beef stew and cornbread and of course corn. "I'll make sure you don't starve; you do know how to use the lantern right?"

"Oh yeah," Brownie says "I have one just like it."

"Ok, you're here and you're safe; I'll be back in a bit."

Forty-One

They eat everything Carol brought, without saying a word.

Louise says, "What do we do with the dirty dishes?"

Brownie says, "Who cares? This could be our last supper. One of the kids that was helping us to pick rocks out of the stream said, he feels like we are cattle being driven to the slaughter. We are fodder for the cannon; that's what he said."

Mark says, "Fodder for the cannon, what does that mean?"

"I asked him the same thing. He said it is like filling a pipe with tobacco, the tobacco is fodder for the pipe; like the men in the Civil War marching into cannon fire, fodder for the cannon. It's like I've had puppet strings attached to my whole body for the last three or four days. Like just now, I wasn't hungry, but I ate a lot; it was good, but even if it wasn't I would have eaten it anyway; because I am supposed to. Do you know what I mean?"

Christine says, "But the strings brought us together, Brownie. Whatever it is it's worth it, I have you, even if it's only for a day or two." Christine starts to cry and Brownie puts his arm around her. "You are right, Christine; it's worth it, because we found each other."

"Enough of this," Walt says, "I know what I'm going to do; I'm going to light this fire and stay up all night, nothing is going to take me by surprise."

Everyone agrees that is the plan; to stay up all night. Betty and Sandy say they may never sleep again, but what they don't know is that in a few hours, they will be sound asleep. Every group in the camp, and in fact everyone in the whole county, is about to experience the deepest sleep of their lives.

Forty-Two

The time Victor spent at the base armory wasn't wasted; he knew just what he wanted, and what he didn't want. He didn't want the M-16's; the rifle had improved in recent years, but he couldn't get over his mistrust of them. Victor wanted something simple, reliable and proven. There were no AK-47's in stock, so he chose two well maintained WWII 30.06 M-1 Garands. Victor fired two clips from each rifle at a target 50 yards away; every shot hit the center black of the targets.

He selected a pair of 45 caliber pistols and test fired them also. Victor is pleased with his selections, simple and reliable, they just work. That's what he wants in firearms and knives; he is extremely pleased to find a pair of Camillus Cutlery Marine Corps combat knives, the best knives in the world. He plans to keep his knife.

At the highest point on the ridge, Ivan and Victor are keeping watch on the power line access road. They are expecting Nikolai and at least one of his associates to try to disrupt the gathering. They have been here for several hours and have had plenty of time to scout the area and plan their ambush.

Ivan says, "When they reach the kill zone, I'll take out the driver; you get any others, Victor; hopefully, there won't be more than three." Victor is, of course, the better shot, being one of the top assassins in the KGB. The Russians assigned to the American team are not at all squeamish about killing comrades that are about to ruin not only world peace, but all of mankind.

Ivan spots movement on the road. "Green and white vehicle coming this way." He says, "Three subjects; the diver is a female." The green and white Volkswagen "Thing" stops exactly where Ivan expected, in the center of a wide spot in the road; a construction vehicle turn-around.

Nikolai steps out of the passenger door, he takes two steps and he stops and stretches. The perfect opportunity doesn't go unnoticed. Victor takes his shot, - click. Ivan takes his shot, - click. Two misfires with two different rifles, back-to-back. What are the odds of that happening?

Nikolai looks straight up to where Ivan and Victor are concealed. He stares for a long moment, then walks to the clearing and spends another moment looking at the little tent city below. His two associates join him and seem to be listening intently as he points and gives orders.

The woman nods and retrieves the vehicle. She stops to let them in, then proceeds at a fast clip across the field. The woman driver stops within their sight, on the ridge side of the rock pile and immediately starts rearranging the lashed-on pine branches to conceal the side of the vehicle they are looking at.

The two men are busy unloading what looks to be a large amount of equipment and carrying it to the opposite side of the rock pile. The finishing touch she applied impresses both Ivan and Victor, she placed rocks on the hood and trunk, also in front of the wheels, the vehicle completely disappears from view.

Victor removes the defective rounds from both weapons and inspects them, he hands one bullet to Ivan. "Perfect firing pin strike dead center and deep, my guess is defective primers." They both bury the bullets point down.

"That doesn't make any sense Victor; the Americans certainly know how to make bullets that work."

"I know, that's why I don't trust anything but my knife right now."

"I'm not sure any of our weapons will work Victor. It doesn't make sense, but maybe we are meant to fail and Nikolai is meant to succeed."

"That's not like you, Ivan. Are you telling me that you don't have a plan?"

"No, I don't. There is more than one force at work here. Take the American lunatic Knapp for example, and our lunatic Nikolai. It's the same thing, evil and meant to stop the plan from succeeding. The bullets not firing definitely concerns me. How much control over this event do we have?"

"It seems obvious to me Ivan. We have to get up close and personal, we'll have to use our knives."

"I don't like knives Victor, but go on."

"After dark, we use our skill to cover the distance – unseen. When we are close enough, we can try the 45's; they have a reputation for never misfiring, but right now I don't trust them. If they don't fire, the click will announce we are there. Maybe their weapons will work and then we are done, or at least we lose our surprise. I say we trust nothing, but ourselves our knives and the element of surprise. It should be dark enough in maybe three or four hours, but I say we wait until the middle of the night. Are you ok with my plan, Ivan?"

"Yes, I agree Victor, but I intend to spend the time reviewing our options. I don't like knives, never have. Unless I can think of something better, we will have to go with it. I'm going to close my eyes and think, if I drift off wake me ten minutes before our zero hour. I hope the hell I can think of something better."

The pile of stones at the edge of the field is not unusual in this, or any other farmer's field, anywhere in the world. Generations of farmers have been picking up rocks as they work and tossing them into piles. The stone pile offers concealment in plain and open sight.

The men are out of Victor's view; apparently, they are setting up and digging in out of his sight, on the other side of the pile. The woman is in plain view; she is using an army-style entrenching tool, at the rear of the stone pile. She is working steadily and placing the dirt she removes in an arc, in front of her hole.

"Ivan, you awake?"

"Yes."

"The woman has been assigned to cover their flank. She appears to be efficient; this could be a problem."

Ivan takes the field glasses from Victor and has a look.

"A problem yes, Victor, but the dirt embankment she is making obstructs her view on the west side; see?"

"Yes, it will be a long and difficult approach, but yes, I see. She has a blind spot."

Nadia is ordered to dig in, at the rear and cover their flank. To her way of thinking it is good news, she would prefer as much distance as possible between herself and Nikolai. Before they drove across the field he had said: "Victor and Ivan are here, I sense it."

Well, they certainly have Russian names; Nikolai knows them and perceives them as a threat. Very important information, they are probably here to kill him. Could they be the way out she is looking for? Maybe she thinks. If she stays away from her commanding Officer Nikolai, she might live through this thing.

Nadia is thinking all of this through, as she steadily works on her foxhole. She knows her future and her fate are tied to this night When it is finished, it is more of a defensive trench than a foxhole, and it is almost dark.

Nadia scans the ridgeline with binoculars, looking for the two agents that Nikolai says are there; so far, she has not seen them. She believes they are there, the question in her mind is would it be in her best interest to report their presence? Perhaps she will let them advance; then what? As she is having these thoughts, Nikolai startles her by jumping into her trench.

Nikolai leans a grenade launcher into the far corner and says "I trust you know how to use this?"

"Yes, Comrade."

"Good, use it only on my order. Gennady is going to relieve you for a moment; I want you to come forward and get briefed on our situation." Nadia gets out and hands the binoculars to Gennady, as they trade places. She has been so preoccupied with her task and her thoughts, that not once did she look behind herself during the last two hours.

The forward defensive position is almost identical to her defensive trench; probably a result of similar training that is deeply ingrained in all agents. She is wondering if Nikolai helped with the real work. The answer is not long in coming.

"I have just returned from scouting the area; we are in the right place. There are fourteen campsites down there, each with six to eight young men and women who are of the right age. The problem is, they are spread out over an acre of land; too widely separated for what I have in mind. My instincts tell me they will gather together somewhere, either tonight or in the morning. I see four possibilities; there are two large barns and a church nearby. We wait until they are grouped together, and take them out as one target."

"Comrade Colonel, the barns and the church, what is the fourth possibility?"

"That's right my dear, you don't know; I will tell you. The situation is incredibly complicated, yet completely simple. Let me start with my original briefing and orders. I was briefed in Moscow six days ago by Yuri Andropov, Chairman of the KGB I was told the assignment is of the highest priority and that the team had been handpicked by Brezhnev himself. It fell to Chairman Andropov to choose the colonel for the mission and to arrange the logistics. I am his choice. The Chairman was highly agitated and red in the face, as he told me the details. Yuri regained his composure and slid a thick file across the desk. This is what he told me; he said the folder he was made aware of only that morning. It is ultra-top secret, eyes only."

"Chairman Andropov told me, according to the file we are being threatened with extermination by alien beings; one week from tomorrow if we do not comply with their demands. Allegedly, the Americans received the same threat. And, the threat applies not only to our two countries, but to the entire world if we do not comply. He said this with a raised eyebrow. I have never seen an alien Nikolai; and, I have to consider the possibility that the Americans are running an elaborate ploy aimed at one of General Secretary Brezhnev's weakness. They say we are to stop testing our nuclear weapons and reduce our overall arsenals by 80% by the signing of the treaty they are calling SALT. He told me the signing of the treaty is scheduled for the 26th of May, tomorrow, in Moscow." He said, "Quite a coincidence; and you know what I think of coincidences Colonel." "Basically, we are to both agree to deep reductions in our nuclear capacities. Just as we are on the verge of surpassing America's military might!"

"Chairman Andropov told me that he chose me for my strength and detection. He also confided in me that Brezhnev is in poor health; and, that he is positioned to take over as General Secretary when Brezhnev dies. Andropov is thinking like he already has this responsibility. The Chairman looked me in the eye and told me my mission is to protect Mother Russia in all ways. My orders are to gather intelligence and to deny the Americans any advantage. He told me to use his desk and he gave me a full two hours to review the files."

"When he returned, this is what he told me." "You have your orders. Do not trust the Americans. As always, gain as much information as possible. Divulge nothing. If the children are of superior genetic stock, ideally, they should be on Russian soil. Or dead to deny the Americans any chance of genetic superiority. I have seen to it that your gear is properly packed and that transportation is arranged, dismissed."

"I have been working very hard, ever since Nadia; it is almost over. The fourth possibility Nadia, is a spacecraft comes from the sky. Well, if that were to happen the open field in front of us would be the best place to land."

"What about the two agents you mentioned, Ivan and Victor?"

"Traitors! I would have never chosen them! They have abandoned me, and Mother Russia! I will have them shot! They have defected to America; now we treat them as the enemy. I believe they are on the ridgeline behind us. Stay sharp and on the lookout, that's your job."

"We are to use our weapons on the young Americans?"

"Yes! That's the one thing that is clear. The young ones down there, are in some way genetically superior. You may not know this, Nadia, but our country has been working on this for a very long time. Eliminate the weak and only allow the propagation of the strong and intelligent. We are to deny them of superior breeding stock."

Nikolai hands Nadia one of the pairs of night vision binoculars. "One more thing, I want you to scan the area of the wide spot in the stream, in the bushes near the large tree."

"Do you see anything?"

"No, Comrade Colonel."

"On my reconnaissance, something caught my eye in that area, a movement, a glint, something. I believe we have another watcher there, and he's good. Take the Starlight vision glasses with you and return to your post, be vigilant."

Nadia's stomach is more than a little uneasy, as she positions herself back in her trench. She coughs and heaves as quietly as she can over the side. After a moment she leans back and wipes her mouth.

Gennady kneels next to her and says "You don't look well; can I get you some water?"

"Yes, first tell me; are you sure this mission is officially sanctioned?"

"Stay still, I'll be right back."

Gennady returns with a wet rag and a canteen. He leans in close and says; "No, I am not sure. I now know I made a mistake in not calling our memorized phone number. I have been thinking; Ivan and Victor, they are efficient and experienced. They have a repetition for always finding a way to succeed. I find it difficult to believe Ivan and Victor defected, especially Ivan. I mean; what would they be doing here if they did defect? I must get to a phone and make that call."

"How are you going to do that?"

"Listen I can only say this once. I am going to make that phone call and there is only one way I can think of. It's not great, but it's the only idea I have. At the first sign of dawn, I am going to knock Nikolai unconscious with the butt of my rifle. You are going to tie him up and stay out of sight until I return with an answer."

"What about -"

"Stop, no time; we will have to improvise. Remember, first light." Gennady gets up and says, "I will bring you some victory pills. You must stay alert. A continuous scan of the rear is necessary."

Nadia takes several deep breaths to try to calm her nerves and stomach. It didn't work. She rearranges the dirt covered wool blanket she is using for a false wall; she has an unobstructed view in all directions. She scans with the American made Starlight binoculars, nothing. The first hour passes slowly and then time seems to speed up. She is full of energy and ready for action. It is just after 2 am when she sees them, crawling on the ground entering the cornfield.

Shit, should she signal them? What the Hell is the proper signal? How can she tell Gennady without alerting Nikolai?

Someone touches her on the shoulder, it's Gennady.

"Here." he says. He hands her a Hersey bar and two more pills. "Consume both; this is no time for drowsiness."

"They are coming."

Gennady has a look. "Give them two short flashes with a red lens, repeat every two minutes. When they are thirty meters out, engage Nikolai in conversation. I will take him out and give Ivan the signal to advance."

"Gennady! Is everything alright back there?"

"Yes, Comrade Colonel."

Gennady pats Nadia's shoulder and returns to his post.

Nadia installs the red lens in her flashlight and gives the signal.

Ivan and Victor both freeze in place when they see the red light.

"What the hell?" It's Victor, "That's the acknowledge transmission signal. It doesn't make any sense."

"She is not shooting and that's a good sign, advance Victor." They continue to advance ten meters at a time.

They are getting close, thirty meters? Close enough. She is about ready to move forward and implement the plan when a wave of complete exhaustion hits her. She feels like she is about to pass out. Nadia remembers the victory pills she is still holding in her hand. She pops them into her mouth and chews. The taste is awful. Her legs buckle and she falls to the ground. Her last thought is poison, I have been poisoned.

Forty-Three

The sleep comes much earlier and more gently for the valley below and the tent city, maybe because they are going to need the sleep for what is to come.

It happens slowly over a one-hour period. Christine is the first one to go inside the tent but of course, she won't go without Brownie. That's the way it goes. Two by two, the couples go into the tent. They snuggle and immediately drift off to sleep with the sound of Gray Kitty loudly purring.

Zippers, it's funny how the sound of a tent being unzipped can so seem loud when the night is quiet and still. It is like a zipper concert with all of the tents being unzipped at almost the same time. Just as our entire crew tumbles out of our tent carrying boots and jackets, the clouds break revealing a bright more than half moon. In the distance, we see kids already walking toward the top of the hill. The boys are able to get their boots on while standing, but the girls have to sit at the picnic table to lace theirs.

John says to Sandy, "Come on, we are going to have to run to catch them as it is."

"Well, I guess that's what we get for having the last tent in the back. I'm not sure I want to go, I'm scared."

"We don't have a choice Sandy, and don't be scared. I'm excited, our lives are about to be changed; I know it."

"Yeah, or ended; but I know what you mean John, I'm ready."

Brownie holds his hand out to Christine and pulls her up. He gives her a strong hug and it's contagious, every couple gets a sincere and loving hug.

Walt says, "Come on, we don't have to run, we just have to walk fast. They are walking slowly; waiting for us to catch up, see?"

Of course, Walt is right. The whole cluster of kids, that we've still not met, is slowly moving up the hill. They are intentionally letting everyone catch up.

"Hey John, doesn't this seem familiar?"

"Nope, I have never done this before."

"No, I mean, it's like before, in the swamp. It's quiet, too quiet and still. No crickets, frogs, nothing. It's like nature herself is terrified. And we are being pulled, like before."

We are walking just as fast as we can. The moon disappears and it is dark, but only for a few seconds; there are strange lights in the sky.

Mark says "Is that a tow truck? What's a tow truck doing in the sky?"

The whole group has stopped, and we are all looking up and pointing. We catch up and can hear what they are saying, there is a lot of chatter, but one phase is repeated by several – including our entire group.

"Do you see what I see?"

There is a ship in the sky, and it is huge. It seemed to be the size of a Navy ship; a battleship or maybe more like an aircraft carrier. It soundlessly floats in the sky; it does not make sense. The lights that circle the ship are unlike any we had ever seen. The lights are mesmerizing; fascinating in their colors and patterns. A multicolored beam of light, about the size of a tractor tire, emits from the bottom center of the craft to the ground. The ground it touches boils with lights and colors.

"Holy shit!"

Again, there is another round of "Do you see what I see? Do you see that?" Everyone confirms they are seeing the same thing, and it's real. One of the boys in the group ahead yells; "It's an anchor, they threw out an anchor!" Then, another strange thing happens. The craft splits in two. The number of lights circling the ship doubles, as the top half slowly separates and floats upward. It makes a little wobble and darts straight up. It disappears in the blink of an eye.

Many smaller disc-shaped craft rise from the top of the still huge ship and circle the area. They also have rings of multi-colored lights and move like no airplane or jet could. Some shoot straight up, like the other half of the giant ship did just a moment earlier. One of the smaller crafts floats to the ground just ahead of us, a ramp lowers and we watch, mesmerized. Automatically, we form up in a column of two's and walk forward.

Naturally, the column is made up of couples, the pairs that had been intentionally mated together for what would be; life. Betty and I are at the rear of the line, shuffling forward with the rest of the group. Everyone in the column, including us, is saying the same thing "Run! I want to run!" The urge to run is unbelievably strong and urgent. But I can't run, and nobody else can either.

 Every sense in our bodies is on overdrive. Our feet are working again, but not in the way we want them to. We are walking toward the ramp. The fight or flight instinct is fully engaged; except we can't fight - or flee. One step at a time, the line moves toward the disc and the ramp. Our feet stop moving when a strong beam of white light emits from the side of the ship to the ground. It's like someone holding a flashlight and pointing it at the ground and then raising their hand causing the beam to move toward us.

The beam travels like that until it gets to the first pair. It moves up and across their chests. They are accepted and levitated, up and across the remaining distance to the ramp. They are gently set down and walk under their own power into the ship. The forty-nine remaining pairs take one step forward, and the process is repeated.

The time for talking is over; no one says a word more. But I can still think. I am thinking maybe they will fix my eyes. Will we get to go into space? Will we ever come back? What are they going to do to us? I won't let them hurt Betty.

I remember trying to burn every detail into my mind; I don't want to forget anything and that works up to the time that Betty and I walk up the ramp. We are not meant to remember the details of what goes on inside, powerful mind blocks are a part of the plan. It is hard to remember what you are forced to forget. Apparently, there are a few weak points with their mind blocks. Terror, anger, and love maybe because these are the strongest human emotions, they are the hardest to cover up.

Terror, I can remember being terrorized, lying naked on a metal table, bright lights shining down and being unable to move. A machine of some sort lowers and attaches to my head, and another one to my private parts. That is terror; it brings me almost wide awake and ready to bolt. They hit me with another dose of whatever they use to keep us under control. The memory is there, unblocked in my mind.

Anger, there are funny un-human looking guys bent over my naked body – poking, prodding and hurting me. I think of the swamp, the police, and the man I thought was a general. I think about what the kid at the stream said, about us being fodder for the cannon. It all clicks, and I realize we have been set up like bowling pins; and it pisses me off. I am almost wide awake again; I want to beat the hell out the little bastards hurting me. Again, they put me down, but I get to keep the memory.

Love, I am worried about Betty. I can't see her; they better not be hurting her. I try to get up and find her, but they put me down again. The memory is there, for better or worse, all of those memories are there.

Forty-Four

Nadia opens her eyes and slowly realizes that she isn't dead. She can move a finger and, with an effort, turn her head and look up. It's not dark anymore; the sun is just above the horizon and the clouds to the east have a reddish color. A thought comes into her head, red sky in the morning sailors' take warning, a storm is coming.

The time, where did the time go? It must be about four hours that have passed. Did everybody pass out like she did? She is able to push herself into a sitting position then awkwardly stands. She needs to know what Nikolai is up to.

Both Nikolai and Gennady are laying the ground and they are not moving. Her senses and control over her body are returning; she must check on them. Nadia is able to get out of her trench and take one step toward them when something unbelievable happens. There is a brilliant light in the field ahead; it's so bright she has to shield her eyes with her arm. The light goes out almost as fast as it came on; and when she looks again, the entire group of young Americans is standing in the field, looking bewildered.

She kneels next to Gennady and shakes him. He is starting to come around, but not fast enough; she needs him. She pours water on his face and he comes fully awake. "What happened? Why is it daylight?"

"Look, look over the edge!"

Gennady pulls himself up and looks. "Shit! How did that happen?" He is startled by Nikolai who is now peering over the edge next to him.

"Perfect! It is ordained! Fate and destiny smile on us!"

"Nadia, retrieve your weapon! Gennady aim left center; Nadia, right center. I will take the middle. Gennady and I will advance and take out any survivors." He looks at Nadia, "You will bring the vehicle for our escape. Get ready and bring your weapon forward; now!"

Nadia is back in her trench in a flash; adrenaline and the victory pills have her senses and body in high gear. She picks up the grenade launcher and glances toward Gennady; he is looking back at her; his eyes look sad. He gives a slight shake of his head; he is saying he is sorry their plan did not work out. The grenade launcher she is holding becomes hot, burning hot. She drops it and hears Nikolai say, "Ready!"

Instinct and a little hint from above save her life. At that instant Nadia leaps out of her trench, she knows she must get to the other side of the stone pile. Three of her best strides get her almost there.

"Aim!"

One more stride and she launches her body forward like she is diving into a pool, she is aiming for the side of her truck. She doesn't quite make it.

"Fire!"

Her body is stretched out, and in mid-air, when the explosion happens. She won't know it until sometime later, but when the first trigger was pulled, every piece of ordinance exploded. Not just the rocket-propelled grenades that Nikolai and Gennady were holding in front of their faces – but Nadia's grenade launcher, and the duffel bags of extra ammunition, as well. Nadia has saved herself from the huge explosion, but not from the rocks that rain down.

Ivan and Victor saw the light and the young Americans return; and, they were close enough to hear Nikolai. When he said, "Ready," Nadia jumped up and sprinted away, as fast as she could run. When he said, "Aim!" they instinctively knew to turn and dive to the ground themselves. Somehow the explosion wasn't a surprise to of any of them. They are lucky to be far enough away and to have the pile of rocks to deflect the blast away from their positions.

When the rocks and debris quit falling, Victor looked up and could see through the dust that the woman was injured, maybe badly. "Victor! There are men approaching from the stream! Get your field glasses!"

"What do you see Victor? Should we shoot them?"

"No, it is Captain Duffy and a big man that I don't recognize. Captain Duffy, I trust. Let them handle that end. They are on our side and are checking on the young Americans. I say you check and see if there is anything left of Nikolai and I will check the woman."

Before he moves forward Victor pops a yellow smoke grenade; yellow is the pre-arranged signal for medical evacuation. They split up and Ivan goes around the rock pile, rifle at the ready.

Victor goes to the woman; she is almost completely covered in rocks, the biggest one is on her leg. Victor lifts the large rock straight up and tosses it aside. He picks at the smaller rocks covering her. The last one to be removed has her cheek and face pinned down. He gently lifts a rock the size of a soup bowl from her face. She is unconscious but breathing; she is still alive. The woman has a nasty cut on her head and it is bleeding profusely; head wounds do that. Her dark hair with grey streaks is matted with blood. When she opens her eyes, she is dazed, her mind is somewhere else. She speaks but not in English, in Russian.

"Отец, брат, Мне так жаль, я попробовал. Они лгали, лгали."
"Father, Brother, I am so sorry, I tried. They lied to me, they lied."

Victor is not shocked by her Russian, but impressed with her honesty. He completely understands what she is saying. He answers her in the same language. "Это все права мои дорогие; вы не с ними. Я помогу Вам получить ответы на ваши вопросы." "It's all right my dear; you are not with them yet. I will help you get answers to your questions."

Nadia's eyes clear and she tries to get up, Gennady gently holds her back. "Stay still;" he says, "listen, helicopters are coming; there will be medics, let them look at you."

"My truck, I want my truck!"

"Your truck is badly damaged, it looks like there's a ton of rocks on it or, I should say, in it."

"I don't care! It is parts; I want the parts!"

Victor gave her a smile, probably the biggest smile since his face had been slashed with a knife, maybe his biggest smile ever. To find a woman such as this, on an operation in America, in the middle of a cornfield; it is amazing.

Nadia tries to smile back but coughs instead. She regains her composure and asks him. "Have you ever been to Montana?"

Forty-Five

When the light went out, we are standing in the top field, the same spot we were drawn to last night. We are tightly packed together and it is early daylight. Betty and John are both by my side and we are all gasping for air, like we have been underwater for too long. After about the third or fourth deep breath, there is a different kind of bright light – followed by a terrific boom. It is an explosion, a big one. Other than the flash and the loud noise, no harm comes to any of us.

The rocks and debris raining from the sky all fall short of us, then it is still. We are safe; or are we? Two men are running toward us from the stream, and we can hear helicopters coming. Any trace of shock, surprise, or drowsiness is fast fading. The tight knot of young Americans steps outward, like stepping out of a crowded elevator; then, we separate into our original groups.

Captain Duffy's friend, the cop Sullivan, starts talking to the bunch at the rear; then Captain Duffy comes around to our side. "Hey guys, you gave me a scare for a minute there; is everybody all right?"

Before we can even answer all conversation is drowned out by helicopters six of them, in a line and low to the ground. They fly directly over us; two bank left, two bank right and the remaining two fly over us again, at a higher altitude.

John says, "Do you see the guns sticking out of those things? They are on our side, right?"

"We wouldn't be standing here right now if they weren't. You have been caught up in a top-secret government operation, but it's over now; it's done. I'm going to explain everything to you, but first, we have to take a helicopter ride to our base." Captain Duffy pops a green smoke grenade and explains that it's the safe to land signal."

Christine says, "I'm not leaving without my cat; she is around here somewhere."

"I'll look for your cat; you just get on the chopper and do what the crew tells you to do. You won't believe how much fun it is to ride in those things. Here they come, get ready."

The thump, thump, thump of helicopters approaching gets louder and louder until we can feel the vibrations. These are a different type of helicopters than the ones that flew over us before; they are big, and not all the same color. A blue one with a red-cross lands first – almost directly on top of the yellow smoke. The next one lands in front of us; the rest land in an arc around the group. Two men with red cross armbands stepped off the first helicopter, and one man from each of the others.

Captain Duffy turns around and speaks loudly, "All groups stay together; you all will have your own helicopter. Follow your escort, please."

Once we get in the air, I realize Captain Duffy is right; it is the best kind of fun to take a ride in a real military helicopter. We sit on a long bench seat made of canvas strips and look out the open door. There are two uniformed men with us, in the cabin standing by the doors. The one with more stripes on his shoulder talks loudly over the noise, "We like to fly with the doors open, unless it's cold or raining. I will leave it up to y'all; do you want the doors open or closed?"

"Open!" It is all the boys. The girls didn't say anything, but they are smiling and holding on to us like we are their seat belts. For me, it is the first time I've felt safe since the bridge. I mean, it seems like the whole US Air Force has our backs, and we have new friends. I remember my dad telling me once "You're lucky if you have enough true friends to count on one hand." I'm sure that I need both of my hands to count my true friends now. Does that make me lucky?

It doesn't take long to get to where we are going. We can see the base out of the open door, and it's huge. It's not just the buildings that go on forever, but miles of open asphalt and concrete with jets big, huge, and small scattered about. There is a cluster of them at the end of the runway. Are they about to take off?

The helicopters land in the same pattern as when they picked us up in the cornfield. This time, the half circle is around four blue buses. The same escort that helped us get on board, helps us down and that's a good thing, because it's a big step. He lifts the girls down and gives the boys a strong arm to hold on to.

He speaks to everyone in a normal voice, he doesn't have to shout anymore. He says, "This is a big base; we are going to have to use the buses and golf carts to get to where we are going." Then, he said something that took me years to figure out he thanked us for our service.

It is almost unnatural that 100 teenagers aren't talking non-stop, but I think we are all tired, tired of being overwhelmed.

Betty whispers to me, "My ears are ringing." "Mine are too" I tell her; "I sure hope that goes away; I hate the ear ringing thing." About that time my earlier question is answered the jets at the end of the runway are taking off, one after the other, on the runway behind us. The loud roar overtakes everything else. I say to Betty, "You hear that?"

"Yeah."

"Well, I guess we're not deaf then. They must have been waiting for us to land; our helicopters must have had priority."

Walt's face is pressed to the bus window, watching the jets take off. "I want to fly one of those big bastards. No, the smaller ones, the fighters yeah, the fighters. Look at the power!" The smaller fighter jets are barely airborne when they angle straight up and take off like a rocket.

The bus starts up and begins to move. I have been trying to see as much of the other teenagers as I can, but my view is limited to my window. A helicopter is next to us with both doors open; the kids are exiting the door opposite me and boarding their bus. They seemed about like our group, not smiling, but content and doing what they are told.

There are two other groups on the bus with us and it seems funny we aren't introducing ourselves or interacting in any way. There are some whispers, but Walt's comments about the jets are the only words uttered out loud.

I remember the official cars and the possible military involvement with our interrogation in the swamp; and, I'm not sure everything is alright after all. Maybe it's the United States Air Force that is messing with us; shit. I glance at John who is in the aisle across from me, he gives a slight shake of his head; I can tell he is thinking the same thing, and he is not sure either.

The buses park near the flagpole and a long double line of golf carts. It looks like maybe this is a parade ground and the front entrance to the base. The driver opens the door and stands at the white line facing the rear of the bus. He speaks loud enough for everybody to hear, "From here on its golf carts to get to where you are going, and believe me it beats walking, it's a big base. Come on, let's step out. We have lots of carts; so, four to a cart will work out nicely." He steps off the bus and we obey and follow four to a cart.

It works out that John and Sandy, and Betty and I, are in the first golf cart. We are moving toward the entrance. Our new escort doesn't say a word as he drives us through an entranceway. Surprisingly, on the other side of the door is a large atrium, it looks like a shopping mall with stores and a post office lining the side walls.

At the center of the floor is a large circular emblem, it says Department of the Air Force on the top half and the United States of America, on the bottom. At the center of the emblem is an eagle and a seal of lightning bolts. Emitting from the edge of the circle are three sets of different color lines, pointing to three different tunnels in the distance; we go straight. We are waved through a checkpoint and two thick, steel bank-vault type doors.

The roadway gets narrower, but there are still doors with writing on them on both sides of the hall. I can see there is an intersection ahead where the group of lines part. We go to the right, following the red line with small white crosses in the center. The road angles down and starts to curve to the left, we are going deeper into the ground. Ahead, the hallway or road comes to a T intersection. Two large double doors stand open to reveal a gigantic hospital-type room.

There are too many white-coated and uniformed men and women to count. One man and three women say good morning to us and walk alongside the cart, to the opposite side of the room. The room is packed with examining tables equipment, and cabinets of all sorts.

The white-coated man speaks. "This is it, our little corner of paradise. I'm Dr. Axelrod and this is my nurse, Lieutenant Moxom. We also have Sergeant Fitzpatrick and Corporal Whitlow assisting with the paperwork." They all say good morning as they are introduced. The doctor nods and nurse Fitzpatrick pulls a white curtain around our little square of the room. "This won't take long; I need one volunteer up on the table. The rest of you, take a seat."

"Let's get this over with," it's John. He sits on the table and nurse Moxom takes his blood pressure, pulse, and temperature. Dr. Axelrod pokes around with his stethoscope, checks his eyes, and uses a cotton swab in his mouth. At that point, John looks at me with a big question mark in his eyes. Dr. Axelrod says "A blood sample and we are done." John looks at the ceiling while the nurse draws his blood. John asks, "Is everything all right?" Dr. Axelrod assures him that everything looks normal. "Hop down and have a seat next to Corporal Whitlow."

I go next; it is the same thing no, it's different because I am intently listening to the questions being asked of John. "What is your date of birth? What city were you born in? Please spell your full name. Parents full names and spelling? Address? Social security number? "

"I don't have one." "That's ok, you will."

Sergeant Whitlow is typing all of the information into a funny looking typewriter and doing it without even looking down at the machine. About the time nurse Fitzpatrick is drawing my blood, Corporal Whitlow tells John "That's it, were done; next." My nurse puts a band-aid on my arm and says "That's it honey, we're done." She helps me down and I sit in the chair that John just vacated. The process is repeated again with Sandy on the table, and me with the question lady.

Betty goes last and she is not happy. She wants to know what the hell is going on; she wants to call her dad. The only answer Dr. Axelrod has to her questions is that there will be a very official meeting in one hour that will include everyone involved. Questions will be answered and she can call her dad afterward.

Betty says; "I feel dirty, not just dirty. I feel like I have been violated by aliens dirty. All the hot water in the world might not get me clean." Dr. Axelrod answers her. "I don't know anything about that my dear, but shower and fresh clothes are next on the list."

"Sergeant Fitzpatrick will escort you to the showers. Afterward every one of you, including those who came on the helicopters with you, will attend a high-level meeting classified in fact. I know no details about it, except you are all to attend. You're done, sit with Corporal Whitlow for a moment please, and I will get you on your way."

Betty endures the question lady and Sergeant Fitzpatrick can tell the atmosphere is getting tense; she tries to lighten the mood by dramatically opening the curtain and saying, "Your chariot awaits you! There is a water cooler down the hall and a luncheon is planned after the meeting. Please, we are two hours away from being done. After that, you can make phone calls and arrangements will be made to get you home."

"Come on; let's get you cleaned up and to the meeting." She climbs into the front seat next to the driver and we sit on the other two bench seats behind the sergeant. The cart takes us deeper inside the facility and stops at a bank of elevators. Sergeant Fitzpatrick pushes the call button on the elevator with the largest steel doors. The cab arrives and is plenty big enough for our cart and three more. The sergeant pushes the number four button and I notice that we are already on level two. The door opens to a large, busy lobby and on the floor is the same eagle / lightning bolt seal that we saw at the entrance; there is one difference, there is a compass and a set of numbers embedded in the colored lines. We turn left and continue down the corridor. Every fifty feet or so there is another set of numbers and another compass.

I can't help but ask the sergeant in front of me what the numbers mean. "The numbers are quadrants; everyone at this level is either an avatar or has been trained in maps. The numbers and compass allow us to easily orient our position in the complex. It works the same way in the air or underground."

We emerge into what looks like a large recreation room, but no one is recreating. There is a TV, tuned to a news channel, Walter Cronkite is talking. There are two pool tables, along with ping pong and card tables; vending machines line the opposite wall. Our cart driver makes a sharp left and parks. He gets out first and the sergeant hands him two clipboards. "Come on guys, the men's showers are this way." Sergeant Fitzpatrick gets out holding other two clipboards "Come on ladies, the women's showers are on the other end; everyone remember our cart number 318, we are going out in the same order we came in."

Betty says, "Hold on; we are waiting for the rest of our crew. I made a mistake by not saying it before; it's our rule to always travel with at least half of our group. We can't go anywhere one or two at a time; it has to all of us, or four at a time." She gets out and stands, holding her ground. The rest of us stand with her. The next cart to come is the rest of our group.

Walt, Brownie, Louise, and Christine join us. They are smiling and seem a lot more excited than we are. "Did you hear?" Walt asks.

"Hear what?"

"The president, President Nixon, he's here! We're going to meet the president!"

Sergeant Fitzpatrick puts her finger to her lips in the – shh sign. "It's true, we're trying to keep it quiet. Who told you? We're you raising hell?"

"I was not cooperating; I wouldn't let the doctor touch Louise or me, and I wouldn't answer their questions either. A captain came in,

Captain York. He said, basically, we had just been drafted and we are to do as we are told. He said the President of the United States would personally explain it to us in less than an hour."

John asks Walt, "Do you believe him?"

"I do, somehow it makes perfect sense."

Two more carts pull up.

"Ladies, I will escort you to the showers; men, please follow Corporal Benson. We are getting pressed for time." The driver of the second cart hands the sergeant two clipboards, she gives a slight nod of her head and starts walking.

Betty leans over and gives me a kiss. "I want my shower, bad."

"Go."

John says, "I damn sure want a shower too; let's do it."

There is a man with a cloth tape measure around his neck standing at the entrance.

Corporal Benson hands him the clipboards. Tape measure man takes one clipboard and study's it, then he hands it back.

"John?"

"Yeah."

"Your towel and personal hygiene kit are on the bench; I just need a few measurements."

With the practiced moves of somebody that has done it before he measures John's neck, arms, waist, and inside seems. Every measurement called out is recorded on the clipboard by Corporal Benson. "Please take off your boots and let the corporal get your shoe size, it's one thing the service is very good about, proper fitting boots."

Clipboards are exchanged.

"Mark?"

"Yes."

He does the same thing to me but even quicker; a line is forming at the door.

Forty-Six

The shower is wonderful, but it seems impossible to get clean. It is like something isn't washing off. After not enough time in the shower; we are ordered out.

"Wrap it up guys, there are men waiting. Your uniforms are ready, let's move it!"

All four from our group emerge from our individual shower stalls at the same time, with towels wrapped around our waists.

The man speaking is definitely in charge. He is an older man and he had a lot of stripes on his shoulders with a chest full of ribbons. He has an assistant, a one stripe private that is in charge of a rolling cart of neatly folded clothes, boots on the bottom rack.

The officer consults his clipboard. "Stevenson!"

The private pulls the appropriate pile from the cart and puts the boots on top. He hands them to me. The same thing is repeated with Walsh, Brown, and Piper. We get dressed in the locker room and use the sinks.

At the bathroom entrance, a camera is set up on a tripod aimed at a chair that is pushed back against the white wall. A man in a blue uniform says, "I need to make your picture for the file sit, please." He takes two pictures, one with the fancy camera and one with a handheld Polaroid.

After that, we go back to where the carts await us. We are the first ones in and the first ones out. We had a chance to talk for a minute. John says, "I like my boots but I'm not crazy about the uniforms. Does that mean we are in the army now?"

"Air Force" Walt says.

Brownie says "I don't remember signing anything about joining the Air Force."

"Did any of you guys go to the movies lately, to see the new movie The Godfather?"

"I did," Brownie says, "I wish I could forget about the rich guy who woke up in the morning with his horse's head in bed with him; he didn't do what the Godfather asked. The horse was a prize winner and his most valuable horse. The way he woke up, slowly to blood on the sheets and his horse's head, that blew my mind."

"Yeah, that one, I'm talking about the part where the Godfather says he is going to make him an offer he can't refuse; that. Think of all the strange shit we have just been through and the fact we are at an Air Force base; four stories underground and we are going to meet the President of the United States."

"That's what is going to happen; President Nixon is going to make us an offer we can't refuse. My guess is we will be in the Army, Air Force, Marines or whatever the hell he says in about an hour."

"We're too young to be in the service."

"Think so? You have never heard of an executive order, have you? The president can make them and it is like a king's law; except the public will never know about it if it is classified or labeled top secret in the interest of national security. I think that's what we have been a part of; Captain Duffy told us that when he said we were a part of a top-secret government operation. Either we are going to come out of this smelling like a rose or we're bad screwed. It's one or the other; I'm not sure which."

"Here comes our girls." They are being ushered along by Sergeant Fitzpatrick, brushing their hair as they walked.

"Feel better?" Walt asks Louise.

"Yes, but I'm not crazy about these clothes, I'm glad they are clean, but I don't want to look like everybody else."

"Me either," Christine says, "I don't want to look like a Xerox copy and I miss my makeup. I can't believe they took my picture like this."

Sergeant Fitzpatrick looks at her watch and says, "Ok, your whole group is here and we need to go." With her right hand, she gestures toward the carts. We get into the same carts, in the same order and start to roll deeper inside the facility. There is only one line in the center of our tunnel, a white one with a basketball and an arrow embedded in the line, along with the quadrant numbers.

The tunnel curves to the left and we pass two-armed MP's, standing at attention then there are two more. We are there, at the basketball court. There is no doubt about it, this is it. Six serious looking guys in suits are guarding the entrance to the court. Two in the tunnel and four more in the concourse entryway, an Air Force man in dress blues collects the clipboards and disappears through the double doors.

He comes out after a few seconds and says, "I can only allow two at a time." Betty and I get out; we are to be the first ones to go. The doors to the basketball court are opened for us and we pass through them. It is what I hoped to see.

President Nixon is standing there with a happy smile. He has a grin that I never again saw duplicated in any photograph of him, before or since. He shakes my hand, then Betty's. He puts one hand on my left shoulder and the other on Betty's right. He speaks directly to us in a soft voice. "Congratulations, I am so proud of you! I personally want to thank each of you."

"You don't know it yet, but you have done your country a great service and I'm confident you will have the opportunity to contribute much more. I have plans, great plans, for this group. I intend to tell you all about it, but first I have ninety-eight more to greet. This is General Brandon and General Yeager; you will spend time with them later. Please have a seat, this won't take long."

He nods to the doorman. John and Sandy walk in. The generals step forward to introduce themselves to Betty and me. The general named Yeager only says; "Pleased to meet you."

The general named Brandon is much more enthusiastic; he seems thrilled we are here. His voice is familiar it's the nicer guy from the swamp. He walks with us to the end of the bleachers and says he will always be available to us anytime, day or night. In my mind, there is no doubt about it. The Air Force has to be involved in what happened to us from the beginning. General Brandon is the one that insisted that we "Walk that way".

He nods to the corporal that drove our cart, Corporal Benson. Benson hands each of us a clipboard that is much thicker with paperwork than the last time we saw it. My new Polaroid picture is on the top right side and a Bic pen is clipped next to the picture.

We climb the stairs almost to the top. I slide between the rows first and Betty follows me, leaving room for John and Sandy to sit next to us. By the time we are seated, John and Sandy are making their way up. I am watching them climb the steps and look past them to the basketball court. My eyes settle on a woman in a wheelchair, she has a cast on her leg and her head is bandaged.

There is a man with her, but I can't see his face because he is on the opposite side of her and leaning in close, talking. He looks familiar; I know why. He turns around and looks back at us. It is only a second or two, but it is enough. He has seen me and I have seen him, again. It's the mean bastard with the accent, my swamp interrogator.

Three of the four of us are bubbling with excitement, I pretend to be. Walt and Louise are climbing the steps; it's Walt I want to talk to. He makes the most sense when he talks. I catch his attention and wave him over to the row below us. I want to be able to lean over and talk to him. I know I have time, even I can figure out if President Nixon greets two couples a minute, it's still going to be about twenty minutes before we find out anything. Brownie and Christine slide in next to Walt and Louise and I notice there are two other couples already on the steps.

Walt isn't interested in talking, his interest is in the papers on the clipboard and he has already flipped the first page.

Good idea I think, what are all of these papers?

I start to read. The first page is basic information, then a few pages of medical status, with charts that make no sense to me. The next page is a shocker. It is a Confidential Presidential Citation. It's signed and dated with today's date. At the bottom, under President Nixon's signature, is a handwritten entry. It simply says, 'To be kept with employment file, do not copy.'

A thick employment application for the Department of Defense is next. It is already filled out and had a red "APPROVED" stamp at the top of the first page. The last page is the enlistment oath. My full name is printed at the bottom; a red X and a signature line above it.

I am elbowed in the ribs by Betty. The large untalkative group seems excited and is now the opposite of quiet; they are loud and talking nonstop. It looks like the one hundred are here.

Betty says, "Did you read this? The president is going to give us a job; mid-level pay grade. Louise says that's about ten thousand dollars a year!"

I tell her that sounds like a great ending and a great beginning at the same time.

Christine is acting particularly excited and Betty leans over to hear what she is saying. I look to see if my interrogator is still there, he is and there is another man standing with him now. I glance at John; he either hasn't noticed, or doesn't recognize the men.

Betty leans back and turns to me.

"What did Christine say?"

"She said her cat is here. The veterinarian sent out for cat supplies and is keeping it separate from the dogs. She is a healthy young cat and Christine can take it with her when she leaves; she sure is happy about that." Sandy is calling Betty's name and she turns to see what she wants.

I use the opportunity to lean over and ask Walt what he thinks.

He says, "It looks to me like we are going to come out of this smelling like a dozen roses. The last page, that's the twist and we will be required to sign it. That will be the offer we can't refuse. Mid-level pay grade? It doesn't sound like a bad deal to me, at all."

"Maybe not so bad I say; we could be set for life, right?"

"Yeah, it looks that way."

Forty-Seven

"Good morning, ladies and gentlemen." It is General Brandon's voice booming through the loudspeakers.

"I am General Brandon, commander of this base. This meeting will mark the end of a very stressful time between our country and our present adversary, the Soviet Union. I can tell you the world is safer today because of all of you."

"It is going to take more than just this meeting to explain what has happened in the last few days. General Yeager and I plan to spend time with each, and every one of you. It is our hope to guide all of you to a successful future. Now, it is my pleasure to introduce the man that made this possible; the President of the United States Richard M. Nixon."

"Good morning, I have much to tell you and little time to do it. Let me start like this, there is a lot I need to tell you, but I can't. I can't because all of what I have to say is classified. Ultra-Top Secret, in fact. The only way I can legally share this with you is if each of you has a Top-Secret clearance. Usually, this type of clearance is reserved for high-level Department of Defense employees, a few government contractors, and fewer politicians."

"My solution to the problem is an Executive Order. A highly classified Executive Order, it is my plan to bring every one of you into the Department of Defense at a mid-level pay grade. You may keep this job for life. As of now, only two days a month will be required; reporting to either General Brandon or General Yeager."

"There is one more requirement. The story of what happened in the last few days is sworn by oath to never be divulged. It's a hell of a good deal for you, and I'm afraid I must insist. You will find a signature page on the last page in your file. Sign it and pass the files to the end to be collected. Clear the room of anyone not directly involved, that includes MP's and my secret service detail. Now, if anyone chooses not to sign the paper, now is the time to tell me; we can fix it."

Nobody moves, stands up, or says anything.

"Good. Please stand and raise your right hand. I will now administer the enlistment oath; repeat after me."

"I, (state your name), do solemnly swear that I will support and defend the Constitution of the United States against all enemies, foreign and domestic; that I will bear true faith and allegiance to the same; and that I will obey the orders of the President of the United States and the orders of the officers appointed over me, according to regulations and the Uniform Code of Military Justice. So, help me God."

"You are now sworn to secrecy regarding what has happened. I must warn you that violation of the oath will result in extreme unpleasantness; life in prison or the death penalty. No trial is required at this level."

"I myself cannot disclose it. Can you imagine the political advantage I would have if I could take credit for saving the world? But I can't, no matter what. The satisfaction I take is for the future of my Country. The members of this group are an important part of the future of the United States."

"I am going to give you a brief summary of what happened. If I was telling this to any other audience there would be laughter and a good deal of skepticism, but not this group; you will understand and not even think about laughing. What happened is that General Secretary Brezhnev, of the Soviet Union, and I were visited by alien beings the "Others" we call them. We call them that because, there are more than one species visiting our planet."

"The "Others" that visited Brezhnev and me are the group in control of what ultimately, is the destiny of the Earth; they call the shots. The "Others" are concerned about our growing nuclear stockpiles and the fact that so many nuclear devices are being tested. They said we are poisoning the planet and soon, the planet Earth will be damaged beyond repair. It is unacceptable to them."

"The "Others" made us an offer we couldn't refuse. We had seven days to comply with their demands or, they would release a plague that would kill every human on Earth, and start over. They said they have done it before, more than once. Believe me, the "Others" are quite convincing when they make a point, or in this case a demand. Their demand was two-fold."

"First, the Soviet Union and the United States had to agree to, and sign a very binding treaty; we had no choice. We had to agree on certain measures, with respect to the limitation of strategic offensive arms. We did as we were told."

"The second condition, involved everyone in this audience. One hundred young men and women, of minimum childbearing age, from both the Soviet Union and the United States were to be provided again, with specific conditions."

"These young men and women were chosen by the "Others" and could not be substituted. The youths were to come of their own free will; they were guided by the "Others" to specific government sites, again chosen by them. The reason you fifty pairs of young women and men were taken, was to ensure human genetic stock, in case the rest of mankind had to be eliminated. This was also the situation for the Soviet Union."

"Our two countries were forced to work together, and not without complications. The end result is an agreement between our countries and the "Others." We have been granted a fifty-year lease on our planet."

"Fifty years."

"That means in 2022, a new lease will be required for human life to continue on our planet. At that point in time, all of you sitting before me will be about sixty-five years of age. It is my desire, and my plan, to have each of you in positions of influence. When that time comes – I trust in all of you to make the decisions that will favorably affect the outcome for the United States and our world. I know it is a heavy burden and secret to keep, but I want to point something out to you. In many ways, you are the luckiest group on earth."

"Why?"

"Because the mates you are paired with, are perfect matches for each of you. I suspect the offspring you produce will be, in some way special. To that end, there are only two or three things that will leave proof that we existed on this earth. What you accomplish, what you write, and most importantly, your children. Your courage and patriotism will continue to flow through your descendants."

"At a young age, all of you are well positioned with good jobs, mentors, and the power to make the most of your lives. I thank you for the service you have rendered for your country, and I thank you in advance for your service yet to come."

"Are there any questions?"

Walt had been waiting and hoping for this opportunity. He jumps straight up and asks his question.

"Sir; I would like a driver's license."

President Nixon glances at General Yeager, then smiles as he looks up at the young man standing on the bleachers.

"I can do that son; how would you like a pilot's license to go with that?"

THE END

Made in the USA
Middletown, DE
02 March 2024